SOULFUL SERENADE

Hillary didn't know if things would ever look bright again. She had thought she'd finally found the man of her dreams, but it looked as though she'd attracted another nightmare instead. Brandon already haunted her daydreams. So why not welcome him into her nightmares, as well? What a deliciously sexual haunting that would be, she pondered as she got out of bed and went into the guest room.

As she slipped into the bed in which Brandon had slept the previous night, she felt his presence all about her. She felt the warmth that had held her intimately close that very morning. If she slept in this bed, where he'd slept, maybe she wouldn't feel the pain of missing him so much.

What a way for the nightmare to begin. . . .

**BOOK YOUR PLACE ON OUR WEBSITE
AND MAKE THE ARABESQUE
ROMANCE CONNECTION!**

We've created a customized website just for our very special
Arabesque readers, where you can get the inside scoop on
everything that's going on with Arabesque romance novels.

When you come online, you'll have the exciting opportunity
to:

- View covers of upcoming books

- Learn about our future publishing schedule (listed by
  publication month and author)

- Find out when your favorite authors will be visiting a
  city near you

- Search for and order backlist books

- Check out author bios and background information

- Send e-mail to your favorite authors

- Join us in weekly chats with authors, readers and other
  guests

- Get writing guidelines

- AND MUCH MORE!

Visit our website at
http://www.arabesquebooks.com

To Eddy

SOULFUL
SERENADE

Linda Hudson-Smith

Linda Hudson-Smith

Blessed Quietness
September 20, 2000

ARABESQUE
BET BOOKS

BET Publications, LLC
www.bet.com
www.arabesquebooks.com

ARABESQUE BOOKS are published by

BET Publications, LLC
c/o BET BOOKS
One BET Plaza
1900 W Place NE
Washington, D.C. 20018-1211

First Printing: August, 2000

10 9 8 7 6 5 4 3 2 1
Printed in the United States of America

This book is dedicated to my loving, devoted husband,

Rudolph A. L. Smith

Rudy—

Steadfastly, you remain the wind beneath my wings, my anchor in the port of storms. Together, bravely, we've fought the numerous firestorms that have threatened to consume our lives over the past twenty-five years. Through it all, we've reigned victorious, as our love for each other continues to bring us through the white-hot flames unscathed. Constantly, with each passing day, we grow stronger in our love and commitment to God and to each other. Separately, we're winners, together, we're unstoppable, unbeatable champions.

I love you endlessly.

In loving memory of the loved ones who have gone on before us in search of the light:

Grandma & Grandpa Grinage and Grandma & Grandfather Hudson. Aunts Dorothy, Mary, Essie, and Lessie. Uncles Lowe, Carl, Arthur, Lee, Oscar, Bill, Ollius, Clarence, and Charles. Cousins Larry, Shirley, and Charles. Friends Ms. Wilimina, Levinia Hylton, and Joyce Hadden.

ACKNOWLEDGMENTS

My Father in Heaven: Thank you for the bounty of blessings you have so lovingly bestowed upon me. As for my phenomenal accomplishments, the glory is all Yours. Without You, I am nothing. With You, I can be anything I so desire. Thank you for loving me unconditionally.

Members of the United States Armed Forces & Their Families: Thank you for all that you put on the line to protect the citizens of the United States, twenty-four-seven, three-hundred-sixty-five days a year. The heavy sacrifices that you make on our behalf will always remain unrivaled.

Mary Wright & the Arabesque Team: Thanks from the depths of my heart for all the hard work and determination each of you gave to the Armed Forces Tour 2000. We should be proud of the extraordinary way in which we joined together to accomplish our mission, a surefire team effort.

Lupus Support Group, Oklahoma City, OK: Thank you for allowing me to come in as a guest speaker at your support group meeting. It was such a rewarding session for me.

Lupus Support Group, Houston, TX: Thanks for receiving me with open arms. Your warm embrace was heartfelt. I wear with great pride the lovely T-shirt that you presented to me.

My Sisters, Marlene, Donna, Candace & Sherry: Girls, I don't dare write another line without acknowledging the tremendous support you four have given me in marketing my first novel, ICE UNDER FIRE. Thanks for pushing my novels as if they were your very own. I love you.

My Brothers-in-Law, Jesse & Russell: As you are brothers to me, thank you for loving my sisters. Thank you for loving me and supporting my publishing efforts.

Melanie, AKA Magic Fingers: Thank you for keeping my hair healthy and always looking good. Thanks also for critiquing my literary works.

The Rialto Hair Biz Crew, Melanie, Willetta, Toni, Ursula, Donna & Glen: Your support of all my endeavors, as well as me personally, has always been tremendous. Thank you so much.

Publicist, Julia Shaw: Words cannot adequately express how much I appreciate you and all that you do on behalf of myself and the other Arabesque authors on a daily basis. Therefore, I'm not going to even try. Just know that your efforts and contributions do not go unrecognized.

Jacquelin Thomas: Thanks for all the support you've given me throughout the first publication process. The book shower your Focus Group held for me was absolutely the best.

Dr. Lloyd Walker & Staff: Your generosity is overwhelming. Thanks for advertising and selling my books in your office. Your unwavering support has meant a lot to me. You guys are great!

Photographer, Leroy Hamilton: Thanks for the marvelous photo shoot you pulled off on such short notice. The end results were absolutely amazing.

Q's in the Baldwin Hills Mall: Thanks for the fantastic makeup session that you did on me prior to my photo shoot. Your expertise came through brilliantly in the finished products.

One

Club Rojo, a very trendy southern California night-spot, overflowed with beautiful people of all ages. Rhythm and blues blared from the massive speakers as the clubgoers rocked to the soulful beat. While the wall-to-wall beveled mirrors reflected their images, the overhead mirrored globe shimmered sparkles of dazzling light over the dance floor. Flickering off and on, the colored strobe light animated the gyrating dancers in its flashing illumination.

It was Friday night, and everyone appeared to be gearing up for the weekend, Hillary Houston noticed as she stepped inside the door of the popular nightclub. Men had stripped away their ties and opened the collars of their shirts, in hopes of shedding their buttoned-down, nine-to-five, stuffy decorum. Women, making high-fashion statements in barely-there skirts, low-cut dresses, and curve-hugging slacks, had gallant hopes of meeting Mr. Right.

Reaching into her purse, Hillary pulled out a twenty-dollar bill and handed it to the man at the door to pay the cover charge for herself and Cassandra Paige, her best friend. "As usual, this place is slamming, Cassie. It looks like all the brothers and sisters in southern California are in this one club. I hope we can find a decent table," Hillary remarked, holding out her hand to be stamped.

"We better hope we can find a table, period," Cassie quipped, looking around for a place to sit. "Bingo, there's one right over there." She pointed at the only empty table in sight.

The two women rushed to the other side of the club, claiming the table just before another group of women, who'd spotted it at the same time, could make their way through the throng. Hillary and Cassie quickly pulled out two of the four chairs and slid into them with ease.

Noticing the group of women glaring at them from across the room, Hillary smiled sheepishly at Cassandra. "I'd say we got real lucky, Cassie, but it looks as though we've made a few enemies."

Cassandra's dark brown eyes twinkled with devilment. "Well, that's not our problem if we just happen to be swifter on our feet. They'll get over it. I love your outfit. I've never seen it before. When did you buy it?"

Hillary's honey-brown eyes danced with amusement as she recalled how she nearly had to pour her curvaceous hips into the forest-green leather pants. "I bought this outfit last year, when the fall fashions first came out. It was a perfect fit at the time, but it looks as though I've gained a pound or two." Hillary removed the matching biker-style jacket and smoothed her stark-white shirt into the slim waistband of the hip-hugging slacks.

Cassie showed an even set of pearly whites as she smiled brightly. "The pants don't look all that tight to me, especially when you consider what some of these other bimbos are wearing. I don't know how some of them can even breathe. The entire outfit looks great on you."

Hillary smiled affectionately at her dearest and oldest friend. "Thanks, Cassie."

Hillary Houston and Cassandra Paige, inseparable

childhood friends, had grown up in the small community
of Washburgh, Pennsylvania. Sharing the same age and
matching petite frames, they'd often been referred to as
the Bobbsey Twins. Over the years they had grown closer
than a lot of siblings. Though their personalities differed
greatly, each temperament complemented the other.

Hillary was effervescent yet somewhat reserved. Cassie
had more energy in her little finger than most people
had in their entire body. The definition of shy completely
escaped Cassie, and she rarely met any strangers who
stayed strangers. Although too trusting at times, Hillary
had a real knack for living her life to the fullest. Every
moment had to count for something worthwhile. Both
women had a great sense of humor. While Hillary used
diplomacy and tact in annoying situations, Cassie said
whatever came to mind. Hillary was slow to anger, but
Cassie could fly into a rage without a moment's notice.

Before purchasing town houses in the same complex,
the two friends had shared a two-bedroom apartment
while they worked to further their educational and career
goals. Both had grown up in the church, disliked phony
people, and were extremely loyal to one another.

While engaging in lively conversation, Hillary sipped
on a club soda and Cassie nursed a rum and Coke. A
dark shadow suddenly towered above them, and the two
women looked up, their incessant chatter coming to an
abrupt halt.

With eyes as black as raven feathers and as mysterious
as the dark side of the moon, the sinfully sexy man stood
at least six-foot-two. His velvety, clean-shaven face looked
as though it might have been polished with liquid
bronze, Hillary marveled.

"Hello, ladies," he greeted cheerfully, his voice as
deep as the bass tones that drifted loudly from the dance-
floor speakers. "How are you doing this evening?"

"Fine," both women said in unison.

"And you?" Cassie asked, flirtatiously, batting the long sable brown lashes that matched the color of her pixie-cut hair.

Revealing strong, even, white teeth, the stranger offered a generous smile. A smile that sent Hillary reeling.

"Great," he responded. "Would you two ladies mind if my friend and I share your table? He's on the phone at the moment. As you can see, there isn't another free chair in the house."

"That's fine by me," Cassie offered, looking over at Hillary for her approval.

As the handsome stranger fixed his raven-black eyes on Hillary, she nearly gasped out loud. "What about you? Do you have any objections, miss?"

Hillary wasn't all that interested in having anyone at their table, but this handsome man positively intrigued her. Nothing about him seemed to warrant a cold shoulder. "It's okay with me," she finally managed, tossing him a bewildered smile.

He pulled out a chair and sat down. "My name is Brandon David Blair." He then looked straight at Hillary. "And yours?"

She swallowed hard as she extended her hand to him. "Hillary Houston. Pleased to meet you, Brandon."

"Cassandra Paige," Cassie chimed in before he had a chance to inquire her name. "Nice to meet you, Brandon David Blair."

"It's my pleasure. Do you ladies come here often?"

"Only once in a while," Cassie offered. "We've been here a few times, but we're not much on hanging out in nightclubs. We indulge in club outings once every few months."

Brandon showed a definite interest in Hillary. "It's a nice place. I don't come that often myself, but my pal insisted that we come here tonight. I'm glad he did. I'm sure you hadn't noticed, Hillary Houston, but I've had a hard time keeping my eyes off of you."

Usually articulate, Hillary couldn't think of a suitable response. She cast her luminous, honey-brown gaze in his direction. Her flawless copper-brown complexion reflecting embarrassment, she nervously tossed back her glossy curtain of chestnut-brown hair. It fell below her slender shoulders, shimmering with flaming auburn highlights and framing her pretty face.

When Brandon Blair first appeared at the table, Hillary's glance at him had been cursory. As she risked another look up at him, she could see that he wasn't at all like the average pick-up artists she'd encountered in the past. *He's certainly handsome enough,* she considered. The magnetic pull from his dark, smoldering eyes made it difficult for her to tear her gaze from his fabulous looks. She watched as he ran exquisitely tapered fingers through his smooth, sable-brown hair. Unconsciously, she licked her lips, wondering what it would feel like to thread her own delicate hands through his clean-cut mass of thick waves.

As though he had read her mind, his full, sensuous mouth curved up in a devastating smile, causing Hillary's blood to rush from her head. "Are you sure you're okay with this arrangement, Miss Houston? You look a little uptight."

"I have no problem with it, as long as everyone understands we're just sharing a table." Hillary couldn't help imagining what it might be like to share his bed.

He grinned. "My, my, Miss Houston, I can see that you possess the gift of tact. Are you always this blunt?"

Hillary gave him a wry smile. "That's an interesting statement coming from you, considering you've been blunt from the moment you sat down."

"Well, pretty lady, when at first glance I can see far beyond a woman's outward beauty, I simply cut to the chase. At the risk of being blunt again, I'm intensely attracted to you. I'm also interested in getting to know you." His tone was unshakably confident.

Although Hillary thought his comments were a bit near the edge of her tolerance, she felt her insides turn to putty. "As for getting to know me, you may be getting into something you just might not be able to handle."

He leveled his eyes at her. "Miss Houston, I somehow get the feeling that you just might be right. But all the same, I'd love to get to know you better."

The sincerity in his voice made Hillary glad she hadn't responded to him with sarcasm, but that didn't mean she didn't feel a need to practice a certain amount of caution with this gorgeous male animal.

She extended her hand to him once again. "Nothing ventured, nothing gained."

Fully expecting him to shake her hand, Hillary looked stunned when he raised her hand to his mouth and brushed a feathery kiss over the back of it. No matter how charming she thought his gesture, she successfully hid the immense pleasure his soft lips aroused deep within her. He smiled broadly for the first time, and she felt a sharp intake of breath. As his smile illuminated his entire face, Hillary basked in it, as though experiencing the afterglow of making ardent love to him.

Interrupting the highly flammable moment, Cassie gasped loudly, drawing the attention of her two companions. Hillary looked beyond Cassie and saw the extremely good-looking reason for her friend's very audible reaction.

The approaching man entrapped the two women in his pleasant, steel-gray gaze. "I see you found a table, man. Not bad, not bad at all." Offering Cassie a radiant smile, the new arrival sat down next to her. "Hello, I'm Aaron Samms."

Aaron appeared even taller than Brandon. His body

was muscular, his smile engaging. From the look in Cassie's eyes, Hillary could see how pleased her friend was at making his acquaintance. Being her usual forward self, Cassie wasted no time in making that fact known as she made the proper introductions.

"Gee, Aaron, you're as handsome as your friend over there," Cassie cooed. Hillary gave her friend a look that said "at ease, girl," but Cassie didn't even seem to notice.

Brandon sensed Hillary's sudden quandary. "Miss Houston, may I have this dance?" He was intent on making sure Aaron knew which of the two ladies held his interest.

"Why, Mr. Blair, I think I can manage that."

As Brandon flashed Hillary another disarming smile, she suddenly felt helplessly weak. Had they made the right decision in letting these two charming roosters invade the hen house? Though eager to make contact with Brandon's hard body, she felt glad for the upbeat tempo of the song that played. Cassie and Aaron had already moved to the dance floor, yet Hillary hadn't even seen them leave the table. The magnetic pull of Brandon's dark eyes held her rapt attention, as he appeared to be just as absorbed in her wholesome beauty.

Conversation on the dance floor was next to impossible due to the volume of the music. Hillary looked surprised when she saw that Brandon had positively no rhythm. Highly unusual for a brother, but he seemed not to notice, and appeared truly comfortable with his performance on the dance floor. Hillary had a hard time keeping her own rhythm since he was totally out of sync with the music.

Hillary glanced over at Cassie, who appeared to be enjoying herself tremendously. *Isn't that what we came here for?* Hillary quietly contemplated. She then promised herself to loosen up and go with the flow. All of a sudden, when the music switched to a popular slow song, the very thing she'd been anticipating with some uncertainty, Brandon had her in his arms. Without warning, her entire body stiffened as he gripped her waist.

"Relax, Hillary, I'm not going to bite you. We're only sharing a dance."

Embarrassed, Hillary realized that he'd somehow sensed her feelings of reluctance. As she began to relax, she remembered her promise to loosen up. In her opinion, Brandon definitely showed more polish in the art of the slow dance.

Hillary really hadn't expected to meet anyone special this evening. Now that she had, she wasn't sure what to make of it. A prior relationship that lasted all of two months had turned out to be a disaster, leaving her markedly distrustful. Hillary had dated a few other guys since then, but none of them had earned her attention beyond the first date. She also had several male friends, but their relationships were strictly platonic. Was it going to be more of the same with Brandon? She had to wonder. Somehow, she didn't think so, especially if Brandon proved to be as charming as he seemed. Though she further relaxed her body, she felt the need to remain somewhat guarded.

Hillary allowed her body to melt into Brandon's. As his lower anatomy gave rise, his arm tightened around her waist and he rested his chin in her hair. It smelled wonderful, reminding him of a patch of sweetly scented wildflowers. The feminine scent of her perfume smelled even better than her hair.

Leaning her head against Brandon's unbuttoned shirt, Hillary nearly sneezed when the curly hairs of his massive chest made contact with her delicate nose. Her nose twitched a few times, but she stilled the urge to sneeze all over him. The embarrassment of such an occurrence would've been too much. Though she had a few problems with allergies, she could only hope that she wouldn't develop any allergies to Brandon Blair, real or imagined.

"What are you beautiful ladies drinking?" Aaron asked, once they were back at the table. After getting the others' responses, he summoned the waitress to the table. While waiting for the drinks to arrive, they engaged in light conversation.

"If it's not too personal, what line of work are you in?" Aaron asked Cassie.

"I'm a buyer for an exclusive women's boutique. I also do my own fashion designs in my spare time."

"Sounds like you keep pretty busy."

Cassie smiled sweetly. "I have so much energy, I need to be on the move all the time. I possess an inherent talent for fashion design. After moving west, I landed a job right away at an exclusive women's fashion boutique as a buyer. When patrons learned that I'd designed the outfits I wore, I found myself with more clients than I could handle. My label, Creations by Cass, has already earned a lot of recognition."

"She hopes to have her own fashion design company one day," Hillary interjected.

Aaron directed his attention to Hillary. "What about you, Hillary? Where do you work?"

"I'm a high-class call girl." Hillary's straight face belied the laughter she held inside. Cassie fought hard to keep herself from cracking up. Aaron appeared stunned.

Normally filled with radiating warmth, Hillary had her own patented personality. Her stunning figure and glowing beauty, which had claimed Brandon's immediate attention, mirrored the beauty she possessed within. Though she had the ability to draw people into the circle of her exuberance, at times her sense of humor went way over the top.

Brandon didn't take his eyes off of Hillary as he bit down on his lower lip. "I do commend you on your sense of humor. That was a good one." The look on his face said that he hadn't bought her response for a second. Aaron, still not sure if what she'd said was true or not, appeared to be in a state of shock.

Hillary touched Aaron's arm briefly. "You can relax, Aaron," she soothed. "I was just being flip. I usually take that approach when I want someone to get lost."

Brandon's ears immediately perked up. "Can I take that to mean you want us to get lost?" Brandon interjected.

She smiled. "No. I don't want you to get lost. I was just having a devilish moment. Aaron, I'm sorry for being so flip. To answer your question honestly, I'm a junior executive in the public relations/marketing department of a major airline."

Aaron sighed with obvious relief. "I must admit that you had me going. Sounds like you two have bright futures. I wish you ladies all the success in the world."

"Six months prior to Cassie joining me here in California, I landed a job with Atlantic Pacific Airlines," Hillary went on to explain. "After being offered the position, I switched from day classes to night classes, while earning my bachelor's degree in public relations and marketing. Once I completed my educational goals, I was promoted to my current position."

"We quickly established ourselves as professionals," Cassie added.

Possessing the voice of an angel, Hillary's first love was singing. She sang in nightclubs on the weekends for a short time, but she'd given it up when all too often she'd become the target of drunken patrons' affections. Though she was now an inactive member of a special choir, others still engaged her to perform at special occasions. When she became inundated with school and work, she'd given up on a singing career. It seemed as though performing was not in the cards for her, but it would always be in her blood.

"Brandon's an architectural engineer. He manages his own firm. In business, he's as aggressive as they come. It's that same enterprising technique that makes him highly revered among his colleagues," Aaron told the two women. "He knows exactly when and with whom to turn on and off his indelible charm. Under his brilliant direction, BDB Architectural Design puts out the finest designs money can buy."

Not only is Brandon handsome and extremely well packaged, he's packing brains as well, Hillary mused inwardly. In her X-rated thoughts, she couldn't help wondering what else he packed. Hillary didn't know how far this night might take her into the future, but she was more than willing to find out.

As for his personal relationships, Brandon had finally realized the same tactics he used in business just wouldn't work in a romantic situation. At thirty-two, he was still trying to mold a style that would best fit his personal and intimate interests. His inability to separate his dealings in his working relationships from those in his personal ones was never more evident than right now. Though four years his junior, Hillary Houston actually made him think before he jumped in with both feet. It seemed that she could become the only real challenge he'd ever had in a personal relationship, a prospect he deliberated with relish.

Brandon rubbed his hands together in an enthusiastic manner. "Since my partner here is singing my praises, I think it's only fitting that I return the favor. Mr. Samms is a junior partner in a very prestigious law firm." Brandon's boasting showed deep pride in his best friend's glowing accomplishments.

Impressed, Cassie whistled under her breath.

Aaron looked a little embarrassed. "Of the two of us,

I'm the most reticent, but I didn't make it through law school on good looks. I can be both ruthless and a gentleman in the courtroom."

Brandon slapped Aaron on the back. "Not only is he all that, he's meticulous in his preparation of a case. Aaron studies and researches case histories relentlessly. He uses every resource available to him. That's what makes him one of the best lawyers around."

As the two couples slipped into an easy comradeship, they talked and laughed as though they'd known one another for years. They were so caught up in their conversations, they didn't even notice when the lights came on to signal the closing of the club. It only became apparent to them when the waitress came to clear the table. The foursome then headed for the parking lot.

Standing in front of Hillary's car, they continued their individual conversations.

"Well, pretty lady, as for all of us being total strangers, I feel this evening turned out to be fantastic. I even enjoyed our sparring sessions. I do love a challenge. I have to give it to you, kid, you're sharp," Brandon complimented, running his forefinger down the side of Hillary's face. "Very few people can hold their own against me, especially in the department of humor. So I'm going to concede this contest as a draw."

"A draw?" Hillary inquired haughtily. "You know I won hands down. However, this has been a fantastic evening for me, as well. Thank you for sharing your time with me."

He smiled lazily. "I should be thanking you. This is the first time I completely forgot about business. I didn't check my answering service the entire evening. Do you think we could do this again, real soon?"

"I think that would be nice."

Brandon wrote his phone number down for Hillary and handed her the pen to write her own. "This doesn't have to end right now. It's only two-thirty. Why don't we all grab something to eat?" Brandon suggested. "A cup of coffee will keep us alert for a little while longer."

Hillary looked over at Cassie. Surprised to see her and Aaron locked in what appeared to be a very passionate kiss, she quickly decided the situation needed to be diffused. She frowned slightly. "With regret, I have to decline your offer. I have to get up early to prepare a proposal that has to be presented to the senior executives of my department by the middle of the week. I'm really sorry."

Smiling seductively, Brandon hid his disappointment. "I fully understand, but the next time I won't let you off the hook this easy."

"Cassie," Hillary shouted, "dear friend, it's time to go. We need to get some rest." She prayed that Cassie wasn't going to challenge her. Cassie needed a time-out, whether she knew it or not, Hillary surmised.

Reluctantly, Cassie pried herself loose from Aaron's embrace. They also exchanged phone numbers and promised to stay in close contact. As Brandon kissed Hillary lightly on the cheek, she felt her body temperature soar a few degrees. Seated inside Hillary's midnight-blue Corvette, they waved to the two men as they drove off into the darkness. Brandon and Aaron watched as the powerful car sped away.

Discussing in detail what they'd learned about the guys, Hillary and Cassie talked nonstop all the way home. Though Hillary thought the two men were intelligent, charming, and handsome beyond belief, she was well aware of a man's knack for being artificially charming. Especially the men born and bred in Los Angeles.

Looking worried, Hillary glanced over at Cassie. "I was stunned to see you and Aaron kissing with such passion."

Cassie looked slightly abashed. "I just couldn't help myself. Somehow it seemed right. You know I never get that familiar with anyone I've just met, but Aaron is not just anyone. I have a darn good feeling about him."

Hillary clucked her tongue. "Cassie, I understand that all the right vibes were there, but let's face it, we really don't know who or what we're dealing with here. I'd like us both to approach these friendships with some degree of caution." Hillary's tone lacked conviction.

Cassie punched at her thigh. "You're right, as usual. We should be careful, but Aaron turns me on in a way that I've never been turned on before."

"I know the feeling . . . and that's what scares me silly."

Arriving at the complex, Hillary pressed the remote-control button that opened the security gate. She waved to the guards as the car passed the security shed. Since they hadn't discussed sharing sleeping quarters, Hillary headed the car in the direction of Cassie's unit.

"We'll talk tomorrow, Cassie. I'm really beat," Hillary responded to Cassie's offer to join her for a hot cup of tea. She watched until she saw Cassie safely inside, then drove on to her own place, only a short distance away.

Stopping in front of her unit, she pressed the remote-control button that opened the garage door. Pulling the car into the garage, she parked it, cut the engine, and closed the door.

With her feet screaming to be free, Hillary rushed into her three-bedroom town house and immediately kicked her shoes off. Tossing her purse on the hall credenza, she walked through to the front of the house.

The walls of the spacious town house, painted in a glossy antique ivory, suggested an expansive spirit of openness and airiness. Nestled on top of plush rose-pink carpets, the bone-white chairs and sofa were cut from the finest leather. Rose-pink miniblinds covered the windows. Embracing the living areas in a refreshing breath of spring coolness, the mint-green accents had a calming effect on a weary spirit. Sandwashed coffee tables, a fine creation of wood blended with glass, completed the contemporary decor.

A twinkle appeared in Hillary's eyes as she recalled all the insufferable months it had taken for her and Cassie to find homes they could afford to purchase without burying themselves under the weight of heavy mortgage payments. Each of their parents had been more than willing to chip in on the down payments, but they'd insisted on making the real-estate purchases entirely on their own. Offering many of the amenities they were both interested in, security being the most important, the Palm Court Town House complex had been affordable and within proximity of each of their jobs.

Once they'd taken a sweeping tour of the entire complex, there wasn't any doubt that they'd found the perfect living quarters. Waiting to find out if their loans had been approved had been the most difficult part, Hillary recalled, as she climbed the winding stairs.

Deep lavender and glacier-blue accents set against ecru walls and bone-white French bedroom furnishings washed the master bedroom in coolness and unstructured serenity. Deep lavender bedding evoked moods perfect for reflecting and dreaming. French doors opened onto a balcony overlooking one of the complex's three azure lakes.

While stripping out of her clothes, Hillary checked the answering machine on the bedside table. Finding nothing urgent on the taped messages, she headed for the shower. After a brief respite under the hot water, she dried off quickly and sprinkled scented bath powder over her body. The mid-length gown she slipped into was done in cream-colored silk. Lastly, she brushed her hair into a ponytail.

Before diving into bed, she opened the balcony door and said her prayers. She felt so exhausted that she couldn't even pick up a book, let alone read, which was her normal bedtime routine. Bone-tired, she turned off the bedside lamp and nestled under the warm down comforter.

Hillary had a few titillating thoughts of the extremely handsome Brandon David Blair as she made herself comfortable. She nestled her head onto the goose-down pillow, and her eyes became so heavy that she couldn't keep them open any longer. Turning on her side, she immediately dozed off.

The top was down on Brandon's white Mercedes-Benz as he cruised down Highway 1. He had to admit to himself that he'd been quite taken with Hillary Houston, as he reflected back on the evening. She seemed to be one dynamite lady. Brandon grinned when he thought about the statement she'd made about him *getting into something he might not be able to handle.* As he had earlier, he couldn't help wondering if she'd been right. He'd never taken to someone so quickly. It felt as though he'd known Hillary Houston all of his life. As he pulled through the gates of his coastal home, he knew he had to call her before he went to bed.

Brandon parked the expensive car and sped into the house. Inside his bedroom, he quickly picked up the phone. Looking at the business card that had her home phone number written on the back, he put his call through.

Hillary had no idea how long she'd been asleep when the shrill sound of the telephone interrupted her serenity. Bolting upright, she reached for the receiver. "Hello," she responded drowsily.

"Hello, pretty lady," came the bass response from the

other end. "It's Brandon. I just wanted to make sure you girls got home safely. I hope I didn't wake you." He sounded apologetic, as if he knew he'd awakened her.

"You did wake me," Hillary retorted much too quickly, "not to mention the fact that the phone ringing at this hour scared me to death. I resent the intrusion," she lashed out. She regretted her rudeness the instant the cutting remarks crossed the phone line. Ashamed of her horrible attitude, she momentarily buried her head under the covers. There was a long moment of uncomfortable silence.

"I see you carry that sharp tongue of yours to bed with you, as well," he joked.

She sighed, relieved to hear that he didn't sound a bit put-off by her rude behavior. "Brandon, I'm really sorry. It's just that I was sleeping so well. Once I awaken, I have a hard time getting back to sleep. You didn't deserve my wrath. It's really thoughtful of you to call to see that I'd made it home. Thanks for caring."

Though tempted, she avoided the urge to be flippant, fighting hard to keep from telling him what she really thought. She'd been getting home by herself for as long as she could remember, not to mention that she couldn't imagine who'd suddenly appointed him as her keeper.

Not wanting to turn him off, especially when she had every intention of finding out exactly what turned him on, she was glad that she'd successfully controlled her urge to be coy. They talked a couple of minutes longer, then a major bout of fatigue started to take over her entire body. Her arms and legs felt heavy and her eyes kept closing.

"I'm really enjoying our conversation, but I'm going to have to go. My jaws are as tired as the rest of my body. Even my skin and hair feels tired. I rarely stay up this late and I know how moody I get when I don't get the proper rest."

He laughed at her comments. "Hillary, please, just one more thing before you go. Can I persuade you to have dinner with me later this evening?"

Hillary hesitated for a minute as she pondered his request. "I think I'd like that."

"Great! Is six-thirty a good time?"

"Seven would be better." She was determined to be the one to set the rules. She wasn't ever going to give up her control to any man. If she remained in control of herself right up front, she wouldn't have to worry about things getting out of hand later on.

"Seven it is. I'll call you at a decent hour to get your address." The humor in his remark didn't escape her as they signed off on the promise of talking later in the day.

Surprisingly enough, Hillary fell right back to sleep.

Two

Hillary had fully intended to sleep until noon, but she awakened to the incessant ringing of the doorbell. It had to be Cassie or a neighbor, she figured. No one else was able to gain access to the complex without going through security. Still feeling sleepy, she had the urge to pull the comforter over her head and ignore the bell. Instead, she dragged herself out of bed and slipped into the raspberry silk robe that matched her gown.

She dragged herself to the door like a zombie and looked through the peephole. Cassie stood there looking like she'd just gotten out of a revitalizing tank. Hillary opened the door, and Cassie bounced in like a newly blown-up beach ball.

"Cassie, for goodness sake, have you never heard of Alexander Graham Bell?" Cassie looked at her friend in bewilderment. "You know, the guy who invented the contraption called a telephone."

Cassie laughed. "Good morning to you, too. You're in rare form today."

"Cassie, I'm a walking zombie. We were out till the wee hours of the morning. And if that wasn't enough, Sir Brandon took it upon himself to call to see if we'd made it home safely. Is there no peace?"

Cassie was slightly offended by Hillary's snippy disposition. "Girlfriend, you definitely need an attitude adjustment. I'm sorry for intruding in your space. I'll come back after you've made the necessary adjustments." Cassie turned back to the door, her tail between her legs.

"No, Cassie, wait. I'm the one who is sorry. I'm just plain worn out. Work was a bear this week, not to mention the mess with that Cash character. I also have a presentation to deliver to the senior executive of my department on Wednesday. I just feel overwhelmed. Cassie, please forgive me. Come on in the kitchen while I fix us some hot tea."

Cassie smiled as she hugged her best friend. "You know I understand. I haven't been your friend all this time without knowing when to be sensitive to your moods."

Hillary hugged Cassie back. "Thanks. I can always count on you to be there, Cass. Still, that's no excuse for taking my frustrations out on you. I'll try to do better. I also ripped into Brandon earlier."

Cassie's eyes grew sympathetic. "Lighten up, girlfriend. You're acting like you do this on a regular basis. Everyone has a bad day or two now and then. You've certainly survived through plenty of mine."

Hillary frowned. "Yeah, but that still doesn't make it right."

Cassie sat at the kitchen table chatting nonstop about the previous evening. After Hillary poured the tea, she pulled out a chair and sat down.

"Aaron called before I left the house. He asked me out tonight."

"Did you accept?" Hillary could already see the answer Cassie had given him glowing on her face.

"Take one educated guess." They both laughed. "Did you and Brandon make plans for this evening?" Cassie probed with a bit of reluctance.

Hillary frowned. "As a matter of fact, we did, but I'm not sure we should've."

"Hillary, for heaven's sake, why not?"

"I'm more than intrigued with him and I think he's an okay guy, but he seems so sophisticated in the ways of the world. I'd feel more comfortable if we double-dated a while, Cass. I'm not sure I'm ready to be alone with such a handsome charmer."

Cassie sucked her teeth. "Hillary, you know as well as I do that you can double-date a hundred times and you still might not get to know the true person. When people are alone together, they have a tendency to be more real with one another. If a man is going to attack you, of course he's not going to do it with witnesses. My instincts tell me that Aaron and Brandon are real brothers. I don't think you need to worry."

Hillary shook her head from side to side. "Cassie, what is the method to your madness? You have an irrational answer for everything."

"I resent you calling me irrational," Cassie charged, pretending to be offended. "If anyone is irrational, it's you."

Exasperated with how the conversation was going, Hillary crossed her arms in front of her chest. "Cassie, I simply call it as I see it, yet I'll concede that some of what you've said makes sense. But not all of it makes sense to me."

"So, is it settled, are you going to see Brandon this evening?"

Hillary rolled her eyes. "Yes. As much as I hate to admit it, being alone at dinner with Brandon seems much more appealing than watching you and Aaron mooning over each other all evening."

Grinning, Cassie clapped her hands. "All right! That's my girl. You won't regret it."

After two cups of tea and a light breakfast consisting of boiled eggs and toast, Cassie left to do some shopping.

She had invited Hillary to come along, but Hillary had too many things to do and too little time to do them in.

The minute Cassie left, Hillary immediately busied herself with her household chores, starting downstairs and working her way up. Saving the dusting for last, she vacuumed the carpets, cleaned the mirrors, and freshened up the bathrooms. An hour later, satisfied that everything looked sparkling clean, she went back downstairs to the living room.

Hillary grabbed a pillow, placed it under her head, and stretched out on the sofa. She saw how late it had gotten and realized that Brandon hadn't called. Worried, she wondered if he'd changed his mind about dinner. She couldn't blame him. She hadn't been in the most pleasant of moods. Besides being tired, Hillary knew her bad moods had everything to do with her problems at work.

For the past several weeks she'd been suffering through sexual harassment by one of the department heads, namely Alexander Cash. Thinking about the situation at work depressed her since she didn't have a clue what to do about it. When the phone finally rang, she was glad for the timely diversion. She couldn't help hoping it was Brandon Blair.

"Hello, Hillary speaking."

"Hillary Houston, this is the man you've spent the entire day dreaming about." Her body tensed slightly. "Hold on, pretty lady, I can feel your troubled spirit coming right through the phone. I was only kidding. The truth of the matter is . . . I've spent the whole day dreaming about you."

His soothing voice relaxed her as she laughed at his flirtatious comment. "Brandon Blair, you were almost slashed by my razor-sharp tongue. And I just finished sharpening its outer edges."

While laughing at her colorful humor, Brandon

thought about what it might feel like to have her warm tongue wrestling with his own. He closed his eyes to savor the pleasant image. On the other end of the line, she found herself enjoying his delicious throaty sounds.

Brandon forced his mind back to reality. "Are we still on for tonight? Before you answer, let me tell you that I have one incredible evening planned for you."

As if that bit of news might influence my decision, she thought defiantly. "Yes, Brandon, I'll be expecting you promptly at seven. At two minutes after seven, you become yesterday's news."

He laughed. "Hillary Houston, I can see that you're going to be quite a challenge. So I'm putting you on notice. I love a good challenge. In fact, I thrive on them."

Does anything put this guy off balance? she wondered. She gave him her address and explained the complex's security measures before they bid one another farewell.

As Hillary lathered her petite body with a fragrant shower gel, she wondered what surprises the evening might hold. Feeling squeaky clean, she dried off thoroughly and slipped into a comfortable robe. She then headed back down to the family room, where she plugged in the blowdryer. As she sank down onto the couch, she flipped the television on.

One of her favorite old movies was showing: *Cabin in the Sky,* starring Ethel Waters. She remembered watching it many times with her parents as a child. The movie was already in progress when it suddenly dawned on her that she hadn't eaten anything since the meager breakfast she'd shared with Cassie. Jumping up from the sofa, she ran into the kitchen for a light snack, hoping she wouldn't spoil her appetite for dinner.

With sandwich and cold drink in tow, Hillary settled down to watch the movie. It was then that she realized she hadn't heard from Cassie, which made her wonder if she was okay. Then she remembered that when Cassie got into the malls, she lost all sense of time. That somehow made her feel confident that her friend was just fine.

Halfway through the movie, the doorbell rang, and Hillary immediately thought of Cassie. As she looked through the peephole, she saw Bob, one of the complex's hired messengers. He held a long white box wrapped with a beautiful pink ribbon. She opened the door and greeted him warmly.

"Good afternoon, Miss Houston. I have a delivery for you."

"Wait a second," she requested, before taking off to get some money for a tip.

Smiling, she handed him the money, thanked him, and closed the door.

Hillary carried the box into the family room, where she set it down beside her on the sofa. Eagerly, she freed the box from the large bow that held it secure. Inside the box were at least two dozen beautiful, long-stemmed deep pink roses. The beauty of the blooms simply took her breath away as she just about destroyed the envelope getting at the card.

The card read: JUST SOMETHING TO REMIND YOU OF ME UNTIL TONIGHT. Brandon's signature peered up at her from the bottom of the card. Beside herself with joy, she ran to the kitchen to search for a vase, hoping she'd find one large enough to hold all the roses.

To her delight, she found the perfect one. She filled it with water and carried it back to the family room to arrange the delicate flowers. Something floated to the floor as Hillary lifted the roses out of the box. When she looked down, she saw the most perfect pink rosebud attached to a card with writing on it, and she bent down to pick it up.

The card simply read: FOR YOUR LOVELY HAIR. Deeply touched by the beautiful sentiments, she felt tears well up in her eyes. She'd never had anyone make her feel so beautiful and so special. She was tempted to pinch herself to see if she was really awake. Hillary's first instinct was to call Brandon to thank him, but she thought better of it. She felt way too emotional over the roses, and her voice just might tell how high her emotions ran. She wasn't ready to reveal the vulnerable side of her to anyone. No, she decided, she'd wait until she saw him to thank him.

"Hillary, it's me. I just got home. Girl, I saw so many things I wanted, I had a rough time making up my mind."

Hillary smiled wryly as she plopped down on the bed for a short chat on the phone before getting dressed for her date. "Cassie, you always have a hard time making up your mind. What did you finally decide on?"

Cassie gasped loudly. "I found the most gorgeous dress you have ever laid your eyes on," she enthused, describing it in detail.

"Cassie, it sounds like your dress is divine. I'm sure Aaron will appreciate all your efforts."

"He'd better, especially if he knows what I know."

The women made plans to get together with their dates at Hillary's, agreeing to meet at one A.M. After promising each other to take things cautiously, they rang off.

The fuchsia-colored taffeta dress Hillary pulled from her closet had a full skirt and a wraparound off-the-shoulder collar. Its wide belt had rhinestones on the buckle. The diamond teardrop earrings her parents had given her as a gift sparkled with life as she lifted them from the black velvet box. Also fuchsia in color, the kid leather shoes and bag she'd chosen had been specifically purchased to match the dress.

Hillary slipped into fresh panties and pulled on a strapless rose-colored slip. Carefully, she pulled on quicksilver-colored silk pantyhose, which shimmered on her shapely legs as she walked over to her dressing table and sat down to tackle her hair and makeup. Having made the decision to wear her hair down, she brushed it thoroughly and pushed one side behind her ear. Picking up the delicate little rosebud, she secured it behind her ear with a rhinestone comb.

Hillary dabbed a small amount of foundation onto her face with a sponge and sealed it with loose translucent powder. With a wide makeup brush, she lightly dusted her high cheekbones with a rose blush and added a deep fuchsia lipstick to her luscious mouth. How appropriate that Brandon had chosen pink roses, she reflected quietly. It was as if he'd known what color she would wear. She knew that to be impossible, yet she liked to think that he had.

Lastly, she reached for the dress and slipped it up over her curvaceous hips and slender waist. Taking a few steps back, Hillary looked into the full-length mirror to observe the fruits of her careful labor. Pleased with the elegant results, she smiled broadly as she left the bedroom and started downstairs. The phone rang just as she reached the bottom of the staircase.

"Hello, Miss Houston, this is Brian James with security. A Mr. Blair is here to see you. Should I let him through?"

She giggled inwardly. "Yes, Brian. I'm expecting him. Please direct him to my unit," she requested, feeling the skittish butterflies taking charge of her stomach.

"Very well, Miss Houston, I'll direct him over." Hillary hung up the phone and went into the living room to await Brandon's arrival.

Brandon arrived at the door at seven sharp. Hillary loved a man who was prompt. Since she worked in the airline business, punctuality was very important to her.

Smiling, she opened the door. He was even more hand-some than she'd remembered.

She marveled at the medium-gray double-breasted jacket he wore over a pale lavender silk shirt, which had his initials boldly embroidered on the collar. His exqui-site silk tie boasted various shades of gray and purple and his expensive-looking charcoal-gray leather boots sported a high gloss. His elegant attire looked as though it had been specifically tailored to define his broad shoul-ders, slender waist, and strapping thighs.

And he has immaculate fingernails, Hillary declared in-wardly. She had a thing about clean fingernails and good, strong teeth. When Brandon smiled, she got another good look at the most beautiful set of even, white teeth and the healthiest pink gums she'd ever seen.

"Good evening, pretty lady. You're stunning! You're even more beautiful than I remembered," he offered, echoing her very own sentiments about him.

She smiled sweetly. "Thank you. Good evening, your-self. You must have read my mind. I had thought the same thing about your looks. Sometimes people look al-together different from when you first meet them in a darkened room." As he stepped into the tiled foyer, he leaned forward and landed a light kiss on Hillary's fore-head. She blushed. "Would you like to come in for a few minutes, or should I just get my wrap?"

Without passing comment, Brandon moved further into the hall and waited to follow her lead. As he looked all around him, he took notice of her exquisite taste. "You have a great place here. Mind if I ask who's your decorator?"

"Just little old me," she cooed softly.

Just as he felt the rushing heat that Hillary caused to arise inside of him, he felt the warmth emanating from the rose-pink and mint-green of her surroundings. "Well,

I see one more talent that you possess. And, lady, I'm eager to find out what else is in that arsenal of yours."

Amused and touched by his overt flattery, she led the way into the spacious living room. "Thank you for your compliments, Brandon. Flattery will put you right on the top of my list."

"In that case, I should be at the top of your list before this night is over." He failed to mention that he'd spent the entire day hoping she didn't have a list. His name would soon be the only name on it, he surmised with confidence.

Hillary noticed his eyes zero in on the roses she'd beautifully arranged and placed on the hall credenza. "Mr. Blair," she rushed in quickly, fearing he might pass comment on the fact that she'd failed to phone in her gratitude, "thank you for the lovely roses. They were quite a pleasant surprise for me. Believe me, their beauty lifted my spirits. Tremendously."

He smiled broadly. "Miss Houston, you are most welcome. Somehow I get the feeling you deserve to have anything your heart desires."

Boy, he sure can turn on the charm, Hillary thought, slightly amused. Besides his irresistible charm, he seemed so sincere. Was he indeed a sincere man? She had to wonder as she showed him around the rest of her place. Purposely, she avoided taking him into her bedroom, but she could see by the devilish smile on his face that he'd noticed.

He shot her a thoughtful glance. "I noticed that you showed me every nook and cranny except where you lay your pretty head at night. I'd like to see where you hang out. It would be nice to imagine you in your intimate surroundings when I'm talking to you on the phone." *Especially in the heat of the night,* he added in his thoughts. Reluctantly, Hillary directed Brandon to the master bedroom. Her face became flushed as she watched his eyes skim seductively over her bed.

He whistled softly. "Hill, this is a spectacular room, beautiful just like you. Your whole house emanates warmth. You've really done a fantastic interior decorating job."

She noticed how he'd shortened her name and she rather liked the familiarity it brought. She thanked him again and quickly retreated from the room. Something about standing in her bedroom with the atrociously sexy Brandon Blair caused her pulse to quicken. She heaved a sigh of relief as they descended the winding staircase.

He glanced at his gold wristwatch. "Hillary, we have reservations for eight-fifteen. We'd better get going."

Hillary grabbed a light wrap from the hall closet as they headed for the door. Brandon secured the house before directing her to his white Mercedes-Benz.

She hadn't seen his car the night before, and his choice in what she considered extremely expensive but very reliable transportation impressed her. He opened the car door for her and she slipped into the soft leather seat with ease. The plush interior of the car matched the dark blue convertible top.

"Brandon, this is a lovely car. I've always wanted a convertible, but I've been so afraid of the top getting slashed."

He situated himself in the driver's seat. "I've had the same fear, but this model comes with an interchangeable hard top. It's the same color as the body. Was that your Corvette you were driving last night?"

"It is. Since I'm afraid of the ragtop, I opted for the model with a sunroof. It doesn't allow me to get as much fresh air as I'd probably get with the convertible, but I'm very satisfied with it." Hillary positioned herself so that she faced him. "Where are we having dinner?"

His dark eyes held a hint of mystery. "Pretty lady, it's

a surprise." There was a touch of mystery in his tone as well. "You'll see when we get there."

Hillary loved the ambiance of mystique that this evening promised and which Brandon's tone seemed to suggest. They rode in silence the rest of the way to their destination.

As her head rested against the seat's back, her eyes closed, her thick eyelashes fanning across her lower lids. Though her loveliness threatened to engulf him, Brandon took the opportunity to study her whenever he could. How he'd love to kiss her full, ripe lips. He licked his own as though he could taste her on them.

Brandon pulled the car into the valet parking lane of a large hotel located in the heart of Hollywood. As he reached over to gently brush his lips across Hillary's cheek, she opened her eyes and tossed Brandon a smile that caused his heart to skip a beat. A few moments of silence ensued before he jumped out of the car and dashed around to the passenger side to open the door for her.

The valet attendant reached the passenger side at the same time he did, but Brandon made it very clear that he had it covered. After helping Hillary out of the car, he handed the attendant the car key. Placing his hand gently under her elbow, he directed her into the hotel. While he felt the niggling urge to steal a kiss from her luscious mouth, his outward appearance remained cool and sedate.

Inside the elevator, Brandon pressed the button labeled TOP OF THE TOWER. Although Hillary had already heard wonderful things about the five-star establishment, still, she was impressed. As they stepped off the elevator, they floated into a vision of beauty she couldn't have begun to imagine. The restaurant, famous for its excellent cuisine, had a revolving tier with a panoramic view of Hollywood and its dazzling surroundings. In the or-

chestra pit located in the center of the restaurant, a trio
played Top 40 hits. Several ficus trees decorated with tiny
white lights provided moderate lighting.

The tables dressed in fine white linen and bathed in
soft candlelight created a wonderfully romantic aura.
Waiters wore black tuxedos, crisp white shirts, black bow
ties, and black cummerbunds. Waitresses wore the same
formal attire, only with long black skirts. The entire restaurant appeared to be one continuous window. One
could see for miles and miles when the city was free of
smog. It was a crystal-clear night in Hollywood.

Hillary felt as though she'd been transported into the
center of a fairy tale. She quickly became intoxicated by
the luxurious surroundings. Making sure Hillary stayed
close to him, Brandon approached the reservation desk.
He gave the hostess his surname and she instantly led
them to a table in the revolving section of the restaurant.

Brandon first ordered drinks from the waiter who
stood by patiently. He then reached over and put Hillary's hand gently in his. "Hill, is this place to your satisfaction?" His sweet breath lightly fanned her cheek.

The way he said the shortened version of her name
made Hillary tingle all over. "Yes, Brandon, but I
would've preferred McDonald's." He laughed along with
her. "I can't imagine anywhere being any lovelier than
here. You've made an excellent choice. Thank you for
bringing me here." *I keep finding myself thanking this man,*
she thought quietly.

The waiter arrived promptly with their drink order.
Hillary had ordered her usual club soda with a twist of
lime and Brandon had ordered the same. He usually
drank Chivas Regal, but with such precious cargo to care
for, he wouldn't even consider drinking alcohol and driving. He was only an occasional drinker, and he rarely
imbibed outside the comfort of his own home. While

engaging in light conversation, they discussed their families, jobs, and goals in life.

Brandon looked surprised. "I can't believe that you moved to California only a few years ago from a small western Pennsylvania town. You seemed to be quite knowledgeable in the history of my native Los Angeles. It sounds as if you know as much about my beloved city as I do."

"It only sounds that way. I love to study the history of the places I travel to. How was it growing up in a big city like L.A.?" Though they had discussed ambitions and such, Hillary had purposely failed to mention her lifelong aspiration of becoming a celebrated recording artist.

He grinned. "It only seems big to those who haven't lived here all their lives. Nowadays, the native Californians have grown few in number, but my parents still live here. I grew up in Los Angeles, but I own a home in Malibu."

Hillary was surprised that he resided in a prestigious beach community. That someone so young had accomplished so much astounded her. While discussing all the things they liked to do in their leisure time, they both were delighted to discover they had a lot in common.

The waiter appeared to take their dinner order, causing the conversation to end abruptly. Hillary ordered boneless breast of chicken, sautéed in a delicate wine sauce. Besides a Caesar's salad, she chose sautéed mushrooms and wild rice. Brandon ordered prime rib of beef, medium well. He also ordered the same side dishes as Hillary, but added a mixed zucchini dish steamed in lemon butter, opting for Italian dressing on his garden salad. As the waiter departed, Brandon asked that a bottle of nonalcoholic champagne be delivered to the table. Savoring each and every bite of the superbly prepared meal, Brandon and Hillary ate in complete silence, each in wondrous awe of the other's presence.

Thirty minutes later, full and satisfied, Hillary pushed back from the table.

"That's the most exquisite meal I've ever eaten," Hillary praised.

"My sentiments exactly. I'd heard about the great food and the fantastic atmosphere this restaurant offers, but this surpasses anything I ever imagined. To top it off, I have the most beautiful companion to share it with. The atmosphere pales in comparison to your loveliness."

Hillary was elated by the fact that he hadn't been there before. Knowing he chose to bring her here on their first date made her feel even more special, if that were possible. This man could charm the sweet out of candy, she reflected warmly. Brandon could steal her heart without making the slightest incision.

Spotting the small dance floor in the center of the restaurant near the orchestra pit, Brandon smiled. "Hillary, would you care to dance?"

She smiled. "I'd like that very much. I could use some exercise to get rid of some of those delicious calories I just consumed."

"I hope that's not the only reason you agreed to dance with me."

"No, Brandon, it isn't. I enjoy dancing with you." *As long as it's a slow song,* she added in her thoughts, stifling the urge to laugh.

Brandon walked around the table and gently pulled her up from her chair. Putting his arm around her tiny waist, he guided her to the dance floor. The jazzy music, soft and dreamy, floated through the room. Pulling Hillary in very close to him, he held her tight. When he pressed his lips to her left temple, Hillary closed her eyes and nestled her head against his broad chest. Though she was much shorter than he was, he thought they made a striking pair.

Brandon whispered softly into Hillary's ear, but she

honestly didn't hear a word he said. She was simply lost in the music and the warmth radiating from his strong body. His Aramis cologne filled her nostrils with a tantalizing, manly smell, the clean, fresh smell of the scent he wore making her want to nestle her nose in his neck.

When the band took a break, they headed back to the table, with him holding on to her as though she might suddenly disappear from his grasp.

"Pretty lady, what would you like do now? I'm very open to suggestion."

Hillary scowled. "Brandon, I forgot to mention it, but I promised to meet Cassie and Aaron back at my place after our date. I hope that wasn't too presumptuous of me. I meant to mention it long before now."

He grinned. "That's fine by me. But I have to ask. Is this a built-in mechanism you and Cassie have to ensure your safety with Aaron and me?"

Hillary had to laugh. Was she an open book or what? "How perceptive you are. I can't deny that we discussed safety issues. Please don't take it personally. There are a lot of crazies out here. Cassie and I are two single, small-town women living in a big, bad city. We've always felt it necessary to look out for one another. I hope you're not offended."

He placed his hand on top of hers. "Hillary, you and Cassie sound like two very sensible, rational females. I find it refreshing that you two care so much about one another to do whatever it takes to ensure each other's safety. Friends are indeed a rare breed. I, for one, am glad that you and Cassie have each other. No, Hillary, I'm not offended. Quite the contrary. What time are we supposed to meet them?"

Hillary glanced at her watch and saw that it was already ten-forty-five. Where had the time gone? she wondered, realizing she'd been completely lost in the tender moments of the evening. "We had agreed on one o'clock. Is that okay with you?"

He nodded. "That's perfect. We'll have almost two hours alone. Why don't we just move over to the lounge, Hill?"

"That's fine by me," Hillary responded sweetly.

With the bill taken care of, he walked around to pull Hillary's chair out. Hand-in-hand, they walked into the lounge, where they found two seats close to the bandstand.

He pulled out her chair. Wanting to study every detail of her beautiful face, he seated himself directly across from her. Content with just conversing and listening to the music, Hillary and Brandon remained off the dance floor.

Suddenly, the music stopped, and the reed-thin bandleader stepped to the microphone. "Good evening, ladies and gentlemen. Thank you so much for joining us this evening. For you that frequent the lounge, you know that once a week we ask the audience to share their talents with us. Tonight is the night! If there is anyone in the audience who can sing or play an instrument, and would like to entertain us, please raise your hand."

Hillary looked all around the lounge, but no one was volunteering. As the bandleader sent out another plea, she had a strong urge to raise her hand, even though no one else did. "Come on, I know there's at least one or two people out there who have a special talent."

As Hillary's hand rose, involuntarily, she knew she couldn't have helped herself if she'd tried. When she looked over at Brandon, she saw the shocked expression on his face.

The bandleader's face showed obvious pleasure. "I knew we had some talent in the house," the bandleader enthused. "Young lady, could you please come forward?"

Speechless, Brandon stood as Hillary left her seat. He watched as she walked toward the bandstand in what appeared to be slow motion. When the bandleader reached out for her hand to help her onto the bandstand, Brandon felt a pang of impetuous jealousy rip right through him.

The man introduced himself to Hillary as Barry Tolbert, asking her name and special talent. Hillary told him she would sing. He then asked her to tell him what song she wanted to perform so he could make sure the band could play the music. With his brief interview with Hillary over, Barry walked back to the microphone.

"Ladies and gentlemen, we present to you the lovely Hillary Houston. She will perform "The Look of Love" from the hit movie *Casino Royale*. We all know that one, don't we?" As he summoned Hillary to the microphone, he adjusted it to her height. Stepping back from the microphone, he took his place with the band.

The band cued up and the first notes began. Hillary looked over at Brandon and saw that he still appeared to be in a state of shock. *I know he's praying I don't make a fool of him,* Hillary thought nervously. Sure that he didn't want to be embarrassed by her, she flashed him a reassuring smile and he appeared to relax.

Three

Hillary closed her eyes and began to sing soulfully, sweetly, angelically. Immediately captivating her audience, Hillary drew the room into a hushed reverence. At some point during the song, she opened her eyes to glance over at Brandon. Beaming, he nodded his approval.

Just as the last note was sung, the room came to life with a roar. People clapped and cheered and wolf whistles came from every direction. Feeling the same unadulterated peace she always did when she sang, Hillary stepped down from the bandstand.

The bandleader quickly summoned her back. "Young lady, you need an agent—that's if you don't already have one. Please feel free to come back and join us anytime." Barry stepped back to the microphone. "Wow! That was fantastic!" Drowning him out, the thunderous applause broke out again.

Hillary had been in her element, and was glad that she'd taken the risk.

As Hillary made her way back to her seat, Brandon stood up, waiting until she sat back in her chair to sit himself. Looking at her with unreadable eyes, he stared but said nothing, causing Hillary to question what she thought she'd seen in his eyes before. Thinking that she really had embarrassed him, she felt hot tears threatening an outright revolt. After what seemed an eternity to her, he finally looked as though he was about to speak.

He took her hand. "Hillary Houston, never, ever would I have guessed that you could belt out a song the way you just did. You are absolutely incredible! You have some voice. Hill, you've missed your calling. You should be in the studio."

She blinked hard. "Brandon, are you saying that I didn't embarrass you?"

He looked downright puzzled. "Embarrass me? Heavens no!" he exclaimed. "I've never felt so much pride. It's overwhelming to know that such a beautiful creature with the voice of an angel is here with me. Just take a look at my chest when I walk out of here with you on my arm."

The threatening tears somehow escaped and began to flow down her cheeks. "I'm so relieved to know you're pleased." Her voice trembled with emotion.

In a flash, Brandon leaped out of his seat when he noticed her tears. Kneeling down in front of her on one knee, he looked at her with genuine concern, cupping her face in both his hands. His touch felt so tender to her. "Pretty lady, why the tears? You should be ecstatic. You were wonderful out there. You've got to believe me when I tell you how proud I am of you. You got it going on, girlfriend!"

She laughed at the way he'd expressed himself so exuberantly. "Brandon, some people cry when they're sad, some cry when they're happy. I just happen to be one of those who do both. Let me assure you that this mixture of tears is born of relief and happiness. Relieved that you're pleased with my performance . . . happy that you're here with me."

Brandon looked at Hillary with such tenderness. Gently, he pulled her into his arms and kissed her thoroughly. If Hillary had any doubts about his sincerity, they quickly disappeared during this incredible exchange. When he finally freed her mouth from sweet captivity, she felt the strong urge to pull him back for more. Instead, Hillary glanced at her watch, unable to believe how fleet the time had been.

"Brandon, we need to go. It's almost twelve-thirty."

He responded by getting up to pull her chair out. He then draped her wrap around her shoulders. Unable to help himself, he pulled her to him for one more kiss. "Let's go, beautiful," he whispered, looking deeply into the honey-brown eyes that melted his soul.

Eager to compliment her on her performance, several people reached out their hands to Hillary as she passed by.

"Do you sing anywhere on a regular basis?" one lady asked.

"I'm afraid not. Tonight's performance came on impulse."

Graciously, she thanked each person that approached her as they made their way to the exit. Just as they reached the elevator, Hillary heard her name being called. When Brandon turned around to look, he wondered why the fast-approaching gentleman had called out to his date. Hillary's eyes went straight to the man's elegant appearance. The handsome stranger already had his hand extended when he reached the couple.

"My name is Eric St. John, Miss Houston. I just wanted to let you know that your performance positively thrilled me!" Hillary smiled, but she couldn't help noticing Brandon's restless movements. If this guy made one wrong move, she feared that Brandon would be all over him. St. John reached into his inside jacket pocket and pulled out a business card, which he handed to Hillary. It said he was an agent for a major recording company.

"Miss Houston, are you under contract with anyone?"

Flattered by his comment, Hillary smiled. "No, Mr. St.

John. Most of my experience is church choir related. I have tried my hand at a couple of nightclubs, but I could never get used to the atmosphere, especially when drunken patrons got out of hand."

St. John flashed her a boyish grin. "Miss Houston, your experience, or lack thereof, is not a problem. Your magnificent voice takes care of all that. If you ever decide to take your voice seriously, please give me a call. I believe I can make great things happen for you. You're one lucky man," he said to Brandon. "Not only is she beautiful, she has major-league talent."

Brandon thanked him, even though he didn't like all the attention St. John so eagerly showered on Hillary. In his opinion, St. John had held on to her hand a little longer than necessary. Brandon quickly scolded himself for acting like a jealous lover, especially when he and Hillary had barely established themselves as friends. Friendship wasn't all that he hoped to have with her. Something told him that Hillary was the kind of girl he'd been praying for nightly.

While pondering the events of the past couple of hours, Brandon was very quiet in the elevator on the way down to the lobby. Hillary was rambling on about how she couldn't believe what had just happened when she noticed that Brandon seemed terribly preoccupied. She felt a little hurt, wondering what had happened to all the pride he'd professed earlier.

She sighed heavily. "Men! Who can figure them out?" she mumbled under her breath.

They arrived at the lower level and quickly approached the valet area. Within seconds of Brandon handing the attendant his ticket, the Benz was at the curb. Brandon rushed around the car to open the door for Hillary, coming just short of knocking the attendant over. Hillary got the distinct impression that he didn't want the valet to open the door for her. She'd gotten the same impression earlier, but it was now confirmed. His actions puzzled her, and gave her cause for serious concern.

By the time Brandon had eased the Benz into freeway traffic, Hillary had decided against making an issue of his reluctance to allow the attendant to open her door. Instead, she rested her head back against the seat and glanced at the quartz clock. "I see we're going to be late. Cassie will be beside herself with worry."

"Hillary, relax," he rasped in irritation, "I'll have you home in no time."

Hillary was taken aback by what she thought she'd heard in his voice, but she ignored that, too. She'd had too good of a time to allow a sparring session to ensue. It suddenly dawned on her that Brandon might be jealous of Eric St. John. She prayed that there wasn't even a remote chance she might be correct in her assessment.

Tyrone Thompson, the successful businessman with whom she'd been briefly involved, came to mind. Once she could see past all his effervescent charm, she had discovered that Tyrone was possessive and jealous . . . and he hadn't trusted women any further than he could throw one. He had trusted Hillary even less simply because of her beauty, he'd told her. He had detested the fact that Hillary was often the center of attention everywhere they'd gone.

Hillary had called the relationship off after enduring two insufferable months of endless embarrassments and smothering possessiveness. That was the same time she'd vowed to never again involve herself with a jealous, insecure man. Not in this lifetime!

Now it looked to her as though Brandon had some of the same tendencies toward jealousy as Tyrone had. But it wasn't going to take her two months to get him out of her life, she swore inwardly. If he continued to display jealous behaviors, he would have to go, too. In her opinion, a jealous man equaled a weak man.

It hadn't hurt her in the least to rid herself of Tyrone. She hadn't been in love with him. But she knew it would be a devastating defeat to her heart if Brandon forced her to send him away. Although she didn't think herself in love with him, the potential for her to fall hard for him was great. Something about Brandon David Blair caused her heart to flutter out of control—and she wasn't ready to let that heady feeling go. To keep from jumping to any more negative conclusions, Hillary closed her eyes and mulled over the entire evening.

There had been many tender moments and she relived them all. With the exception of his jealousy act, Brandon had been a perfect companion in every sense of the word. Nothing could spoil this evening for her, not even Brandon's seemingly pensive mood. When she felt a crazy mood of her own coming on, she quickly warded it off and drifted into a light sleep.

Feeling guilty for snapping at her, Brandon looked over at his companion. *Not only does she have the voice of an angel, she is an angel,* he thought warmly. It surprised him when she didn't call him on the sharp tone he used with her. He knew he'd better not try it again. *She may be an angel, but that tongue of hers should be registered as a lethal weapon.*

Just as they pulled up to the gate of her complex, Hillary awakened. Immediately, she reached into her purse and handed him the key card since she kept the remote in the car. Brandon steered the Benz through the gate and parked in the visitor's slot in front of Hillary's unit.

"You seem really tired," Hillary said, breaking the interminable silence. "So if you'd like to pass on getting together with Cassie and Aaron, I'll certainly understand."

Brandon stretched across the seat and brought his face intimately close to hers. "Hill, this date could go on forever and it wouldn't disturb me one tiny bit. I get a power surge every time I get close to you." He flashed her what she considered to be a trademark exclusive to him, his disarming smile. It seemed his mood had passed, which relieved Hillary.

Fleetingly, she pressed her lips to his forehead. "Let's do it!"

Taking the keys from Hillary's hand, Brandon opened the door and stepped aside. "After you, pretty lady." She entered with him close behind. He secured the door before following her into the living room.

"Brandon, have a seat anywhere you like. I'm going to run up to check to see if there's a message from Cassie."

Hillary ran up the stairs and checked the machine, but there weren't any messages. A little apprehension crept in, but she dismissed it immediately. "Cassie will be along soon," she told herself calmly.

Hillary returned to the living room, surprised to find Brandon seated on the leather couch looking fully relaxed. His eyes were closed and he'd removed his jacket. While observing this fine specimen of a man, Hillary stood quietly. As she inhaled his scent, she felt every nerve in her body come alive. *This might very well turn into a dangerous liaison,* she thought. Though his jealousy concerned her, she thought he might just be worth the risk she was considering taking. But why would a man who seemed to have everything going for him be jealous of anyone?

Hillary finally stepped into the room. Before taking a seat, she inserted an easy-listening cassette tape into the cassette player, and soft music penetrated the silence. He opened his eyes slowly. When he reached his hand out to her, his smile broadened.

Instantly killing the sudden urge to fall into his lap, she smiled back at him. "Before I join you, would you like something to drink?"

His eyes held a dangerously sexy glint. "No thanks, Hill. I'm thirsty, but I'd prefer to have my drink from your sweet mouth. His taunting voice was low and seductive.

Hillary felt her hands shaking and decided to sit down before her legs started, too.

Sitting down next to him, she looked him square in the eye. "Everything that looks sweet isn't always sugar-coated."

He saw her pert remark as a challenge. "Why don't you move a little closer so I can find out firsthand?" Obeying his softly spoken command, she moved closer to him. The doorbell pealed just as their mouths came close to a fiery union. Startled, they pulled apart.

Hillary laughed heartily. "Saved by the bell," she quipped, dashing out of his reach before he could stop her.

Brandon moaned. *Aaron, buddy, I'm going to have to talk to you about timing.*

Hillary greeted Cassie and Aaron at the door with enthusiasm. Cassie was her usual bubbly self, Hillary noted. She couldn't help wondering, as she had so many times before, how Cassie managed to have so much energy. Was the girl on speed or what? But Hillary knew better. Cassie had always been a high-level, energetic person.

Cassie planted a quick kiss on Hillary's cheek. "Where's the hunk you went out to dinner with?"

Hillary cast Cassie an imploring look. "In the living room, Cassie. Please be on your best behavior."

Cassie rolled her eyes. "Best behavior? What's that?"

Aaron and Hillary hugged each other. He then shook his head and smiled. "Hillary, your friend is charged with dangerously high volts of electricity. I hope I can keep up the pace. One thing is for sure, I'm going to die trying."

Hillary laughed. "Aaron, if you can keep up with Cassie, I'll buy you dinner."

Aaron shook Hillary's hand. "It's a deal."

Hillary and Aaron joined Cassie and Brandon in the living room, where Cassie's mouth seemed to be moving a mile a minute. Aaron just smiled at Hillary and shrugged his shoulders.

Much to Hillary's surprise, as they discussed their evening, Brandon shared the story of her singing at the restaurant. She wasn't going to mention it for fear that it might put him in his earlier mood. She wasn't positive his mood swing had to do with Eric St. John raving about her singing, but he'd been fine up until that point.

"I've been trying to get this girl to do a demo forever. It would take a cattle prod to move her in that direction," Cassie charged, turning to face Hillary. "On a serious tip, you need to give this St. John guy a call. At least you'll find out if he's just blowing smoke."

Hillary frowned. "Cassie, let's just drop it. I have no intention of calling Eric St. John. I have enough to do already."

"Hillary, would you mind letting me hear a sample of this incredible voice everyone is raving about?" Aaron asked.

Hillary gave Brandon a questioning look, which she immediately regretted. She was her own person, she reminded herself. She didn't need his permission to do anything.

Hillary owned several cassette tapes with just the music to a variety of popular songs. Walking over to the stereo, she plugged the microphone into the system and selected a fabulous musical rendition of "Lift Every Voice and Sing." As the words to the song slipped effortlessly out of Hillary's mouth, her eyes closed and she totally lost herself in the music.

The second she finished, Aaron and Cassie both

clapped loudly. Still under the magical spell of her angelic voice, Brandon remained silent.

"Hillary, I think Cassie's right," Aaron said excitedly. "You need to make that phone call. I would definitely be a major fan."

"Thanks, Aaron, but you can keep your opinions to yourself since no one asked for them," Hillary retorted. Aaron looked genuinely hurt. "Aaron, I'm just kidding," she quickly added, feeling sorry for him. "Thanks for the vote of confidence. But if you're going to hang out with Cassie and me, you're going to need to hone your skills in sarcasm."

Aaron smiled, looking a little less nervous. "I'm beginning to see that."

Cassie laughed out loud. Hillary normally would've left poor Aaron to wonder if she'd been serious or not, but Cassie was glad that Hillary had told him she'd been teasing. Brandon thought both women's wits were more than a handful as he quietly observed their behavior.

Hillary turned the soft music back on, then sat down next to Brandon. Aaron and Cassie retreated to the kitchen to brew a pot of herb tea.

Brandon slipped his arm loosely around Hillary's shoulders. He drew his mouth close to her ear. "Baby, that was beautiful," he whispered. "I don't want to run the risk of getting slashed by that razor you call a tongue, but I have to agree with Cassie and Aaron. Make that call."

Hillary smiled. "That's a generous statement. Thank you. However, I'm happy at my nine-to-five. And I love having my weekends free. When I was younger, I dreamed of nothing but becoming a professional singer," she added wistfully. "I'm an adult now and I've long since dispensed with my childhood fantasies. But I'll always have a passion for it. I've always thought I could heal the world through the gift of song." She swiped a tear away before it had a chance to fall.

Brandon drew her face closer to his. "Sweetheart, never let go of your dreams. I strongly sense that the inner child in you is still very much alive. Don't ever change that quality about you. I find it most intriguing."

Feeling overwhelmed by Brandon's statements, Hillary rested her head against his chest. Glad that Cassie and Aaron had moved into another room, he held her tightly as he stroked her hair gently.

Hillary broke the enchanting spell she and Brandon seemed to be under when she looked at the clock and saw that it was four-thirty in the morning. She frowned. "Look at the time," she remarked, as her other guests entered the room. "I don't know about you guys, but I'm ready to have a long love affair with my bed."

Everyone agreed it was time to go home, and Cassie and Aaron gathered their things and started for the door.

"Aaron, I trust you will see that Cass gets inside okay." Hillary sounded like a mother hen.

Aaron grinned. "Don't worry, Hillary. I'll make sure Cassie is safe and sound before I leave."

"Thanks, Aaron, I really appreciate that." Hillary hugged the couple before closing the door behind them.

Brandon came up behind Hillary and gathered her in his arms. "Did that speech about leaving include me? Or were you just trying to get me all alone?"

"Mr. Blair, as much as I hate to burst your bubble, that statement definitely included you. I'm exhausted." She paused suddenly, looking as though she was straining to hear something. "Listen, did you hear that?" she whispered.

"Hear what?" he whispered back, gearing himself up

for combat, in case an intruder had somehow gained unlawful access to her home.

"My bed's calling me. 'Hillary, Hillary, please come and warm me up. I'm so cold,' " she chanted sweetly.

Brandon roared, feeling immediate relief. "Pretty lady, you never cease to amaze me. I get the message. Loud and clear."

He pulled Hillary back into his arms and gave her a gentle kiss. As it escalated to full-blown passion, she responded with all that was within her. But panic arose inside of her, and she quickly broke his embrace, pushing him toward the door.

Unable to get enough of her delicious lips, he kissed her again. "I'll call you tomorrow."

"It's already tomorrow," Hillary reminded him. "Don't bother to check since you already know I'm safe. Make sure it's late in the afternoon when you do call."

Brandon still couldn't tear himself away. "Pretty lady, till we meet again. This is the most unbelievable first date I've ever been on."

Hillary blushed as she stifled an embarrassing yawn. "I feel exactly the same way. I'll be looking forward to your call later on in the day."

He leaned into her for one more kiss. "Good night, Hill, or should I say good morning?" He finally had to drag himself away, especially when Hillary once again steered him toward the open door.

Hillary straightened the room and put all the loose pillows back in place on the sofa. She turned off the stereo and all but one light as she made her way to the kitchen, where she pulled out a carton of vanilla ice cream. One scoop of ice cream before bedtime had become a habit, but so far it hadn't done much damage to her figure. Once she'd retrieved the ice cream scoop and a spoon from the drawer, she pulled out a plastic bowl. Taking the bowl over to the table, she sat down and polished off the ice cream. In less than ten minutes she was at the sink rinsing out the bowl.

The evening certainly had been full, she thought as she climbed the stairs. And more delightful than she had ever dared to hope. As tired as she felt, she still dragged herself into the bathroom for a quick shower. She desired to soak her feet in a tub of hot water and Epsom salts, but she was sure she couldn't stay awake that long.

Hillary had just stepped out of the shower when the phone rang. Sure that Brandon couldn't have gotten home that quickly, and expecting to hear Cassie on the other end, she picked up the receiver.

"Hello, Cassie, good night, Cassie. I'm going to bed and you should go, too. I'll hear all about your exciting evening tomorrow, but not before late afternoon. Got it?"

"Sorry, pretty lady, but it's not Cassie," the familiar voice came over the line. "Before you get in a huff, I was sure you hadn't gone to sleep yet so I decided to call you from the car." Hillary remembered seeing the phone earlier. "I just wanted you to know that I think you're incredible!"

Hillary fought hard to contain her excitement. "Brandon, you make it so hard for me to get upset with you. I think you're incredible, too. Now hang up and get home safely." The laughter she was becoming all too familiar with rang sweetly in her ear, then the line went dead.

Still wet from her shower, she grabbed a towel and dried off thoroughly. After slipping into burgundy silk boxer shorts and matching T-shirt, she stripped the rose and the rhinestone comb from her hair. Hillary gave her hair a brisk brushing and secured it in a ponytail. Once in bed, she flipped off the bedside lamp. Seconds later she jumped back out of bed and knelt down to say her prayers. Hillary Houston had so much to be grateful for.

Back in bed but unable to sleep, she thought about her stimulating encounter with Eric St. John. He seemed genuinely impressed by her performance, but that was just one performance, she told herself. Could her voice really pass the true test of time? While thinking of all the reasons why she'd always wanted to become a recording artist in the first place, she nearly broke down and cried.

Money had little to do with Hillary's desire to sing professionally. She'd always been possessed by a need to minister to the world through the gift of her voice. While growing up, she'd sung in the church choir and had been a member of the glee club. Hillary felt that songs of love could be healing, uplifting, and deeply spiritual, but reaching the masses through her God-given talent seemed to be her one "impossible dream."

Could St. John really help make her lifelong quest a reality? she wondered for the hundredth time. Before drifting off into a peaceful sleep, she remembered how incredibly good it felt to perform in front of a live audience.

Four

Hillary finally arose at two-thirty in the afternoon. She looked at the clock and freaked. She should've been up long before now. She'd never slept in this late. As she pulled herself up in bed, she relaxed her back against the headboard, smiling at her instant thoughts of Brandon.

The blinking light on the answering machine caught her attention, causing her to hope that Brandon was the caller. After propping a pillow behind her head, she played her messages back. The first message came from Cassie. Then she heard her mother's voice. The strangest call of all came from Alexander Cash. Disappointment set in when she didn't hear a message from Brandon. It was hard for her to believe that the phone had rung so many times without her having heard it once.

Hillary dialed Cassie's number, but after several rings the answering machine picked up. Leaving a message for Cassie to return her call, she dialed her parents' phone number. Jackson Houston, her father, answered on the first ring.

Hillary's face beamed at the sound of his loving voice. "Hi, Daddy! How are you today?"

"Fine, honey. How are you? Your mother tried to get you earlier, but you didn't answer. Are you okay?"

"I'm fine, Daddy. I was still asleep when Mom called.

Cassie and I were out until the wee hours of the morning. We both had dates last night. Where's Mom now?"

"Hold on, sweetheart. I'll get her for you." Hillary listened as her father yelled out for her mother to pick up the extension.

"Hi, Hillary. I called you earlier but didn't get an answer." Alice Houston's gentle voice always made Hillary smile. "Were you out?"

"I was here, but I was dead to the world, Mom. I had a hot date last night. It lasted until the early morning hours."

"Oh! Anyone we know?" Alice asked, highly curious about Hillary's date.

"No, Mom. I just met Brandon Blair Friday night at a club called Club Rojo. He asked me out afterward. Cassie had a date with his friend, Aaron. Before you ask, we were careful."

Leaving nothing to Alice's imagination, Hillary told Alice all about Brandon and their fantastic date. She then listened to Alice's motherly advice, which she'd heard thousands of times. Before hanging up, Hillary made a promise to see her parents within the next few days.

Dreading the next call, she hesitantly dialed Alexander Cash's number. When Alex also answered on the first ring, she had a strong urge to hang up on the last person in the world she wanted to talk to. Talking to him would no doubt leave her bitter with anger.

Nervously, she tossed a pillow up and down. "Hello, Alex. This is Hillary. You phoned?" Her tone was intolerant and cold.

He released a throaty laugh that sounded positively vulgar to Hillary. "You didn't have to identify yourself, Miss Houston. I would know your sexy voice anywhere."

She gritted her teeth. "Alex, you said you needed to talk to me about something important. Cut the innuendoes and spill it," she demanded impatiently.

"Woman, don't you ever relax?"

"Alex, for the last time, spill it. I don't have time for this," she retorted sharply. Hillary already felt far beyond exasperated.

"Okay, okay. Cool down. It's not that serious. I called because I have some new figures on the advertising proposal. I thought you should have them before you finished up your monthly report so you can include the recent changes."

"Let me get a pen and a notepad. Hold on."

Although his voice and everything about him annoyed Hillary, she talked shop with Alex for the next forty-five minutes. After thanking him for the new information, she abruptly hung up, robbing him of the chance to say anything else irritating. Grateful that her conversation with Alex was over, Hillary sighed deeply. The man had a way of keeping her terribly on edge.

While relaxing in his posh beachfront home, Brandon was in deep thought. Hillary Houston was the main focus. Sensing that she was no ordinary woman, he somehow knew that he'd need to handle her with extreme care. In his opinion, Hillary came off as a very self-assured woman, but he suspected that deep down inside she was extremely vulnerable. Something had told him she was someone special from the moment he'd laid eyes on her.

He couldn't count the number of times he'd picked up the phone throughout the course of the day to call her. Afraid of crowding her, he'd aborted each call. She seemed to be a woman who needed plenty of space, and he didn't want to run the risk of invading it.

Brandon stood up and walked out onto the spacious terrace, where he dropped into a lounge chair. As he listened to the pounding of the surf against the rocks, he couldn't help wishing that Hillary were there with him to enjoy the magnificent display of nature. He couldn't imagine anything more erotic than making love while listening to the tranquilizing sounds of the surf, especially with someone you cared deeply for. He didn't need to be a genius to know that he'd already begun to feel that way about Hillary.

As he went over the previous evening in his mind, he caught a chill every time he thought of the sweet taste of her lips. He could almost smell the sexy scent of her perfume. The revelation of her many talents fascinated him. Each second he'd been with her had brought new and exciting discoveries.

He smiled to himself when her singing performance came to mind. She had the voice of an angel, yet she remained so modest about it. He recalled how she'd had the crowd at the restaurant panting for more. Still, she seemed so unaware of the effect she'd had on her listeners. He couldn't believe she'd chalked her performance up to *impulse*. Confessing inwardly to himself that this girl stirred his blood, he let out a loud expletive and went back indoors.

Without further delay, he picked up the phone and quickly dialed Hillary's number, hoping she wasn't already asleep. He'd wasted too much time. "So much for space," he uttered aloud. "I need to hear that woman's voice or I'll be no good the rest of the night."

"Hello," Hillary greeted.

"Hello, pretty lady. It's Brandon."

She let out a sigh of relief when she heard his voice, hoping he couldn't hear her pounding heart. All day she'd toyed with the idea of calling him, but she'd thought he might need some space, too. "Brandon, how are you? It's nice to hear your voice."

"Not half as nice as it is for me to hear yours. What have you been up to all day?" Hillary quickly ran down her itinerary for him. "Sounds like you've accomplished quite a bit."

"You're right. I'm really pleased to have successfully tackled so much considering I didn't get up until late. I've just about completed the proposal I told you about. I hope to finish it at work tomorrow. What have you been doing with your day, Brandon?"

"Actually, I had some work to catch up on as well. For the most part, I've just been relaxing and thinking about you. I've picked up the phone at least a dozen times to call you, but I'm concerned about crowding your space. I have no intention of pressuring you. I know you want us to take things slow. I respect that."

Pleased to learn the reason he hadn't called earlier, Hillary smiled. "Brandon, I would've welcomed your call. I'm pretty up front, as you well know. If you call and I'm busy, I'll tell you. I know I've been rude when you've called before, but that was due to the lateness of the hour and sheer exhaustion, nothing personal. Please accept my apology for the time I was rude. I really enjoy hearing from you."

Her honesty and forthrightness touched him. "No apology necessary. But if you insist, I accept."

Hillary and Brandon engaged in heavy conversation, including her curious inquiries about his home. He only gave her a few minor details, yet they were enough to cause her to imagine him in his own surroundings. Hillary was the one who finally ended the conversation, but not before they made plans to see each other the next evening.

Before calling it a night, Hillary called Cassie again. The phone seemed to ring an awfully long time before Cassie finally picked up, sounding as though she'd been asleep.

"Cass, it seems we've been playing phone tag all day. What are you doing? You sound half asleep."

Cassie laughed. "I'm laying here thinking of ways to seduce Aaron."

Hillary grinned. "I just bet you are! I think he'll be easy. Don't you?"

"I'm not sure since I didn't get to first base last night."

Hillary pretended to be shocked. "Why, you little hussy! You can't seduce Aaron, at least not before I seduce Brandon. I need a little more time. Give me another day or two." The two women dissolved into laughter. "If they could hear us talking like this, they would probably drop us like hot potatoes."

Cassie sniffed. "I doubt it. Them two boys seem hot to trot. Aaron was steaming in his clothes last night. He said he needed a cold shower."

"Knowing you, Cassie, he probably did."

Cassie feigned injury at Hillary's remark. "Now you know I'm not that kind of girl, but I can dream, can't I?"

"Little do they know, we'd probably run for the hills if they propositioned us." Cassie laughed loudly at Hillary's right-on-target remark.

The two women joked and laughed for a while longer. As they discussed their plans for the following day, Cassie informed Hillary that she'd be seeing Aaron. Once again, they both vowed to take it slow.

Cassie seemed as taken with Aaron as she was with Brandon, Hillary surmised. As she'd done before, she wondered where these relations were heading. Hillary climbed into bed as visions of Brandon danced in her head, keeping her from falling right off to sleep.

Hillary awakened to the sound of the alarm clock. Eager to get her day started, she leaped out of bed. Reaching into her closet, she pulled out a navy blue double-breasted suit and a red silk blouse. A pair of red shoes was chosen to complete her outfit, before she hopped into a brief but brisk shower.

Considering how little rest she'd gotten over the weekend, she felt surprisingly full of energy. After pulling all of her hair straight back, she French braided it and secured it with a red decorative clasp. Once she'd applied her usual light cover of makeup, she made a dash for the stairs.

Downstairs in the kitchen she fixed a slice of whole wheat toast and drank a glass of fresh orange juice. After gulping down her meager breakfast, she ran back upstairs to get her briefcase. She then rushed out to the garage.

The twenty-minute drive to work was pleasant. For some reason she didn't mind the traffic this morning, but she suspected that it had a lot to do with the wonderful weekend. Parked in her assigned spot in the multilevel parking structure, she secured her car and headed for the elevator. On her way to her office, Hillary grabbed a bottle of unsweetened orange juice. She then stopped briefly to talk with Lois Jacobs, the new receptionist for her department.

"Good morning, Lois. How are you?"

Lois smiled brightly. "Fine, thanks. How are you this morning, Miss Houston?"

Hillary flashed Lois a refreshing smile. "Really great for a Monday morning," Hillary practically sang out. She gently grasped Lois's hand. "Lois, it would be nice if you could get used to calling me Hillary. I know you've only been here a couple of weeks, but I already consider you one of us. This department runs on team effort."

Lois seemed embarrassed by Hillary's offer. "That's so kind of you. But, Miss Houston, you're an executive. I'm only the receptionist."

Hillary briefly touched the woman's hand again. "Lois, you know a receptionist or a secretary is the backbone of every office. Titles mean nothing to me. It's how you relate to people that counts. Please feel free to call me Hillary."

Lois's eyes turned moist. "Thanks, Hillary. Thanks for making me feel so comfortable around here. I'm going to enjoy working for you."

Hillary gave Lois a warm hug. Her warmth and sincerity put the woman at ease. "I hope we become good friends, Lois."

While making her way to her office, Hillary spoke to several of her coworkers. Before settling into her office, she put her things away. From her briefcase she removed the file that held her proposal and headed for the private executive library, where she'd do more research to put the finishing touches on her marketing report.

Two hours of steady work in the library had caused her hands to cramp badly. While she massaged the kinks out of her hands, the door suddenly opened and she looked up. Cold chills raced up and down her spine. Her worst nightmare stood there. Alexander Cash, thin and wiry, her archenemy . . .

Alex closed the door behind him and walked over to where she sat. Eyeing her as though he was selecting a steak at the local meat market, he pulled out a chair and sat down across from her. "Good morning, Hillary."

She refused to raise her head to acknowledge her adversary. "Miss Houston, to you," Hillary responded coolly.

His laugh was hard and brash. "Testy, testy! Didn't we get any over the weekend? I can remedy that for you— after we enjoy a nice cozy dinner at my place," he taunted, his voice nasty with sarcasm.

Hillary saw a rainbow of colors before her eyes. This was the last straw. Before she could stop herself, she leaped out of her seat, knocking the chair over in the process. Before he could breathe another word, she was right in his face. Surprising herself, she grabbed Alex out of his chair by his shirt collar. Alex was about five-foot-six compared to her five-foot-four.

"Listen, you weasel!" she screamed in a high-pitched voice. "I'm sick and tired of your sexual connotations. Enough is enough! I've tried to handle this in a diplomatic way, but you haven't afforded me that luxury. I'm not interested in you, Alex, and I never will be." Alex tried to speak, but she cut him off. "Shut up, Alex! I'm talking and you will damn well listen to what I have to say." Looking at her in total bewilderment, he swallowed hard. Had he bitten off more than he could chew? She looked ready to kill.

"Alex, I don't know how many other women you have done this to, but this is your final attack on me. If you so much as look at me in the wrong way, I'm going to bring you up on sexual harassment charges." She breathed deeply as she gathered her tumultuous thoughts.

"Keep your nasty remarks to yourself. I'm not interested in hearing them. I don't think Mr. Asher would take this too kindly if I told him. I haven't mentioned it to him so far because I really don't want to be responsible for you losing a good job. If you don't stay the hell out of my space, you're not only going to find yourself unemployed, you may find yourself in the ICU." Her hands shook as she forcefully pushed him back into his chair.

Too shocked to speak, Alex just stared at her in disbelief. Snatching up the papers she'd been working on, she left the room in a hurry, slamming the door loudly behind her. Trembling uncontrollably by the time she reached her office, Hillary closed her door and locked it. Sobbing audibly, she sat down at her desk and lowered her head.

Less emotional now, she quietly thought about the impossible situation in which she'd been placed. It was apparent to her that she'd have to deal with the problem sooner rather than later. Hillary was more upset for allowing others to control her emotions, something her parents had often warned against. She then made the decision to meet the problem head-on should it come up again.

She would no longer be a victim, she vowed.

It startled her when the intercom line buzzed loudly, signaling an internal call. She fully regained her composure before picking up the phone.

"Hillary, there is a Mr. Blair on the line for you. Should I put the call through?" Lois asked.

A call from Brandon both surprised and pleased her. "Please do, Lois. Thank you." Hillary hung up and waited for the call to be transferred to her private extension. Lois immediately followed through.

"Hillary speaking," she answered. The tremor in her voice sounded horrible to her ears, as she dabbed at her eyes with a Kleenex.

"Hello, pretty lady. How are you doing today?" Before she could respond, he continued on. "I hope you don't mind me calling you at work. I know we didn't discuss it. I just needed to hear your sweet voice."

Her smile came easy but weak. "I'm fine, Brandon," she lied. "It's okay for you to call me here. If you have a pencil, I'll give you the number to my private line so you won't have to go through the switchboard. It's not on my business card for obvious reasons." Her voice quivered as she called out the number for him to write down.

"I can understand why you wouldn't have it on your business card. It's always a good idea to have your calls screened. You never know what lunatic might be calling. Hillary, is it my imagination, or are you upset?" He sounded genuinely concerned. "You sound as though you've been crying. Your voice is cracking, too."

His concern caused her tears to resurface. She fought hard to control her emotions. "I just can't get over how sensitive you are to my moods in such a short time of knowing me." She swallowed hard. "I had a small problem here at work, but I think it's settled. However, I don't want to discuss it over the phone. I'll tell you all about it tonight."

"Good. You just answered my next question. Since we're still on for tonight, where would you like to have dinner?"

She briefly pondered his question. "Brandon, if you don't mind, could we just call and have something delivered to my place? I'm not up to going out."

"Is Chinese food okay? I know a great take-out place. I can pick it up on my way to your house."

"That sounds great. I love Chinese food."

"What would you like me to bring?"

"I enjoy most Chinese food, but I don't eat pork and I prefer vegetarian egg rolls. Is that too much trouble?"

"Trouble? Not at all. I'll cook it to order myself if I have to. One more thing—cheer up, sweetheart. Don't let whatever's going on spoil your entire day."

She managed a bright smile. "I won't. I'm fine now. Don't worry. I've got to run."

"Wait!" Brandon shouted. "What time?"

"Is six-thirty good for you?" she queried softly.

"That works for me, the sooner the better. Good-bye, Hillary."

Hillary had several meetings scheduled throughout the course of the day, the first one to begin in ten minutes. Reaching into her purse, she pulled out her compact. After checking her appearance, she repaired her makeup. She noticed how swollen her eyes looked, but she knew nothing could be done about them before her meeting.

* * *

The first meeting lasted a lot longer than anyone had expected. By the time it ended, she had to rush to her next meeting. After nearly falling through the door, attracting everyone's attention, she slipped into a chair in the back of the room.

Mr. Asher, the senior executive of Hillary's department, presided over the meeting. Once all the new marketing strategies had been discussed, Mr. Asher went over the future plans for the company. Hillary missed most of his presentation because the earlier incident with Alexander occupied her mind.

Smiling, Mr. Asher approached Hillary. "Hillary, I may need you to go to a conference in a few weeks. In New York," he instructed in a gentle tone. "The details haven't been worked out yet, but I should have something concrete before the end of next week."

Hillary gave him her best smile. "Okay, sir. I'll be waiting to get my instructions. I love to visit New York, especially this time of year."

Though Hillary loved to travel and would normally be excited when scheduled to go on a trip, the thought of leaving Brandon behind unexpectedly passed through her mind. Considering someone else's feelings when making plans, business or otherwise, was quite new to her.

"I'll wait to hear from you," Hillary said, dashing off to her next meeting.

When Lois told Hillary the last meeting had been cancelled, she decided to use the rest of the day to tackle several other projects. Before returning to her office, she stopped by the break room to purchase a sandwich and a drink to consume at her desk.

The intercom buzzed before she could settle down in her office. *What is it now?* Hillary wondered impatiently.

"Miss . . . uh . . . Hillary, there's a special delivery out here for you. Is it okay to bring it to your office?"

Hillary pushed her lunch aside. "You have enough to do, Lois. I'll come get it." She received special deliveries all the time, so she never gave it a second thought as she got up from the chair.

Out at the reception desk Hillary found Lois hidden behind a huge vase of long-stemmed yellow roses. Unable to believe they'd actually been sent to her, she gasped loudly. As Lois handed the splendid flowers over to her, a bright smile lit up Hillary's eyes.

"Could these be from a new admirer?"

Hillary stuck her nose in one of the roses and inhaled deeply of its scent. "I don't know, Lois. Let's see."

Reaching for the envelope, she ripped it open with one finger. She smiled broadly when she saw that Brandon had sent them. *He must have gotten the address off my business card,* she realized. A rainbow-colored CHEER UP leaped at her from the inside of the card.

Still smiling, Hillary turned to Lois. "I guess we can definitely say these are from the new admirer," she cooed. She then told Lois all the details of how she and Brandon had met.

Lois whistled. "Looks to me like the gentleman has a mission."

Hillary swung her hands at her side. "We'll have to wait and see what that mission is. For right now, I'm going to bask in all this sweet-smelling attention." Carrying the vase of roses back to her office, she placed them where she could take full advantage of their beauty.

Hillary still hadn't finished the project she was working on when five o'clock arrived. Normally she would've stayed late. But tonight, she wouldn't even consider working overtime. After wishing everyone a pleasant evening, she made her way to the elevator.

Seated inside her car, she turned on the engine and

exited the parking garage. Her thoughts returned to the incident between her and Alex as she drove toward home. She rarely lost her temper, but she had to laugh at the way she'd grabbed him by the collar and pushed him down in his seat. If he hadn't been so stunned, she thought he might have retaliated. She couldn't begin to imagine what might have happened had he gotten physical. Silently, she thanked God for not letting it go that far.

Hillary looked at her watch when she reached the inside of the house. It was now five-forty-five. Brandon was due at six-thirty. After putting all her things away, she checked the rooms to see that everything was in place. She then stripped her clothes away as she mounted the staircase.

A quick shower revived her. She then searched for something warm and comfortable to put on. Standing in front of the mirror, Hillary pulled on a hunter-green oversized sweater and a pair of dark green denim jeans. In her opinion, green, her favorite color, seemed to add luster to her chestnut-brown hair and copper-brown complexion.

She freed her hair from bondage, brushed it back with quick strokes, then pulled a few strands over her forehead. After applying moisturizer to her copper skin and a dab of lip gloss to her ripe mouth, she stepped back to check herself in the mirror. Though she rarely wore makeup when having a relaxing evening at home, she was pleased with the results. Six-fifteen, she noted, time enough to make a quick call to her parents, then one to Cassie.

The call to her parents was short and sweet.

"Hi, Cassie. I just wanted to give you a quick call to see what you're up to," Hillary announced cheerfully.

"You're not going to believe this, but I am actually

cooking. Aaron is coming over for dinner . . . he's due any minute. I'm cooking lasagna."

Hillary laughed out loud. Cassie never cooked. "You, the salad bar queen, cooking? I guess we both reneged on our promise to take it slow with these guys. Brandon's bringing Chinese food over. So much for promises."

"Hillary, I feel extremely comfortable with Aaron. I think I'm safe with him. The question should be is he safe with me."

They both laughed, then agreed they'd talk later in the evening. Once again, Hillary couldn't help wondering in which direction these two relationships were headed. The phone rang just as she replaced the receiver onto the cradle. She listened as security announced Brandon. Feeling extremely excited about the evening that lay ahead, Hillary ran to the door to await his arrival.

Five

With his arms full of brown bags, Brandon entered the foyer. "Hi, babe," he greeted, planting a quick kiss on her forehead. Following Hillary into the kitchen, he deposited the food bags on the counter.

Feeling rather bold, Hillary stood on her tiptoes and planted a lingering kiss on Brandon's sweet lips. The look on his face told her that the tantalizing gesture had nearly swept him right off his feet.

"What was that for?"

Looking like an innocent little girl, she turned herself from side to side. "To thank you for the beautiful yellow roses. They completely bowled me over. Are you always this sweet?" she asked, poking her head in one of the brown bags.

He gave her a thoughtful glance. "Hillary, I can't honestly tell you the last time I sent someone roses, let alone twice in such a short period of time."

"Thank you. That makes me feel extra special."

"Pretty lady, you are extra special! More than you know. If sending you roses gets this type of response, you'll have more roses than you can handle."

"Sounds like a serious plan, Mr. Blair."

Seated at the table, they set about the task of opening all the cartons that held every type of Chinese food imaginable. The egg rolls looked light and flaky, the curry chicken smelled heavenly.

The delicious smells made her mouth water. "Brandon, what did you do, order the whole menu?"

Though Hillary had set the table earlier, she'd forgotten the bottle of chilled cider. Excusing herself, she jumped up and retrieved it from the refrigerator.

"Just about. We should have plenty of leftovers to take for lunch tomorrow. I don't know about you, but I never have time to go out for lunch."

Hillary returned to her seat. "I get out every Friday. Several of my coworkers and I have proclaimed Friday as 'out-to-lunch day.' We work hard all week so we figure we deserve it."

For the next half hour the only sound was the tinkling of the silverware hitting the plates.

Hillary arose from her seat to clear the table, but Brandon stood up and moved her aside. "I'll take care of this. You go in the other room and get comfortable. I'll be right behind you." She made no attempt to dissuade him. It probably wouldn't do any good anyway, she surmised.

In the living room, Hillary tuned the television to the Monday Night Football game; the Oilers and the Steelers were playing. She laughed when she realized she didn't even know if Brandon liked sports. If he didn't, he'd just have to suffer through it since she rarely missed a football game. She loved both football and basketball, but she only watched baseball during the World Series. The game was already in progress as she curled up on the sofa.

When Brandon still hadn't joined her after what seemed to be a long time, she went to the kitchen to see what was keeping him. He'd just hung up the dish towel when she appeared. She took special notice of the washed, dried, and neatly stacked dishes sitting atop the tiled counter. *Here he goes again,* she marveled, *doing the absolute unexpected.* Of all the male friends she'd had over for dinner, not one even offered to clean up the kitchen, let alone actually did it.

She looked around the kitchen and smiled at his handiwork. Everything appeared to be in its right place. It seemed as though he'd somehow known where everything belonged.

She gave him an appreciative smile. "You didn't have to do this, Brandon."

He smiled back at her. "I know that. I wanted to. You've had a rough day. You need to relax as much as you can."

"You're really considerate, Brandon. Thank you." Silently, she wished she had a dollar for every time she'd said thank you to him over the last several days.

Hillary tapped Brandon on the shoulder. As he came face-to-face with her, she cupped his face between her hands and planted a staggering kiss on his lips.

The fire in her kiss utterly overwhelmed him, but he was careful not to reveal how deeply it had impacted him. "Okay, lady, let's hit the couch so we both can relax."

Noticing the football game on the television screen, Brandon looked at Hillary strangely. "You like football?"

"Love it. And if you don't, you're S.O.L. tonight. I'm watching this game," Hillary asserted.

"Lady, I love football, but I've never had a date that cared two cents for it. Once again, your depth astounds me."

"Well, you're now dating someone who is passionate about football and basketball."

"Basketball, too? No! This is too good to be true."

"You just try to keep me from watching either and you'll find out. I am Laker-crazy. What about you?"

He sat down on the sofa. "My firm holds Laker season

seats . . . right at midcourt. You and I have a date for as many home games as you'd like to attend."

"I'm going to hold you to that, Mr. Blair."

"By the way, what does S.O.L. mean?"

"To put it mildly, surely out of luck."

He threw his head back in laughter. The melodious sound of it thrilled her silly, causing her to laugh, too. Following her lead, Brandon took his shoes off, then pulled her into him, making sure she was comfortable. However, she didn't stay in that position for long. As the Steelers scored a touchdown, Hillary leaped out of her seat and started running around the room.

"Yes, yes!" she screamed, excited as a kid in a candy store.

Brandon thoroughly enjoyed Hillary's enthusiasm for the game. Her knowledge of it amazed him as she called out penalties, interceptions, fumbles, and various other plays.

He stared at her incredulously. "Incredible! You really do have a passion for the game, Hill. And you really know what's going on out there on the field."

She grinned. "Oh, it took me a while to learn. In the beginning, it was just twenty-two men running up and down the field in very tight pants. I learned a lot from going to my high school football games. The fact that I dated the school's star running back didn't hurt matters."

He looked at her through hooded eyes, but she missed the brief flash of certain jealousy. "You could have kept that last bit of information to yourself," he bristled.

Hearing possessiveness in his tone, Hillary decided not to respond. Hadn't he just mentioned other dates? Or did she have an overactive imagination? She turned her attention back to the game.

The Steelers won, which thrilled Hillary. She had

grown up watching the Pittsburgh Steelers, who hailed from her home state of Pennsylvania.

Brandon picked up the remote control, turned off the television, and turned to face Hillary. "Now, I want to hear about what had you so upset today."

She'd forgotten that she'd told him they would discuss it. Fearful of how he might react to the vulgar subject matter, she was now reluctant to do so. She was also worried that Brandon might have somewhat of a nasty temper, which usually went along with a jealous streak.

He nudged her gently. "I'm waiting. You have my undivided attention, Hill."

"Honey, this story is just too unbelievable. Since I think I have it taken care of, why don't we just forget about it?" she queried hopefully.

"No way, Hill. Anything or anyone that affects you enough to cause you to cry, I want to know about it. Hillary, I'm including myself in that statement. Our relationship won't work if we don't keep the lines of communication open."

So, we're on the same page, Hillary mused giddily. She hesitated a moment before launching into her story. "My problems have to do with someone at work. Alexander Cash is one of the directors in the advertising department. He constantly makes irritating innuendoes to me. . . ."

"What type of innuendoes?" Brandon interrupted.

Hillary swallowed hard and her palms felt clammy as she wrung them together. "Sexual," she announced shakily.

He placed his hands over hers to still them. "For instance?"

Hillary shivered involuntarily. "For example, I was in the executive library working on my proposal this morning when Alex walked in. He said, 'Good morning, Hillary.' Because of past experiences with him, I expected him to say something I didn't like. So I said, 'Miss Houston to you.' He then accused me of being testy because I hadn't had sex over the weekend. He went on to offer his services to remedy the situation. Those may not have been his exact words but his exact meaning came through very clear."

Brandon knew that his control over his temper was on a short leash. He felt like hitting something, hard, as Hillary went on telling him how she'd responded to Alex's crass remarks. Tears ran fast and furious down her face by the time she finished the rest of the story. Her audible sobs tugged viciously at his heartstrings as he held her close to him. He stroked her hair until she'd pulled herself together.

He felt the need to lighten up her mood. "Baby, you handled him valiantly. I can just imagine you manhandling this jerk. You really grabbed him by the collar?" Her delightful laughter told him that his plan had worked.

"Hillary, let me spend the night with you?" His question came from completely out of the blue, which sent her into a tailspin. "In the guest room, of course," he quickly added. "I don't want to leave you like this."

A warning signal flitted up her spine. "Brandon, I'm a big girl. I'll be fine. Having you to talk to helped out quite a bit," she remarked, feeling awfully nervous.

He looked at her with pleading eyes. "I'd still like to stay. I'm not in the mood to drive all the way home, but I could just go to the leased apartment the firm holds. I often end up spending quite a few nights there during the week. Still, that's twenty to thirty minutes away."

He saw that she wasn't moved by his weak argument when she turned the television back on. As she rested her head in his lap, he knew that if he didn't leave now he'd make a fool of himself by begging her to let him stay.

"Come on, Hill. Walk me to the door. It's getting late—and I know you're tired."

She lifted her head from his lap, stood up, and stretched her aching limbs. Her body movements excited him, causing him to pull her close to him. As he explored her mouth with a burning passion, his breathing became ragged and labored. Abruptly, he pulled away and directed her into the hallway.

Thoroughly shaken by his ravaging kiss, she reluctantly opened the door. "Good night, Brandon."

Outside, Brandon leaned on the door, trying to calm his uneven breathing. The kiss had shaken him, too.

Feeling lonely already, Hillary started toward the steps. Surprising herself, she ran back to the door, jerked the locks open, and swung the door open wide. Brandon just stood there, smiling that sweetly disarming smile of his. Glad to see him still there, she flung herself into his arms.

"What took you so long, pretty lady?" he queried, his tone more confident than he felt.

She gave him a haughty look. "You cad! You were waiting for me to come back, weren't you?"

He smiled sheepishly. "Let's just say I'd hoped. Can I stay with you tonight?"

She was practically breathless. "Only if you promise to behave yourself," she warned in a teasing tone. Once he assured her that she'd be safe with him, they turned off the lights and ascended the stairs.

Upstairs, she turned on the light in the guest room and turned the bed down. She then stepped into the hall, opened the linen closet, and removed a fresh towel and washcloth.

Her laughter trilled as she walked back into the guest room. "Would you like one of my nightshirts?"

He loved how easily she dished out the humor. "No,

babe. I sleep in the raw," he taunted, laughing at her blushing face.

Oh, boy, she thought. *I had to ask, didn't I?*

"Hill, is it okay if I take a shower?"

"Sure, no problem."

Hillary disappeared into the hall bathroom, turned the water on, and tested it for warmth. "Brandon, your shower is ready," she called out.

Brandon appeared in the doorway. "Thank you. That was sweet of you."

"My pleasure."

He went into the bathroom and she retreated to her bedroom. The phone rang just as she entered the dark room. Sitting down on the side of the bed, she turned on the light before answering the ring. "Hello."

"Hillary, it's Cassie. I want to tell you something. Is Brandon gone yet?"

"No, he's still here." Should she tell Cassie that he'd be there all night? she wondered.

"In that case, I'll make it quick. I've decided to let Aaron spend the night. I need to know what you think." Hillary laughed uncontrollably.

"Hillary, what the hell's wrong with you? You want to let me in on the joke?" Cassie sounded angry at Hillary's response to her question. "It's not what you think. Aaron is going to sleep in the guest room."

Hillary put her laughter in check. "Cassie, I'm sorry. It's just that Brandon will be staying in my guest room, as well." Cassie busted up laughing, too. "Cassie, do you think they planned this?"

"Who the hell cares," came Cassie's sarcastic reply. "I sure don't. On the serious side, Hillary, I don't really think so. I was the one who told Aaron that Brandon was at your place. He looked genuinely surprised by it." Satisfied that she hadn't been made a complete fool of, Hillary ended the call on a pleasant note.

As she stepped back into the hallway, she could hear the shower still running. Remembering that her dad kept a bathrobe at her house, she rummaged through the guest room closet until she came up with it. After tossing the robe on the bed, Hillary hurried out of the room, hoping Brandon wouldn't return before she could make it to her own space. She wouldn't be able to handle seeing him half-naked, or worse, totally nude.

She was in and out of the shower in a flash. After dressing in an oversized nightshirt, she gave her hair its nightly brushing. As she turned off the light and slipped into bed, she remembered that she hadn't even said good night to Brandon. A light knock came on the door before she'd finished her thought.

"Hill, are you still awake?"

Hillary pulled the comforter up around her neck. "Yes. Come in," she said, hoping she wasn't sending mixed signals.

Brandon opened the door and stepped inside the room. Looking handsome in her dad's white terrycloth bathrobe, he walked over to the bed. Without turning the covers back, he lay down beside her and she nestled her head against his arm. They both felt the dangerously strong current of electricity between them. Neither of them could deny it. As they fell into silence, he rocked her gently in his arms.

He nibbled at her ear. "Pretty lady, dream of me tonight. I'll definitely be dreaming of you." When he didn't get a response, he looked down at Hillary and found her fast asleep. His heart swelled to near bursting. Elated that she'd been comfortable enough with him to fall asleep in his arms, he smiled. The exotic sensations pounding in the pit of his stomach made him weak with desire. He found Hillary desirable in ways that went far, far beyond her ravishing physical attributes.

He released her hair from the loosened band and eased her head from his arms. Trying not to awaken her, he placed her head on the pillow. As he lightly brushed his lips over her mouth, he noticed the slight swelling from the onslaught of earlier kisses. As though he had the power to remove the bruising, he traced her lips lightly with his fingertips. Missing her before he even stepped away from the bed, he returned to the guest room.

Brandon knew he wasn't going to rest as he settled himself in bed. The things Hillary had told him about Alexander Cash had his blood boiling. He remembered how childlike she'd become when she'd been crying. She seemed so vulnerable. "Lord, don't ever allow me to make her cry. I couldn't bear to be responsible for one sorrowful tear," he prayed out loud.

Hillary Houston was the most unique person he'd ever met. He fondly remembered how animated she'd become when the Steelers had scored a touchdown. No woman had ever elicited the type of wild, torrid responses from him that she did. This delicate woman had him beguiled, he admitted to himself. Not only was she sensitive, intelligent, and beautiful, she had a great sense of humor. Not only would he rise up to meet each and every challenge she might present him with, he would enjoy doing so.

As his thoughts drifted back to her situation at work, he wondered how some people could be so insensitive. Hillary didn't deserve to be treated this way. As a matter of fact, no woman did. All things considered, Brandon knew he had to find a way to handle this situation in a very thorough manner. In spite of only knowing her a short time, he accepted the fact that he cared very deeply for her, and vowed to protect her from anything or anyone that caused her discomfort or unhappiness, including himself.

All of his concerns for her didn't mean that he wasn't scared of his feelings. Finding himself in unfamiliar territory frightened him. He had a wall of steel around his heart, but he knew, without a doubt, that the wall had now been penetrated. Regardless of any fears he had for himself, he knew he had to put a stop to Alexander Cash's reign of terror against Hillary Houston.

The bright orange sun slowly peeked through the pastel-tinted clouds. A light breeze blew in through the patio door and ran its fingers through Hillary's hair as she lay sleeping. She appeared at peace. She'd finally drifted into a serene place after a turmoil-filled night. Her sleepless night had been particularly plagued with unpleasant thoughts of Alexander Cash and ugly scenes from her brief affair with Tyrone Thompson.

Hillary awakened to a light knock on her bedroom door. At first she thought she was dreaming. At a firmer second knock, she bolted upright, remembering that Brandon had spent the night there.

Already dressed in the clothes he'd worn the previous evening, Brandon carried a wicker tray into the bedroom. Delicious breakfast smells filled the room. His smile was cheerful as he set the breakfast tray down.

"Good morning, pretty lady." Walking over to the bed, he put his hand gently behind her neck and pulled her forward. Then, reaching behind her, he fluffed the pillows and kissed her forehead before retrieving the wicker tray.

His strength fascinated her as she observed his every sleek move. As he carefully stationed the food tray across her lap, she noticed one of the yellow roses that he'd placed in a bud vase. Could she be having an out-of-body experience? It certainly felt like it. If this was heaven, she didn't ever want to come back down to earth. Was it possible she'd given too much weight to Brandon's jealous outbursts? Did she care enough about him to try to understand what prompted his behavior?

He smiled broadly and winked his right eye. As usual, his disarming smile caused her heart to flutter wildly. His smile had a way of brightening her dimmest outlook.

"Eat up, young lady," Brandon gently commanded, breaking her train of thought. "I suspect that you barely eat in the morning."

She looked at him incredulously. "Right again. How can you understand me so well in such a short time? I don't understand myself half of the time—and I've always been with me."

He slipped into bed next to her. Much like the night before, she didn't feel at all threatened. "Lady, I can't begin to profess that I understand everything about you, but I can promise you this. Understanding you and your needs has become my top priority."

She smiled brightly. "Now that sounds promising. By the way, I apologize for falling asleep on you last night."

"I'm thrilled that you felt comfortable enough with me to do so. You don't ever have to be afraid of me, Hill. I would never intentionally do anything to hurt you."

Hillary smiled and nodded as she delved into the delicious breakfast he'd prepared. "Brandon, why aren't you eating? This is wonderful."

"Normally I don't eat breakfast. I'll grab a doughnut and some coffee at the office. I never have time to make myself a good breakfast."

Brandon removed the tray when she finished and set it on the floor. He lay back on the bed and pulled her head onto his chest. She felt so secure that she stayed in his arms until the alarm clock pierced their tranquility thirty minutes later.

Before arising from the bed, he kissed her mouth ever so gently. "Hillary, you concentrate on getting ready for work. I can let myself out. I'll put the bottom lock on. With all the security this complex employs, I'm confident no one will get to you." He bent over and rained kisses all over her face.

His spirited display of affection left her breathless.

He picked up the tray and headed for the door. "Have a wonderful day. Think of me. I'll call you at work later this morning. You have my private number," he added. "Don't ever hesitate to use it."

"Brandon, thanks for staying with me. It was nice to know that you were right across the hall."

"Anytime, lady, anytime. Good-bye."

"Good-bye, Brandon. I'll be anticipating your call."

Six

Brandon had only been gone a few seconds when Hillary made up her mind that she wasn't going to work. She would work on her projects at home. Atlantic Pacific Airlines afforded their employees the luxury of working at home from time to time, especially if they had a heavy workload. She thought of several projects that had to be completed. Most of the data needed for their completion was in her briefcase. It would be another hour or so before anyone would be in the office. She would call in then.

She tried not to deal with the issues regarding Alex, but deep inside she knew that she didn't have the stomach to face him. He had made her life miserable, but she was just as responsible for the way things had turned out, simply because she'd let him get away with his dirty deeds for far too long. Unnerved by the mere thought of him, she rested back on the pillows and closed her eyes, hoping to block out all the unpleasant memories.

How right it felt having Brandon here all night, she reflected quietly, glad she'd let him stay. He incited her to do things she normally wouldn't even consider. Hillary wondered what was happening to her. Knowing it wouldn't take much to figure it out, she laughed out loud. The man had stolen upon her mind like a sweet dream.

Brandon had somehow navigated his way into her heart.

As she thought about Cassie, she imagined her and Aaron sitting on Cassie's patio having breakfast despite the coolness of the morning. Cassie loved to eat her meals on the patio while enjoying the beautiful gifts of nature. Hillary hoped that everything was okay with her dear friend.

While the birds outside her window chirped a peaceful melody, Hillary reset the alarm and drifted off into a light sleep.

Brandon looked around the spacious firm apartment where he kept several changes of clothes. The furnishings consisted of those often found in leased executive suites: an off-white contemporary sofa and chair, small dinette set, king-size bed, bookshelves, desk, and wet bar. The entire setting was too austere and businesslike for his taste.

A short time later, smartly attired in a moss-brown textured-wool three-button suit, brown and beige herringbone shirt, and brown-and-white striped silk tie, Brandon carefully studied a map of the city as he carried on a phone conversation with his secretary, Marissa. Once he'd given Marissa detailed instructions, he left the apartment and returned to his car.

He steered the car onto a road that took him in the opposite direction of his office, his face grim and his jawbone rigidly set. After approximately thirty minutes of driving, he turned onto the street he'd pinpointed on the map.

He parked the car and walked to a large apartment complex, where he scanned the tenant directory. Finding the name he'd been looking for, he entered the building and caught the elevator. Arriving at Apartment 412, he rang the bell and stood back to await an answer.

A small-framed black man with dark brown hair and

tinted eyeglasses opened the door. Behind the glasses, his eyes appeared small and beady. Sure that this was the man with whom he wanted to make contact, Brandon mechanically straightened his tie and put his game face on.

Alex looked curious. "Hello, can I help you?"

Brandon stared at Alex without expression. "If you're Alexander Cash, you can," he stated, his tone rather emphatic.

Alex looked perplexed as he tried to figure out who this strange man was. "I'm Alex. What can I do for you?"

"Mr. Cash, may I come in? What I need to say should be said in private."

When Alex seemed reluctant to let Brandon in, he drew out a business card and handed it to him. Alex studied the card a moment. Deciding that he should hear what this man had to say, Alex stepped aside.

Inside the well-maintained apartment, Brandon remained standing. Standing gave him a better advantage when confronting an ugly situation. "Mr. Cash, I'm here to see you about a personal and very dear friend of mine, who also happens to be a client," Brandon explained, intentionally leaving out Hillary's name.

Alex squinted his beady eyes. "And may I ask who we are talking about?"

Purposely, Brandon paused before giving Cash a name. "Hillary Houston. Does that name ring a bell with you?"

Alex's olive-brown complexion turned as pale as a ghost's. Coughing nervously, he took a few minutes to regain his badly shaken composure. "What about her?" His tone now dripped with surliness.

"It's my understanding from a source close to the situation that you harass her on a daily basis. To be more specific, you sexually harass her," Brandon stated clearly.

Cash remembered "Attorney at Law" on the card he'd been given. Had Hillary filed a lawsuit against him? he wondered. Then he recalled that Mr. Samms had said a source close to the situation—not Hillary, making him wonder who else knew about this.

Choosing his words carefully, Alex leaned on a brown reclining chair. "Mr. Samms, just what is it you're after?" Alex's gaze wandered around the room, looking everywhere but directly at the man who confronted him.

Moving quickly, with confidence, Brandon closed the space between himself and Alex. His unexpected move caught Alex off guard, causing him to flinch. "Mr. Cash, I think it would be in your best interest to stay clear of Miss Houston. If I hear about one more outrageous thing you've said or done to her, there will be a lawsuit slapped on you so fast you won't know if you're coming or going. Consider yourself on notice," Brandon warned with deadly calm.

Alex cleared his throat. "Mr. Samms, I think this has been blown all out of proportion. Hillary Houston is a paranoid neurotic. She thinks every comment directed at her has sexual overtones."

Brandon fought hard to remain calm, when all he really wanted to do was bash Alex's face in. "Mr. Cash, I warned you. You have just attempted to slander Miss Houston's name. You can count on a sexual harassment case being filed against you. Today!"

Alex realized his tactics hadn't worked as he swallowed the bitter taste in his mouth. "Hold on, Mr. Samms. I think we can work this out. I will agree to stay clear of Miss Houston, but mind you, I'm not admitting to anything. I just want this unpleasantness over with as quickly as possible. You have my word. Now, can I have your word that no lawsuit will be filed?"

Brandon couldn't believe the nerve of this character. "Mr. Cash, you're in no position to make deals with me. If I had my way, the CEO of your company would've been notified and a lawsuit filed the very moment this

came to my attention. I think you've had fair warning.
Mr. Cash, I do play hardball. I play to win. I'm going to
turn your past inside out. I will leave no stone unturned.
If you have a history of this type of behavior, you can
surely believe it's going to become your worst nightmare.
You are preying on innocent women," Brandon spat out.

With his business finished, Brandon turned and
stormed out the door. Out in the hallway, he hit the wall
hard with his fist, relieving some of his pent-up anger.
Pain shot through his wrist as he pressed the DOWN elevator button. He shook his hand out vigorously to ease
the aching.

Seething with anger, he got into his car and steered
it in the direction of his office. As he drove, he thought
to himself how clever it had been to use Aaron's business
card. It seemed to have had a definite impact on the
outcome of the entire sordid mess.

Hillary picked up the phone to call her office and
dialed straight through to Mr. Asher's private line.

"Asher here," her boss answered in a pleasant voice.

"Good morning, Mr. Asher. This is Hillary."

"Morning, Hillary. How are you?"

"I'm fine, sir, thank you. I called to let you know I'm
going to work at home today. I'll be presenting my proposal tomorrow and I also have a few other projects that
need my undivided attention. I need to work without all
the interruptions at the office."

"That will be fine, Hillary. I appreciate you calling."

"Thank you, Mr. Asher. I'll see you in the morning."

"Hillary, is everything okay with you?" he asked before
she could hang up. "I've noticed that you don't seem
yourself these days. Is something troubling you?"

His statement shocked her. *Maybe I should tell him what's
been happening and get it over with,* she considered. When

she thought of Cash losing his job, she decided she didn't want to be responsible for that particular occurrence.

"Mr. Asher, you're right. I have been a little preoccupied, but I think it's just the jitters over my presentation tomorrow. A lot is riding on this proposal. I'm just feeling anxious about it." She wasn't particularly fond of lying to her boss, but it was the lesser of two evils.

"Hillary, you know I have total confidence in your abilities. You will do just fine," he assured her. "You're a bright, articulate young woman. I see you having a great future with this company."

"Thanks for the vote of confidence. I'll be okay. See you tomorrow morning, sir."

"Good-bye, Hillary. Have a pleasant day." Mr. Asher felt that something more than the proposal bothered his brightest young executive, but he decided not to press the issue.

Though Brandon had been at his office for quite some time, he'd just found time to check his schedule. He had a meeting in an hour. Deciding he would call Hillary first, he went into his private office and closed the door. He dialed Hillary's private office number and let it ring several times before hanging up. Hadn't she said she'd be anticipating his call? *Maybe she's in the ladies' room,* he thought, busying himself with some papers on his desk.

Ten minutes had passed when he dialed her office again, but still no answer. Hoping the receptionist knew where to locate her, he dialed the main number.

"Atlantic Pacific Airlines. How may I direct your call?"

"Marketing department, please," he requested kindly. A brief silence ensued before the cheery voice of the department's receptionist came on the line.

"Lois speaking. May I help you?"

"I sure hope so. Brandon Blair calling for Miss Houston."

"I'm sorry, but Miss Houston is not in today. May I take a message?"

He felt panicky over her absence from work. "Do you know where I might locate her?"

Lois suddenly realized that this was the man Hillary had just started dating. "She's working at home today, Mr. Blair. You can try her there," Lois suggested.

"Thanks, Lois. You've been a big help."

As he punched in Hillary's home number, he couldn't help wondering if the mess with Cash had kept her from work today. He must have really gotten to her for her to miss work. He should've nailed that sucker when he had the opportunity.

Hillary's sweet voice immediately calmed the storm he'd brewed up inside of him.

"Hillary, I've been worried sick about you. Are you okay? I called your office only to find out that you didn't go to work."

Hillary sighed wearily. "Brandon, you might think I'm a coward, but I couldn't face Cash today. I'm ashamed of the way I allowed him to make me behave. Instead of reacting to this bad situation, I should've merely acted on it."

"Lady, you've got nothing to be ashamed of. You did what you had to do. Don't give that wretched guy another thought."

"Maybe so, but I felt so bad I decided to work at home. I thought I'd get more work done here than at the office. I guess I used work as a way to keep from dealing with this situation, yet I know it has to be dealt with. I've made up my mind to do so should it reoccur."

"Hillary, I'm coming over right now. Don't leave."

"That isn't necessary, Brandon. I know you can't drop everything to play nursemaid to my wounded emotions."

"Nursemaid, hell! I'm coming over . . . that's final. If you choose not to let me in, I'll cross that bridge when I get to it." Not waiting for a reply, he disconnected the line.

"I need to put this man in check. He's out of control," she uttered aloud.

As she thought about his reaction, she had to admit to herself that it felt nice to have someone other than her family care about her. It felt nice to have someone other than her father to protect her honor. It felt nice to have a seemingly decent man in her life, period.

Since it was lunchtime, she walked into the pastel-bright kitchen to fix something to eat for herself and Brandon. Opening the refrigerator, she pulled out all the ingredients that would make a halfway decent meal. Using tender roasted turkey breasts for fillers, she made plump sandwiches, lathering them with mayonnaise. Filling a glass bowl with shredded lettuce, cherry tomatoes, and sliced cucumbers, she tossed it with vinaigrette dressing. Once she'd squeezed the fresh lemons for lemonade and added the water, she garnished it with lemon slices and red maraschino cherries. Just for color, she added a few slices of lime.

The phone rang and the low burring sound annoyed her. *So much for interruptions,* she thought, wondering how all these people knew she was at home. Lois came to mind, and she made a mental note to give her specific instructions on how to handle her phone calls when she worked at home.

"Hello," Hillary practically grumbled.

"Miss Houston," came the sullen voice, "this is Alex Cash." Hillary immediately tensed up, and he sensed it. "Please don't hang up. I called to apologize."

His comment really stunned her since he'd never admitted to any wrongdoing. His wanting to apologize came as a big shock to her. "Alex, I can give you two minutes. Speak," she commanded, sitting down at the kitchen table.

"Hillary, I didn't realize I've caused you so much discomfort. After your lawyer left this morning, I had time to really assess my behavior. I now realize I've been really cruel to you. I hope we can work this out without a lawsuit."

Hillary couldn't get past "lawyer," knowing she'd have to be coy to get more information. She had a sneaky suspicion that Brandon had involved himself, which made her feel as if a Mack truck had broadsided her.

"Which one of my lawyers did you meet with—and where?"

"Aaron Samms. He showed up at my place early this morning."

His response disturbed her. She couldn't help wondering if Cassie had put Aaron up to this. But why would she do that without talking to her first? No, this wasn't something Cassie would do. There was male ego involved here. This was totally unacceptable. Whoever was responsible, she'd have a hard time recovering from the sickening blow she'd just been dealt.

"Hillary, I hope it doesn't have to go that far. I'm truly sorry."

"You damn well should be sorry, yet I can't help but wonder if this change of heart came about as the direct result of a lawsuit being threatened. Contrary to popular belief, women don't like to be treated as sex objects, or pieces of meat. Alex, you can be very charming when you want to be. You need to work on the nice guy routine a lot more and drop the sexual dominance act. Give it a chance. You just might find out that people will respond to you in a more positive way."

Alex was scared to death of a lawsuit. "You have been

gracious. I hope my apology and the change in my behavior will be enough to settle this."

Hillary detected the stress in his otherwise obnoxious voice. "As far as I'm concerned, this is the end of it. But I promise you, if you ever do or say anything to me with sexual overtones, I'll go straight to Mr. Asher. Then my lawyer will be instructed to file a lawsuit against you."

"Do you think you could call your lawyer and tell him it's settled?" Alex asked, hoping she'd agree.

Hillary sighed. "Yes, Alex. I'll take care of it. One more thing before we end this conversation. Could you describe the lawyer that came to see you today? I want to make sure it was Mr. Samms and not his law partner."

Alex described Brandon Blair to a T, right down to his highly polished leather boots, which confirmed Hillary's suspicions.

Her blood ran cold.

Before she hung up, she reassured Alex that she'd call her lawyer and inform him of her decision. With her blood pressure at an all-time high, Hillary went up to her bedroom and threw herself across the bed. She was angry as hell's fire.

Who did Brandon Blair think he was? She still couldn't figure out how Alex got Aaron's name . . . unless Brandon introduced himself as Aaron. How could he do that? What made him think it was his right? she wailed inwardly. Thinking back to the conversation she'd had earlier with Mr. Asher made her wonder if Brandon had spoken to him about Alex. "Oh, God, please don't let it have gone that far," she prayed. How could she handle all of this insanity? The whole mess seemed too much to bear.

Thirty minutes later, when security called to announce Brandon, Hillary jumped off the bed and ran a brush through her hair. She then rushed downstairs to await his arrival.

As she opened the door to Brandon, he tossed her that disarming smile she'd come to love. But she had every intention of wiping that sexy smile right off his face. Permanently, if necessary.

He kissed her cheek. "Hi, pretty lady. I've been worried about you. I'm glad to see for myself that you're okay."

She tossed him an impatient glance. "I told you earlier I was okay, but I'm glad you're here," she effected nicely. They'd eat lunch before she let him have it right between the eyes, she decided. "Come on in the kitchen. I prepared lunch for us." Her tone of voice carried a blend of reserve and agitation.

He was puzzled by her reserved demeanor, but decided not to make an issue of it. "Great," he replied, following her into the kitchen.

He sat down while Hillary pulled all the food out and set it on the table. She then took the seat directly across from him. Other than his compliments on how good the food tasted, they said very little to each other, causing the tension between them to mount.

Once the food had been devoured, he helped her clear the table. They washed and dried the dishes together. After putting everything away, they moved into the living room.

Brandon sat down on the sofa. As he reached to pull Hillary onto his lap, she jerked away from him, shocking him in the process. He immediately became quite wary of her mood.

"Did I offend you with my gesture?"

She sat down next to him. "The truth of the matter is, you're doing quite a bit to offend me."

He got that puzzled look again. "Would you mind telling me how?"

Knowing she couldn't make her position clear in such proximity, she quickly distanced herself from him. Brandon had a way of using his effervescent charm to snuff out her anger, but he wasn't going to get off so easily this time.

She eyed him suspiciously. "Do you know anything about a lawyer visiting Alexander Cash today?" The look in her eyes warned him not to lie.

A light came on in his raven-black eyes as he shifted uncomfortably in his seat, resting his palms on his thighs. "As a matter of fact, Hillary, I do. Please, before you go off on me, allow me to explain. That's why I came here."

"You have the floor, Mr. Blair. Or is it Mr. Samms?"

He definitely saw the need to proceed with caution. Otherwise things were going to blow up in his face. Hillary didn't seem the type that could be easily placated, so he was going to steer clear of that approach.

"Babe, I've been very upset about this Cash character ever since you first mentioned him. Last night I laid awake trying to figure out how anybody could do this to another person, especially you. No woman deserves to be sexually harassed by a man."

He got up from the sofa and paced the room. "I knew you didn't know how you should handle it, but I knew it had to be handled. I made a vow to protect you from anyone or anything that caused you discomfort . . . and I didn't exclude myself. So I went to have a talk with the man. The only thing I regret about this entire mess is that I didn't discuss it with you first. I know I should've."

His handsome face grim with regret, he came over and sat on the arm of her chair. "Reflecting back on today's events, I realize I took a lot for granted. I admit that I didn't consider how you'd feel about me intruding in your private affairs. I'm a very compulsive person. I was consumed with finding a way to put an end to your nightmare as quickly and as effectively as I possibly could. My intentions were all good."

In spite of all the anger she felt, she carefully considered her response. Understanding his frustration with her situation, she took a few seconds to put her emotions in check. The last thing she wanted to do was come unglued in front of him.

"Brandon, I know your intentions were good, but the road to *hell* is paved with good intentions. Knowing you want to protect me makes me feel good. But, Brandon, you can't fight my battles for me. I would've eventually handled this sensitive matter, but you stripped me of my right to do just that. I make my own decisions, in my own time. If you're to be a part of my life, you'll have to respect that I'm an adult, too. I merely trusted you with a confidence. I didn't ask you to find a solution. I feel betrayed." Tears flooded her eyes, though she'd tried to hold them back.

Wiping her tears away with his fingers, he looked as injured as she felt. "Hillary, I'm sorry I hurt you. I can see the pain in your eyes. Would you like me to leave and give you a chance to sort all this out?"

She sniffled. "I think that would be best. But I have two more questions before you leave. Why did you tell Alex you were Aaron? And how did you find out where Alex lived?"

Brandon heaved a huge sigh. "He seemed reluctant to let me in so I thought if I presented myself as a lawyer, it just might give me the edge I needed. I never told him I was Aaron. I just handed him Aaron's business card. All I can say to the second question is that I have my sources. Now can I ask you something?"

"Shoot."

"How did you find out?" *Dumb question,* he thought. It had to be Alex. No one else had been present.

"I have my sources!" *Payback,* she thought irritably.

Not used to having his own answers thrown back at him, not to mention the sharp tone she'd used with him, he stared at her through narrowed eyes. Hillary totally ignored his petulance as she arose from her seat and started for the front door. At the door, when he brushed her lips with his, she waged a major battle within herself to keep from responding.

He eyed her intently. "Pretty lady, I know I handled this badly. I hope you can forgive me. I can't feel any sorrier than I already do."

Hillary simply opened the door. She knew her gesture was rude, but that's how she felt. He touched her cheek with the back of his hand and stepped outdoors. Neither of them spoke another word, neither of them knowing if they were going to see each other again. Both appeared to be hurting as she shut the door on his retreating back.

Taking the steps two at a time, she started to enter her bedroom, but turned around and went into the guest room. As she dropped down onto the neatly made-up bed, she pulled a pillow into her arms. Unexpectedly, she caught a whiff of Brandon's expensive cologne. Aching inside, she inhaled the manly scent that made her senses whirl with longing. Hillary hated the idea of Brandon being yet another man who seemed to want to take control of her life. She wasn't so desperate for a man that she had to give in to his senseless whims, but her lonely arms were telling her that she just might be wrong. No, she wasn't desperate for a man, just hopelessly desperate for Brandon Blair!

Recalling how Tyrone had tried to make her feel so inadequate, especially when it came to certain decisions she'd made, she flinched. He would forcefully insinuate his own ideas about the way things should be done, but she'd soundly rejected his archaic brainwashing techniques.

She would also reject Brandon's ideas for her life, in the same decisive way.

Hillary didn't think Brandon was the same sort of man as Tyrone, but any similarities to the highhanded businessman she once dated were more than she could swallow, more than she cared to put up with. For sure, Brandon possessed a jealous streak; the one thing she hated the most. A jealous person signified a lack of confidence, though Brandon had enough confidence for an assembly of men. It just didn't add up for her. To take her mind off Brandon, Hillary jumped off the bed and went into the third bedroom, where she sat down at the desk and pulled out her workload.

The blush-rose nuance of her office/den harnessed a tonic effect, making it the perfect setting for getting things done. The leaf-green accents, connecting Hillary to nature, grounded and freshened the spirit of the room.

Eight bells, she noted as she put everything away and left the office. She'd finished her presentation for the next day, along with several other projects. She hadn't eaten since lunch, she realized, but her appetite no longer existed. The only thing she had an appetite for wasn't available to her at the moment: Brandon's sweet, fulfilling kisses. Crossing the hall, she entered her bedroom. After undressing, she grabbed her robe and went into the bathroom. Her head throbbed like crazy, so she took a couple of aspirin before returning to the bedroom. Before getting into bed, she turned on the television. This was going to be one long, lonely night, she concluded.

Though interested in the movie she'd turned on, she couldn't concentrate on it for thinking about what had transpired between her and Brandon. Maybe she'd been a little too hard on him, she thought. But not being hard enough had everything to do with the reasons for this mess she found herself in in the first place. She needed to talk to Cassie, her best friend, her always-available confidant. Picking up the phone, she dialed the number in haste.

"Artie's Pet Shop."

Hillary may have thought she had the wrong number had she not been used to Cassie's antics. "Hi, Cassie, it's me. I need to talk."

"You sound terrible, Hillary. What's wrong?"

"I think Brandon and I just had our first fight."

"What the heck over?" Cassie asked with concern.

Hillary explained the details of her troubles with Brandon.

Cassie was impressed by Brandon's ingenious idea. "I think that's hilarious. He cares—and you should try to see the good in it. Using Aaron's business card was brilliant."

Hillary frowned. The last thing she needed to hear was Cassie singing Brandon's praises, even if she did have a point. "Cassie, why don't you come over for dinner tomorrow?" Hillary had changed the subject, not wanting to hear any more conversation regarding Brandon. "We can just kick it like old times."

"We have a date if you'll fix spaghetti. I know I just had lasagna, but I love your spaghetti sauce."

"Absolutely. Spaghetti it'll be. Cassie, I'll be looking forward to us having dinner tomorrow. Good night."

"Good night, Hillary. Try to get a lot of rest. Things will look brighter in the morning."

Hillary didn't know if things would ever look bright again. She had thought she'd finally found the man of her dreams, but it looked as though she'd attracted another nightmare instead. Brandon already haunted her daydreams. So why not welcome him into her nightmares, as well? What a deliciously sexual haunting that would be, she pondered as she got out of bed and went into the guest room.

As she slipped into the bed in which Brandon had

slept the previous night, she felt his presence all about her. She felt the warmth that had held her intimately close that very morning. If she slept in this bed, where he'd slept, maybe she wouldn't feel the pain of missing him so much.

What a way for the nightmare to begin. . . .

Seven

Hillary was ready for work in record time. After making the bed, she tidied the room and gathered all the materials she'd need for later. Deciding not to bother with breakfast, she entered the garage and backed the car out. Entering the freeway, she could see that traffic looked a mess. It remained bumper-to-bumper all the way in to work, the last thing she needed.

However, she made it to work with fifteen minutes to spare, an hour before she had to make her presentation. As she passed through the reception area, she noticed that Lois wasn't at her desk, so she proceeded to her office. An array of heady scents bowled her over when she opened her door. The entire office had been filled with colorful flowers. Every type of bloom one could imagine had been arranged all around the spacious room. A large greeting card sat in the center of her desk. Her fingers burned with anticipation as she ripped the envelope open.

The special occasion card began with: I'M SORRY I HURT YOU. . . .

With scalding tears running down her face, she read the note he'd handwritten at the bottom. *Brandon has done it again,* she thought in utter bewilderment. He'd made her feel as though she were the most important person in the world. Without giving it a second thought, she rummaged through her purse to locate his private number. Assuming he'd already be at work, she dialed his office number.

She thought his voice sounded harried when he answered. It also had that scratchy sound to it, as if he had a sore throat. "Brandon, it's the woman you've spent the entire night dreaming about," she mocked sweetly. His wonderful laugh drifted into her ear, making her happy she'd called.

"Pretty lady, you don't know what this call means to me. Are you okay?"

She fingered one of the velvety rose petals. "I'm just fine. These flowers in my office have a lot to do with it. How did you get someone to deliver them so early?"

"I didn't. I delivered them myself—and Lois helped me put them in your office. She seemed reluctant to do so, but when I told her this was my way of apologizing to you for making a big mistake, she agreed to help me."

His ingenuity astounded her. "So now you've got my coworkers conspiring against me to help you get back in my good graces."

"Tell me something. Did it work? Am I back in your good graces?"

"Without a doubt!"

"Does this mean I've been forgiven?"

"Exactly."

"Lady, I was worried I'd blown this relationship before I had the chance to spoil you rotten."

She felt the warmth of his smile. "Let's forget about what happened yesterday . . . and start from today."

He felt one hundred percent relieved. "Can I see you tonight, Hill?"

"I'm sorry, Brandon, but I already have plans for this evening." A palpable silence infiltrated the phone line.

"I guess I missed out."

She felt sorry for him because he sounded so sad. "Brandon, Cassie is coming over for dinner tonight. If you'd like, I'll call her to see if she minds if you join us." *Darn,* she thought with annoyance. Why had she given in to his whims so easily? She should've made him sweat a little longer.

"You wouldn't mind doing that, Hill?"

"I offered, didn't I?" What else could she say now that she'd put her foot in? "I'll call you right back."

"I'll be eagerly awaiting your call."

Immediately after speaking with Cassie, Hillary called Brandon back and told him everything was set. Cassie would bring Aaron along if he was free. After doing a quick check on her appearance, she left to deliver her proposal. On her way to the boardroom, she ran into Lois.

"I was really taken by Mr. Blair's charm. I hope you don't mind me letting him into your office," Lois said.

"Don't give it another thought. He has a way of making you do the unthinkable. I'm happy you helped him out."

"You're so lucky. Brandon is even luckier."

"Thanks, Lois." Hillary then took the opportunity to give Lois phone instructions for when she worked at home.

The presentation of her proposal went off without a hitch. Hillary impressed Mr. Asher—and he told her so. Several of the other senior executives also spoke of the brilliant job she'd done. Pleased with things, she decided to reward herself by taking the rest of the day off. Back in her office, she cleared up a few matters that needed her immediate attention.

Before taking leave, she returned all the phone calls that had come in while she was out.

* * *

At the local grocery store, she picked up everything needed to make spaghetti. Moving into the produce section, she selected vegetables for a salad. In the bakery department, she purchased a loaf of freshly baked French bread. She then proceeded home.

Twenty minutes later, upstairs in her bedroom, she changed into jeans and a royal blue cashmere sweater. As she ran a quick brush through her hair, she smiled, remembering that Brandon had freed her hair from its band the other night. When she'd noticed her hair band on the nightstand the next morning, she knew it hadn't gotten there on its own. Before heading to the kitchen, she slipped a bathrobe over her clothes.

Downstairs in the kitchen, she busied herself preparing the meal. Realizing she hadn't purchased a dessert, she thought about the tart green apples in the refrigerator. They would make a wonderful apple pie.

While cutting the crisp fruit, she fought the urge to eat it. She loved to eat green apples with salt. Thinking about all the apple trees she'd climbed when she lived back East brought a lot of fond memories to mind, making her miss the easy lifestyle she'd enjoyed on the East Coast.

As the spaghetti sauce simmered, she put the pie into the oven. She cut the vegetables for the salad and quickly tossed the greens. The salad dressing could be added later by her guests. Hastily, she cleaned up after herself and went into the living room.

Curling up on the sofa, she opened up a fashion magazine. The new fall fashions looked stunning. Fall and winter were her favorite seasons. She loved to wear warm sweaters and fall plaids. She missed the seasonal changes of the East Coast, but she had no intention of moving back there.

* * *

Awakened by the phone, fear gripped Hillary when security informed her that her parents had arrived. Her parents never came without calling first, which made her afraid that something had happened to someone in her family. Running to the door, she stood there until she saw her parents' car come around the bend. Full of apprehension, she ran outside and patiently waited until they emerged from the car.

"Mom, Dad, is there something wrong?" she inquired anxiously.

At five-foot-five, several inches shorter than her husband's six-foot-one frame, Alice Houston was a slender, graceful woman. She had the same chestnut-brown hair as her youngest daughter, though hers was mixed with broad streaks of gray.

Alice reached for her daughter's hand. "No, Hillary. Everything is just fine. Dad and I were in the area so we decided to stop." Hillary's breath escaped in a sigh of relief. Alice's fawn-brown eyes gleamed with uncertainty. "I hope we didn't come at a bad time. We've really missed you."

Hillary frowned. "It's early yet. How did you know I was even home?"

Alice looked sheepish. "I called your job earlier."

Hillary laughed as she led the way inside. "Okay, I get it. You guys were worried about me."

Possessing the finely tuned physique of a marine, Jackson Houston's dark brown eyes lit up with glee as he tousled his silvery curls. "Yes, Hillary, we were concerned. We know a lot has been going on for you at work. We wanted to make sure you were okay."

Before they sat down, Hillary put her arms around both her parents and gave them a hug. As she sat down with them, she began filling them in on all the latest happenings at work. She held up admirably while speaking of Alexander Cash.

Jackson was visibly upset over the sexual harassment business, but he didn't comment. He trusted her to handle it in her own way. They were proud of the way she handled her professional and personal life. In fact, they were proud of the way they'd raised all of their six children, proud of the wonderful adults they'd grown up to be.

Rubbing his stomach, Jackson sniffed the air. "Hillary, what smells so good?"

"It's spaghetti sauce and an apple pie. I'm having guests for dinner."

Alice looked at her husband with dismay in her eyes. "Jackson, we did come at a bad time."

Jackson pursed his lips as he stood up. "Hillary, we can come back another time."

Hillary jumped to her feet. "Mom and Dad, you're welcome here anytime. I'd even like for you to stay for dinner. I have plenty of food."

Alice looked uncertain. "We'd love to stay if you're sure it's okay. We don't want to interfere with your plans. We wouldn't feel good about doing that."

Surprised at her mother's reluctance, Hillary draped her arm around her shoulders. "I wouldn't have it any other way. If you'll excuse me, I need to make a phone call."

Hillary felt the situation was a little complicated, only because she wasn't sure how Brandon would respond to meeting her family. She'd call and tell him that her parents were there. He could make his own mind up about coming to dinner, but her parents were staying. She would put the ball in his court. The next move was up to him.

She walked into the bedroom and closed the door behind her. As she glanced at the clock, she hoped she could reach him in time.

After several rings, Brandon answered the phone, sounding out of breath.

"Blair here."

"Hi, it's Hillary."

"Hi, pretty lady. You just caught me. I was out the door when I heard the phone ringing. I knew it was the private line. It has a different ring from the other phones. Is everything okay?"

"Brandon, my parents are here. They showed up unexpectedly." While waiting for his response, she nervously bit down on her lower lip.

"Hillary, what are you really saying here?"

"That I invited them to stay for dinner and I wanted to let you know. I want you to be able to make your own decision about meeting them. I certainly will understand if you want to cancel our plans."

"Hill, do you have a problem with me meeting your parents?"

"Of course not. That would be silly."

"In that case, I don't have a problem with it either. I would be honored to meet the two people who are responsible for such a beautiful young woman."

She felt enraptured. "Honey, they've been wanting to meet you, too." It was only the second time she'd used an endearment toward him . . . she liked the way it sounded.

"I love it when you call me that. It gives me an incredible rush."

"Good. I'll remember to use it more often."

"I'm on my way. Keep my seat warm for me. Can I bring anything?"

"Just that disarming smile of yours."

"Good-bye, precious."

Hillary quickly returned to the family room, where her

parents eagerly awaited her arrival. As they sat talking about everything from A to Z, it was easy to see that Hillary adored her dad. Jackson had a way of anticipating her every need. She could talk to him about anything, but she was more reserved with her mother.

Alice Houston had a tendency to be negative about a lot of things. Hillary and her sisters often wondered if their mother's negativity was due to a bad experience of some kind, but they were never able to find out for sure.

Hillary's guests all arrived at the door at the same time. After steering her friends into the living room, she introduced Brandon and Aaron to her parents. While everyone got acquainted, she slipped into the kitchen to put the finishing touches on her meal.

Brandon appeared in the doorway a few minutes later. Walking up behind her, he put his arms around her waist, squeezing her tightly. "Precious, I've missed you so much. I'm glad you decided to give me a second chance."

She lost herself in the warmth of his arms. "There was never a question of a second chance. I had to sort everything out in my mind, but I'll admit to being damn angry with you. I just felt I had to make myself clear."

Nuzzling the side of her neck with his nose, he turned Hillary around to face him. "Pretty lady, I promise I will always communicate my intentions to you."

He sounded sincere enough, she thought, smoothing his hair back. "I thought we closed this subject earlier. I want to focus on today. The past doesn't figure into the equation."

He kissed her with a desperation that matched her own hunger for him. "Point well taken."

Hillary and Brandon joined the rest of her guests, where her mother and Cassie could be heard talking up a storm. Jackson and Aaron didn't seem to have a clue what the two women chatted on about, Hillary noted with a smile. It turned out that Alice had been filling Cassie in on the daytime soaps. Though Hillary eagerly joined in their conversation, she kept an eagle eye on her father as he talked easily to Brandon and Aaron. A good sign, she mused happily.

Jackson Houston was a man of few words, saying even less if he didn't care for someone, she knew. He was never rude; he just wouldn't have much to say. Comfortable with how well things seemed to be going, she left the room to put the food on the table. Cassie and her mother followed along behind her. Alice bubbled like a newly opened bottle of champagne as she told Hillary and Cassie how handsome she thought the guys were. She also mentioned how comfortable her husband seemed to be with the young men.

Everyone rushed to the table when Hillary announced dinner. Once Jackson offered the blessing, the small group engaged in light conversation as they partook of Hillary's excellent culinary skills.

"Mrs. Houston, did you teach Hillary to cook like this?" Brandon asked.

"I'm sorry, Brandon, but I can't take any of the credit. Mr. Houston is the chef in our house. She learned to cook by hanging out in the kitchen with her dad."

Brandon turned his attention to Jackson. "Mr. Houston, you've taught her well."

Jackson smiled. "Thank you for your generous comments, young man."

Half an hour later, when everyone was too full to eat another bite, chairs were pushed back from the table. No one had room for dessert except Jackson. Hillary promptly went into the kitchen to cut him a slice of pie.

Joining his daughter in the kitchen, Jackson opened the freezer door and removed a carton of vanilla ice cream. As he waited for Hillary to cut the pie, he brought up her relationship with Brandon. Hillary gave him the upside and the downside of their budding romance.

"Keep a level head—and always follow your heart, honey."

Knowing that this was his way of telling her to take it slow and to be careful, Hillary smiled with endearment at her beloved father. She could tell by his comments that Brandon had won Jackson's approval, which made her ecstatic. Jackson Houston's approval wasn't won easily.

The phone rang just as she finished wiping her hands on a paper towel, and she picked up the kitchen extension. It was Mr. Asher calling to inform her that the plans for her trip to New York had been firmed up. He would discuss all the details with her the next day. After a few moments of unimportant office chitchat, she bade him a good evening.

The rest of the evening with her guests turned out to be pleasant. Everyone seemed to get along so well with one another. When it was time for everyone to leave, she and Brandon walked her guests to their cars. While Hillary kissed everyone good night, Brandon told her parents how honored he was to have met them. As he shook hands with Jackson and gave Alice a light peck on the cheek, Hillary noticed Aaron's eyebrows rise at Brandon's gesture toward her mother.

Brandon never got involved with his women's families, Aaron knew. *He's a goner,* Aaron thought, as he helped Cassie into his car. He wasn't sure if Brandon knew it himself, but he sure enough did. The signs were all there.

Dropping down on the sofa, Brandon wasted no time in searching out Hillary's mouth. He wanted to hold on to her for as long as he could. He'd convinced himself earlier that he'd lost her over the Cash incident. He had no intention of losing another precious second.

As time moved on, Hillary appeared to be in deep thought, Brandon noted, wondering what she was thinking about. He'd asked her a question, but she hadn't even heard him. He nudged her shoulder. The blank stare she gave him put him on high alert. "Earth to Hillary. Pretty lady, where are you?"

She scowled. "I was trying to find the right words to tell you something."

Thinking that she'd changed her mind about continuing their relationship, his entire body grew tense. He studied her intently. "Tell me what?"

She rested her head on his shoulder. "Honey, I have to go out of town to a conference."

Relaxing his muscles, he allowed his breath to escape. "Where is it . . . and when do you have to leave?"

"New York. I'm scheduled to leave in two weeks."

"How long will you be gone?"

"Probably for an entire week. I will know more tomorrow."

"Hill, I can't be without you for an entire week," he protested.

She smiled at his expression of agony. "You'll manage, I'll manage, and it will be all the sweeter when we get together again." She looked at him and laughed. "Don't look so pained. It's only a week."

He poked out his lower lip. "I am in pain. Why shouldn't I look the part?" Pulling his head into her lap, she kissed him deeply.

As he thought of how much he would miss her, he tried to find the words to ask her if they could spend the rest of the time until her departure together. "I want you to come home with me tonight." Though he'd tried to speak calmly, his words had gushed out hastily. "I need to be with you. I need us to be together."

His request surprised her. "Brandon, I do have to go to work until I leave, you know."

He ignored her terse response. "I'll drop you off each day and pick you up. I can rearrange my schedule to accommodate yours. I want us to be together until you leave."

"I'm not sure if that's such a good idea," she hedged. "You've caught me completely off guard here, you know."

"Give me one good reason why it's such a bad idea."

Hillary thought his question over. She could give him twenty reasons; all of them legitimate. "I don't know, Brandon. It's such a tall request."

He sighed. "Hill, it's not that big a deal. I just want to pamper you," he countered. "I want to show you how good you and I can be together."

She blew out a ragged breath. "You're really making this difficult for me." She truly wanted to accept his offer, but would it be a wise move?

"Hill, I promise to be on my best behavior. You can have all the space you need. Please come home with me. The surf is magnificent at this time of year."

She sighed. "Yes, I'll go, but if it doesn't work out, I'm not going to stay," she said with certainty, hoping she wouldn't live to regret such an impulsive decision.

"That's a given, Hill." He couldn't believe his luck as he hugged her much too tightly. When she protested loudly, he realized he'd nearly smothered her.

They spent the next half hour cleaning the kitchen and putting the house back in order. Upstairs in her bedroom, while she packed her things, he lay across the bed watching her every move. Once everything was taken care of, they secured the house and went outside to where his car was parked.

"Would you like me to put the top down? It's a beautiful evening."

Loving the feel of the wind in her hair, she eagerly agreed to his suggestion. As they drove out of the city, Hillary took special notice of the spectacular view.

A short time later, Brandon expertly steered the Benz onto Highway 1. Normally he drove a lot faster; the car was built for speed, but he wasn't taking any chances with her safety. Reminding him of the deep pink roses he'd given her on their first date, her cheeks had come alive with color. As the sweeping wind incited a riot in her lovely hair, he saw that she didn't seem to mind. The sparkle in her eyes told him she was as excited as he was.

As Brandon finally pulled the car into the gates that led to his beach property, her breath escaped in a loud gasp.

"Brandon, I had no idea. I've never envisioned such splendor. This is not a house. It's a mansion. I can't believe you live all alone in this much space." Her eyes danced merrily as she looked up at the huge house.

"Believe it, babe. It's true."

Brandon Blair had lived with many women, but not in this house. He had designed and built this house for only one mistress. Unfortunately, he hadn't found her yet, but he somehow felt that the absence of a mistress for Blair House just might be over. Easing the Benz into the three-car garage, he cut the engine and jumped out.

For the next half hour or so Hillary was in complete awe as she went from room to room, in eager anticipation of the beauty she'd discover next. She thought that Brandon had excellent taste and that the huge house was extravagantly furnished. The colors in the rooms were in direct contrast to those in her own home. While her house was done in soft pastels, Brandon's was done in manly tones of various shades of burgundy, blues, and grays. Splashes of white brightened the spirit of the rooms.

As Hillary sank down into one of the plush navy-blue

leather chairs, she surveyed all that her eyes could take in. She felt totally out of her element, but she felt a peace that surpassed all understanding. It was like she and the house shared something special in common. For sure, they had Brandon in common.

While Hillary continued to look around, Brandon brought her things in from the car and deposited them in the master bedroom. He was going to insist on Hillary sleeping in his room and he'd take one of the guest rooms. He knew she'd probably try to argue the case, but it wasn't going to do her any good. After her stay was over, he wanted a constant reminder of her having slept in his bed. Just the thought of her in his bed caused his loins to ache.

Eight

Brandon returned to the front of the house. Lifting Hillary from her comfortable position in the chair, he carried her into the family room. Carefully, he lowered her onto the white Greek imported Flokati rug laid out in front of the marble fireplace. Excusing himself for a moment, he built a fire, then joined her on the floor.

Drawing her onto his lap, he held her securely with one arm. While exploring her enchanting beauty, he showered her face, neck, and arms with tender kisses. He stroked her hair, and Hillary enjoyed the tingling sensations rumbling deliciously through her entire body. As his tongue teased her ears with quick darting movements, Hillary fought in desperation to keep her sanity. Lifting her off his lap, he pressed her back into the rug and continued the passionate assault on her mouth. Her senses reeled. Careful not to frighten or offend her in any way, Brandon practiced extreme caution in his explorations of her staggering sensuality.

Hillary was more to him than just a conquest, he reminded himself. Overcome by the delicious sensations invading her body, she trembled. Thinking that her shaking limbs were due to fear, he immediately acknowledged that she might very well be waving a red flag. Though he put himself in check, he couldn't resist kissing her once more. Even when her response to his kiss seemed to belie his earlier thoughts, he sat up and drank in the lovely vision that was Hillary Houston. For several tension-filled moments, they just stared into one another's eyes.

Bringing himself back to earth, he excused himself, rose up from the floor, and disappeared into the cavernous kitchen. Hillary watched after him, looking as though she'd fallen into a trance.

Upon his return, he carried two cups of hot tea to where she lay quietly.

After allowing the hot drink to cool a bit, he lifted the mug to her lips. "Hill, would you like to go out on the terrace to enjoy the surf?"

She rose to her feet. "I can't think of anything I'd like to do more."

I sure in the heck can, he thought mischievously.

As he opened the sliding glass door, the sounds of the surf rushed forth and embraced her ears. The moment Hillary stepped outside she fell speechless, but her eyes spoke volumes. Enthralled by the beauty before her, tears burned in her eyes.

She turned to Brandon. "Have I just died and gone to heaven?" she asked, turning her attention back to the pounding surf.

Walking up behind her, he drew her back against his broad chest and encircled her tiny waist with a quiet strength. "No, pretty lady, you are very much alive."

Lifting her hair, he massaged her neck with warm, wet kisses. As she turned around to face him, her body involuntarily betrayed her. She melted into him like hot candle wax. The incendiary contact nearly singed the hairs on her elegant neck, leaving her bewildered and breathless.

Though the beach appeared to be only a stone's throw, Hillary surmised that it was actually several yards away.

Steps located on both sides of the terrace led down to the water. Brandon had easy access to the water's edge.

"Can we walk down to the beach?" she asked, breaking the enchanting moment.

"Absolutely. Let me get a couple of sweaters." Brandon disappeared into the house to grab two heavy sweaters from his bedroom closet.

Returning with the sweaters, he dressed her in one, then put his own on. Ensuring her warmth, he put his arms around her and pulled her close before taking the steps.

They walked as close to the water as they could get without actually getting wet. Their faces sparkling with the mist from the ocean, Brandon and Hillary appeared lost in the moment. Suddenly, they stopped and faced one another. As they fell into each other's arms, their lips met in a heated rush, their hearts embraced.

Unable to get enough of her sweet mouth, he picked her up and carried her back into the house as he continued to hold her mouth captive. Stopping briefly, he deposited her into the plush leather chair where he'd found her earlier. Without uttering a word, he disappeared again.

Hillary felt breathless. When she heard Brandon calling her name, she traveled in the direction of his voice. Her search for him led her to the master bedroom.

He smiled when she entered the room. "Babe, you need a warm shower. Don't want you to catch a chill."

He lifted her suitcase onto the bed and flicked it open in one rapid motion. "Pretty lady, get your night things out while I run the shower."

He moved further into the bedroom, then into the adjoining bathroom, where he turned on the shower. He then left the room so she could prepare herself for bed.

After her shower, she dressed in a pink satin gown and robe. Leaving her hair loose, she brushed it with hard, even strokes. Feeling tired, she lay down on the king-size bed. Completely relaxed in the masculine surroundings, she looked out onto the beach and watched as the high tide rolled in. In a matter of seconds, the melodious lull of the surf lured her into a sweet, peaceful sleep.

Brandon had just finished his shower in one of the guest bathrooms. After thoroughly drying off, he dressed his lower body in winter-green silk boxer shorts and left his chest bare. Once he'd put on a velour bathrobe of the same color as his shorts, he brushed his teeth. Rushing back to Hillary, he stood quietly in the doorway of his bedroom, watching her intently as he tried to determine if she was asleep. He was in deep thought when her sweet voice drifted across the room.

"Honey, how long have you been there?" she asked drowsily.

He drew in a shaky breath. "I just got here, pretty lady. I was afraid you were asleep. I didn't want to disturb you, but I'll admit it was difficult not to."

He strode over to the bed and lifted her up. Glad that his housekeeper had been there earlier, he turned the bed down. After positioning her in the center of the bed, he climbed in with her and pulled her close to his body.

"Sleep, pretty lady. You're safe with me. I haven't forgotten my earlier promise."

Moving even closer to him, she burrowed her head into his chest. Reaching inside his robe, she stroked his thick chest hairs. Her tender touch made him shiver in delight; her hands felt so soothing, so marvelous. Minutes later, when Hillary's limp hand fell away from his chest, his heart nearly failed. Knowing she fully trusted him made him glow with contentment.

Hillary had floated away on a fluffy cloud of cotton candy. As soon as Brandon realized she was asleep, he slipped out of bed, making sure she was well covered before he turned to leave. He actually hated to go into another room, but he'd made a promise to her. Just as he eased the door open, Hillary awakened.

She looked at him through sleep-filled eyes. "Please don't go. I have faith in the promise you made to me," she uttered timidly.

He looked astonished. "Hill, are you saying you want me to sleep in the same bed with you?" In response to his question, she pulled the covers down, inviting him back.

In slow motion, he walked to the other side of the room and lit the candle inside the Shepherd's lamp. While the flames from the lamp and the bedroom fireplace engaged in a seductive slow dance with the shadows on the wall, he slid back into bed with her. Putting her arms around him, she lowered his head between her perfectly rounded breasts.

Hillary awakened before the sun rose. Noticing that Brandon had turned over onto his back sometime during the night, she propped her head on one elbow to watch him sleep. He was still dressed in his robe, but it had come open. Smiling, Hillary took the opportunity to explore his half-nude body. Had he selected the green attire just for her? she wondered. She couldn't remember if she'd told him it was her favorite color.

As she watched the rise and fall of his broad, hairy chest, she fought the temptation to kiss him awake. She couldn't believe how incredible last night had been for them. She'd never met anyone with such raw passion. He had trembled almost violently under her touch. To her, it seemed that all the nerves in his body had been exposed. A warmth spread through her entire body as she recalled the same trembling from her own body when he'd touched her so tenderly, so deeply, so intimately.

Hillary crept quietly out of bed. She'd forgotten her slippers, so she slid her tiny feet into Brandon's and headed for the sliding glass door. At her request, the door had been open all night long. She eased the screen back and slipped outside.

Once she'd removed the plastic covering on the thickly padded lounge chair, she dropped down onto the lounger and sat quietly to wait for the sun to make its grand appearance.

Half-awake, Brandon turned over and reached for her. Shaken to find her not there, his eyes searched the room for her loveliness. He then arose from the bed to look for her on the balcony. Smiling broadly, he moved in her direction. He joined her in the lounge chair, and she snuggled herself tightly against his body. Wrapped in the warm blanket of one another's bodies, they watched in reverence as the dazzling sun appeared over the smoky-gray horizon.

Hillary grabbed her clothes and retreated to the bathroom. "Don't fix me anything to eat. I've been filled by your passion."

Brandon smiled all over himself as he ducked into the spacious walk-in closet to retrieve his own clothes. Satisfied that he had everything he needed, he went to the guest room to shower and dress.

Dressed in a classy heather-gray pinstriped business suit, Hillary went in search of Brandon. When she found him, she wrapped her arms around his waist. While looking around at the glossy, ivory-colored island-style kitchen, she saw that all the appliances were a shiny copper-brown. It made a delightful contrast with the ivory-beige walls. Lovely kitchen, she mused.

She nudged his ear with her nose. "Is it okay if I make a couple of phone calls?"

He tilted his head back and kissed her chin. "Hill, you

don't need to ask to use the phone. As long as you're not calling another man."

She looked at him and raised her eyebrows. "Funny you should say that. That's exactly what I intended to do. How far is the nearest pay phone?"

Nothing in her voice indicated that she was putting him on. The look on her face confirmed how serious she was. "Babe, I was just having fun. Use the one in the bedroom if you'd like." Without further comment, she turned and left the room.

When is he going to learn not to bait me? Their relationship was going to be one challenge after another, she sensed. But she'd learn to handle Brandon. He somehow seemed worth her efforts. She knew she couldn't change him—or any man, for that matter—but she thought she'd hang in there a bit longer. Sometimes things had a way of working themselves out.

Just to send him the message that she couldn't be controlled, she'd intentionally left Brandon to figure out if she was calling another man. She also had doubts about his statement of "just having fun."

Hillary called Cassie first. As they talked about their evenings, Hillary described Brandon's home to her. Like Brandon, she left a lot of details out, hoping Cassie would one day see it for herself.

When Hillary called through to Mr. Asher's office, she informed him that she'd be into the office in a couple of hours. She then asked about her travel arrangements, learning that they'd been taken care of. After terminating the call, she returned to the front of the house.

Brandon was out on the terrace. The air felt cool as she stepped outside and walked up behind him. She easily sensed his pensive mood. Was it what she'd said earlier? *He shouldn't get in the kitchen if he can't stand the heat,* she mused. Bending over, she kissed the back of his neck. Reaching behind him, he pulled her around, onto his lap.

Though his eyes wore a moody covering, he kissed her mouth gently. "How did you sleep last night, pretty lady?"

She stretched her arms out. "Like a rock. Your bed is too comfortable. You're really spoiling me, Brandon."

"I told you that was my intention from the very beginning. Are you sure you won't let me feed you?"

She kissed the tip of his nose. "Honey, you've been feeding me since the day I met you. My bread basket is full and my ego is overweight."

He laughed at her humorous assertion. "Did you talk to Cassie this morning?"

She rolled her eyes at him. "Don't even go there. You don't ever give up, do you?" As her expression turned somber, he knew she'd seen right through his ploy.

Frowning, she eyed him intently. "I have a problem understanding something, Brandon. Maybe you can explain it to me."

"What's that, pretty lady?" he asked, yet he already knew what was coming.

"I don't understand how we could've spent such an incredible evening together, not to mention the awesome time we spent sharing the sunrise, yet you don't seem to trust me. Just where are you coming from, Mr. Blair?"

The distinct pain in her eyes struck him hard, making him feel ashamed. She didn't deserve his mistrust. Had he been projecting? He couldn't help thinking about the many women he'd played around on in the past. Payback seemed imminent. If anyone could pay him back, he knew that Hillary Houston was the only woman that ever had that type of power over him.

Not wanting Brandon to see how much his mistrust had injured her, she moved away from him. Feeling the need to cool off, she decided to take a short walk on the beach.

Disappointed in himself, he moved quickly down the stairs to go after her. Catching up to her, he spun her around to face him, pulling her roughly into his arms. "Hill, I'm sorry. I seem to be saying that a lot. You've said a dozen thanks and all I've been saying is sorry. It's not that I don't trust you, but I need you to understand that all these soul-deep emotions are so new for me. I've never had the feelings that I have for you for anyone. You might be able to say that I've been a bit of a Casanova in the past."

He briefly thought about the woman he'd just recently put in the past and the young girl of long ago. "To be honest, I fear that I may get it all back through you. But it helps me sort things out when you confront me. I'm glad you don't let me intimidate you."

His confession had somehow deepened her respect and admiration for him. "I appreciate your candor, but this is new for me, too. You need to let go of the past. If we hold the past in one hand and the future in the other, what are we holding on to the present with?"

She astounded him. "Hill, I can always trust you to be up front. I'm glad you don't pull any punches. I really wasn't sure if you were going to call another man, so I let it upset me."

She clucked her tongue. "You're the one who brought up the bit about the man. Do you think so little of me that you would think that I'm capable of such a thing? I told you I was calling a man because I was. It just happened to be Mr. Asher, my boss. I'm not used to reporting my every move to anyone. I have no intentions of starting now. So, if you have any hope of us having any type of relationship, you've got to get your act together. When I'm emotionally and romantically involved with someone, they have my loyalty and my undivided attention. Now that I've said all I'm going to say on this particular subject, I'm ready to leave for the office."

Reaching for her hand, he put it to his mouth, as his

eyes communicated to her all the words that his mouth couldn't.

Both Hillary and Brandon were quiet on the drive to the city, yet they each wondered what the other was thinking. Hillary thought she might have said too much, while Brandon thought that he hadn't said enough. Suddenly, without the slightest warning, he swerved the car onto the shoulder of the road, scaring Hillary half to death. Putting the car in park, he turned to face her.

"Hillary Houston, I think I'm falling in love with you." He'd been toying with the idea of telling her how he felt about her all morning. Glad he'd finally gotten it out, he sighed deeply, wiping his forehead with the palm of his hand. Too stunned to speak, she stared at him in disbelief.

Gently, he brought her face into both of his hands. "Did you hear what I said?" he asked in a choked voice.

"Of course I heard you. I just don't know what to say."

"Does my confession bother you?"

"It stunned me, that's all. I didn't have a clue you felt this way. Do you mind telling me when you came to this end?" Awaiting his answer, she rubbed her thighs nervously.

He held back his emotions. "I've been questioning my feelings for a couple of days now. When you trusted me enough to allow me to sleep next to you, and I did without even trying to make a move on you, I knew I was in deep."

"Does that scare you?"

"Hell, yeah. It scares me to death. But what scares me more than that is to imagine life without you now that I've found you. I need you in my life. You make my days much brighter. You make it all worthwhile."

Hillary's smile spoke of understanding. "I feel flattered that you think you're in love with me, but I believe *think* is the operative word here. Please don't concern yourself with losing me. For now, I'm here to stay. As you once stated, as long as we keep the lines of communication open, our relationship has a chance for survival. Maybe we're bogging ourselves down with too much analyzing. Let's just go with the flow and see what happens."

After kissing her gently, he grinned widely and pulled the car back into the flow of traffic. "Babe, you can be my anchor in any storm."

Exhaling a steady stream of breath, she felt relieved that the conversation hadn't gotten any heavier. It was the type of conversation that could put the fear of God in her.

Twenty minutes later, when Brandon dropped her off at her office, she promised to call him as soon as she was free to leave.

In the elevator, Hillary went over their conversation in her mind. Fortunately or unfortunately, she didn't know which, she was way ahead of him. She was already in love . . . the type of love that never, ever died.

While making her way to her office, she spoke to several of her colleagues. She then stopped by the reception desk to have her usual chat with Lois.

"You look radiant. Anything to do with Brandon Blair?" Lois asked.

"Oh, yeah," Hillary sang out. "I'll keep you posted, Lois."

Smiling, Hillary walked into her office. After putting her things away, she put her feet up on the desk to relax. Her office seemed bare after all the flowers she'd received, but she was happy that she'd donated them to a local nursing home.

While getting some papers in order for Lois to file, a knock came at the door. "Come in." She looked startled to see Alexander Cash opening her door.

Alex just stood there, smiling meekly. "Good morning, Miss Houston. May I talk with you for a few minutes?"

Though wary of him, she remained calm, taking note of the respectful manner in which he'd addressed her. "Good morning, Alex. How can I help you?"

Making direct eye contact with her, he shuffled his feet, then pulled out the chair in front of her desk. "Miss Houston, I've been pretty disturbed by all that has transpired between you and me. You don't deserve the way I've treated you. I'd like to explain something. Then maybe you could give me some advice. Do you have a few minutes?" He knew this showed nerve, but he had to try to make amends.

Out of sheer curiosity, she said, "Alex, I'll make the time. Go ahead and tell me what's on your mind."

He wore an uncomfortable expression. "I'm sure you've noticed my short stature. It has been a problem for me all my life. I have been teased and called every conceivable name you could imagine. Trying to make up for my size, I've always been an overachiever. But once I achieved my goals, the emptiness returned. My achievements didn't matter to most of the women I was interested in. They just didn't want me, based solely on the fact that I'm short. Miss Houston, I just became sick and tired of all the rejections."

He lowered his head dejectedly. "I believe being rejected by women, including my mother, was what started my harassment of women. I think it's my way of getting to them before they even have a chance to reject me. What do you think I can do to get out of this awful habit?"

Though overwhelmed with his story, she knew she'd have to choose her words carefully. "Alex, I must say that your story is an incredible one. I also have to commend you on having the courage to come in here and bare your soul to me. I respect you for that."

When Hillary saw that Alex looked very nervous, she did all she could to put him at ease before she continued the conversation. "Alex, I know this happens to a lot of people. Believe it or not, it happens to women, too. I'm not all that tall either, and I've been teased mercilessly by others as well, male and female alike. But you have to learn to put it in proper perspective, or it will destroy you. I'm going to quote something a great man once said, but I'm not going to use his exact quote. I'm going to tie it into your situation.

"A man should not be judged by his size but by the content of his character. Alex, I think that should pretty much sum it up for you. You have to be who you are and not what people want you to be. You can't please everyone. So don't even try."

Hillary offered him an encouraging smile. "When you look in the mirror and you like what looks back at you, that's the only thing that really matters. Alex, self-esteem comes from within—no one can give it to you. You're a very intelligent man, and I can honestly say that you called my attention to your so-called shortcomings by your actions, not by the way I perceived you. There are always going to be prejudices. That's life. But I do suggest that you seek counseling for your Napoleonic complex. I've always told you that I thought you could be a great person if you would just lose the macho-man image. I hope my comments have been somewhat helpful.

"Thank you for your honesty, Alex. I found it most refreshing. No one else in this office building will have any knowledge of what was discussed here today. You have my word."

Alex looked like a man who'd just released a heavy burden. "Miss Houston, thank you. As I said the other day, you've been so gracious. All along I believed that you were different from anyone else I'd met, but I still feared that you'd reject me, even as a friend. After the way you calmed my fears about the lawsuit, I knew I was right. That kindness is what gave me the strength to tell you all this today. Thank you, Miss Houston. I hope that one day we can be friends."

"Alex, I'd like that very much. What is past is past. People who work together should try to get along. If you're sincere about us becoming friends, I no longer have an objection to you just calling me by my first name."

Moving hurriedly around the desk, Alex gave Hillary an awkward hug. Responding in kind, she graciously allowed his innocent display of affection. Wearing an inquisitive expression on her face, she watched him slip out the door as quickly and as quietly as he'd entered. After several minutes of mulling over her conversation with Alex, Hillary buzzed Mr. Asher on the intercom to see if he was free.

Seated comfortably in Mr. Asher's office, she spent the next hour with him as he filled her in on all the details regarding the upcoming conference. Though the meetings would end by Wednesday, he'd arranged for her to stay in New York through the weekend, knowing how much she loved to visit the Big Apple.

Just before her workday ended, she called Brandon to let him know she was free to leave. She would meet him outside. In view of what Alex had told her, she thought it best. She didn't want Brandon to make Alex feel intimidated, or to cause a break in their newfound common ground. One day she would tell Alex who Brandon really was. Knowing how much time Brandon needed to get across town, she went out to the reception area to talk to Lois.

"Well, Lois, it looks like you'll soon be rid of me for a short while," Hillary joked. "I'm going to a conference in New York."

"Oh, Hillary, I'll miss you. You're one of the few people around here who gives me a break. A lot of the others around here think I should know the whole operation after only being here a few weeks."

Hillary patted her on the back in a nonpatronizing way. "Lois, I think you're doing a great job. Let's have lunch when I get back. I'll arrange with Mr. Asher for us to have some extra time."

Lois beamed. "That would make me very happy. We can get better acquainted."

A thoughtful look crossed Hillary's features. "Lois, how does Alexander Cash treat you?"

Lois flashed Hillary a glowing smile. "He's been one of the nicer ones. Why do you ask?"

"No special reason. I was just curious."

Lois suddenly got a strange look on her face. "Is Alex married?"

"No. Now it's my turn to ask you why."

"I just think he's sweet. He's taken the time to show me a few shortcuts to getting things done—and he's helped me out with several of the computer programs."

Hillary found this bit of information very interesting, to say the least. "Does his height bother you in any way?" She didn't want to put Lois on the spot, but her need to know was greater than the risk.

"That's absurd," Lois said, sounding as though she was offended by the question. "I don't make judgments on the outer appearance of a person. It's what's inside that concerns me the most. Do you have a problem with his height?"

Hillary smiled gently. "No, sweetie. I just wanted to see if we shared the same views on that particular issue. I'm glad to find out that we do." Hillary gave Lois a warm hug.

They shared a few laughs and light conversation before bidding one another farewell. Hillary left the reception area and went downstairs to meet Brandon.

Nine

Brandon pulled up to the curb at the same time Hillary walked out of the building. Exiting the car, he opened the passenger door and kissed her before returning to the driver's seat.

He looked over at her and smiled. "Want to get some lunch, Hill?"

She nodded. "That sounds divine."

He grinned. "So your bread basket is running a little low, huh?"

"Nope, not in that sense. But I realize my body needs fuel. My stomach has been growling for the last half hour."

"There's a nice cozy restaurant near the house. We can go there."

"That sounds nice." She put the seatback down a little, hoping to relax the tension in her body.

All these late nights were getting to her. But she was excited about going to New York. Besides that, she felt that she and Brandon needed a breather from one another. His jealousy still gave her cause for concern. Though he'd explained himself, she felt there was something more to it. She'd have to watch this vice of his very closely. He didn't appear to be the type of man who might have insecurities . . . unless he'd been really hurt. Perhaps Brandon's heart had been badly bruised by someone. Just the thought of him loving another woman that much made her a little crazy. Her tortured thoughts were interrupted when Brandon pointed out the neon-painted kites flying high above the coastline.

The scenery down Highway 1 was breathtaking. She loved all of the southern California beaches. How nice it would be to fly so freely with the wind and the sky as constant companions, she mused. Losing herself in the wind would be a fascinating experience.

Arriving at the restaurant, which was set very close to the water's edge, Brandon pulled into the valet parking. Much to her surprise, he allowed the attendant to open her door. *Perhaps he's learned something,* she thought.

Inside the restaurant, Brandon requested window seating, but was told by the hostess that they'd have a few minutes to wait before a window table became available. They sat down and made light conversation until a hostess came to escort them to their seating.

As they started toward their table, Brandon stopped Hillary in her tracks. Taking her in his arms, he kissed her with all the passion in him. Embarrassed by his blatant display of affection, especially in such a public forum, Hillary couldn't stop herself from blushing.

Determined to get into her blood, Brandon had made up his mind he'd show Hillary just how much he cared about her before she left on her trip. He knew he'd miss her; he wanted her to miss him just as much. This was the one woman he wasn't about to let get away. Hillary Houston was worth fighting a fierce battle for.

Hillary ordered broiled salmon with herb butter, and Brandon ordered grilled lamb kabobs with steamed vegetables. They both decided on club soda with lime for their beverage.

The food arrived in minimal time. Knowing every second spent together was precious, they hurried through their meal, eager to be alone with each other.

* * *

Back at the beach house, after changing into comfortable, warm clothing, they walked on the beach, holding each other close. Stopping to sit down on a wooden bench, Brandon pulled Hillary's head onto his shoulder.

"Hillary, I'm going to miss you. Did you find out how long you'll be gone?"

"The meetings will be over that Wednesday, but I'm considering staying on until the weekend. I haven't been to New York since last year. I have a few places I'd like to visit. I'm going to miss you, too. The last few days have been wonderful. I credit that to you."

Brandon kissed her forehead. "I'm glad to hear you say that. I know I've had a few moody moments, but I'm going to deal with the issues we've discussed. I plan to work on them while you're gone. I want to be in your life for a long time. I'm going to do whatever it takes to make you happy."

Surprised by his comments, Hillary lifted her head from his shoulder and looked deeply into his eyes. "Brandon, you don't need to change for me. Honey, you can't make another person happy. An individual's happiness is the responsibility of that individual. If a person is happy with his or herself, they can be happy with someone else. I work on me on a daily basis. You will find that I can be pretty moody, too. We'll just have to learn not to take each other's moods personally. If one of us sees that the other one needs space, we need to honor it. If there are things about yourself that you don't like, work on them for yourself. Not for someone else."

He shook his head. "Hill, you are wise beyond your years. That's what I like about you. You take the time to reason. You think things through. I'm an honor student in compulsion. By the time my common sense takes over, it's too late. I think you and I could have a great future."

Sensing that things were getting too heavy, she allowed her mischievous streak to take over. "Brandon, let's walk over near the water. I want to get my feet wet." He didn't have a clue as to what she was up to.

After moving closer to the water, she bent over to take her shoes off. While Brandon did the same, she ran a short distance into the surf and splashed him with water, catching him completely unaware. As soon as he recovered from the splash of cold water, he retaliated. The battle didn't stop until they were both completely drenched. Laughter and screams rang out on the beach when they saw how silly they looked. Picking up her shoes, she ran toward the house. She was almost to the steps when Brandon caught up with her. He gently tackled her before she could begin her ascent. Lying on the ground, they played and romped in the sand like two kids.

With both hands pinned over her head, he took full advantage of kissing her mercilessly. Her strength surprised him when she flipped him over. She'd never told him she'd taken a few Judo lessons. Once she managed to get on top, she put a handful of sand down his clothes. They wrestled and teased each other until total exhaustion took over.

"We need to go in, Hill. We're soaked. I don't want to take any chances with you getting sick." He gave her a wicked smile. "Hmm, maybe that's not such a bad idea. Then you'll have to cancel your trip to New York."

She wagged her forefinger at him. "Don't get that into your thick head. I have to go to New York whether I get sick or not. I have a job to do, Mr. Blair," she huffed.

"Just a thought."

Inside the house, Brandon went off to draw her a bath. After sprinkling the tub with the perfumed crystals he'd purchased earlier in the day, he filled the huge oval tub with steaming hot water. The plush white velour bathrobe he'd purchased for her was adorned with a beautiful gold lamé stitched crest. Inside the crest, embroidered in navy blue thread, were her initials. He hung it on the back of the bathroom door, hoping she'd like it. After lighting several candles, he went to find Hillary.

Still dressed in her wet clothes, Hillary was sitting on the terrace. Lifting her from the lounge chair, he carried her into the bathroom. When she saw the lighted candles and the bubble bath, she giggled in delight. Her lilting laughter simply put him on a natural high.

"Brandon, I'm going to lose myself in this heavenly bath. You scoot so I can get started. The water's just the way I like it, steamy hot."

She snuggled her petite body deep into the water till only her head could be seen. Putting her head back on the soft bath pillow, she relaxed her body. While pondering the last couple of days, she came to the conclusion that she could live like this every day. She definitely enjoyed all the pampering that Brandon generously gave her, and more than enjoyed the company of the man behind the pampering.

In the kitchen, Brandon opened a bottle of nonalcoholic wine. After pouring a small amount into a crystal wineglass, he carried it into the master bedroom. Before knocking, he took a few calming breaths. Her nakedness was more than he dared to think about. Finally, after a few silent oaths, he knocked on the bathroom door.

"Hill, I have something for you. Cover yourself for a minute."

She giggled. *If he's bold enough to come in here, I'm going to be bold enough not to cover myself,* she told herself. However, when Brandon opened the door, her false bravado disappeared. He set the wineglass on a gold decorator shelf and retreated in haste, unable to see much of Hillary for the bubbles and washcloth she'd draped over her breasts. He didn't need to see. He had a vivid imagination.

As she sipped the wine, she kept the bath heated by periodically running the hot water. After washing her body and hair, she stood under the shower to remove all the suds. Then she panicked, remembering that she didn't bring her robe into the bath with her. Looking around the spacious bathroom, she spotted the white robe on the back of the door. She stepped out of the tub and reached for it. Seeing that the initials on the robe were hers, she hugged it to her. Brandon had somehow managed to think of everything.

Since their playtime in the sand had caused major fatigue to set in, instead of looking for him, she turned the covers back and slipped into bed. Still dressed in the robe, she reached for the remote control and turned on the huge television screen built into one wall.

Wondering what was taking Hillary so long to come up to the front of the house, he entered the bedroom to check on her and saw that she was sound asleep. Though her hair was still wet, she'd brushed it back and had pinned it to the top of her head, he noted, turning the television off. He took one last glance at his sleeping beauty.

Back in the family room, he tried studying one of his architectural manuals, but to no avail. He couldn't get Hillary out of his mind. His concentration had been totally destroyed. What would he do when their time was up and she was three thousand miles away?

Unable to be away from her for one more second, Brandon returned to the master bedroom. Finding her still asleep, he slid in beside her, but she didn't even stir. He fell asleep as soon as his head hit the pillow.

* * *

They spent the next several days in sheer bliss. They rose to sunrises and held each other through spectacular sunsets. They talked endlessly about anything and everything. Brandon couldn't beat Hillary at Scrabble, and she couldn't beat him at chess. They listened to romantic music and watched television until the wee hours of the morning.

She sang for Brandon and he did a mock striptease to music. No calls came in and none went out. Both avoided discussing her imminent departure.

Sitting quietly through the Sunday sunrise, they had curled themselves up together in the safe haven of the balcony watching the huge whitecaps roll in to greet them. The ocean seemed as disturbed this morning as they felt. In fact, the entire morning had been drenched in melancholy.

Hungrily, he tasted Hillary's mouth, his body taut with tension. His eyes searched hers for some sort of sign that would tell him she was as desperate for him as he was for her. As her body pulsated from Brandon's intense caresses, she knew in her heart what he hoped for. She also knew she wasn't ready to fulfill his needs. Brandon read, acknowledged, and accepted the apology he saw in her tear-filled eyes.

"Hillary, I know you still have to pack. Maybe we should be getting ready to leave."

Was he trying to get rid of her since she wouldn't fulfill his needs? A sharp, stabbing pain landed in her midsection at just the thought.

"Hill, I'd like to spend the night at your place. I want to take you to the airport tomorrow. I know this may be prolonging our agony, but I believe it would be more agonizing with you there and me here. Especially when we could be together. What do you think?"

His comments immediately dispelled her painful thoughts. Hillary put her arms around him. "Honey, what took you so long?" she asked, loving to throw his very own words and actions back at him.

Fondly, he remembered saying those exact words the first night they spent together.

Their moods now considerably lighter, they moved into the master bedroom, where they packed their clothes for the trip back to Hillary's. Locked away from the world, they would have one more marvelous night of solitude. Just as they were about to leave, Brandon's doorbell rang. Looking at Hillary, he shrugged his shoulders.

On the way to the door, Brandon hoped that the model he'd recently broken up with hadn't decided to become confrontational. She hadn't been too happy with his decision for them to just be friends. She'd even warned him that she would get even. He didn't want anything to upset the wonderful times he and Hillary had shared. At least, not until he had a chance to fully explain to Hillary how things had been between him and Lisa. The last time he'd seen Lisa Baxter was several weeks before he'd even met Hillary, but he knew that Lisa still saw their relationship as unfinished business by the messages she left on his voice mail.

At the door, he viewed the security screen before opening it. Smiling broadly, he opened the door to Aaron and Cassie.

Cassie's eyes were wide with disbelief. "Brandon, your grounds are gorgeous. I can't believe the size of your house. It's huge. It seems so private and peaceful way out here."

Brandon laughed at the way Cassie rolled her eyes. "It's all that. I really love it out here. I can shut out the world when I need some privacy. Hillary loves it here, too. We've had a great time together."

Cassie giggled. "Where is Hillary?"

"Come on in. She's in the bedroom packing."

Brandon shook hands and exchanged pleasantries with Aaron before he ushered his guests into the family room. As he took Cassie on a short tour of his home, her reaction to each room was pretty much the same as Hillary's had been.

Brandon tossed his arm around Cassie's shoulder. "Come on, Cassie. Just follow me. I'll lead you to your best friend."

As they passed through the family room, Cassie kissed Aaron softly on the mouth. "Keep it warm for me, cowboy," she said in a lusty voice. "I'll be right back."

Aaron laughed. "I'll be waiting."

Brandon took Cassie down the long corridor to the master bedroom. When they walked into the room, Hillary turned around to see who had come in.

"Hi, I'm Cassandra Paige. Nice to meet you." Both Hillary and Cassie laughed. "It seems like we haven't seen each other in ages. I thought I'd better introduce myself."

Hillary smiled as she hugged her dear friend. "Cassie, it does seem like forever. I've missed you. As soon as I get back from New York, we'll have a girls only night."

"That sounds good to me, Hillary. We have to catch up on so many things. I'm going to miss you while you're away."

"I'll miss you, too. I wish you were going with me, Cass."

Back in the family room with Aaron, Brandon sat down with his friend after Aaron had declined his offer of something to drink. "We've had an incredible time together. Hillary is wonderful. I don't know what I'll do when she's away."

Aaron could see how happy his friend was. "I know exactly how you feel. Cassie keeps me laughing. I've told her how good she makes me feel."

Brandon grinned. "It sounds like we're in pretty deep, yet I don't feel as though I'm drowning. But we both know that I've got some unfinished business to attend to."

Aaron nodded, more concerned with Brandon's other conundrum, Lisa Baxter. "Better you than me. I'm glad that Miss High-and-Mighty Lauren Jamison dumped me. Her and Cass's personalities are worlds apart. But you really need to reiterate your position to Lisa, in a hurry. By the way, I'm in love with Cass. I'm in ocean-deep, pal. I fell for her the minute I saw her smile."

Brandon wasn't surprised when Aaron told him he'd fallen in love with Cassie from the onset. Though he didn't voice it, Brandon was sure Aaron had already guessed how he felt about Hillary. It appeared they were *both* in ocean-deep. Even though Hillary hadn't given a voice to her own feelings for him, he hoped they would eventually end up on the same page.

Losing all thought for time, Hillary and Cassie had a ball laughing and talking. They were just about caught up on everything that had happened during the course of the week.

"Brandon and I have plans to visit my parents and sisters. Would you and Aaron like to join us?"

Cassie nodded her approval. "I think Aaron would love that, but I'll ask him so he won't think I'm starting to take his cooperative nature for granted."

Hillary finished packing her things; then they left the room to join the guys.

Minutes later, when Aaron eagerly accepted the invitation to go visiting with their friends, he and Cassie went out to Aaron's car and waited for Brandon to back out of the garage. Immediately afterward, the foursome left to caravan back to the city.

Back at Hillary's house, after spending several hours with her family, Brandon relaxed downstairs in the family room while Hillary was upstairs getting her things together.

The weather would be very cool, if not cold, in New York, Hillary figured. After packing several business suits, evening clothes, slacks, and a couple of heavy sweaters, Hillary stuck a pair of leather gloves into the pocket of her winter coat. Two warm but fashionable hats were thrown into her bag as an afterthought.

Finished with her packing, Hillary joined Brandon in the family room, where he was watching *60 Minutes,* one of his favorite programs.

Momentarily dragging his attention away from the program, Brandon pulled her into his arms. Nestling up close to him, she put her head on his shoulder. When *60 Minutes* was over, Brandon switched off the television set. Walking over to where she kept her music selections, he selected a homemade tape labeled "Love Songs." As soft, romantic music filled the room, they cuddled together and listened to the sweet ballads of love.

Brandon lifted Hillary's chin. "Pretty lady, I'm interested in having an exclusive relationship with you. How do you feel about that?"

Feeling all warm inside, Hillary smiled. "I must admit that I've been wondering where our relationship was going. We hadn't discussed it and I didn't know how to bring it up. I knew we'd eventually have to talk about it.

But let me make sure I have this straight. Are you saying that you want us to only see each other?"

He kissed her forehead. "You got it. I don't want to share you with any other man. Is that possible?"

Hillary felt breathless as she studied his handsome face. She loved him. More than anything, she wanted an exclusive relationship with him, but she had to be sure he was sincere. "I think that's possible if you're sure that's what you want. I don't want you to commit to this if there's any possibility you can't keep it. I don't want to be hurt by anyone."

He hugged her fiercely. "Baby, you won't be hurt. I will come to you if I feel we need to make changes and I want you to tell me if you feel the need to change things." Reaching into his pocket, he pulled out a set of keys and handed them to her. "These are the keys to my heart and my castle. Use them as you see fit."

Hillary looked at him incredulously. "Brandon, I can't accept these. You have a right to your privacy. I could never just walk into your house."

He'd expected her to put up a fight. "Baby, you can come to my house whenever you like. I want you to have them." Hillary still refused. "What if you just use them when I know you're coming, or if I'm out of town and you just want to enjoy the beach? And in case of an emergency," he added.

Reluctantly, she accepted them under those conditions. She knew she'd never use them unless it was an emergency, or when he knew she was planning to visit.

Although they shared many kisses and caresses through the rest of the evening, Brandon didn't allow himself to get out of control. He'd accomplished too much to do something stupid now. Despite the fact that he wanted her so much it hurt, he knew she wasn't ready, and he was willing to wait for however long it took. It would be worth it if it was meant to be.

Arising from his seat, he turned off the stereo. He then picked Hillary up from her comfortable spot and carried her up to her room. As they mounted the steps, Brandon's pager went off. Looking at the digits on the screen, he scowled.

She noticed the gloomy expression on his face. "Is it important?"

"It's nothing that can't wait until tomorrow." Yet it was something that he thought he'd already taken care of. Shutting out the nature of the page, he kissed her nose.

Depositing her in the middle of her bed, he kissed her senseless. He then left the room to take a shower in the guest bathroom.

Finished with her bedtime routine, Hillary could hear the water still thumping in the hall bathroom. She couldn't help wondering if Brandon would ask to sleep with her tonight. Though she felt secure with him, she was a little afraid that she might be tempting the hand of fate. She wouldn't invite him in if he didn't ask, she decided. After turning off the light, she eased her body under the covers.

As he'd expected, Hillary was asleep when he returned to her room. Lightly, he kissed her eyelids anyway. Although he went back into the guest bedroom, he'd wanted so much to slide in next to her. Knowing he'd want her too much made him opt for the guest room. Besides, he had a lot on his mind, a lot to settle.

Once in bed, he had a chance to think about the number on his pager. It belonged to the woman he'd been seeing before he'd met Hillary. Despite the many messages that she'd left for him, he hadn't phoned her back since he'd started seeing Hillary regularly. He didn't know how he was going to make Lisa understand that it was over between them, and had been over for a long time. But he knew that he'd have to convince her once and for all.

Brandon had met Lisa Baxter, a high-fashion model, at a party several months prior to meeting Hillary. Lisa was a nice enough person, but she seemed so needy and she didn't stir his blood or his intellect the way Hillary did. He knew he'd been unfair to her by not telling her it was over long before he'd actually done so. Here he'd made a commitment to Hillary for an exclusive relationship, yet he hadn't even mentioned Lisa to her. He knew he owed Hillary an explanation, but he dreaded telling her about Lisa and the fact that she was still trying to hold on to him.

However, he knew he had to handle Lisa while Hillary was gone. He quickly made up his mind that he'd first set Lisa straight for the last time, then he'd discuss the whole matter with Hillary when she returned from New York. With everything settled in his mind, he slept.

Arising the next morning before Hillary, Brandon slid into bed beside her and pulled her into his arms. Still half-asleep, she looked up at him and smiled. "Honey, I missed you. I'm glad you're here."

He brushed her lips with an intense kiss. "I missed you, too, babe. I knew you needed your rest so I just took the guest room. I also needed to think about a few things." A lot of things, he added in his thoughts.

She looked at him hard. "You sound so serious. Is everything okay? Is there something you need to talk about?" She hoped he hadn't changed his mind about them having an exclusive relationship.

He pulled her closer to him. "I am serious, serious about you. Girl, your going away has got me stressed. I don't know how I'm going to deal with missing you. I like having you right here at my fingertips."

He kissed her collarbone, making her shiver with longing. "When you're this close to me, I can kiss you like this." He kissed the side of her mouth. "And like this," he uttered wantonly, kissing her full on the lips.

Feeling a fever rising in her flesh, she pushed his head back into the pillow. "How about like this?" she murmured, connecting her lips to his in a long, staggering kiss.

He drew her up his body until his lips were level with her navel. As he flicked his tongue in and out of her navel, she squirmed atop him, causing his lower anatomy to harden like a rock. The desire to go even lower was so tempting, but he knew she wasn't ready for that either. Fighting the demands of his body, he rolled her over on her back.

He looked into her eyes. "One last kiss, then I'm going to let you get ready for your trip."

"Promise?"

He answered her with one long passionate kiss. Then he released her. Much to her dismay, he'd kept his word.

Forty minutes later, dressed in comfortable traveling attire, Hillary took a last-minute inventory before they went out to the car. After stowing all her luggage in the trunk, Brandon maneuvered the car out of its parking place and out the security gates.

Soon after Hillary's plane took off, Brandon raced at top speed to his new destination. When he pulled up to a huge, ultra-modern condominium complex, he dialed a number on the call box and spoke to someone briefly. The gate opened and he pulled in. Jumping out of his car, he rushed toward one of the doors. After ringing the doorbell, he stood back and waited.

A tall, gracefully slender brunette opened the door, wearing a wide smile upon her sultry mouth. As Lisa Baxter slipped her willowy arms possessively around Brandon's neck, he knew that hard times lay ahead of him.

Ten

The flight to New York had been long and uneventful. Once the pilot effected a smooth-as-silk landing at JFK, Hillary gathered up all her belongings and deplaned. Inside the terminal, she headed for the baggage claim area. Eager to locate transportation to the hotel, Hillary hadn't bothered to look around her until a strange man approached her. She looked quizzically at the stranger who waved a cardboard sign in the air, a sign that had her name written in bold, black letters.

"Madame, are you Miss Hillary Houston?"

"Why . . . are you asking?" she asked hesitantly.

He smiled. "I've been engaged to take you to your hotel in Manhattan."

Providing transportation was unusual for her company. She usually took a cab, she mused, continuing to stare at the sign with obvious curiosity. "By whom?"

He took a list of names from his breast pocket. "Madame, a Mr. Brandon Blair from BDB Architectural Design requested our services."

His thick French accent certainly added a flair for the dramatic, Hillary thought, looking astounded. *This is too much,* she cried inwardly. "Are you serious?"

He nodded. "Yes, madame. I am quite serious," he assured her handing her the list of names to see for herself. She glanced at the paper and laughed. By the merry twinkle she saw in the jolly Frenchman's eyes, she thought he was amused with her.

Just as he had so many times before, Brandon had done it again. "I'm sold," she told the chauffeur. "I'm ready to go if you are."

Taking her things from her arms, he guided her to the baggage claim area. Just in case Hillary had somehow missed the sign with her name on it, Brandon had given the company a full description of her, the chauffeur told her, when she asked why he'd chosen her to approach.

As she stepped out into the crisp air of New York, she inhaled deeply, allowing the cool air to fill her lungs. She enjoyed the wind in her hair as she remembered all the reasons she loved fall and the East Coast.

The chauffeur opened the door to an ivory-white Lincoln Town Car limousine, and Hillary nearly fainted. She'd never had the pleasure of riding in a limo before. This was just too much for her to take in all at once. Each day that she'd known Brandon had held untold surprises for her. He'd never once mentioned hiring a limo.

Oh, how she'd miss him, she thought, conjuring up in her mind his disarming smile. A warm sensation rushed to the most intimate parts of her body, making her sweat. Sinking back into the rich creamy leather seat, she looked out the window. As the chauffeur expertly maneuvered the limo into the heavy flow of traffic, the car glided smoothly through the busy streets. Her eyes, wide with excitement, moved from side to side, taking in the sights of the Big Apple.

Brandon had certainly kept his word regarding spoiling her rotten, she thought happily. Then, a look of sadness suddenly came to her honey-brown eyes. How long would the fairy tale last? Thoughts of her ending up with a broken heart caused her stomach to quiver slightly. Just as the chauffeur pulled the limo up to the door of the magnificent Essex House Hotel, she sighed with discontent. This was where she'd spend the next week. All alone, she thought sadly.

In its splendor, New York could be a dangerous place, as could any big city, especially for a woman alone. The Essex House, located on Central Park South, was within easy striking distance of Broadway. Cabs seemed to be in abundance in and around the hotel area, she noted.

After checking in at the desk, she accepted the key to her room. A friendly bellboy directed her to the elevators and followed with her luggage. She saw that her room was located near the top of the hotel when he punched in the floor number.

The bellboy reached for the key and opened the door. Hillary seemed amazed to find that she'd been booked into a suite, another unusual occurrence. She could see the splendor of the rooms as she walked over to the window. The view of the magnificent skyline was out of this world. Finally coming out of her trance, she said her thanks to the bellboy and handed him a tip, closing the door behind him.

Giggling like an adolescent, she ran and leaped on the massive bed. Looking up at the ceiling, she yelled, "I'm the luckiest girl in the world!" Her only other desire was that Brandon could be there with her. While rapidly stripping away her clothing in preparation for a long, hot shower, she foolishly indulged herself in a few moments of wishful thinking.

The twenty-minute shower left her feeling fresh and rejuvenated, but her stomach growled with a ravenous longing. She crossed the room and picked up one of several hotel brochures from the desk. Once she read all the choices for dining, she decided to eat in one of the hotel's fine restaurants.

Hillary carefully dressed herself. The superbly tailored winter-white, wool crepe trouser suit had a double-breasted jacket with decorative pockets, and boasted peaked lapels, pearlized buttons, and a weskit front. The pleated trousers hugged her hips gracefully. A short necklace of gold leaves tenderly embraced her neck and the double-leaf earrings hung delicately from her ears. Earlier, when she'd brushed her hair, she'd left it loose so that the ringlets fell softly below her shoulder. Satisfied that she looked her very best, Hillary headed for the elevators, ready for a sumptuous feast.

As she stepped into the unoccupied car, she pushed the LOBBY button. Sliding her back against the metal bar, she waited for the car to descend to the lower levels. The car came to an easy stop on the twenty-third floor and a well-tailored, handsome gentleman entered the elevator. Somehow, the man seemed familiar to Hillary, but she couldn't remember where she'd seen him.

"Hillary Houston! Fancy meeting you here. You do remember me, don't you?"

She looked perplexed. "I don't know. You look so familiar, but I can't seem to place you." A slight frown creased her smooth brow as she racked her brain.

He extended his hand. "I'm Eric St. John. We met at the Top of the Tower in Hollywood."

Recognition immediately flashed in her eyes and she smiled radiantly. "Why, yes, I do remember. How are you?"

He grinned broadly. "I'm just fine. I've been frantically trying to locate you. I waited and waited to hear from you after I gave you my card, but to no avail. What are you doing here in New York?" Before she could answer, the elevator came to a complete stop.

Without giving her the chance to respond, he asked, "Are you meeting someone?"

"No. I'm just going to have something to eat."

"Miss Houston, I would be honored if you would join me for dinner."

As thoughts of Brandon's jealous behavior crossed her mind, Hillary suddenly became unsure of herself. Trying to decide what to do, she stole a guarded glance at St. John. He seemed harmless enough. Besides, they'd be dining right here in the hotel. What harm could come from having dinner with this charming brother? *None,* came the inward response. Knowing how much she hated to dine alone, she decided to accept his invitation.

The smile she gave him reached to the depths of her honey-brown eyes. "I'd love to join you for dinner, Mr. St. John."

Seated at a lovely adorned window table, Hillary and St. John resumed their conversation. She answered his earlier question of why she was in New York and he shared with her his reasons for being there.

"Miss Houston, have you thought any more about the things I said to you the last time we met?"

She looked a little embarrassed. "I'm afraid I haven't. And please call me Hillary."

"If you'll call me Eric." Smiling, she nodded. "I can't understand why you don't seem to take your talent seriously. I know a lot of people who'd kill for the opportunity to be considered by a major recording studio. Please tell me why you're not one of them."

"I just haven't had the time to pursue it. I did early on, but I guess I decided I didn't have what it takes to make it big. It's really a tough business."

"I'm here to inform you, Hillary, that you have exactly what it takes. While we're waiting for dinner, I will tell you what I can do for you. Are you willing to listen?"

Dazed with excitement, Hillary nodded again. "I can't see any harm in listening," she commented timidly.

Eric St. John outlined, in painstaking detail, exactly what he could do for Hillary Houston. As she sat quietly, listening intently, the man sitting across from her told her all the things she'd spent most of her life dreaming about. Not once did he pull any punches.

"The recording business is definitely not all glamour. It's very hard work. The work is rigorous and extremely demanding, but the rewards, monetary- and personal-wise, are without boundaries, Hillary."

Then he spoke about marketing, packaging, public relations, all the things she was familiar with in her present line of business. She was spellbound under his direction.

"I can make you a *superstar*, Hillary Houston."

Shivers of excitement and fear raced up and down her spine at the same time. This was so unreal, yet she felt that it was deeply based in reality.

He briefly covered her hand with his. "I believe it was your fate to come to New York at this particular time. This is your chance to become the celebrated recording artist you've always dreamed about. I can make it happen for you!"

Now that he was finished, Hillary actually believed in all he'd said. Her eyes misted with emotion. Did she dare hope? Did she bite the bullet? Unbelievable thoughts rushed through her head like a torrential rainstorm.

"Eric, I'm overwhelmed by your presentation, yet I still have so many doubts." Her voice had quavered when she'd finally spoken. Staring him straight in the eye, she licked her suddenly parched lips. "Am I understanding you correctly? Are you making me an offer here?"

His smile was warm and sincere. "Hillary, I never make an offer I can't deliver on. There are a lot of details to work out, but if you're willing to give it a try, yes, I'm making you an offer. We'll take things as far as we can."

The mist in Hillary's eyes spilled over onto her cheeks as she reached for St. John's hand. "Yes, I'm willing to try! Yes, yes, I am," she cried excitedly.

He became so excited he knocked over the water on the table, but nothing was damaged. When the waiter appeared to tend to the spill, St. John ordered a bottle of the restaurant's finest champagne. Unable to bottle her excitement, Hillary giggled out loud.

Moodily, Brandon pondered his heated confrontation with Lisa Baxter, his now finally confirmed ex-girlfriend. He felt bad that she'd been hurt. Why was it never his intention to hurt anyone, yet he always seemed to manage to do so? He wondered if he'd end up hurting Hillary, too, which was something he'd never be able to bear. He'd never had any illusions about Lisa and himself, but he felt ashamed when he thought about her having been just someone to pass the time with. He'd known from the beginning that Lisa was much too shallow for him. Then why had he let it go as far as he did? he questioned himself.

Hillary was a different story altogether. She was the only woman he'd ever let into his private domain, his castle. He'd often longed to share those romantic sunsets and sunrises with someone, but no one had fit the bill until he'd met Hillary. No one made him feel like she did. But how could he be sure she wouldn't end up hurting him?

Hillary could never hurt anyone, he thought, laughing to himself; it just wasn't in her nature. But he'd thought the same thing about someone else, long ago. Stifling his thoughts, he opened his briefcase and rifled through it until he found Hillary's New York itinerary. He then dialed the number to the hotel, asking for her room when the operator came on the line. The phone in her room just rang and rang.

Feeling uneasy, he hung up and dialed the hotel again. This time he left a message for her to call him when she returned. New York was on EST, he thought. When he looked at his watch, his uneasiness grew. It was after eleven P.M. on the East Coast. He knew she'd arrived safely since he'd asked the operator if she'd checked in.

While tuning out the evil voices in his head, voices that incited his jealous streak into action, he told himself he had nothing to be jealous about. He then turned out the lights in the den and went off to the bedroom to take a shower. He wanted to be totally relaxed, and in bed, if and when she called back. He also wanted to find out where she'd been all this time and with whom, he finally admitted.

Hillary and Eric had a wonderful dinner, but they'd completely lost track of the time while making plans for Hillary to attain her dream, the dream of her life.

Noticing the time, she said, "Eric, I need to be getting back to my room. I have an early morning meeting."

He smiled as he got to his feet. "All right. I'll see you to your room." Walking around the table, he pulled out her chair.

Hillary had noticed that several of the diners had been glancing in their direction all night. She now saw that heads turned when he guided her from the restaurant; they did make quite a handsome African-American couple, she had to admit.

Inside the elevator, Eric leaned against the metal railing. "Tomorrow I have to go to the recording studio. How would you like to come with me to get a feel for what goes on there?"

She gasped with excitement. "Eric, that would give me great pleasure, but I'm in meetings until three o'clock in the afternoon."

He shrugged his shoulders. "That's okay. I have to be there all day. I'll come back for you around four. How does that sound?"

She grinned widely. "It sounds like a great plan. I'll be waiting in eager anticipation."

At the door of her room, Eric bade her a good evening. She thanked him for a wonderful evening and the extraordinary opportunity he'd presented to her.

"The pleasure was all mine, Miss Hillary Houston, my future superstar!"

Finding the entire evening unbelievable, Hillary allowed the intentionally suppressed detonator in her mind to explode the moment she closed the door to her suite. Not caring who heard her, she roared out loud as she danced and jumped around the room. After calming herself, she undressed, hung up her suit, and took another hot shower.

As she came back into the bedroom, wrapped in nothing but a towel, she noticed the red light flashing on the phone. Immediately, she called the front desk to retrieve her messages. It completed her evening to find out the caller had been Brandon.

Hillary poured herself into a sage-green silk chemise with a beautifully fitted bias cut, scooped front, low back, and crisscrossed straps. She loved her body to be surrounded by blissful, luxuriously silky lingerie. The background on the matching kimono was the same sage green but had a floral scroll print of peach and aqua.

She laid the robe at the bottom of the massive bed and climbed in. While making herself comfortable, she reached for the phone and dialed Brandon's phone number. The line was busy. Placing the phone back on the hook, she lay back against the pillows to allow herself time to once again digest all the wonderful experiences that had filled her day. Before her mind could sprout wings, her beautiful thoughts were interrupted by the sharp jangle of the telephone bell.

"Pretty lady, I've been waiting to hear from you."

"Hi, honey. I called you back, but the line was busy."

"Oh. So that was it. I took the phone off the hook while I showered. I miss you, babe. Tell me about your day."

Excitedly, Hillary gushed into the phone most of the details of her trip. "Honey, that was so incredible of you to order a limo. I'm going to be devastated when you stop spoiling me."

She could hear the grin in his voice as he assured, "You don't have to worry about that. I'm enjoying it as much as you are." She then told him about her flight and the beautiful hotel suite she was staying in. "Where were you when I called?" he asked, reluctant to do so but unable to quash his mounting need to know.

She approached the subject of St. John very carefully. His ears wide open, Brandon listened intently to her story. When she finished, she could feel his tension coming right through the phone line.

"I thought we were exclusive. I thought we'd made a commitment to one another."

Hillary could almost see the bright-green jealousy his voice carried. "Brandon, I'm not dating St. John. I just shared a meal with the man. Please don't spoil my day by acting like a jealous idiot."

Her name-calling incensed him. "Hillary, I'm sorry if you think I'm an idiot," he countered sharply.

"Don't twist my words either. I didn't know going exclusive meant I couldn't have friends. Aren't you happy about the news I just gave you?" A long silence greeted her as he tried to regain his composure.

He sighed. "Yes, Hill, of course. I'm ecstatic for you. I didn't mean for you to get the impression that I wasn't. I just don't like the thought of you being with another man, a stranger, especially so damn far away from home."

His childish behavior irritated her, and his asinine whining grated on her last nerve. "Brandon," Hillary shrieked, "we just shared dinner in the hotel dining room. I thought we had cleared the trust issue. I guess I was wrong."

He took a deep breath. "Hill, it's not you I don't trust. It's St. John."

Impatiently, she slapped her forehead with an open palm. "You don't have to trust St. John! Just trust and believe in me. Is that too much to ask?"

"It isn't. And I do trust you. I care so much for you, I can't help being protective of you. Forgive me. Please finish telling me the rest of your good news."

Feeling she'd already said way too much, Hillary decided not to tell him about the studio trip scheduled for the next day. Instead, she told him some of the things that St. John had told her, engaging him in small talk for a few minutes more. Then, after telling him she'd talk to him the next day, she hung up.

Starting to feel the delayed effects of the few sips of champagne she'd had, she moaned. Because she didn't drink at all, the champagne affected her a lot, but Brandon's bad attitude had affected her more. Hoping to have a peaceful night's sleep despite the fact that she and Brandon hadn't parted on a perfectly good note, she nestled under the cool linens.

Right after receiving an early wake-up call from the front desk, Hillary carefully selected her attire for the meeting, then took her shower.

In less than an hour she dressed in an autumn-brown V-neck tunic draped over a slim-waisted skirt. Cut from the softest of cashmere, the tunic had a ribbed button placket and large patched pockets. Big gold hoop earrings dangled from her ears. Aside from her watch, she wore no other jewelry. The suede pumps she wore on her feet matched the color of her outfit.

Having ordered a light breakfast from room service,

she moodily picked at the food. Still brooding over the conversation she'd had with Brandon, she shoved the food away. Arising from the chair, she grabbed her briefcase and headed for the door.

The phone rang just as she was on her way out. Tossing her briefcase on the bed, she raced across the room and picked up the receiver.

"Hillary here," she greeted, her voice lacking its normal luster.

"Good morning, pretty lady. I wanted to hear your voice before you started your day," Brandon said warmly.

It's only seven A.M. here in New York, she thought. That meant it was only four-thirty in California. "What are you doing up so early?"

"Hill, I couldn't let you start your day upset."

His assumption piqued her interest. "Who says I'm upset? I'm doing just fine. I have a meeting to attend. And I never let anything interfere with me doing my job."

Her distant tone tugged at his heartstrings. "Hill, I didn't call to make you angry. I just wanted to let you know I'll be thinking of you throughout the day."

She felt herself soften. "I'll be thinking of you, too. I really miss you, Brandon David Blair. Believe me, you have nothing to worry about," she assured him.

"That's what I keep telling myself. Now that you've told me, I have to believe it."

She thought he sounded humble. "Honey, I have so many warm memories to keep me safe till I'm in your arms again. That's enough for me."

"Thanks. I needed to hear that. I love you, pretty lady! Have a nice day." He hung up before she could respond to his heartfelt confession.

Even though he'd disconnected the line, she held on to the phone. Had he said he loved her? She knew he hadn't said, "I think I'm in love with you." So, sure she'd heard him correctly, she allowed her spirits to soar sky-high. Smiling all over herself, she grabbed her briefcase and left for the meeting.

Brandon sat very still by the phone. He had finally said it, and it was all so true. He loved her with all his heart and soul. He loved her with every fiber of his being. The words had slipped out so easily, so naturally. He felt no regrets. But would the truth set him free? Would the truth finally free him enough to conquer his demons of old?

Whatever she did with those three monumental words was up to her. He wasn't about to take them back. He would go on telling her, each and every single day, how much he truly loved her. He could only pray that she'd one day love him in return. He'd already figured out that life would never be the same for him again. Without Hillary, he wouldn't have much of a life. He'd just have to figure out a way to curb his jealousy. She wouldn't stand for it much longer, he knew. Once again, he found himself vowing to protect her from any undue distress.

Eleven

Hillary's business day ran smoothly. She was a big hit with all of her conference colleagues. One female colleague had even dubbed her "Miss Confident and Lovely." Her enthusiastic personality had a profound effect on everyone she'd come into contact with. Everyone seemed eager to make her acquaintance, especially the men. At the end of the business day she had more invitations to dinner than she had time left in New York.

A wonderful lunch had been prepared for all the participants in the meeting. All during the meal, Hillary had other things on her mind, like going to the recording studio. Having politely declined all invitations to dinner, she rushed back to her room to prepare herself for her engagement with Eric St. John.

Promptly at four o'clock, Eric arrived. She was ready and waiting. They talked easily with each other in the elevator. Eric was known for his dynamic sense of humor. Another beautiful limo waited at curbside to whisk them to their destination. When she saw the limo, she once again thought of how she could get used to this way of life. Chiding herself on her fanciful thoughts, she made a silent oath to keep her head screwed on straight.

In a short span of time they arrived at the studio. Eric guided her into the building that housed the recording studio, which was located on the very top floor.

Peace engulfed her when she stepped out of the elevator. In awe of the plush surroundings of the studio, she felt as if a new fairy tale was about to unfold. Eric gave her a grand tour before guiding her to the room that held the sound booths, where a young man about twenty-three or so sang into one of the many microphones.

Perched on a stool in the sound booth, she listened to his melodious voice. His strong, beautiful tones strummed her ears seductively. She watched the buzzing activity as several people scurried about her, making sure everything ran smoothly.

By the time the young man finished his exquisite performance, Hillary was giddy. Little did she know that St. John had plans for her when he invited her into the area where the young man had been singing.

Smiling, Eric draped his arm around her shoulder. "Hillary, would you agree to do a song so everyone can hear your fantastic voice?"

His request rendered her speechless. Unable to fully register his intentions, she stared at him for several seconds. "I wasn't prepared for this. I don't know if I can handle it," she confided to him, her eyes smoldering with uncertainty.

He nudged her gently. "Of course you can. Tell me one of your favorite songs." Hoping to squash her uncertainty, he continued to offer her encouragement in a soft tone.

"Somewhere Over the Rainbow," she responded shakily.

"Great song. Hold on while I have someone find the music to it."

Eric disappeared into the sound booth for a few seconds.

Smiling, Eric came back and stood before Hillary. "Okay, honey. You're on." His face showed his eager anticipation for what he was about to experience. He'd never forgotten the magical sound of her voice.

Though she was a nervous wreck, she stationed her slender body in front of one of the microphones. As the music began, she felt her old friend, Peace, take her hand. While hitting every note with expert precision, she saw that all eyes were trained on her. Hillary sang her heart out as her angelic voice reached out and delicately caressed the ears of her listeners. The response in the room was deafening when she finished singing the last note. Just as in her many dreams, everyone cheered and clapped loudly.

"St. John, you've got another winner," she heard someone yell. "This girl is a dynamo! How the hell do you do it?"

Eric's grin stretched from ear to ear. "I was born with an ear for outstanding talent," St. John replied cockily. "This beautiful sister is headed for superstardom!"

As if on cue, the loud cheering started up again.

While Hillary spent time at the studio with St. John and his team, they talked freely about her talent, and the "contract" word came up several times. Eric wanted to get her signed before anyone else grabbed her, but she explained that she'd have to talk things over with an attorney before she signed anything. Things were moving way too fast for her, and she desperately needed to catch her breath.

Later in the day she was also told that they had several songs lined up that her voice would definitely do justice to. Eric and his team had her head spinning by the time she left the studio.

In a deep state of shock, she couldn't begin to fathom what had just happened to her. She needed to get some advice right away, before this whole thing snowballed out of her control. Rushing inside her suite, she quickly placed a call to Cassie. As she shared the events of the past hours with her friend, Cassie tried desperately to keep from screaming through the phone. Hillary told Cassie she needed to talk to a lawyer, and that she was scared to death. Cassie told her Aaron was there. Cassie then yelled for him to listen in on the extension.

Breathlessly, Hillary told her story to Aaron.

He let out a loud whistle. "Hillary, you definitely need representation. Have you talked to Brandon about all this?"

She lowered her eyelashes. "No, Aaron. He doesn't even know I went to the studio."

"Does he know about St. John being in New York?"

"I told him last night. Aaron, he gets so jealous whenever I mention another man. Can you shed some light on this for me?"

Aaron, remembering to stay loyal to his good friend, approached her question with caution. "Brandon is a space cadet where you're concerned. Lately, I don't think he knows if he's coming or going. Give him time, Hillary. These feelings he has for you are foreign to him. But I can promise you this: he only has your best interest at heart. As far as what's going on in New York, don't sign anything till I get a chance to do some research on this company. I'll get back to you tomorrow. Does Cassie have your number at the hotel?"

"She does."

"Okay. You just sit tight. I'll get on this right away. Hillary, I think you need to call Brandon and tell him what's going on," he advised. "I'd hate for him to hear this from anyone other than you." In all the years they'd been friends, Aaron had never seen Brandon act so possessively, yet he understood it from Brandon's very slanted point of view.

Aaron had put her mind at ease, and she sighed with relief. "I'll call him now. Cassie and Aaron, I truly don't know where this is all going, but I do know I'm feeling overwhelmed by it all. I just hope Brandon will understand the situation. I'm really worried about his jealous outbursts. I couldn't take it if it destroyed what I think we could have together."

"Hillary, sweetie, if Brandon feels about you the way I think he does, he will support you in this," Cassie consoled. "It may take him a little time to get used to it, but I feel confident he'll come through for you."

"Thanks, Cassie. I'm so happy I have you to count on." Hillary was so close to tears, she signed off before her voice gave her away. She calmed herself before putting her call through to Brandon.

Brandon answered right away, and she went straight into explaining all that had gone on. When she was through, she could tell that he was fighting his demons bravely, yet he gave her as much support as he was capable of.

"I'll get with Aaron to see what he's learned about St. John's company. Even though it's a major recording company, I feel it needs to be investigated thoroughly. Don't sign anything, not until you have adequate representation. Aaron and I have direct access to several contract lawyers," he told her.

"I miss you," she said, her voice sounding small and frightened. Doubts about becoming a recording artist had begun to set in. She knew she'd be taking on a monstrous amount of responsibility, if in fact she decided to sign with St. John.

"I'm in your corner, Hill. We'll work things out together. I truly love you." His confession made her heart sing, but she was still too stunned to respond.

Late into the evening Brandon still sat quietly, staring into space. He was happy for Hillary, but on the other hand it created a new fear for him. He knew if she entered the entertainment world that her time would no longer be her own. They would no longer be afforded the spontaneity to which they'd become accustomed. He thought of the many lonely hours that he might have to spend without her. The many men she would come into contact with frightened him even more. They were just getting their relationship off the ground; now it appeared it was going to be put on hold. Were failed relationships to be his lot in life?

Brandon sighed heavily as he picked up the phone. He jabbed hard at the phone buttons, determined not to let his relationship with Hillary fail.

"Aaron, it's Brandon. I talked on the phone with Hillary earlier. She told me what's going on in New York. I want you to check this thing out from top to bottom. I want to know everything there is to know about St. John and his company."

"I plan to do exactly that. I've called a few people already. So far it seems on the up and up. It's not unusual for a record company to ardently solicit someone of Hillary's talent. They'll pull out all the stops to get her signed. How are you handling all this?"

Brandon blew out a ragged breath. "I'm dealing with it. There are so many aspects to consider here. I'm trying to keep my personal feelings in check. You know how I feel about Hillary. I'm going to have to make her interest my top priority. If I don't support her in this, I could very well end up losing her."

"You're right about that, pal. Hillary deserves one hundred percent loyalty from you. Listen, Cassie had a great idea. She thought we should all fly to New York to give Hillary our support. She and I have already taken this week off. We were going to drive up the coast toward San Francisco. So, what do you think?"

He smiled brightly. "I think it's a brilliant idea. I was

even thinking of asking her about my joining her for the rest of the week. Her conference is over tomorrow, but she's thinking of staying on through the weekend. I can't help but wonder if she'd be offended if we all barged in on her."

"Brandon, I'll have Cassie give her a call and feel her out about us coming. How does that sound to you?"

"That might work. At least we'd know if we were welcome or not. Do me a favor. Don't mention my coming. If she seems open to the idea, I want to surprise her."

"So you want us to lie to her?" Aaron asked pointedly.

"No. I just don't want you to tell her the whole truth. Is that so hard to understand?" Brandon asked, his tone rude.

"Not really. I guess you know what you're doing. But I do hope that if she'd rather we don't come, you'll respect her wishes."

"Aaron, pal, you worry too much. I'm working very hard on respecting Hillary's wishes. I admit I have a long way to go. I'm so used to having it my way, I've never taken the time to consider what someone else may want. Believe me, I know my way won't work with her. She's made that very clear. I'll be waiting to hear from you."

"Pal, we've always been up front with each other and I have a need to be just that. Your jealousy is one problem. Needing to be in control is another."

Brandon was surprised by Aaron's comments, yet he knew he'd hit the bull's-eye.

"You're not in control here, man. And you really need to think about whose priorities you're talking about making number one. I don't think Hillary expects you to make her a priority, but she's going to expect understanding and respect. She's not one of your clients. She's not the type of woman that you inwardly fear. I hope you're listening, man."

"How could I help but listen. You've managed to take

the air out of my arrogant ego. I needed that. Thanks, man. I'm glad we're friends. If I didn't know better, I'd think you'd taken private lessons from my father. Trust me, I'm working hard on my fears." Their laughter seemed to ease the heavy weight they both carried.

The conversation then turned to one filled with jokes and light banter. They'd been friends for so long, there wasn't too much that one couldn't say to the other. The two men were always mindful in showing each other the utmost respect.

Suffering from fatigue, Hillary was already in bed, but the tension in her body wouldn't allow her to rest. So much had happened in such a short time. One minute her mood was up, the next minute it was way down. She, too, had been giving her relationship with Brandon a lot of thought. She had some of the same fears that he did.

She turned on the television, thinking that a good movie might chase some of her fears away. She'd just started to relax a little when the sharp ring of the phone startled her. *The hotel needs to do something about these phones' bells,* she thought irritably as she picked up the receiver. The shrill sound was much too annoying.

"Hi, girlfriend, it's Cass. Is something wrong? Your voice sounds so strange."

"There's nothing wrong. The phone bell sounds so shrill. It scared the daylights out of me," Hillary said, chewing nervously on her lower lip.

"I want to run something by you real quick," Cassie said, hoping Hillary wouldn't see through her game.

"Okay. I'm all ears," Hillary responded.

"Aaron and I have been discussing your situation quite a bit. We thought we might fly out to New York to give you some moral support. How do you feel about that?"

"Oh, Cass, I've been praying for that very thing. I'd

be forever indebted to you and Aaron. I'm afraid I'm not handling this situation well at all. I'd been thinking of calling you to ask you to come out. I didn't ask because I knew you and Aaron had planned a trip up north. I thought it would be selfish of me to interfere."

"Aaron and I can go up north any old time, but New York is a different story. I've never been there. This would be a great opportunity to take a bite out of the Big Apple and to be supportive of you at the same time."

"Cassie, I feel a hundred times better already. I just wish Brandon could come. I thought he'd offer, but I guess he's pretty busy. I'm aware that he can't just drop everything to be with me, but it doesn't stop me from wishing."

Bingo! Cassie thought. She'd caught the fish without even baiting the hook. However, she did feel a little guilty about agreeing to set up her best friend.

"Cassie, are you still there?"

"Yes, sweets. Just thinking."

"Do you have any idea when you might get here?"

Cassie laughed a little. "We did take the liberty of checking the airline schedule, just in case you agreed. There's a flight we can get on first thing in the morning. It's an Atlantic–Pacific nonstop. It arrives in New York around three o'clock P.M. And I did reserve a couple of seats. But the reservations will automatically cancel at midnight if I don't call back to confirm. I'm also eager to check out this airline you work for and rave about so much."

"Cassie, I'm so excited. My last meetings are tomorrow. What about hotel reservations?"

"Aaron is going to handle that. He's going to see if there is anything available where you're staying, or close by."

"Most of the people who are here for the conference will be checking out tomorrow. Plenty of rooms should be available. But, Cassie, I have to warn you, the rooms here are very expensive but extremely beautiful."

"That's what I told Aaron. He just shrugged his shoulders. He told me money is no object when it comes to us. We deserve only the best."

"How sweet! You guys are really getting along famously. I'm really happy for you."

"I have to agree. Aaron makes everything so easy, but I've had nagging doubts from time to time. The more I'm with him, the less I doubt. I was even going to mention to you that I thought we should cool it. I felt like we were losing control of ourselves and they were taking us over. I just might be wrong. You and I are both pretty strong-headed when it comes to relinquishing our control. I think we'll be fine if we keep level heads. Aaron has spoiled me rotten. And I heard about the limo bit. Aaron pretty much tells me what Brandon tells him, but I know Aaron would never break Brandon's confidence."

"I think you've got something there in Aaron, Cass. But we better get off this phone. I can't wait to see you guys. I still wish Brandon were joining us." Hillary laughed. "I can't believe I'm acting this silly. Our relationship hasn't even begun to peak yet."

"Hillary, you're not being silly. You know he'd come if he could've gotten away. Don't worry about it. You'll be back home in a few days."

With their plans settled, they said their good-byes.

Before getting into bed, Hillary adjusted the ringer on the phone to low. Hoping to have everything sorted out by the next day, she said her prayers and settled in for what would hopefully be a good night, even as tears ran down her cheeks.

Seated at the long table in the hotel's conference room, Hillary looked radiant despite her tearful night.

She wore a caramel-brown Buscati's tailored silk coat-dress, above the knee in length, with padded shoulders. Its buttons were made of tortoise shell. On her small feet she wore rust-brown suede pumps, and oyster-white hose on her shapely legs.

Rising from her seat, she smiled before addressing the conference participants. Every eye in the room was glued to her. While giving her presentation, she spoke eloquently. She had no difficulty in making herself clear. Using graphics to outline her projections, she explained Atlantic Pacific Airlines' latest marketing proposal in a very articulate manner.

For such a young woman, she exuded confidence. For close to an hour she held her peers' undivided attention, in a way that showed her outstanding professionalism and her ability to make her points precise.

She received a healthy round of applause when she finished. As she was the last speaker, her colleagues flocked toward her to offer congratulations on her presentation. Though the conference was officially over, a reception would be held in one of the hotel suites. Before entering the reception suite, Hillary glanced at her watch. It was already after three, she noted. Excitement took her over. She would be seeing Cassie in a short while, and she could hardly wait. She also liked to have Aaron around. It somehow made her feel closer to Brandon.

She surveyed the crowd as she crept quietly into the hotel suite to join the reception. Several of the men noticed her come in and they all made a beeline right for her, eager to get her anything she needed. Fending off the other suitors, one extremely good-looking black guy approached the small gathering.

"Miss Houston, I need to speak to you privately for a moment. I need you to clear up something for me."

Hillary stared at him in amazement. She'd never seen

such a gorgeous creature. If he'd been a woman, he would've been considered beautiful, she marveled.

He extended his tawny-brown hand to her. "I'm Anthony Sinclair." He held on to her hand until she politely removed it from his firm, warm grasp.

She smiled brightly. "Pleased to meet you, Mr. Sinclair. What can I clear up for you?" she inquired, noticing how quickly the other men had moved away. His very presence seemed to demand respect.

He winked, grinning. "Miss Houston, you looked as though you needed rescuing. I thought I'd oblige you. Those men looked like they'd rather have you for lunch than this grand feast here," he said, eyeing the lavish buffet.

Hillary snorted under her breath. "Mr. Sinclair, I can assure you that I'm not a damsel in distress. I can be tactfully brutal if the need arises. I wouldn't have had any trouble handling myself with those gentlemen, or for that matter, any wolf in sheep's clothing."

He totally ignored her pointed reference. "I can see that now. Tell me, Miss Houston, are you free for dinner tonight?"

"Why, Mr. Sinclair, you flatter me," she said in an artificial Southern accent. "But the truth of the matter is, I'm otherwise engaged this evening."

Enjoying her pretentious Southern accent, he gave a smile that nearly split his face wide open. "Miss Scarlett," he taunted mockingly, "will you be staying on in New York for a few days? If so, perhaps you will join me another evening?"

Hillary enjoyed the flamboyant exchange as well. "Mr. Butler, I truly hate to disappoint you, but I have already made plans for the rest of my stay in this beautiful city."

His expression grew somber. "I see." Reaching into the breast pocket of his superbly tailored sports coat, he withdrew a business card and handed it to her. "Miss

Houston, should you find yourself lonely . . . please call."

Hillary raised both eyebrows. "Mr. Sinclair, I think hell will freeze over before I get lonely enough to call on you," she said sweetly. She'd realized early on that Sinclair was stuck on himself; she loathed that in any man.

He seemed totally surprised by her sweet retort. "Well, I guess I've just experienced firsthand your brutal tact."

She seductively batted her eyes at him. "You, Mr. Sinclair, get an A in perception." Hillary smiled smugly as she turned from him and walked away.

He stared after her in total bewilderment.

While mingling with the crowd, she found herself stealing covert glances at Sinclair. Why did such an incredible-looking man have to be such a jerk? She just might have enjoyed sharing a meal with him. When she thought of her commitment to Brandon, she scolded herself. After excusing herself from the busy throng, she returned to her suite.

Inside her suite, she called the front desk to get her messages. There was one from Mr. Asher and from Mr. St. John, but none from Brandon. The message from Eric St. John was read as urgent, and she called him right away.

Her smile danced in her eyes when Eric came on the line. "Hello, Eric. It's Hillary, returning your call."

"Hi, Hillary. How are you?" His anxieties just up and left him at the sound of her delicate voice.

"Just fine. Thank you. What can I do for you?"

"Hillary, I'm in a bind. One of my singers is ill. She was to perform tonight at a very ritzy supper club here in Manhattan. Could you fill in for me?"

Stunned by his request, she had to take time to catch her breath. As she gripped the phone tightly, her hands began to tremble. "Eric, I don't know what to say."

"Just say yes. Hillary, this would give you an opportunity to get a feel for a large crowd. This place is packed every night. It could also help you make up your mind about a recording contract, not to mention the wonderful experience you'll have. Say you'll do it," he coerced.

She took a deep breath. "I'm having a hard time saying no. Maybe it's what I need to help me decide, but I have some friends flying in from California. Can you get them a table?"

"Front row seats, honey! So, do we have a deal?"

"Yes!" she exclaimed excitedly.

"Hillary, wear one of your finest. As I said, it's a ritzy joint. I'll drop the song program off at the hotel for you. Break a leg, honey! And get there early."

The trio from California entered the lobby of the Essex House Hotel. Cassie and Aaron went to the desk to check in. After asking his companions to give him some time before they saw Hillary, Brandon went off to locate a phone.

Locating one of the house phones, he dialed Hillary's suite.

"Hello," Hillary responded with an abundance of cheer, expecting to hear Cassie's voice.

"Hill, it's me. How's it going?"

"Brandon, I'm so pleased to hear your voice. Everything is just fine. I didn't expect to hear from you this early in the day."

"I know, babe. I was missing you terribly."

"Honey, I miss you, too. I wish you were here. It's so lonely without you. I guess Cassie and Aaron should be here shortly. Maybe they'll take my blues away."

"Hill, do you want me to come to New York? I could catch the first thing smoking." He deliberately enticed her.

Hillary gasped as butterflies filled her stomach. "Brandon, I have wanted to ask you to come to New York since the day I arrived. I know you're busy, but it would be so nice." Holding her breath, she awaited his response.

"Say no more, pretty lady. I'll be there before you can blink. Let me run. I'll call you as soon as my plans are firm."

After disconnecting the line, she ran around the room laughing and screaming. "Yes, yes!" she shouted until she heard a knock on the door.

"Who is it?" she shouted through the closed door.

"It's room service, Miss Houston. I have a delivery for you."

A little disappointed because she'd hoped it was Cassie, Hillary flung the door open. The young man before her held a bouquet of blood-red baby rosebuds. He strode across the room and she followed, watching as he put the roses into an empty vase. He then filled it with water from the wet bar.

When the young man started for the door, Hillary turned around to face the exit. It was then that she saw Brandon leaning his strong, sexy body against the door-jamb—and he wore that incredible moonbeam of a smile.

Shrieking loudly, she sprinted across the room to his waiting arms. She held onto him in desperation, not caring that he'd duped her. Tilting her chin upward, Brandon rained kisses all over her face. He'd missed her more than he'd even realized. At some point during their reunion, the delivery man had discreetly removed himself from the room and closed the door behind him.

Picking her up, Brandon carried her to the bed. Lying down, he pulled her on top of him. Hillary didn't resist as they clung to each other passionately, kissing each other until they were both breathless. As his tongue savored the taste of her inner mouth, he rolled her over and covered her with his body. Their hands were all over each other. When she tried to speak, he silenced her words with his sweet mouth.

Tilting her head back, he took advantage of her creamy neck, nipping her gently with his teeth, making her lustfully unstable. When Brandon slipped his hand inside her dress to cup her breast, she didn't move a muscle. During his exploration of her body, she moaned and cooed softly into the stream of his warm breath.

Making love to Brandon was to be her fate, she already knew.

Holding her away from him, he examined her lovely face, as though he'd never seen her before. Her beautiful hair was in disarray, her eyes sparkled, and her cheeks were flushed.

"I love you, precious," he whispered softly in her ear. "You have come to mean the world to me."

Gently pulling his ear to her mouth, she nibbled at his lobe. "And I love you," she said in a sweet, gentle voice.

Overcome by her confession, he let his sunlit smile enter her heart on silver wings. How he'd longed to hear those very words coming from her lips. Brandon's dark eyes held a misty, wistful gaze, and he couldn't tear them away from her beautiful face. As her wholesome beauty and sweet innocence impaled his heart, Brandon tried to clear the frog in his throat.

"Hill, you're the love of my life. I've wanted to hear you say that you love me since I told you how I felt about you. Now that you've said it, I never want you to stop. Hill, I'll do my best to be deserving of that love."

Hillary's eyes filled with tears as she wrapped her arms around his neck. "Brandon, you're already deserving of it. You've been so very good to me. I'm not just talking material-wise, either. You've been good for my soul."

He kissed her eyelids. "I'm glad to hear that, Hillary. I recently told Aaron that I'd found my soul mate. Hill, since we're confessing, I have something I need to tell you before it drives me over the edge."

Her expression sobered. "Honey, what is it?"

In short, Brandon told Hillary all about his brief relationship with Lisa Baxter.

"We had a heated confrontation when I went over there, the day you left. It's been over for us for some time, but she hasn't been able to accept it. After our discussion the other day, I'm sure she accepts it now. I didn't mean to hurt Lisa. And I have no intentions of hurting you in that way."

She pulled away from him. His confession had upset her, and she truly felt sorry that Lisa had been hurt. Hillary looked him right in the eye. "How can you say you won't hurt me, Brandon? According to you, you didn't mean to hurt Lisa either."

He cleared his throat. "That's a fair enough question. The difference here is that I'm in love with you and I wasn't in love with her. I never, ever told Lisa that I was in love with her. She never spoke of loving me."

She cut her eyes at him. "You should've at least returned her phone calls. And you should've been up front from the start, with both of us. We've been seeing each other for weeks, and this is the first time this has come up. Why is that?"

He ran his hand through his hair. "I wasn't even seeing Lisa when I met you. It was over between us long before that. I didn't see any point in encouraging her by returning her phone calls and such. I had made it clear to her that the relationship no longer worked for me. I'm not going to sit here and put her down, or go into all the reasons why it wasn't working. It just wasn't what I wanted."

She began to understand his dilemma, which didn't sound too much different from what she'd gone through with Tyrone when she'd ended their relationship. The desperate phone calls and messages had been endless. Brandon was damned if he did, damned if he didn't, she concluded.

"The threats Lisa has made against me cause me the most concern."

He tried to calm her fears. "Lisa's reaction was to the rejection. She regretted the threats she'd made against you, especially after I made her see that you had nothing to do with anything between us. We both knew our relationship wasn't the lasting kind. I have to say this again, I never meant to hurt her. And we did part as friends."

Hillary could see that he was truly sorry he'd allowed the relationship to go on after he'd known it wasn't going anywhere. The regret was there in his eyes. He'd succeeded in convincing her that he hadn't meant to bring pain to Lisa. Hillary was a woman first. She didn't like it when her comrades got hurt callously, but that didn't seem to be the case in this romance-gone-bad saga.

Hillary glanced at the clock and leaped off the bed. "Brandon, have Cassie and Aaron arrived? I forgot all about them. I feel so ashamed."

He grinned. "Don't worry, sweetheart. They understand. I asked them to give us a little time alone," he said, pulling her back to him.

She shook her finger at him. "You have everyone conspiring against me. I'm going to have to remind Cassie where her loyalties should lie."

Laughing at the funny expression she wore on her face, he rubbed her back in a circular motion. "Babe, Cassie is the most loyal friend you could ever have."

She nudged his chin with a closed fist. "I know that, silly. I just like harassing her. How many people would drop everything they've planned to fly to New York to give their friend moral support? With the exception of Aaron, of course."

"Cassie and Aaron are the best," he declared.

"Come on, Brandon, let's go. I'm dying to see Cassie. We always miss one another when we're apart for too long."

"If I can have one more kiss, we can go." Falling on top of him, she kissed him until she'd temporarily satisfied her hunger for the taste of his mouth and his for hers. He stood her on her feet. "Okay, pretty lady, let's go find the other dynamic duo."

Hillary shrieked with joy. She couldn't remember ever being happier than she was now as they ran to the elevator and took the car down to the twenty-fifth floor.

Twelve

Standing at the door of Aaron and Cassie's room, Brandon knocked hard. Cassie opened the door, and she and Hillary immediately fell into each other's arms. As they hugged and giggled like two adolescents, Aaron and Brandon watched in amusement.

How could they both have gotten so lucky, at the same time, with two best friends? Brandon wondered. The four of them had grown so close, he reflected with warmth.

After all the joyous greetings, Hillary explained about her upcoming performance. Everyone was in a state of shock, but they all agreed that it was a great way for her to test her wings. There was no doubt in Brandon's mind that she would soar on her solo flight.

"Hillary, do you want me to get my own room?" Brandon asked, once they were settled back in her suite.

She laughed. "Do you want to lose your life?"

Brandon chuckled. "I was hoping you'd want me here with you. I'd go crazy in another room. I'll pay for this one."

Hillary shook her head. "Honey, it's already taken care of. Mr. Asher was adamant about the company paying for everything. He's really a wonderful boss."

"He knows what he has in you as an employee. He's going to lose it if you decide to leave the company."

Hillary hadn't even given that a thought. Wondering what else she hadn't considered, she felt a flutter of apprehension right in the center of her stomach. Rapidly dismissing her fears, she looked over at Brandon.

"I think you should take your shower first. I take forever. But then again, so do you."

He ducked into the bathroom. "I'll make it quick." Though he hadn't voiced his opinion, he would've preferred them taking a shower together.

A devastatingly beautiful black velvet dress was Hillary's choice for her performance. Gilded with braided gold along the off-the-shoulder, deeply plunged neckline, the dress had stand-away ruched sleeves secured discreetly with elastic. The fitted bodice had back smocking and the skirt flared at the hem.

Not wanting Brandon to see it until it was on her body, she carefully slipped it back into the dress bag. To complement the dress, she'd chosen a pair of gold-and-black tiered drop earrings and sheer black hose speckled with gold. Around the edges of the black velvet pumps was the same braided design that adorned the neckline of the dress.

As soon as Brandon emerged from the spacious bathroom, she grabbed the dress and her lingerie and ran into the bathroom. He laughed at how quickly she'd disappeared, glad he'd brought his tuxedo. From what little Hillary had told him about the place at which she'd be performing, he understood it was a first-class establishment.

While dressing himself in a Pierre Cardin tuxedo, tailored to fit his body superbly, he took special care not to wrinkle his attire. The crisp white shirt had been tailor-made as well, accenting his broad chest nicely. Gold cuff links boasted his initials.

* * *

While putting the final touches on her hair, Hillary swept most of it to the top of her head and pinned it loosely all around. She then laced a slender gold braid through the style and brushed several strands of hair forward to hang in tendrils around her lovely face. She also pulled a few tendrils down around the nape of her neck.

After applying her usual light covering of makeup and a terracotta blush to her cheeks, she applied a light layer of matching lipstick to her full, succulent lips. Finally, she slipped her slender body into the beautiful dress. She was as devastatingly beautiful as the dress she wore. To finish her grooming, she generously sprayed on Shalimar by Guerlain of Paris, a special gift from Brandon.

As she stepped from the bathroom, smiling brilliantly, Brandon's pulse raced wildly. He let out a shrill wolf whistle. "Hillary Houston, you are bewitching. You become more beautiful each time I see you," he hailed proudly.

His entire appearance was heart-stopping as he moved across the room with the gracefulness of a gazelle. On his body, the formal attire screamed "class." He was an impeccable specimen of a man, Hillary mused with delirious joy.

"Honey, you are definitely prejudiced."

He swept her into his arms. "Damn right! But that doesn't make you any less beautiful. You're a femme fatale in that dress! I love it." His dark eyes shone with a near-blinding brightness. "I don't know if I want to share all this beauty with anyone tonight. Perhaps we should stay in."

She clucked her tongue. "Sorry, darling, you don't have a choice." Hillary was learning just how to put Brandon in his place—tactfully.

He stuck his lower lip out in a pout. "I want to kiss you, but I don't want to mess your lipstick up."

She flirted with a wide-eyed innocence. "I have plenty of lipstick, big boy."

Taking her comment for the invitation it was, he kissed her gently. Her parfum was wild and exotic. When he'd first smelled it at the cosmetic counter, he thought it should've been named "Hillary."

When the limousine arrived, compliments of St. John, the foursome was downstairs in the lobby, ready and waiting.

"We all look like a million bucks," Cassie dared to say, smiling sweetly.

Cassie wore a gorgeous backless dress of black crêpe de Chine. Aaron looked as striking in his black designer tuxedo as Brandon did. The two couples looked as though they were made for each other. The guys were as handsome as the girls were beautiful.

The Manhattan Supper Club was every bit as ritzy as Eric had said—and it was packed with patrons. Waiting until after her friends were comfortably seated at a center-stage table Eric had reserved for them, a nervous Hillary departed for backstage, where St. John waited for her.

Eric was a little nervous himself when she finally appeared. He greeted her with enthusiasm as he slipped his arm around her shoulder. "I wasn't sure if you'd gotten cold feet at the last minute. It wouldn't have been the first time something like that had happened. Singers with very little public experience often suffer from stage fright," he told her.

"I'm very nervous," she told him with a smile, "but I never once considered not showing up. I just hope everything goes okay."

"It will. I'm confident that once you make your debut, you'll be as professional as anyone in the business. I remember how well you were received at the restaurant in California. I know you'll be embraced warmly here. New Yorkers always appreciate a fine talent. To cheer you on, I'll be at the table located right at center stage."

"I'm going to give it my all. It'll be comforting to me to know that you'll be there should I need moral support."

Eric allowed her to take a few minutes to rehearse before looking over the music program together. St. John couldn't wait till she was singing songs written exclusively for her talent. He gave her another small but effective pep talk, telling her she would do just fine. After thanking her for bailing him out, he left to take his seat.

Trying to calm her nerves, Hillary thought of all the times she'd performed solo in the choir. This time should be no different, she thought. *Give them all you've got. Just add a little extra sass and lots of pizzazz,* she told herself quietly.

Hillary knew it was show time when she saw the man in the white tuxedo.

The master of ceremonies took to front and center. "Good evening, ladies and gentlemen. We're honored to have you join us. We have a real treat in store for you. Many of you came to see Miss Gina Rawlings. Unfortunately, she's ill. However, Miss Hillary Houston will entertain you tonight. This beautiful young woman hails from Los Angeles, California, via western Pennsylvania. I can assure you her talent will surpass everything you've come to expect from our grand entertainment. Please join me in giving Hillary Houston a warm New York welcome. Miss Hillary Houston!" he announced excitedly.

Hillary felt as if her heart were playing hopscotch inside her stomach. Nervous couldn't begin to describe how jittery she felt. She said a silent prayer as she stepped to center stage. As she took a moment to smile at her friends, Brandon flashed her a reassuring smile, which seemed to say, "You can do this." Both Cassie and Aaron gave her the thumbs-up sign.

Most of the songs Eric had selected for Hillary were soft ballads. As the soothing music entered her very soul, she drew in a calming breath. Captivating her audience from the onset, she commandeered her voice through a dazzling spectrum of harmonious pitches. Hillary awed her listeners as she took them through a range of emotions.

Purposely tantalizing the crowd, she moved her body with slightly seductive swaying motions, which were meant to drive the males crazy. While moving her hands and body in a hypnotically suggestive way, she hit notes that she didn't even know she was capable of. It felt as though an angel had entered her soul and taken control of the performance.

For the next thirty minutes, the world was Hillary's stage. The soft lighting all around her illuminated her natural beauty. Hillary's rich, sultry voice expertly held her audience captive.

Her most willing captive was Brandon.

Upon finishing the last song, she stepped back from the microphone. The audience went wild, overwhelming her with cheers and whistles. Stepping forward, she bowed gracefully. The cheers and clapping kept coming. Using the stage as a model would a runway, she covered each area of the stage just like a professional.

Eric St. John was beside himself with joy. He knew he'd found a rare, precious gem in Hillary.

Stepping back to the microphone, she lifted it from its stand and began speaking. A hush immediately came over the crowd. Everyone seemed intent on hearing what this lovely young woman had to say.

"Thank you so very much. You've been extremely gracious. I've never experienced such a warm outpouring of support. You have my undying gratitude."

The crowd was back on their feet as she took a last bow before disappearing into the wings. Her face wet with tears, Hillary watched the standing ovation from behind the curtain. She was elated, overwhelmed by such a positive response. Just as she knew Brandon was her fate, she knew singing was, as well.

Eric St. John walked up behind her and grabbed her around the waist. Turning her to him, he hugged her tight. "Hillary, you're one incredible lady! Honey, you've got to give them one more song. They're going crazy out there. Do you think you can handle another onslaught?"

She hugged his neck. "Eric, I can handle just about anything tonight," she dazzled.

When Eric escorted Hillary back on stage, the crowd, still on their feet, grew louder and louder. Hillary stepped to the microphone. As before, a hush came over the entire place.

Lifting the microphone, she once again mesmerized her audience. It was obvious that her confidence had already grown by leaps and bounds. The magnificent encore had the crowd eating right out of her hand.

St. John carefully studied the effect she had on her audience. It was phenomenal. Not wanting to risk her getting away from his company, he wanted to sign her before she left New York.

Brandon Blair appeared to be in seventh heaven. Hillary never ceased to amaze him. He felt so blessed to have her love. He, too, had watched the effect she'd had on the audience. But now, while she sang with all the passion she was capable of, he couldn't take his eyes off her as she lovingly manipulated her ardent listeners. He thought her movements on stage were graceful and seductive. Brandon particularly enjoyed how she'd looked at him when she'd sung the love songs.

She made him feel as though she was giving him his very own private, intimate concert.

He'd also studied Cassie while her friend performed. He could see that Cassie truly loved Hillary. Her eyes shone with love and admiration for her best friend. Aaron, too, seemed genuinely moved by Hillary's extraordinary performance.

Hillary joined her three friends at the table. Brandon stood as he saw her approach. Putting his arms around her, he pulled her to him and kissed her tenderly. Cassie and Aaron hugged her next, giving their praises and congratulations.

"Hill, you were wonderful! You captivated everyone in this place. I just want to go on record as your number one fan. I will support you in every way I can." Stretching across the table, Brandon planted a gentle kiss on her forehead.

"Thank you, Brandon. I appreciate your support. I know this isn't going to be easy on us, but if our love is as strong as I believe it is, we can get through anything."

"And so we will."

While several people stopped by the table to rave over Hillary's performance, much to Hillary's surprise, the sexy and beautiful Anthony Sinclair sauntered up to the table, looking fabulous. A slinky, gorgeous redhead hung onto his arm.

His eyes flirted openly with Hillary. "Miss Scarlett," he addressed, using the Southern drawl she'd mocked him with earlier, "I had no idea. You're a lady of many faces. You were as brutal with your audience as you've been with me, but in a much kinder, gentler way."

Feeling a little uncomfortable with the situation, Hillary thanked him. She then introduced him to her friends. The embarrassment she felt over seeing Sinclair was clearly etched on her face. Sinclair congratulated her once more before returning to his table.

Brandon closely watched this too-pretty man. His jealousy was trying to get the best of him as he tried to figure out the dialogue between Hillary and the stranger. What had he meant about Hillary being brutal with him earlier? he wondered. Because Hillary looked very uncomfortable, he couldn't help wondering if she may have broken the commitment they'd made to one another. Sinclair had called Hillary Scarlett. What was that all about? Though he decided to drop it until later, he had every intention of finding out what the man had been spouting off about.

Smiling as though nothing unusual had occurred, he turned his attention back to his friends. Deep inside he burned with conflict.

The dynamic foursome talked and laughed until the wee hours of the morning. Had the evening been prearranged weeks ago it couldn't have turned out better, Hillary mused, grateful to St. John for such a fine evening. Eric truly had integrity.

Before they left the establishment, Eric asked Hillary if she could perform the rest of the week. Since her friends had flown all the way from California to be with her, she thought she should spend the rest of her time with them. She just wanted to relax and have a good time. Eric was disappointed when she declined, but he didn't try to sway her, which she appreciated.

Inside the limousine, Brandon asked the driver to give them a short tour around the city. Manhattan was still very much alive despite the early morning hour. Enjoying the bright lights and the active nightlife participants, they rode for an hour or so before returning to their hotel.

Back at the hotel, Aaron and Cassie got off at the twenty-fifth floor while Hillary and Brandon proceeded on to their floor.

Inside the suite, Hillary flopped down on the sofa. "Brandon, I'm drained."

She smiled invitingly at Brandon as he sat down next to her. "I guess so. You had one hell of a night!"

She nestled her head on his chest as he lifted her feet and placed them across his lap. "I guess you could say that."

He removed her shoes. While tenderly massaging her feet, he planted kisses up and down her legs. "Hill, are you ready to go to bed?"

She got up from the sofa and stretched her hand out to him. "I certainly am."

Standing before the mirrored dresser, she removed her earrings. Walking up behind her, he wrapped his arms around her waist. Their eyes, ablaze with passion, met in the mirror. Watching her closely, he reached around to her back and pulled down the zipper on her dress. It fell to the floor in a heap.

She wasn't wearing a bra, and he felt a sharp pain in his chest. Her body was beautiful. Cupping her breasts in his hands, he kneaded them gently. As his touch sent a jolt of electricity throughout her entire body, she tossed her head back against his chest. Bending his head forward, he sought solace from her sweet mouth. Moaning softly, she stretched her hands upward until they nestled in his wavy hair. Turning her around to face him, he looked deeply into her eyes, searching for approval to continue. Her passion-filled eyes gave him the answer he sought.

Lifting her into his arms, he carried her to the bed. After placing her in the center, he slid in alongside her. Skillfully, he removed the rest of her clothing, his breathing becoming heavy and ragged. While intently studying every inch of her, her beauty impaled his heart yet again.

Slowly undoing the buttons on his shirt, her hands trembled with excitement as they sought out his thick chest hairs. Hillary experienced an aching throb from her innermost passage as Brandon acquainted himself with every inch of her soft flesh. With their passion at a fever pitch, he rolled over briefly and removed the last vestige of his clothing. She gasped as her eyes made contact with his hard, muscular body. Her eyes traveled the full length of his body, resting momentarily on his male hardness. As he continued to excite her, expertly manipulating her most intimate, inner self, Hillary clawed desperately at his strong back.

Before he was no longer able to control himself, he took time to slip on protection. Then he slipped gently into her comfort zone. There was no doubt in his mind that he was the first, which brought him uncontrollable pleasure. Uniting with Hillary had not only awakened him physically, but spiritually as well.

She moaned softly as Brandon completed the delicate act of penetration. Though she experienced a minimal amount of pain, inconceivable pleasure soon replaced the slight discomfort. In perfect harmony with Brandon throughout their blissful union, Hillary mindlessly arched her body to draw him in closer. Fully engrossed in giving each other pleasure, they moaned from the sheer ecstasy of their lovemaking.

Their climax was so much more than they could've ever imagined. Hillary swore she heard a symphony while Brandon saw flashes of thunder and lightning, with a rainbow at the end of the heavens.

For sure he'd found his pot of gold.

He rolled her on top of him. "Precious, I love you deeply. You've made me the happiest man alive. I hope I live up to all your expectations of me."

He hadn't noticed her tears until he felt the moisture on his chest. Tilting her face upward, he looked into her face and became alarmed. "Precious, did I hurt you somehow? Why are you crying?"

Because of her heartfelt emotions she couldn't speak. She buried her head into his chest as her body was racked with sobs. As a horrible feeling of helplessness struck him, he questioned himself about the signals he thought he'd received from her, stroking her hair with one hand and massaging her back with the other.

Much calmer now, she lifted her head until her eyes were level with his. "Honey, you didn't hurt me," she said, her voice quaking. "I'm just overwhelmed by the deeply satisfying pleasure I just experienced. My body is sated. I made the decision regarding this union earlier today. I have no regrets. I truly love you. The depth of my love for you makes my decision right for me."

Relieved beyond belief, he kissed her bruised lips until she gasped for air.

Just before dawn Hillary pulled Brandon out of bed and had him pull a chair over to the window where they could observe the magnificent view of the city lights. With her positioned snugly on his lap, they watched the sun rise majestically over New York. Gently, he rocked her in his lap until she fell asleep. Careful not to awaken her, he carried her to the bed, laid her down, and nestled himself in close beside her.

Awakening to find Brandon looking down at her, she smiled into his dark, mysterious eyes. Bending his head, he possessed her mouth with a wet, passionate kiss. She gave herself up to the delicious warmth that engulfed her. Oblivious to everything around them, except for one another's burning desire for fulfillment, they became entangled in an ardent lovemaking session, but not before he made their union a safe one.

Peaking, they screamed each other's name. Their explosive climax was even more powerful than the last. Neither of them wanting to pull apart, they clung desperately to each other, hoping this moment of exquisite ecstasy would never end.

Fulfilled, they took a brisk shower, but the coolness of the water wasn't enough to douse the fire burning between them, causing them to seek pleasure yet again.

Afterward, Brandon gently lathered her body with her favorite scented soap. He then washed her hair until her scalp tingled. She later performed the same services for him.

Squeaky clean, they emerged from the shower to dress.

For the rest of their stay in New York, the two couples took in many of the sights and pleasures of New York. To get a real feel for the city, they used public transportation. While touring Central Park in a horse-drawn hansom cab, they stopped briefly to ride the carousel.

Touring Lincoln Center for the Performing Arts was especially interesting to Brandon. The buildings had been designed by some of the nation's finest architects. Rockefeller Center was a real treat for everyone. Hillary and Cassie especially loved the underground shops and restaurants, where they purchased several souvenirs to take to their families and friends.

Hillary was overly excited by Radio City Music Hall. She couldn't help wondering if she'd ever perform there. During the course of their stay, they visited other attractions, such as the Statue of Liberty, Empire State Building, World Trade Center, and Trump Tower. Cassie enjoyed the Garment District tremendously, and Aaron found Wall Street quite intriguing.

Toward the end of their visit, the foursome eventually visited Broadway, the "Great White Way." They easily became captivated by the dazzling array of theater marquees. That same evening, standing in front of a pizza parlor window, they watched in fascination as the pizza-makers tossed their dough high into the air. There was a show going on at the Apollo Theater in Harlem, but they were denied access because it was already filled to capacity.

As it was the last night of their mini-vacation, Brandon and Hillary had just finishing pampering themselves with a long, sizzling hot bubble bath. After giving one another an erotic lotion massage using scented lotions and hot oils, they settled down to enjoy a final night of television in the Big Apple. Admittedly, they were too tired to do anything else.

Brandon lay down on the bed and flipped through the channels, trying to find a suitable program to watch. Bundled up in a Staffordshire robe in a delicate pastel floral print with ivory cuffs and collar, Hillary rested with her hair splayed across his chest. When Brandon first saw her in the robe, he told her she looked like a cuddly bouquet of flowers.

Snaking his arm around her, he pulled her head higher onto his chest. While making sure she had a good view of the television set, Hillary nestled into his chest comfortably. They quickly became engrossed in a movie. The only sounds in the room came from the television. Hillary thought of how much she'd love to stay in his arms forever. Still elated over the fact that Hillary had wanted him with her, Brandon felt his soul was at peace.

Taking his eyes away from the television, he looked down at her. He felt deeply touched when he saw her lower lip quivering as she fought stoically to keep from crying. Pressing his lips softly to her temple, he stroked her hair, and she found comfort in his tender caresses. Knowing he understood her emotional state, she released her tears freely.

When the movie was finally over, he pulled her on top

of him and allowed her to free the rest of her pent-up emotions. Though he felt like crying, too, he kept a tight rein on his feelings.

"Are you feeling better?" he sympathized.

"I am. I've seen *Imitation of Life* a thousand times, but it gets to me every time. There is so much prejudice in this world. I wish I could rid the entire planet of it, but all I can do is make sure I treat everyone as a human being. There is only one race of people: the human race," she asserted with passion.

Brandon kissed her forehead. "I understand your feelings, but I don't think we'll ever be rid of it. It's too deeply rooted and it sprouts new growth everywhere as it spreads the deadly disease of hatred to everyone it touches."

"Very nicely stated," she complimented drowsily.

Seeing that she was ready to fall asleep, he turned off the television and all the lights. Curling up next to her, he watched her through adoring eyes, stroking her gently until he could hear the even breathing that told him she'd fallen asleep.

Thirteen

Back in Hillary's home, she and Brandon dropped onto the sofa in sheer exhaustion. The length of the flight and the time change had already gotten to both of them.

"Hill, come home with me tonight," Brandon requested, his voice tired and a little hoarse.

"I think I should stay here. I have so much to do to prepare for work tomorrow. If we stay together tonight, we'll accomplish nothing."

Reluctantly, he nodded. "I guess you're right, but I don't want to be without you. I've grown accustomed to your face."

Hillary laughed at the old cliche. "Absence makes the heart grow fonder," she responded in turn.

Brandon moaned. "You don't believe that one yourself. Or do you?"

"As a matter of fact, I do. I know while I was in New York without you, I accepted the fact that I loved you."

"Well, pretty lady, in that case, I believe it, too." Wrapping his arms around her, he pulled her close. "I love you, too—and I knew that long before you were absent."

"Sometimes it takes longer for some than others. We aren't all lucky enough to be so damned impulsive," she quipped.

He grinned. "That sharp tongue has a familiar ring to it. For a while I thought you'd gone soft."

"Fat chance!" They both chuckled loudly. He then silenced her laughter by covering her mouth with his, drawing her into a passionate kiss.

Just as their breathing became labored, the doorbell rang. Both Hillary and Brandon went to the door. It was Aaron, who'd come to pick up Brandon.

Hillary and Brandon kissed once more and said their good-byes. As Hillary closed the door, a few tears escaped from her half-closed eyes. She knew she'd have difficulty sleeping alone tonight. She'd become accustomed to Brandon's arms, yet she could no longer daydream. She had to tend to her tasks.

During their drive to the coast, Brandon and Aaron became engrossed in a serious conversation. They hadn't gotten a chance to talk much in New York, but both men had plenty they needed to say.

"Aaron, I really hated to leave Hillary tonight. She drives me wild. You know me well. And you know I've always vowed never to let anyone get under my skin this way."

Aaron grinned. "Man, I know exactly how you feel. Cassie has my tail going in circles, too. How did we both get caught at the same time?"

"That's easy enough to answer. We've never met two more incredible women. They're beautiful, intelligent, and they both have a great sense of humor."

"Tell me something, Brandon, were you able to figure out what was going on between Hillary and that Sinclair fellow?"

Brandon's face took on a scowl. "I wish you hadn't asked that question. I've been fighting like hell to keep from asking Hillary about it. They seemed to be enjoying a private joke of some sort. I just hope the joke isn't on me."

"I don't think you have anything to worry about. It's probably best if you let it go. Hillary's not that type of a sister. You need to remember that all women aren't alike."

"You're right. It probably meant nothing, but did you catch it when he called her Scarlett?" Brandon asked.

"Sure did. Cassie even thought that was strange. But she did say that Hillary probably told him that that was her name. Even Hillary has said that she loves to have one up on people that she's not interested in being bothered with."

"Well, I'm sure he knows her name by now. If things keep going the way they are, the whole damn world will know her name," Brandon hissed, cradling his head in his palms.

Aaron glanced over at Brandon. "You sound as though that bothers you. If so, you better get used to the idea. Hillary Houston is about to become a 'superstar.'"

Brandon blew out a ragged breath. "I love Hillary enough to deal with anything that comes our way. I'm not about to give up on her. As long as she's going to be happy, I'm going to be happy for her."

Aaron smiled broadly at Brandon. "Now that's what I wanted to hear from you. Hang in there, partner. Hillary is worth it. She's not going to disappoint you."

So many thoughts went through Brandon's head as he thought about getting away with Hillary again, before she was too bogged down with this recording business. He hadn't even told her he was a licensed private pilot. He wasn't sure how she'd take it. His own mother didn't even know. No other woman had ever flown with him, but he felt almost sure that Hillary's adventurous spirit would love to go up with him.

* * *

Hillary's family had come and gone. She'd called them from the airport while waiting for her baggage to be unloaded and asked them to come to her place. During their visit, she'd shared with them all the things that had transpired over the last few days. She'd especially wanted to talk with her father, who was always able to put things in proper prospective for her.

Once everyone had gotten settled in, she'd told her thrilling story from beginning to end. When she'd finished, the room had taken on a life all its own. The loud screaming and shouting would've made a deaf man hear.

Hillary had laughed at one of her sister's comments. Diane had fondly recalled all the times she'd heard Hillary crooning in her room. Jackson and Alice had beamed when they'd pulled Hillary into their arms. They couldn't have been happier for her. Her lifelong dream would finally be fulfilled.

Promising to be there for her, the rest of her family had hugged her while making a big fuss over her, she fondly recalled. The rest of the evening had been spent with Hillary spinning her yarns about New York. She told them about her friends joining her there. Though she'd talked to her parents while she was away, she hadn't mentioned that Brandon, Aaron, and Cassie were in New York with her. She wasn't exactly sure why she hadn't.

She later had shown them the beautiful gold ring Brandon had given her, and had been teased mercilessly. When her family had decided to stay for a late supper, Jackson and her brothers-in-law, Jesse and J.R., had gone out and gotten food for everyone.

Hillary hadn't been very hungry since she'd eaten on the plane. She had been content just to have her family around her. When Brandon had come to mind, which was often, she'd regretted that she hadn't allowed him to stay with her. Once the food had arrived, the delicious smells had made her hungry, and she'd found herself piling food on a plate.

It was after midnight before everyone left, but one more night in Brandon's arms would've been like paradise. It would've also helped to prepare her for going back to work.

Feeling very vulnerable, she sat in the darkened room and allowed herself to give into the wave of exhausting tears that washed over her. Trying to stop them, she squeezed her eyes shut, and sleep immediately took over.

As soft music wafted through the air, a cool breeze blew in from the half-open patio door. A single candle softly illuminated the entire room. The shadows of the rustling leaves lent an eerie quality to the room. Whispers seemed to be coming up through the floor.

Holding Hillary tightly in his arms, Brandon whispered sweet words of love into her ear. Lying on the carpeted floor in her bedroom, the couple was lost in time. Only air could have gotten in between them. Hillary's soft laughter rang out as Brandon discovered a sensitive spot on her anatomy. She tried to wiggle free from his embrace, but he held her fast, wreaking havoc on the tender spot. She screamed out with pleasure.

Still fighting to break away from his tight embrace, she finally managed to escape. When she looked at Brandon, the look in his raven-black eyes matched the fire in her own.

"I'm so happy you decided to come back," Hillary said. "I can't believe you got all the way home and still felt like driving back here. When you called to say you wanted to come back, I couldn't believe it."

"I can't believe it myself. I was definitely closer to my warm bed, but I couldn't get you out of my mind. Woman, what are you doing to me?"

"You don't know? Let me give you a clue."

Bending her head, she whispered something in his ear. "Now do you know?"

"Boy, was that some clue! You just gave me the evidence I needed to have Aaron bring you up on charges. Would you like to cop a plea?"

"I don't plea bargain. I'm going to make you prove your case. All you have right now is your word against mine."

"I believe I have a little more than that. Would you care for me to present the rest of my evidence?"

"I guess I can stand to be fed a little more bull."

Pushing her back against the thick pile carpet, he made his evidence abundantly clear. Without a doubt, he had his case easily won.

"Miss Houston, how would you like to plead?" he asked, smiling with smug satisfaction.

"Guilty, guilty, guilty! Now come back over here and give me more of your fascinating evidence." Blending into one another with all the right ingredients to start World War III, Hillary and Brandon slipped from this world and plunged into a deep, dark, mysterious place in another era.

She had told him she'd been a witch in another life. He was still collecting evidence for an even stronger case against her. Since she'd told him her many dark secrets, he planned on blackmailing her into staying in his space forever. Never realizing that he was the one being blackmailed, he fell right into the fire. She had prepared him for consumption by the white-hot flames of desire. . . .

With one leg dangling over the edge, her still form was stretched out on the leather sofa. She hadn't had the strength to climb the stairs after her unexpected rainstorm of tears. Drifting in and out of sleep, she could hear bells ringing somewhere off in the distance. The clothes she'd stripped off earlier were haphazardly thrown around the otherwise meticulously kept room.

A car backfired, sending her straight to her feet. As she tried to adjust her eyes to the darkness, the moonlight streaked in through the slightly opened miniblinds to offer assistance. When the coolness of the room reached out to embrace her scantily clad body, she shivered.

Weary from her very real dream, she sat back down on the couch and tried to collect her thoughts and store them in a neat package somewhere in the back of her mind. Unable to accomplish this goal, she wearily picked her clothing up from the floor. After stopping in the kitchen for a drink of water, she slowly climbed the stairs.

She followed her nightly ritual, then dressed in a black camisole and tap pants made of whisper-soft crêpe de Chine, fashioned with ivory dots and lace trim.

Pulling back the covers, she smiled when she noticed the fresh rose-pink and mint-green sheets on the bed. The reversible comforter had been turned over, too. She remembered telling Cassie that she hadn't had time to change her linens, and was touched that her friend had taken care of them.

A dark shadow fell across her thoughts as she climbed into bed. Remembering the reason for her earlier tears brought fresh ones to the surface as it hit her hard again. She'd given up her virginity. But she loved Brandon, and he loved her. Besides, it had been her decision. He hadn't pressured her in any way. She had given her love willingly. Then she recalled all the conversations she'd had with her parents about intimacy and the importance of saving oneself for one's marriage partner.

"Brandon Blair, I love you and I hope I've made the right decision. But if we don't stay together, I have grossly cheated the man I might one day call husband," she whispered into the silence. She closed her eyes, hoping sleep would come.

It was close to two A.M. when she next glanced at the clock. Still, she picked up the phone. The illuminated dial guided her fingers.

"Yes," a voice husky with sleep came over the line.

"It's me," she whispered into the mouthpiece.

"Precious, is something wrong? I've been calling you off and on for hours. I had every intention of calling again, but I fell asleep."

"The only thing that's wrong is you're there and I'm here."

"I can right that wrong, you know. I can be there in no time."

"That sounds tempting, but I wouldn't think of allowing you to drive all the way here this late. I can't believe I even called you so late."

"For you, my hotline is open twenty-four-seven. Hill, why didn't you answer the phone earlier?" She could tell he'd tried to keep from asking that question, but it just wasn't in his nature not to.

She smiled to herself. "It sounds like you have a bad case of 'curiosity killed the cat.' "

He laughed softly. "Am I that obvious?"

"Painfully obvious!" Feeling that he needed to break his habit of wanting to know her every move, she didn't answer his question. She wasn't about to allow him to become a control freak over her life or the events that surrounded it.

He was intuitive enough to let it drop. "Hill, I'm glad you called. I've been longing to hear your voice. And, Hill, I'll never make you feel one ounce of regret over the precious gift you bestowed upon me in New York." It was as if he'd sensed her need to be reassured that she'd entrusted her most valuable possession to someone worthy, someone who would guard it with his life.

"Brandon, thank you. I guess I needed to be reassured. I made the right decision . . . simply because I love you. I hope I didn't disappoint you when we were intimately involved. Did I disappoint you, Brandon?"

"Excuse me? I'm not sure I heard you."

"You heard me—and I'm not going to repeat it!"

Her response let him know he'd heard her correctly, but his disbelief that she'd asked such a question was obvious in his tone. "There's no way you could ever disappointment me. No one could ever fulfill me the way you do. Are you disappointed with the decision you made, Hill?" He sounded fearful.

"I was. But as I felt your smile, when you recognized my voice, my dubious feelings were quickly swept away."

"Precious, I plan to be the one and only recipient of the love you've shown me. Trust me. It will be okay."

His reassuring words swept into her soul and helped it make its peace with her misgivings. "Brandon, I think I can sleep now. I love you."

"And I love you. Dream of me. We'll talk later in the day, angel-of-mine."

Long after their conversation had ended, they both were still awake. She relived the intimacy they'd shared for so many wonderful days, while he indulged himself in exactly the same wonderful memories. Before they finally fell asleep, the Master Artist had already painted another of His beautiful masterpieces across the early morning skies.

On her drive to work Hillary tried to think of the words she would say to Mr. Asher regarding her signing a recording contract. She knew he'd be bitterly disappointed if she were to leave the company. He'd put a lot of time and energy into her career. His faith in her was unwavering, and he considered her his protégée. He'd taken her under his wing from the moment she'd arrived at Atlantic Pacific Airlines.

She got off the elevator and went straight to Mr. Asher's office.

He smiled warmly when she poked her head in the door. "Good morning, Hillary. Welcome back. We've missed your smiling face around here."

She smiled back as she took a seat in the chair in front of his desk. "Morning, Mr. Asher. It's good to be back."

He laid his pen down on his desk. "I've heard nothing but good things about your presentation. Another job well done. I'm proud of you."

"Thank you, Mr. Asher. I feel the conference was a big success. However, there's something else I would like to discuss with you. Do you have time right now?"

"Of course, Hillary. What is it?"

She worried the hem of the lightweight sweater she wore with her fingers. "When I first came here for my interview, I remember telling you about my aspirations to become a singer. Do you remember our conversation?"

He nodded. "I recall us discussing the matter."

She bit down on her lower lip. "Well, sir, it seems that I may have the opportunity to become just that. I've been offered a recording contract with a major studio."

He pondered her words carefully. "I see. I get the distinct impression that you're about to resign here. Am I correct?"

Hillary felt a little ashamed of herself. "Mr. Asher, I just wanted to tell you before you heard it elsewhere. I also wanted to discuss my options with you. I haven't actually signed a contract yet."

His eyes met with hers. "Let me ask you this. Have you made the decision to sign with this recording company?"

"To be honest, I'm leaning in that direction."

Before resuming their conversation, he studied her intently. "Hillary, I'm going to take the liberty to speak frankly here. You and I know each other well enough for me to be up front with you. First off, I am disappointed. I had great plans for you here at Atlantic Pacific. However, I'm not one to hold anyone back. You have my sincere congratulations, and I hope all of your dreams come true."

His twinkling eyes showed his sincerity. "Have you thought of what you will do if this venture doesn't succeed?"

"I've given it a great deal of thought."

"And?" He gestured with his hands for her to continue.

"Sir, I'm prepared to start all over in my trained field should I fail in the entertainment business. I won't have any problem starting at the bottom and working my way back up."

Having received the answer he'd hoped for, he smiled. "In that case, let me make a few suggestions, if I may?" He looked to her for approval and she nodded. "I would like to see you take a couple of months' leave of absence rather than resign. You can continue to renew that leave of absence for up to a year. That way, you don't have to give up your health benefits. We can allow you to pay the premiums yourself. Another suggestion is for you to work part-time until your singing career takes off. If you work at least twenty hours a week, you can keep your full benefits at the company's expense. What do you think?"

Hillary was filled with admiration for this gentle giant who'd become her friend from the very beginning. Elated, she raced around the desk to embrace him tenderly. "Mr. Asher, I hadn't even given your suggestions a thought before now. I've read the policy manual over and over, but I never considered a leave or part-time as an option. Thank you so much for supporting me in this.

I'll never forget you. I'll be there for you anytime you need me, whether I remain an employee here or not. Could I get back to you with my decision? You've shed so much new light on my dilemma."

"By all means, Hillary. I'll be looking to hear from you. Take your time . . . there's no rush. Your position is here as long as you want it."

Hillary nearly skipped all the way down the hall. Asher had thrown her a life raft. When she stopped to chat with Lois, they embraced each other as long-lost friends would.

Lois seemed happy to have her back. "Hillary, I missed you. This place is not the same without you. You bring so much sunshine with you."

Hillary beamed. "That's really sweet of you to say. I've missed you, as well. We'll have our lunch date this week so I can fill you in on my trip."

Lois had a mysterious glint in her eyes. "That sounds wonderful. I have some news of my own. I can hardly wait to share it."

Hillary noticed the mysterious look, which made waiting next to impossible. "Lois, by the look in your eyes, I don't think I can wait."

Lois laughed softly as she leaned over to whisper in Hillary's ear. "I've been going out with Alexander Cash."

Hillary looked stunned. Trying to hide her concern, she took a few moments to mull over Lois's news. "Sweetie, when did all this happen?" Animatedly, Lois told her how it all started and how Alex had first come to ask her out.

Hillary was fascinated by her story. "Lois, you seem so happy. So, Alex has been working on himself." Remembering her vow to keep Alex's secret, Hillary immediately tried to change the subject. She could see that her blunder hadn't gone unnoticed when Lois looked as though she'd already caught on.

"I know all about the trouble Alex caused you." Hillary looked totally perplexed now. "Don't look so troubled . . . Alex told me himself. He also told me how gracious you were in forgiving him. Now I understand why you asked me if his short stature bothered me."

Relieved, Hillary sighed. "Lois, I am thrilled that Alex was able to be honest. It tells me he's sincere in his quest for change."

"He told me about the advice you gave him. It was really sound advice, and I believe it was instrumental in putting him on the right path. He's in counseling twice a week now." Hillary smiled broadly, pleased that Alex had taken her advice to heart. "Hillary, could you please keep in confidence what I've told you? I know Alex wanted to tell you himself, but I just couldn't hold it."

"Your secret is safe with me. I won't let on to Alex that I know, but I think you should at some point. What if I can't pull a surprise act off? Don't start your relationship off with secrets." Hillary couldn't help thinking about the woman Brandon had kept a secret from her. "At any rate, this is such good news. Is he treating you well?" she asked, still a bit concerned.

"Very well. I've seen him almost every night since you left. We've been to the movies, dinner, and bowling. We have a lot in common. I've even taken him to meet my parents."

Hillary's eyebrows shot up. "That's serious business, Lois!" she exclaimed.

"I know. His family doesn't live here. I don't know if I'll ever meet them. I don't think they have much of a relationship," Lois revealed with some reluctance.

"Don't sweat it, Lois. Maybe now that he's in counseling things will change. At least he's dealing with his problems."

"I hope so. Hillary, I plan to take the advice you gave me. I'll tell Alex that I've told you about us. I hadn't thought about it the way in which you put it. I don't want us to keep things from one another." Before retreating to her office, Hillary hugged Lois again.

Immediately busying herself with unfinished projects, Hillary was happy to be back at work. It was a pleasant diversion. During her difficult time sleeping last night, she had missed Brandon painfully. She'd also thought of the many times they might have to be separated over the coming months, but she was determined to make a go of their relationship. He had assured her that he was just as committed.

Surprised that he hadn't yet asked about the exchange between her and Anthony Sinclair, she wondered if he'd been put off by her refusal to say why she hadn't answered the phone. But she really didn't want him to get the wrong idea about Sinclair.

The rest of the week flew by. Hillary practically lived in her office, arriving early and staying late to catch up on all the new projects.

She and Lois had their lunch date on Friday, and Lois was excited by all the news Hillary shared with her, but she was saddened that Hillary might be leaving the company. Knowing that very few people would have the sort of patience and kindness that Hillary had shown toward her, Lois couldn't imagine having a new boss. She would sorely miss Hillary's delightful presence.

The next few weeks were hellacious for Hillary, as well. She was constantly in negotiations with St. John and the attorney Aaron had retained for her. The attorney representing her was Michael Goldstein. He had quite a reputation in entertainment law. He and Hillary had met several times before their negotiations with St. John, but needing more of a feel for what St. John's company offered, he met with Eric and his attorneys a couple of times without Hillary.

Seated in Michael Goldstein's office suite, Hillary listened intently to what the brilliant young lawyer had to say. Tall and prematurely gray, Michael had a head full of tight, unmanageable-looking curls. A lighter gray than Aaron's, his eyes appeared calm. With his legs crossed, Michael sat behind his cherrywood desk in a burgundy leather swivel chair. "I'm satisfied that you're getting a fair shake, Hillary, so I've resumed negotiations with all parties concerned. As you know, Aaron has complete trust and faith in me. He has even sat in on some of the meetings. The other attorneys agreed to his presence as a professional courtesy."

Hillary smiled. "So, it looks as though we are moving forward, at a much faster pace than I'd first expected. How are things looking thus far?"

"Now that I fully realize your marketing potential, not to mention how eager S&J Records is to sign you, I called this meeting to advise you that I only want you to accept a limited timeframe on your contract. I don't want you to limit your options by being tied up with one company for too long a period. We can always renegotiate. Two years would be an adequate start. The money they've offered is more than generous, but I still need to negotiate royalty percentages and a few other perks to sweeten the deal. Confident in my professional abilities to get you one honey of a deal, I've already set the wheels in motion. You're in good hands, Hillary Houston."

Hillary stood up and shook his hand. "I trust that. From what I understand, your stellar reputation precedes you throughout the entertainment world. You come highly recommended. It's nice doing business with you. I've got to run now so I can pack."

Michael got up and walked Hillary to the door. "You

have a great weekend. I hope your boyfriend's surprise for you is a good one."

Having refused to tell Hillary where, Brandon was taking her away for the weekend. The new demands on her time hadn't given them as much time alone as before. She had hurried to get home to ready herself for their excursion. Brandon was due shortly. While packing several types of clothing, she thought she could prepare herself more adequately if she knew where they were going. But she admitted to herself that she loved all the surprises that Brandon loved to give her. After securing her bags and making sure she had everything, she ran downstairs to wait for him. She sat on the sofa and closed her eyes for a brief respite.

Fourteen

Arriving right on schedule, dressed in tan casual slacks and a soft lemon-yellow wool sweater, Brandon looked relaxed and well rested. Hillary wore black leather pants that clung to her anatomy like a second skin. Her silk hand-knitted sweater was a bright, textured mix of stitches. The sweater's deep coral color complemented her coppery skin.

"Hi! I've missed you," she said cheerfully.

He wore a brooding look in his eyes, but it quickly turned to one of appreciation when he checked out her attire. Whistling softly, he kissed her lightly on the mouth. "Hill, I've missed you, too. These last few weeks have been difficult, but I know you've been busy. Ever since those first nights you slept in my bed, that room has been dreadfully lonely. I'm glad we're getting away together again."

Hillary frowned. "Brandon, I hope this hectic schedule of mine won't last much longer. I'm sick of meetings, negotiations, the whole nine yards. Everything should be wrapped up early next week. Then I plan to take a couple of weeks off for myself."

"Will I be included in those couple of weeks?"

She looked at him in adoration. "If you'll have me."

He took her into his arms. "Hill, I'll always want you," he confessed, kissing her thoroughly.

* * *

With the mystery of the destination still intact, they arrived at Van Nuys Airport. She looked at him with questioning eyes, but he just parked the car and removed their bags. Telling her to wait in the car, he disappeared inside a small shedlike building, returning before she had a chance to wonder what was really going on. He picked up the bags and she followed him as he moved in the direction of the private planes.

How romantic! He's hired a private plane to take us away, she thought. She looked around but didn't see anyone else in sight. "Brandon, who's going to fly the plane?"

He laughed nervously. "I am."

She stared at him as her eyes filled with horror. "You're what? Are you out of your impulsive mind?"

He put his hands on her shoulders. "Calm down, Hill. . . . I'm a licensed pilot. You'll be safe with me."

Staring at him in disbelief, she wondered where she'd heard those words before. "Why haven't you told me about this long before now?"

"It never came up, but I thought for sure your adventurous spirit would love to soar through the clouds with me. Hill, I would never put your life in jeopardy. If I wasn't confident in my ability to fly this plane, we wouldn't be standing here." He held her close. "Come on, honey, you're going to love it."

The corners of her mouth turned up in a slight smile. "Now you hear this. If you kill me in this contraption, I'm going to come back and haunt you for the rest of your natural-born life."

He felt his body relax as he laughed at her comment. "That's the spirit, adventure girl! Come on, babe, let's get this show on the road."

He hugged her roughly before they boarded the small

aircraft. After securing her with the seat belt, he returned to the tarmac and untied the aircraft from its chock.

Though filled with apprehension, she wasn't about to let him know how scared she really was. She thought that she needed to have her head examined. She had tried many crazy things, but this was the craziest of all.

Once in the pilot's seat, Brandon directed his full attention to the task at hand as he carefully taxied the airplane onto the runway. After getting approval from the tower, he carefully prepared for take-off.

As the aircraft picked up speed, Hillary's stomach lurched, causing her to silently pray for deliverance from losing her meager breakfast. He'd be deserving of it if she did, she thought churlishly. When the thought of that really happening popped into her head, she laughed. Intense in his manipulation of the aircraft, Brandon kept his focus on the controls.

As the plane left the ground, she held her breath and continued to pray fervently. Once he'd leveled off, she permitted her breath to escape. Oddly enough, it didn't take long before she started to enjoy herself. She even ventured to look out the window. The scenery below was breathtaking as he flew the plane low along the coastline. Wanting to show her something below, he veered the plane sharply to one side.

She gasped in fear. "Brandon, please don't do that again."

He laughed inwardly at her horror-stricken expression. "Sorry, Hill, I didn't mean to frighten you."

In a matter of minutes, she relaxed and began to enjoy herself once again. She found it hard to believe that he'd kept his ability to fly a secret, which made her wonder what other secrets he'd kept. There would always be something fresh and exciting to discover about Brandon Blair, she decided.

They flew approximately two hours before he came in

for a landing. The landing shook her up as much as the take-off. When he nailed his touchdown, she was glad to be back on solid ground. He then taxied the aircraft to the end of the runway. Much to her surprise, he parked the plane right in front of a quaint motel. In front of each room was a chock to secure each plane. *How convenient,* she thought, still amazed at Brandon's ability to fly through the air with no visible markers to lead the way, then land in an airport many miles from where they began.

Hillary thought the name of the motel was certainly fitting. Located on William Moffett, between the airport terminal and Goleta Beach Park, in the city of Santa Barbara, the Pilot House Motel had twenty-four comfortable rooms. He secured the plane, then checked them in.

The decor of the room was attractive and comfortable, and the furnishings were modern, Hillary saw as she took inventory of the room. Once they'd put their things away, he immediately called for a taxi for them to embark on a sightseeing excursion.

Fifteen minutes later, the taxi dropped them off at Stearn's Wharf.

"This landmark was built in 1872. Today, as you can see for yourself, the wharf is the site of many specialty shops and restaurants. There's the fishing pier," Brandon said as he pointed it out. "The view of the harbor and the mountains behind Santa Barbara are excellent from this spot. Just look behind us."

Hillary had never been to Santa Barbara, and she was fascinated by what little she'd already seen. Her breath caught as she looked up at the majestic mountains. Later, after grabbing a quick sandwich, they visited the Mission Santa Barbara.

" 'This mission is know as the "Queen of the Missions." Founded on December 4, 1786,' " he read from the plaque, " 'it's one of the best preserved of all the missions.' " After taking in several other sights, they took another cab back to the motel to rest.

Hillary dressed in the same winter-white crêpe trouser suit she'd worn her first night in New York. Great things had happened when she wore it before, so she now considered it one of her lucky charms. Brandon wore charcoal-gray wool dress slacks, a matching double-breasted jacket, and a pale gray silk shirt. His silk tie was a paisley design of varying shades of black, red and gray. They both looked elegant.

Having hopped into yet another cab, they arrived at Maxi's in Fess Parker's Red Lion Resort a short time later.

The rustic decor offered comfort and warmth, Hillary noted. Before sitting down to dinner, they were escorted to a table in the lounge to have virgin cocktails.

She covered her hand with his. "You're full of surprises, and I love them all."

Her smile made him feel warm all over. "Hill, you deserve only the best. I've been waiting to get you away since we returned from New York. Impatiently, I might add. I'm sorry I sprung the flying on you. My mother doesn't even know. . . . She would worry herself sick. I had intentions of taking you on a short trip first, but I later decided to just jump in with both feet."

Hillary chuckled. "I'm not sure I'd be here if you had told me earlier. However, it was a nice flight. I felt like one of those neon-painted kites we saw on the beach near your house. I seemed as though I was drifting through space. . . . It was a tremendous feeling, a feeling I've never had before."

"I had hoped your free spirit would get the best of you." Her familiar smile wangled its way into his heart with ease. Leaning across the table, he kissed her full on the mouth. "I'm glad that I'm going to have the entire weekend to show you how I feel about you."

Brandon rapidly set about the task of running Hillary a hot bath. After lighting candles in the room and pouring her favorite bath crystals in the water, he laid out the bathrobe he'd given her.

Wondering how she'd gotten so lucky, she sat on the bed and watched him move busily around the room. He took such special care of her. For the most part, he was pretty considerate of her feelings. Ever since the few bumps they'd experienced early on in their relationship, he tried to keep the communication lines open. She appreciated all the efforts he'd made. So far, their relationship looked as though it had an excellent chance for survival.

Adroitly unbuttoning her jacket, he slipped it off and unbuttoned her trousers. He gently lifted her, slid her trousers off, and delicately stripped away her silk camisole. Her nipples hardened when his hand made contact. As he bent his head and drew one creamy breast into his mouth, Hillary moaned in pleasurable agony. Hastily, he removed the last of her clothing.

Picking her up from the bed, he carried her into the bathroom. As he continued caressing her with his mouth, he lowered her into the water. She had a devilish urge to pull him into the water with her, but she was mindful of his expensive clothes.

Her voice stopped him dead in his tracks as he was about to leave the room. "Hey, big fellow, aren't you going to join me?" she asked, her voice low and seductive.

Smiling that all-too-familiar, disarming smile of his, he turned sharply on his heels. "Pretty lady, what took you so long?" She laughed heartily at their private joke.

After hastily undressing himself, he slid into the water

with her, and they lovingly nipped at one another. He was fully aroused before he'd even hit the water. Lifting her up, he adjusted her on his lap. His fingers moved anxiously over her body before he entered her. As the heated contact was made, she threw her head back violently, causing him to thrust deeper. Her eyes were wildly glazed as she moved in perfect rhythm with his muscular body.

She felt weightless as they torpedoed into climax. Trembling all over, she screamed out his name. Thinking that his world had exploded, he cried out her name as their liquid fire flowed into one another, covering them in a blanket of delicious warmth.

She stilled his hand when he reached to turn the hot water on. "No, don't do that. If it gets any hotter in here, I'll melt."

"Hill, I have to warm the water. You'll catch a chill if I don't."

"Honey, we could be in Antarctica, in an ice storm, and I still wouldn't catch a chill. My body is on fire."

He still looked concerned. He removed himself from the water and retrieved her robe. Lifting her from the tub, he wrapped the robe around her and tied the belt snugly.

"You worry too much," she charged. "I'll be fine."

"I know. I'm making sure of it, sassy!"

"Who would've ever thought you were such a fuss box."

He swatted her across the behind with his towel. "I got your fuss box." Screaming, she fled from the bathroom before he could swat her again.

After helping Hillary dress in a slinky black nightgown, he quickly pulled on a pair of black boxer shorts, leaving his upper body bare. With a hairbrush in her hand, she climbed into bed, and he slid in right beside her.

Lying across the bed, he amused himself by running

the brush through her hair. He loved the way it shined. "What do you use on this beautiful chestnut hair to keep it so shiny?"

"Eggs and mayonnaise."

"Are you serious?"

"Quite."

He gave her a sarcastic glance. "We're very talkative, aren't we?"

She rolled her eyes at him. "Maybe you should ask questions that require a more intelligent and in-depth response."

"Flip, are we? Let's see how intelligent and deep you are." He ruffled through his bag until he found the Monopoly board. Laughing, he challenged her to a game.

"Brandon, you have about as much chance of beating me in Monopoly as you had in Scrabble," she said with confidence. "No chance at all."

"Is that a threat or a promise?"

"I never make threats and I don't make promises unless I can keep them," she said pointedly.

"Ooh, Hillary is too bad. I'm shaking from fright," he quipped, laughing at her arrogant expression.

"Okay, cutie pie, put your money where your mouth is. I bet you fifty bucks I slaughter you," she challenged.

He eagerly rubbed his hands together. "Make it a hundred and you've got a bet."

"A hundred it is, and I'm not talking about Monopoly money."

After two hours of serious play, keeping her promise, she beat him soundly.

"Hill, will you take your bet in services rendered?"

"What services?"

He leaned over and whispered in her ear. She looked shocked.

"That was too off-color even for me. You give me the mean green. I prefer that color so much more. It's my favorite, you know. You and your sick thoughts of purple passion border on soft porn."

He feigned disappointment. "Lady, you drive a hard bargain. I think we should . . ."

"Have a rematch," she finished for him. "Not a chance! Just shut up and pay up." He handed her a one-hundred-dollar bill. Waving it in front of his face, she laughed wickedly.

Picking her up over his shoulder, he threw her back down on the bed. Grabbing a pillow, she hurled it at him. They threw pillows until one burst open, casting feathers everywhere. She began to sneeze as the feathers tickled her nose. Because of her allergic reaction to the feathers, he ended up cleaning the mess all by his lonesome.

Lying close to her in bed as they settled down, he decided to risk asking about Sinclair. The exchange between them had been a thorn in his side from the moment it had occurred. "Hill, how do you know the guy you introduced me to at your performance in New York?"

Laughing inwardly, she looked directly at him. *Poor baby,* she thought with amusement, *he just couldn't last another second.* "That jerk? He was in the conference I attended."

"Why did he call you Scarlett?"

She smiled smugly. "I was being sarcastic by talking to him in a Southern drawl. When he asked me to dinner that's the accent I used to deflate his overgrown ego. I'm surprised you didn't ask who he was before now."

"I've been struggling not to."

She giggled. "I guess your bad case of curiosity has returned. You really need to seek professional help," she teased. "Seriously, I had every intention of telling you about him. I didn't want you to get the wrong idea."

"You know how my mind works by now, but I'm improving."

She smiled warmly. "Yes, honey, you are." When she told him about Sinclair telling her to call him if she got lonely, he really enjoyed the response she said she'd given him.

"Pretty lady, I'm not going to worry about you anymore. You can definitely hold your own against the best of men, including myself."

"Remember that the next time you decide to match wits with me, Mr. Blair."

He hugged her gently. "Point well taken."

After talking for a couple of hours, they fell asleep with the television still on. The sun came up just as they ignited each other in yet another passionate encounter.

The morning air was nippy, so they dressed in warm clothing before taking breakfast on the terrace at the Santa Barbara Airport. When they later visited the Santa Barbara Zoological Gardens, Hillary was thrilled with the many exhibits that displayed exotic animals in their natural habitats.

Toward the early part of the afternoon, they ended up in beautiful Chase Palm Park. As they walked along the beach, they held hands, nudging and bumping one another in a playful manner. Having a hard time keeping his eyes off her, Brandon stopped to hold her in his arms, arms that ached to be filled with her tender body.

He tilted her chin upward. "Hill, how has Alexander Cash been treating you since your return from New York?"

A docile smile played around the corners of her mouth. "Alex has been a perfect gentleman. He's dating Lois."

Brandon's eyes looked troubled. "Hillary, how could

you let that happen? You know what that guy is capable of."

She shot him a furtive glance. "Alex has changed. I think he's learned his lesson."

"Hill, the guy needs professional help . . . he shouldn't be around any woman."

"Chill out, Brandon. Lois can handle herself. And he is getting counseling."

He held her at arm's length. "How do you know that?" he asked, both eyebrows raised.

She hesitated long enough to take a deep breath. "Alex and I had a long talk before I left for New York." She then explained the conversation to him.

He let out a low, shrill whistle. "How come you never told me this before?"

"It never came up!"

Recognizing the familiar words that were his own, he shook with laughter. "You don't forget anything, do you? You derive a sick pleasure from throwing my words back at me, don't you?"

Her eyes sparkled with innocence. "Who, me? I haven't a clue as to what you're talking about."

He lifted her into the air and ran toward the water. When he threatened to throw her in the ocean, she fought like a tiger, scratching and screaming at the top of her lungs.

"Put me down," she demanded. Before he stood her on her feet, he took the liberty of assaulting her lips with a brutally riveting kiss. She responded ardently.

Feeling ravenous after a few minutes of playing and running through the park, they located a nearby place to eat.

Over lunch of fried shrimp and fries, Hillary discussed at length her recent dealings with Alex. Brandon didn't have too much to say on the subject, because any talk of Alexander Cash put him in a bad mood. He thought the guy was annoying as hell and shouldn't be dating any woman.

While they browsed through the many specialty shops on Stern's Wharf, Hillary purchased a few T-shirts for her nephews. When a heavy glass paperweight caught her eye, she picked it up to examine it closely. Inside was a beautiful beach scene. As she shook it up, the water turned to white foam, giving off the effect of rolling waves. The beauty of it struck her. As she returned it to its shelf, Brandon removed it from her hand, strode to the counter with it, and purchased it for her.

One more lovely souvenir to add to my collection, she mused with delight. She'd been collecting souvenirs from all of their outings. She now had a collection of napkins, matchbooks, movie ticket stubs, swizzle sticks, and all the cards from the flower deliveries. She kept one petal from each flower delivery pressed in her Bible. She had dated everything she could put a date on.

Finished with his transaction, he tucked the small package under his arm. Outside, where the air was cool and clean, he hailed a cab.

Back at the motel, Brandon and Hillary lay in bed, where they talked incessantly, each making new discoveries about the other. They were in the process of discussing Aaron and Cassie's relationship when Brandon ran his fingers through her damp hair. "Aaron has confided in me that he has fallen deeply in love with Cassie. He has never been this happy. He's one of the good guys. You know, one of those guys women shun for the bad boys."

She looked at him quizzically. "Are you one of those bad boys, Mr. Blair?"

He tousled her hair. "Used to be a *real bad boy*. That is, until I met you. I'm not your classic bad boy, the love-them-and-leave-them sort. I just seemed to get classified that way. I don't disrespect women at all, but I don't believe in lying to them about how I feel either. If a relationship no longer works for me, I'm right up front about it."

"The way you were with Lisa," she tossed out without thinking.

His eyes clouded with pain. "Was that statement meant to hurt? If that was your goal, you achieved it."

She felt awful for hurting his feelings. "No. I didn't mean for that to hurt. I don't know why I said that. I just wish I hadn't."

He twirled a tendril of her hair around his forefinger. "You said it because that's what you were thinking. Subconsciously or not, those are your feelings talking. Do you believe in forgiveness, Hill?"

Her eyes widened. "Of course I do. I was brought up in a Christian home. We were taught that in order to be forgiven, we must always be willing to forgive. The ultimate in forgiveness for our sins is the price that was paid at the cross."

He stroked his chin. "I'm not much of a church person, but I do believe in the man upstairs. Does that bother you to know that I'm not a holy roller?"

She laughed. "Holy roller? Is that how you see church-going people? Or are you just being coy?"

He shook his head. "I really don't know how I see it. I just know some people who talk the talk, but can't come close to walking the walk. They're too crippled in their faith and too blinded by that big old log in their eye to see themselves for what they really are, but they claim to see everybody else's shortcomings. Hill, I know more hypocrites than I care to mention. I truly believe in God, but I'm not sold on religion as a whole. Maybe you can share some of your insight with me."

Pondering his question, she turned the corners of her mouth down. "That's a fair enough assessment for some, I guess. I'd be happy to share with you what I understand about Christianity. Hate to disappoint you, but I'm not a holy roller." She ended on a laugh.

They then scratched the surface of how each felt about marriage and children. When he told her he never wanted children, he waited for what he was sure would be a negative response. But when it didn't seem to bother her, he sighed with relief.

"I used to think that people who didn't want children were selfish. But I've changed my mind since I've seen what a heavy responsibility it is. I do truly love my sister's kids. When my parents baby-sat the kids, I used to race home from school just to be with them. Oh, how I loved the feel of their chubby little fingers in my hair when I held them. Children are indeed a rare, special gift and they should be treated as such. People who don't want children simply shouldn't have them."

Her expression was so soft as she discussed the children, he noted. Her sentiments caused him to have second thoughts about not wanting any babies. Any child of Hillary's would be beautiful, he knew, and he had no doubt that she would be a wonderful mother.

Seated in the aircraft, Hillary waited patiently for Brandon to take to the skies once again. She experienced the same feelings in her stomach that she'd felt before, but she was apprehensive during take-off and landings in larger aircraft, as well. As the plane leveled off, she began to relax.

The flight was as smooth as the first. Two hours later, they arrived back at Van Nuys without experiencing any difficulties. Once again, Hillary was relieved when the wheels touched down on the ground.

After grabbing their things, they headed for the car. When he insisted on her driving his car back to her place, he had to convince her that he needed to relax after flying. As she maneuvered the expensive car into traffic, he pulled out two tickets and waved them in the air.

"Hill, are you up for a Lakers game tonight?" Over-excited, she swerved the car a little into the next lane. Fortunately, nothing was coming. He wiped his forehead with the back of his hand. "Jeez! You can be dangerous when you get excited."

She laughed. "I told you how I feel about the Lakers. I have a hard time containing myself when I think about them."

He grinned as he patted her thigh. "So I see. And I think I have my answer."

Upstairs in her bedroom, they lay down to take a nap before getting ready for the game. Brandon fell asleep immediately, but Hillary felt restless.

She slid out of bed and walked across the room to sit in front of the window, where she watched the ducks swim lazily across the lake. Most of the ducks appeared to be peaceful. Amused by one of the drakes who was trying to take advantage of his female counterpart, she watched as the female warded off the male's unwanted advances. When the male became overly aggressive, the female dove into the water to escape his amorous advances.

"Sister duck, you don't stand a chance of getting away," she whispered, smiling. "You may as well stop running right now. That drake will follow you right into hell."

There were times when she wanted to run, too, but she knew Mr. Blair would pursue her as aggressively as the drake had pursued his lady friend. Unlike sister duck, she knew she'd already been caught. She'd surrendered to Brandon's ardent advances sometime ago, with no regrets.

He was still sleeping peacefully when she grabbed a bathrobe and slipped quietly out of the room and into the guest bathroom for a hot shower.

While basking in the warmth of the hot water that ran over her body, the steam rose rapidly, causing her eyelids to droop. Suddenly, she felt something icy-cold come into contact with her buttocks. She turned around and became startled at what looked like a hand sticking under the shower curtain. The steam made it hard for her to see.

A chilling scream escaped her throat before she recognized what was Brandon's hand holding a handful of ice cubes. Her heart was still in her mouth, making it difficult for her to speak. But her eyes easily cut him to shreds.

He hopped into the shower and gathered her against his nude body. "I really startled you, didn't I? I thought nothing scared you, my lady love."

"Brandon, if you scare me like that again . . ."

Pressing his lips urgently onto her mouth, he cut her off. Intent on finishing her sentence, she tried to push him away, but the harder she fought, the tighter he held her. Realizing it was no use, she relaxed her body against his and allowed him to have his way with her. As she thought of sister duck, she wondered if her feathered friend had finally given in, too.

Fifteen

With her head resting on his shoulder, Hillary and Brandon sped toward downtown. Hillary was uncomfortable due to the fact that she was stretched across the console; the Benz had bucket seats with the console in between. Each time she tried to move away, he would pull her back.

Wearing a deep purple cotton fleece sweatshirt, with a double-ribbed collar and a small Lakers logo stitched on the right breast pocket, she was fashionable. She also wore tight-fitting, five-pocket purple jeans. Her feet were decked out in bone-colored, midcalf leather boots and her head was topped with a purple Lakers cap with gold lettering.

Brandon had on black jeans and a black sweatshirt, with a huge gold Lakers logo in the center. He also wore a gold polo shirt under the sweatshirt. His Lakers cap was black with gold lettering.

After showing his season-ticket parking pass at the gate, he parked as close to an entrance as he could get. Once he'd opened the door for her, he swept her out of the car. While walking hand in hand with her toward one of several entrances, he could feel her excitement growing with each step they took.

Inside the Staple Center, once he'd purchased hot dogs, popcorn, and drinks, he guided her to their seats.

Just as he'd promised, they were seated right at midcourt. Having a perfect view of the Lakers bench, she took the liberty of surveying all the fans that surrounded her and the players who were out on the floor doing a shoot-around. Eagerly, she sought out her favorites. The men looked like giants to her, since she'd never sat so close before. She couldn't wait for the game to begin. While everyone stood as the national anthem was sung, Hillary imagined herself singing at a game.

As the Detroit Pistons were announced, a few cheers and a lot of loud boos rang out. Finally, when the Lakers starters were announced, the fans went crazy. Hillary got to her feet, cheering and shouting as loud as anyone. Amused at her enthusiasm, Brandon enjoyed watching her as much as the game. Each time the Lakers scored, her feet left the ground, and she constantly shouted orders at the players, as though she were the head coach.

A couple of times, Brandon had to pull her back into her seat. He couldn't believe how into the game she was. She was just as knowledgeable about basketball as she was about football. He excused himself to go to the bathroom and hoped they wouldn't kick her out of the arena while he was gone. A few times she'd come dangerously close to the edge of the floor, which was a serious infraction of the rules.

Only minutes after Brandon had hurried back to his seat, he seemed somewhat distracted, Hillary noted. He appeared to be paying more attention to the scoreboard than the game. Puzzled by his behavior, she immediately addressed his distraction. "You seem awfully quiet. Is there something wrong?"

"No, babe. I'm fine," he said without taking his eyes off the scoreboard. She got a little miffed when he didn't bother to look at her when he answered.

Above the noise of the crowd, she heard him call her name. When she turned to look at him, he gestured for her to look at the scoreboard. Her face broke out in a blinding smile as she read the ticker tape.

HILLARY, I LOVE YOU.

Grabbing him around the neck, she hugged him with all her strength. "Honey, that was so sweet of you," she squealed excitedly. "When did you arrange for that?"

"Before we went to Santa Barbara. I wasn't sure when it would come up, so that's why I gave the scoreboard my undivided attention," he said apologetically.

"That explains it. I felt a little ignored. Thank you. That was very special!"

"Lady, you were so into the game, I felt like we were on different planets. You've got nerve talking about being ignored."

She winked at him. "I apologize."

He winked back. "I accept."

With two minutes left in the fourth quarter, the Pistons were up by four, but the Lakers had possession of the ball. While running a fast break, the Lakers point guard passed the ball to the other end. *Swish!* Nothing but net; two more points for the Lakers. The scorer had been fouled and the possibility for a three-point play was at hand. As the scorer poised himself at the foul line, he appeared to be praying.

Swish! Another point scored for the Lakers. All the fans seemed nervously intense. Even Hillary held her breath. Grabbing Brandon's hand, she squeezed it tightly.

With less than a minute on the clock, the Lakers began to play tough defense. One of the top defensive players stripped the ball from one of the Pistons. As he spotted one of the star forwards who was out on the wing leading the pack, he sailed the ball toward him. The forward caught the pass effortlessly. When the ball handler took the ball straight to the defender, the defender moved slightly.

Slam dunk! Lakers by one.

With twenty-five seconds left on the clock, a timeout was taken by the Pistons. After the timeout, the visiting team took the ball at midcourt and was able to get the ball into play. Swarming all over the ball handler like a hive of busy bees, the Lakers made a tough defensive stand, holding the Pistons in check until the game-ending buzzer sounded.

Lakers by one!

Hillary and the rest of the fans were on their feet, going ape. When she released Brandon's hand, he shook it out vigorously to get circulation back into it. It felt as though she'd been holding on to it for dear life.

She laughed as she pulled his hand to her mouth and planted a healing kiss onto it. "Brandon, I thought I was going to perish in the last seconds of that game!"

He flashed her an amused smile. "I know. I thought my hand would, too."

She gave him a smug look. "I'm sorry, honey, but I thought you were invincible," she harassed as they made their way to the exit.

He laughed heartily. "I was until I met you," he countered.

"Do you remember my warning to you the first night we met?"

He grinned. "How could I forget it? I knew I was in trouble when you warned me I might not be able to handle you."

"Honey, I gave you fair warning. It's not my fault that you decided not to take heed."

"I have no regrets, Hill. These have been the best times of my life. I find you quite stimulating." She rewarded his praises with a staggering kiss.

As Brandon neared the freeway, he looked over at Hillary. "Your place, or mine?"

His question surprised her. She thought for sure that he'd be tired of her by now. "Mine, if you're going to stay all night."

"And if I'm not?"

She shrugged her shoulders. "Still mine."

"I thought so."

She rubbed his thigh. "Honey, we have to work tomorrow. We'd have to get up way too early if we go to your place. I want to sleep as late as I can tomorrow. We've had an action-packed weekend."

He placed his hand over hers. "Okay, but this weekend we stay at my place."

"Are you asking or telling me?" she asked playfully.

"I'm telling you, babe."

She slipped her hand under his shirt and growled. "I love it when you take charge." His smile was sultry.

He pulled off the freeway and stopped at a service station. While Hillary sat quietly in the car, fighting sleep, Brandon filled the gas tank. The oily smells in the air around the station made her nauseous. As she thought about the ticker-tape message, she was sure he really did love her. *He let the whole world know tonight,* she mused happily. Of course, no one had a clue for whom that message was meant.

She laughed. Then fear suddenly crept in. She couldn't help wondering how long this would last. It was too much of a fairy tale. All her life she had prayed to find someone to love her as much as he appeared to. And now that she had, she knew the real test was drawing near. She looked at him through fearful eyes as he re-entered the car. Would he rise to the occasion, or would he run scared, especially when her schedule got super-crazy? If she were to reach superstardom, would she lose her handsome lover? She had to wonder.

* * *

At home, in her cheerful kitchen, Hillary fixed Brandon and herself a small snack consisting of fruit and cheese. They drank hot Earl Grey tea before retiring for the night. After a shower with Brandon, she nestled her head onto his chest. While the radio played slow golden oldies, they somehow managed to fall asleep without even attempting to make love. There was more to their relationship than sex, they'd both come to know. They'd become best friends, as well as lovers.

Besotted with more than just the Monday morning blues, Hillary dragged herself down the corridor to her office. Though she'd taken a couple of aspirin before she'd left home, her throat still killed her and her skin felt hot and clammy. In fact, her body ached all over. She attributed her health problems to the many changes of climate she'd experienced in the last few weeks.

With too many projects to tackle, she'd found it necessary to come to work. She rarely allowed herself to get behind in her tasks. After working diligently the whole morning, she paused for a few minutes to accept a call from Michael Goldstein.

"Good morning, Michael," she rasped.

"Morning. Just called to tell you that everything is settled. The contract is ready to sign, but I still need to set a time for us to meet. Aaron worked closely with me on the contract. He's very satisfied with the outcome. We're going to meet with St. John on Friday. As soon as I can set some time aside for you and me to discuss the terms, I'll call you back. Tentatively, I'm looking at Wednesday for us. Will that work for you?"

Hillary checked her calendar. "As long as it's in the afternoon. We have a staff meeting every Wednesday morning."

"I'm going to schedule our meeting for two P.M. Should I need to change it, I'll call."

"Thanks, Michael. Have a good day."

"You, too, Hillary. *Ciao.*"

The call lifted her spirits, giving her the incentive to try to make it through the rest of the day. But a short break was what she needed now. After taking the elevator down to the employees' cafeteria, she purchased some hot soup, hoping it might make her feel better. Not wanting to pass her germs around, she opted to sit in a corner off by herself. As she sat quietly staring into space, Alex approached her.

Alex stood over her chair. "Hi, Hillary. How are you?"

She looked up at him and smiled weakly. "Hi, Alex," she rasped. "You look cheerful this morning. How's it going?"

Noticing the distressing rasp in her voice, Alex looked at her with disquietude as he pulled out a chair and sat down. "Hillary, are you sick?"

She nodded gingerly. "I have a sore throat."

"Why are you here at work?"

"I had a lot to accomplish, Alex. I've never been one to allow things to pile up."

"Is there anything I can help you with?"

She smiled, pleased with his offer. "Alex, I can handle it. I was able to clear up quite a few of my priority projects. If I work through the afternoon, I should be able to clear my desk completely."

Placing his folded hands on the tabletop, he told her all his good news. He also told her that Lois had shared with him the fact that she'd already talked to Hillary about them seeing each other.

"I'm proud of the changes you've made, Alex. And I think Lois is just wonderful."

They continued to converse for a while about him and Lois. Then she excused herself when the cafeteria began to buzz with the lunch crowd. Feeling weak, she walked slowly to the elevator and entered. As the elevator jerked into an upward motion, her stomach lurched violently. There was a wastepaper basket in one corner of the elevator and she reached it just in time, glad that no one was present to witness her gut-wrenching upheaval. Making it back to her office without any more difficulty, she settled in and worked on until the end of the day.

As soon as she entered the house, she fled to her bedroom. Once she'd stripped bare, she took a hot shower and donned a warm pair of flannel pajamas before climbing into bed. Not wanting to be disturbed, she turned off the ringer on the phone.

An hour later, after tossing and turning, unable to get comfortable, she slipped out of bed and searched through her medicine cabinet. Finding some medication from a previous bout with the flu, she popped two pills into her mouth and returned to bed. Immediately, the medicine caused her to become drowsy, which would probably allow her to sleep for several hours.

Awakening in the wee hours of the morning, she discovered that her body was bathed in perspiration and her pajamas were soaked through. When she got up to change into fresh nightclothes, she noticed the flashing signal on her answering machine, but she chose to ignore it. She was too sick to talk to anyone.

By late morning her temperature had risen to a dangerously high level. Recognizing she might be in the danger zone, she picked up the phone to call Brandon. When he answered, she told him how bad she felt and that she might be in real trouble. He promised to come right over and see her.

* * *

Arriving less than thirty minutes later, Brandon let himself into the house with the spare keys she kept in a special hiding place. Taking the steps two at a time, he rushed into the bedroom. Touching her forehead, he realized her illness was more serious than he'd originally thought. Her body burned with fever. Concerned for her health, he stroked her tenderly. "Don't worry, Hillary. I'll take care of everything."

With her cheeks flushed a bright red, she looked up at him and nodded.

Brandon rushed down to the kitchen, where he boiled water for tea. Once the tea brewed, he laced it with fresh lemon and a good dose of brandy. He would stay with Hillary until her fever broke and she was well enough to be back on her feet. He didn't care if he had to temporarily move in with her. He knew she might object to him staying with her for too long, but nothing would stop him from taking care of the woman he loved.

Back upstairs, Brandon positioned himself beside Hillary. "Sorry you feel so bad, babe. But I'm going to be here until you're all better."

She placed her hand over his. "No apology needed. I'm just glad you're here for me. I feel much better knowing you're going to see me through the worst of this."

As his eyes grew dark with longing, he lay down and pulled her snugly into his arms. "I'm happy you called on me, sweetheart, but I don't want to tire you out. Close your eyes and go to sleep. I'll be right here when you awaken."

Obeying his gentle command, Hillary closed her eyes, but she wasn't ready to fall asleep. Being in Brandon's arms was too exhilarating. Although she had fully intended to just lie there and enjoy the delicious warmth of his arms, the sandman was too overwhelming for her to combat. Snuggling up closer to Brandon's strong body, she allowed the sweet arms of sleep to sweep her up and carry her away.

Brandon was sleepy himself, but he couldn't tear his gaze away from her lovely face, the face he wanted to wake up to every morning. Hillary was a woman who was so refreshingly alive, and he didn't think he could go on without her in his life. Now that she was going to allow him to be there with her throughout her illness, he was going to make every moment of their time together stand for something good, something wonderful.

When Hillary hadn't shown any signs of getting better, Brandon had taken her to the emergency room at Columbia Hospital. Although her condition wasn't serious enough for her to be admitted, she'd been diagnosed with pneumonia. Along with being prescribed several medications, she'd been advised to have bed rest for the next few weeks.

Brandon had insisted that she recuperate at the beach house. He'd made arrangements for his housekeeper, Rosa, to help him with her care. Rosa was to come every day for four hours. If he needed to go out for something, he wanted someone there. He'd already made it known to her family that they were welcome to visit at any time.

Though she was now resting comfortably, her skin was still very pale. Allowed to have only clear liquids, she sat up in Brandon's bed as she sipped water through a straw. She felt hungry enough to eat, but she understood all too well that she hadn't gotten to the point where she could keep anything solid in her stomach, tolerating only a soda cracker or two. As she thought about all the trouble she had caused everyone, she knew that her life had been moving at too fast a pace. Normally, she got a lot of rest, but she and Brandon had been running fast and hard over the past few weeks.

Having been diagnosed with pneumonia in both lungs, she now knew she couldn't keep up this sort of pace. It made her question her physical ability to keep abreast of things when she got well enough to sign the recording contract. When her weakened body couldn't keep up with her speeding mind, she drifted into a light sleep.

Two hours later, when Brandon entered the room carrying an armload of magazines, she awakened. She smiled sweetly when she saw his cargo. "You plan to broaden my horizons while I'm here?"

He blew her a kiss. "I guess you could say that. I don't want you to get bored."

She blew him a kiss in return. "I could never be bored with you around."

Having already set up a table near the bed with her toiletry items neatly arranged, he set the magazines alongside the telephone. Anything that he thought she might need was right at her fingertips. As he looked at her, his heart filled with love and pride. She had a way of making him feel so good. She made every part of his life an exciting new adventure.

Cassie had packed a suitcase for Hillary, which she and Aaron had dropped off earlier in the morning before they'd gone in to work. Brandon had cleared some drawer space in his dresser for all of her things. Rosa was assigned the task of keeping her belongings clean and fresh.

Brandon pulled a pair of sea-blue silk pajamas from one of the drawers. Walking into the deep closet, he removed from a hangar the white satin quilted bed jacket he'd purchased for her. Tenderly, he separated Hillary from the robe she'd put on. Cassie had earlier assisted her with a bath. Helping her into the pajamas, he then wrapped her upper body in the beautiful bed jacket.

Instantaneously, she fell in love with it. "Brandon, this jacket is beautiful! Thank you. You're going to have to stop spoiling me."

He shifted his eyes toward her and smiled. "Never!"

She shifted her body. "I'm going to have to be careful not to think out loud."

"I intend to pamper you throughout your stay. Anything that you mention you'd like to have, I'm going to find a way to get for you. So do be careful of what you ask."

Making sure it was the doorbell that he'd heard, he momentarily halted his conversation, waiting to see if the bell rang again. "Someone's at the door, Hill. Rosa's at the market, so I'll have to get it. I'll be right back."

After they exchanged a few pleasant remarks, Brandon showed Eric to the master bedroom, but he didn't enter the room with him. He'd made it a point to respect her right to privacy. He'd told her family and friends they could visit her in his home and he'd meant it. He still wasn't keen on St. John, but he never failed to show him respect.

Eric walked into Brandon's bedroom. Although Brandon had only been gone a matter of seconds, Hillary had already nodded off. Sitting down in the chair near her bed, Eric studied her sleeping form. The expression on his face clearly showed that he was worried about her, not so much about her singing career, but about what she had become to him. He considered her to be a wonderful person and a dear friend. Hillary had shaken up everyone at S&J Records, all for the better, he thought.

He'd been shocked when Michael Goldstein had told him Hillary had taken ill, and he'd dropped everything to come see about her. Although her illness would delay contract signings, her health and well-being were what concerned him most.

As her mouth was very dry, Hillary awakened to reach

for her cup of water. When she saw Eric sitting next to the bed, she gave him a wide smile. "Hello, Eric. What are you doing here? You must have tons of other things to attend to, but I do appreciate you coming all the way out here to see me."

He smiled back. "My main concern is for you. I came to see how you were doing for myself. How do you feel?"

"Much better, thank you. I can't remember when I've felt this awful." She still had a difficult time speaking, and her voice was noticeably raw and raspy.

Eric recognized her difficulty and he got to his feet. "I wish you well, Hillary, but I don't think I should stay any longer. You don't sound so hot to me. I want you to rest, but I promise to see you again, real soon."

She reached her hand out to him. "I'm sorry about this. Sorry we didn't get the contracts signed," she said, near tears. "I hope this delay hasn't caused you and your company too much anguish."

His heart went out to her. "There'll be plenty of time for contract signings. We still want to sign you if that's what you're worried about. You still possess a golden throat even though it's not doing that great right now. Don't worry, the songbird will return."

As he left the room, she thought of how lucky she was to have so many people who genuinely cared for her. So many of her family members and friends had already been out to see her even though Brandon's house was so far removed from the city.

Rosa entered the bedroom as Eric exited. Hillary and Rosa had taken to one another within moments of meeting. Hillary thought Rosa was as sweet as she was round. Decorated with Spanish ornaments, her long, black braided hair shone like the midnight sun. Hillary found her to be the typical motherly type, loving and caring. Rosa kept Brandon's house spotless, and she loved to cook for him as well, she'd told Hillary with pride.

Rosa sat in the chair at the side of the bed. As she talked to Hillary, her heavy Spanish accent made it hard for Hillary to follow all her comments. "*Señorita,* you are too skeeny. I have to put some meat on your bones. Men don't like skeeny women. They like to have something to hold on to. Like these love handles of mine."

Hillary laughed at the expressive way Rosa gestured when she spoke. "Rosa, are you telling me Brandon likes his women pleasingly plump?"

Rosa paused to think before she spoke. "*Señorita,* I've never seen any other woman here in this house but you, so I would not be able to answer that question."

Hillary felt ashamed of herself. She didn't want Rosa to think she was pumping her for information about Brandon's personal life. "I'm not trying to pry into Brandon's private business, Rosa. I was just joking. Please don't get the wrong impression."

Rosa shook like jelly when she laughed. Hillary could see all of her white teeth. "No, *señorita,* I did not think that. You are much too kind for that sort of thing. Do not fret now," she said, patting Hillary on the legs. "You must get well."

Hillary responded by hugging her warmly. "Thank you, Rosa, for understanding."

Brandon stood in the doorway, watching Hillary and Rosa hugging one another. The affection between them gave him a warm rush. Stepping into the room, he cleared his throat. "Rosa, are you taking good care of my lady?"

"Of course, *Señor* Blair. She is a very special young lady. She is very pretty, too. You should hurry and make her your bride."

Brandon was embarrassed at her comment, even though he knew she always spoke her mind. "You take care of Hillary's needs and I'll take care of the rest," he said jokingly.

"Just don't let her get away. If you do, you will be miserable for the rest of your life."

He continued to laugh as he reached out to give her a hug. After returning his affection, Rosa moved out of the bedroom.

Brandon positioned himself alongside Hillary. "Sorry about that, babe, but Rosa has always been blunt. She's a hopeless matchmaker, as well."

"No apology needed. Speaking of blunt . . . I now understand why you and Rosa get along so well."

He laughed. "You should talk, Miss Blunt America." They both fell into laughter as she attempted to slap his arm.

His eyes growing heavy with sleep, he snuggled up next to her and rested his head on one of the pillows. "I'm happy we're together, Hill. I want to take care of you. More than that, I want you to get well. I don't like seeing you feel so poorly."

He couldn't help remembering how her lovely face had sweated so profusely just a few short hours ago. Those moments when she'd burned with a fever high enough to kill a horse were the worst moments he'd ever experienced. He'd never felt that vulnerable in his life. He was so glad that she was here in his bed with him and not lying in some hospital fighting for her precious life. Until now, he'd never known that pneumonia could be treated at home. When the diagnosis had first come, he was sure her doctor was going to admit her to the hospital, but he was relieved to know that her condition wasn't as bad as he'd initially thought. Finally, when the doctor had said he could take her home, he'd had a hard time believing it, but wasted no time in whisking her out of there.

He kissed both of her eyelids. "You're looking a tad better, love. Can I get you anything?"

She played with a lock of his hair. "Nothing at all. I

just feel so sleepy all the time and I'm easily exhausted. I can barely keep my eyes open."

He picked up one of her medicine bottles. "See that little red label?" She nodded. " 'May cause drowsiness' is what it says. Don't fight sleep, Hill. The more you rest, the quicker you're apt to heal. You want to take the bed-jacket off?"

She sat up so that he could help her remove the jacket. "It's so pretty, but I don't think you're supposed to sleep in it. It's for looking cute when you have company."

He grinned. "You're cute with or without the bed jacket. Come here and fall into these arms, woman. We could both use a long nap."

She looked up at him in adoration. "Thanks for being such a great nurse."

Hillary felt much better as she lay in the center of the bed staring into the fireplace. Brandon kept a constant fire going to make sure she didn't catch a chill. As she allowed her eyes to drink in the magnificence of the room, she recalled Brandon telling her that he had designed the entire house. She was proud of his artistic and architectural talents. The magnificent room fit his personality to a T. While her thoughts drifted into a wonderful fantasy, with her as the mistress of the Blair castle, Brandon appeared in the doorway. He brought her fantasy to an abrupt halt before it really had a chance to take on a life of its own.

Looking sexy as ever, he leaned against the doorjamb. "Hill, you have an appointment today with Dr. Caine. Are you feeling up to it?" he asked soberly.

She gave him an enthusiastic smile. "I'm dying to get outside. I need to feel the sun on my face."

"I know, babe. A flower can't blossom without the sun."

After helping her bathe, he made sure she was good and dry before allowing her to don her clothing. She was growing stronger, but she still tired easily. When he saw her struggling with her hair, he gently removed the brush from her shaking hands and brushed her hair briskly. He then tied it back with a decorative band. He handed her the morning dosage of medication along with a glass of juice, and she pulled a face but took it anyway.

Her honey-brown eyes shone with happiness as she thoroughly enjoyed the ride into the city. She'd missed all the beautiful sights the outside had to offer. Seeing nature's splendor in a whole new light made her appreciate it all the more.

The checkup went just fine. Dr. Caine was quite pleased with her progress and he told Brandon that he was doing a fine job taking care of her. Dr. Caine changed some of her medications and discontinued others. After another appointment was scheduled, she and Brandon left the office.

Sixteen

During the drive, Brandon kept checking her for signs of fatigue, but she showed none. Her personality bubbled over with joy, and her eyes were as bright as sunshine, which had helped him to make a snap decision. Brandon smiled as he pulled the car to a halt in front of a beautifully quaint house located in a well-to-do Los Angeles suburb. The lawns around the white stucco house were neatly trimmed, and a variety of flowers and plants bloomed all over the property.

Mystified, Hillary looked over at him. "Brandon, where are we?" Waiting for his answer, she took in the beauty of the fall flowers that graced the long walkway.

Studying her carefully, he blew out a short gust of breath. "Hill, it's time you meet my parents. Are you up to it?"

She was deeply touched. "You bet I am." She suddenly looked nervous. "I hope they approve of me."

He gripped her hand gently. "Hill, they will love you as much as I do."

A petite, smiling woman wearing glasses, her hair done up neatly, answered the door. When she saw her son, her face lit up like a Christmas tree. At that very moment Hillary knew from whom Brandon had inherited that disarming smile. Anna Blair, a retired schoolteacher, opened the door wide to allow them entry. Brandon quickly introduced Hillary to his mother.

Mrs. Blair smiled as she took Hillary's hands. "Hillary, it's so nice to meet you. Brandon has told me so much about you. You're every bit as lovely as he has said."

"Thank you." Hillary felt Anna's kindness and warmth deep inside her heart.

She smiled at Hillary again. "Dad is in the back watching television. Son, he'll be pleased to see you and your lovely friend."

David Blair stood when he noticed that Brandon had a guest with him. Brandon once again made the necessary introductions.

"Hello, young lady," David said in a booming voice, his six-foot-four frame dwarfing Hillary. "You are beautiful!" She blushed. "Come sit down and make yourself comfortable," David offered kindly. "I'm glad we're getting a chance to finally meet you. Brandon's been telling us for ages that he was going to bring you by to see us."

"Mr. Blair, it's nice to meet you and your wife. Thank you for welcoming me so warmly." It made her feel good to know that Brandon had been talking about her to his parents.

As the Blairs smiled at her, Hillary took special note of the resemblance between Brandon and his father. But the credit for that disarming smile of his definitely went to his mother.

It took very little time for Hillary to become relaxed in her new surroundings. The Blairs made her feel comfortable in their lovely home, and they seemed to be a very genuine couple. As genuine as their handsome son, she mused quietly.

The Blairs had been watching a taped recording of a big awards show on television. Mrs. Blair and Hillary engaged in animated conversation, discussing the latest gossip they'd heard about some of the Hollywood stars.

Their conversation never became dull or awkward as they made flattering comments about the stunning fashions worn by the female stars.

Brandon was seated at a large game table talking to his father, a real estate agent, about business. From time to time Brandon stole glances at the two women in his life. He was thrilled to see how well they were getting along.

Quite a long time had passed when Brandon checked his watch. Having kept Hillary out much longer than he had intended, he immediately stood up. "Babe, I think we need to be going. I've already kept you out far too long."

Hillary was saddened by the thought of leaving. She was having a wonderful time. "I am feeling a little tired," she said in a resigned voice. "Maybe we should go."

Brandon directed his attention to his parents. "I'm sorry, but we're going to have to leave now. Hillary is still recovering from the illness that I told you about." Brandon's parents rose to their feet.

Anna draped her arm around Hillary's shoulder. "My dear, I'm so happy to have met you. Please come again, soon." She then laughed. "It is so nice to meet someone shorter than myself for a change," she admitted merrily. Brandon and his father busted up laughing.

Anna Blair was barely a couple of inches taller than Hillary, but she was a woman who stood as tall as any man. Her humanity and service to the community easily made her a giant among men.

Her eyes twinkling with glee, Hillary smiled at Anna. "I find that being short has its advantages." She then winked at Anna, who pulled her in close and hugged her cheek.

Hillary and Brandon left with the promise of returning when Hillary was stronger.

Hillary fell asleep within minutes of getting into the

car. Looking at her with concern, Brandon wondered if he'd risked her health by not taking her home right away. Reaching over to feel her forehead, he decided she was warmer than she should be and cursed himself for being so insensitive. He'd been dying to take her to his parents' house, but now felt that he should've waited till she was fully recovered. Picking up speed, he got her to the house as quickly as safety would permit.

She didn't awaken until he unbuckled the seat belt. Seeming dazed, she looked around her to see where they were. "We're home already?"

Brandon took special note of the word "home," glad she thought of it as such. "Yes, pretty lady, we're home."

He wanted to carry her into the house, but she insisted on walking. Inside, he had a hard time convincing her that she needed to go back to bed, but she reluctantly agreed. Having brought his favorite book of poetry into the bedroom with him, Brandon lay beside her in bed.

While reading several poems to her, his favorite being "How Do I Love Thee," she drifted into a peaceful sleep. After stoking the fire, Brandon quietly removed himself from the room.

On the couch, half-asleep, when the phone rang, Brandon grabbed it quickly, hoping it hadn't disturbed Hillary. "Hello."

"Brandon, this is Mrs. Houston. How is our daughter doing today?"

"Hello, Mrs. H. Hillary is doing just fine. She had her check-up today and Dr. Caine was pleased with her progress. She's asleep as we speak."

"I'm happy to hear she's doing so well. Her dad and I would like to visit tomorrow. Will that be okay?"

"We would love for you to come out. Hillary will be eager to see you."

Alice gave him an approximate arrival time before they rang off. Returning to the bedroom to check on his sleeping beauty, Brandon found her still very much asleep. Without disturbing her, he covered her up and went back to the living room.

The next few days brought Hillary more company than she could handle. Her parents were happy to see how well she looked and they told Brandon he was doing a wonderful job. Her sisters visited later in the week, and Cassie and Aaron had been to see her several times already. Brandon had even tolerated Eric St. John a few more times. After St. John's last visit, Brandon realized Eric really did have her best interest in mind. Brandon's whole attitude changed toward St. John, and he even told him to come back whenever time permitted.

St. John was happy to have gained Brandon's trust, feeling things would be much easier to deal with if Brandon cooperated when Hillary actually started recording. A disgruntled lover almost always posed problems.

For the next week Brandon dedicated himself to caring for Hillary. Rosa prepared delicious meals for them to eat. Though Rosa was used to cooking her native food, she was very competent in preparing nutritious meals that Hillary could tolerate. Rosa promised Hillary that when she was well enough she was going to prepare her a grand Mexican feast. Three weeks passed before Hillary was cleared to return to work.

Seated on the terrace with Hillary parked on his lap, Brandon held on to the woman he loved, dreading her departure. The surf crashed against the rocks below with torrential force while the sun hovered low in the sky, poised to set behind the horizon.

He lifted her chin. "I have an idea. Why don't you lease your place out and move out here with me? It's already been proven that we can live together harmoniously."

She shook her head. "That's not going to happen," she said with a firmness that would brook no argument from anyone other than Brandon.

"Can you tell me why it's not going to happen?"

She brought her eyes level with his. "I don't feel that I have to explain my reasons, although there are many. Living with a man is just not something that I'm interested in."

He eyed her intently. "What *are* you interested in? Are you holding out for a marriage proposal?"

If she'd thought he was serious, she would've been offended. But the laughter she saw in his eyes defied any seriousness on his part. Playfully, she covered his eyes with her hands. "I think you know me better than that, Mr. Blair. If you don't, shame on you. If I'd been holding out for a proposal of marriage, there would've been no free samples."

He looked shocked. "What the hell's that supposed to mean?"

She got up from his lap. "Whatever you want it to mean. I'm going to go to bed now. I want to go home first thing in the morning. I miss my place something awful."

He would've liked to have the chance to argue the points she seemed to be trying to make, but he knew by the look on her face that Hillary wasn't going to give him another ounce of play regarding her reasoning on the subject of them living together.

With nothing but males surrounding her at the meeting for the signing of her contract, Hillary might have been somewhat intimidated if two of her friends and strongest allies, Brandon and Aaron, hadn't attended the meeting with her. Both men were dressed to the nines, and she was extremely pleased with their very professional look.

Dressed in a smart-looking dark blue power suit and a crisp white shirt, Hillary looked sophisticated and classy. She'd recently had her hair cut and styled in feathered layers. Loaded with body, her silky chestnut-brown hair bounced freely about her shoulders each time she moved her head. Dainty diamond studs twinkled in her ears.

Michael Goldstein had the rapt attention of everyone present as he cited the terms that Hillary had asked to be included in her contract. When he stated that Hillary had advised him that she would not agree to do any performances in or near her native Pennsylvania, everyone appeared puzzled by her course of action.

Although Brandon was just as stunned by this highly unusual clause, especially since she grew up in Pennsylvania, he felt that this wasn't the time or the place to question her business decisions. He would wait for her to explain it if and when she decided to.

Hillary stood up when Goldstein finished making his inspiring presentation. She smiled as she placed her hands behind her back. "I want to thank you all for the support and encouragement you've given me through this entire ordeal. And I use the word 'ordeal' because that's exactly what it's been for me. As many of you know, I became ill, which delayed things a lot longer than expected. For a person who's just beginning to realize her lifelong dream of becoming a recording artist, 'pneumonia' is truly a curse word, worse than any four-letter word I've ever heard." Everyone laughed.

"However, the ordeal is behind me now and I'm ready to forge ahead. I'm healthy, I'm happy, I'm excited, and I'm extremely proud to become a member of the S&J

recording family. Now that all parties concerned have accepted the terms and conditions of the contract set forth, I'm ready to get on with the program. If someone will kindly hand me an ink pen, I'll be more than happy to sign on the dotted line."

St. John removed a gold pen from his breast pocket as he came forward. "Before Hillary signs her contract, I'd like to say a few words. As Hillary has stated, this has been some ordeal, but it's been one of the most worthwhile ordeals I've ever gone through. I want and need Hillary to know that her health was always our first concern here at S&J Records. Of course we wanted to sign her, but more important, we wanted her to get healthy, because we consider her a friend and not just someone who's going to make us tons of money. Hillary, honey, we wish you the best of luck. We're going to keep our promise of making you a superstar. And you get to keep the gold pen for when you have to sign all those millions of autographs!" Finished with his speech, St. John hugged Hillary and handed her the pen.

"Thank you, Eric. I'm going to hold you to your promise, and I know you're going to hold me to my end of the bargain, which is to do my very, very best to strive for excellence for this company and for myself. Thank you for the extraordinary gold pen."

As she signed on the dotted line, she saw that the pen was engraved with her initials. Tears fell from her eyes.

As a surprise Brandon had arranged a small, intimate reception for after the contract signing. Hillary's parents and two of her sisters were present, as well as Cassie. Some of her coworkers also showed up for the reception. Mr. Asher, Lois Jacobs, and Alexander Cash represented Atlantic Pacific Airlines, along with several others. Everyone was very proud of her as she worked the room like a celebrated star, but Alice and Jackson were the proudest of their youngest. Hillary's sisters were beaming, as well.

The buffet-style table held a variety of hors d'oeuvres and an assortment of other delectable finger foods. Plump, pink shrimp and lemon wedges rested on a bed of ice chips. Small glass bowls of cocktail sauce were available for dipping. Delicious-looking pinwheel sandwiches filled with different meats were stacked high on silver platters. An array of julienned vegetables rallied around a scalloped bowl of dill salad dressing. The relish tray held black and green olives, pickles, and other pickled delights. In the center of the table, a huge cake decorated with buttercream icing and filled with lemon custard was shaped like a record. All sorts of drinks, alcoholic and nonalcoholic, were being served at the host bar.

The guests milled around the buffet table while Hillary had a private moment with her mother, father, and two sisters, Diane and Jean.

Jackson Houston wiped away his wife's and three daughters' tears. "Come here, my beautiful girls," he commanded, gathering all four women into his arms. "I'm glad these are happy tears we're spilling. I hereby proclaim today as 'Hillary Houston's Day,'" he exclaimed. "We're all so proud of you."

In adoration, Hillary looked up at her father. "I need to tell you what's so awesome about all of this. When I pursued a singing career before, I stayed sick with worry all the time. Then I let go of it completely. When I least expected it, my prayers were all answered. Is that awesome or what? This has been one incredible adventure, and it's only just the beginning."

Alice kissed her daughter's cheek. "Sometimes that's how it is, Hillary. You just have to know when to let go and let God. He does things in His own time. This is by no means luck. Your good fortune is an *undisguised* blessing, as is your beautiful voice."

Hillary's eyes misted up again. "Oh, Mom, that was a lovely thing to say."

"It was, Mom," Diane seconded. "And it's the truth. Well, little sister, looks like you're on your way to stardom." Diane hugged Hillary as she conveyed her sincere congratulations. "I can hardly wait to hear your first song."

"It's my turn now," Jean stated, hugging Hillary to her. "Hillary, baby, I know you're going to be a star and I also know that you're never going to forget where you came from. Keep it real, baby sister."

"Thanks, family. Speaking of keeping it real, I better mingle with some of my other guests. I don't want them to think I've turned into a *snobbish diva* already." Everyone laughed as Hillary left the family group.

Hillary stopped and chatted briefly with several people as she worked the room like a natural-born celebrity. Then she went in search of the man with the raven-black eyes and the devastatingly beautiful smile.

Hillary pulled Brandon along with her when she went to chat with Alex and Lois, but she could tell that Brandon wasn't particularly pleased by Alex's presence. Though he'd accepted their newfound friendship for her sake, he still didn't like Hillary involving herself with Cash.

"I think you two have met," Hillary said. "Alex, I'm sure you already know that Brandon isn't my lawyer. I wanted to clear things up myself and make the formal introductions. Brandon Blair, this is Alexander Cash."

Alex had the good grace to look ashamed. "I'm really sorry for being less than contrite with you. I'm also sorry for the pain and discomfort I've caused Hillary. She has accepted my apology and I hope that one day you can do the same."

Although it came hard for him, Brandon let down his guard long enough to shake Alex's hand. His gracious gesture put Alex at ease, but Hillary was disappointed that Brandon hadn't said whether he accepted Alex's apology or not. She wasn't about to push the issue, since he did at least shake his hand.

Hillary and Lois hugged each other. "You're looking great, Lois. I see that you got your hair lightened. The color looks really good on you." Hillary tugged at Brandon's jacket. "Honey, I know you remember Lois. She's the receptionist in the PR department."

Brandon smiled broadly at Lois. "Of course I do. She helped me win you over by letting me put all those flowers in your office, and I've talked to her on the phone a few times since then. It's nice to see you again, Lois. Thanks for coming to help us celebrate Hillary's record deal."

Besides all the good food and drink served at the reception, Hillary made it extra special when she agreed to do a short performance for her guests. All in all, the reception turned out to be a great success!

While Brandon fixed them something hot to drink, Hillary kicked her shoes off and curled herself up on her sofa. Moisture pooled in her eyes as she reflected back on the day's events, which just happened to be the most thrilling events of her life. Everything had gone as smooth as silk; she had officially been signed to a major recording contract by a major studio.

Brandon brought her out of her reverie with a start when he set two cups of hot tea down on the coffee table. "I have to get the cake. I'll be right back."

Hillary nodded as she reached for the cup. Before she could take the first sip, Brandon appeared with two slivers of cake on one cake plate. He put the plate down before he took a seat beside her. Pinching off a piece of the cake, he held it up to her mouth. She nibbled at his fingers before she accepted the delicious-looking morsel.

He grinned. "You better be careful there, Hill. Sucking on a man's fingers can get you into a heap of trouble."

Her eyes flirted with him. "I like trouble. In fact, my middle name is trouble, big boy," she growled, giving him her best Mae West imitation.

Brandon laughed heartily as he pulled her onto his lap. "I see that I'm going to have to give you something to calm you down. You're on some kind of high there, aren't you, girl?"

She inhaled deeply. "A natural high, sweetie."

He touched her nose with his fingertip. "Well, how does it feel to be validated as a recording artist by a highly successful record company, beautiful lady?"

She placed her left hand over her heart. "Magnificent! I still can't believe this is happening to me, for me. If it's a dream, I don't ever want to wake up. With Michael Goldstein acting as my agent and attorney, I feel as though my career is in extremely capable hands. I was concerned about Michael wearing both hats, but Aaron assured me that I had nothing to worry about. He said that it's not an unacceptable practice, that's it's done all the time. With you and Aaron there to look out for my best interest as well, I'm in a win-win situation."

He kissed her nose. "I think you can put all your worries behind you. Aaron would never tell you something that he himself didn't believe to be true. Goldstein's a highly revered representative of the entertainment world. I'm sure he'll do you proud. When do you have to be in the studio?"

Her eyes lit up like the crown jewels. "First thing on Monday morning. I can't wait. I'm going to work the late afternoons at Atlantic Pacific until I see how things go. Mr. Asher is allowing me to make my own schedule. He's also given me the freedom to work on my projects at home when necessary. Someone else will handle my traveling schedule for the next month, which brings us to the end of the year, anyway."

"Looks like you've got all the bases covered. Now why don't you lay back and relax. Your delicious body has a few bases I'd like to cover. Maybe I'll even score a home run."

Dressed casually in jeans, a UCLA sweatshirt, and white Nikes, Hillary had just about finished cleaning out her desk. Finding it next to impossible to handle both careers effectively, after several weeks of trying her best, she'd decided to take six months' leave of absence to begin the contract she'd signed a few weeks back with S&J Records.

Tears threatened as she looked around the room. With fondness, she thought about all the friends that had been made within these four walls. Hillary knew without a doubt that she'd miss working at Atlantic Pacific Airlines.

Mr. Asher popped his head in the door of Hillary's office. "Hi, may I come in for a second?" he asked softly.

She swatted the tears from her eyes. "Certainly. I'm just about done in here."

Mr. Asher entered the office and sat in the chair across from her desk. She sat in the chair next to him. "Hillary," Mr. Asher began in an emotion-choked voice, "we're all going to miss you. Remember we'll always be here if you need us. You've been a tremendous asset to this company. If you ever get blue, or just plain tired of the hustle and bustle of show business, remember that you have a home with us."

Hillary's eyes sparkled with unshed tears. "Mr. Asher," she said, her voice as emotional as his, "I couldn't work for a finer company, or have a finer boss. You've been my friend and my confidant, right from the start. I will always remember your kindness. I'll never forget all the valuable things you've taught me over my short tenure with this company. Just to name a few qualities, your fairness, your veracity, and your humanity are unrivaled. You took me under your wing and provided me with the space to spread my own wings far and wide. Mr. Asher, this is by no means good-bye. I expect to see you at all my California concerts and any others you can make. You will have tickets for each and every performance."

She leaned over and embraced him. He responded warmly to her gesture, then got up and rapidly departed the room.

Brandon bumped into Mr. Asher as he was on his way out. He could see the tears and the sadness in the large man's eyes. It was best not to approach him at this emotional time, he decided, sure that he and Hillary had just said their farewells. Brandon stepped into Hillary's office, only to find her as emotional as Asher had been.

Gathering her into his arms, he tried to comfort her. "Pretty lady, it's not the end of the world. Friendships are forever."

While Brandon took her things to the car, Hillary went from office to office saying her farewells. Knowing what a hard time she'd have saying good-bye, she'd wanted to pack up when everyone was gone, but Brandon had convinced her that she'd only regret it later. Finding Lois and Alex together in his office, she smiled. Strangely enough, she thought, this was the second hardest encounter that she'd have to experience.

Hillary and Lois dissolved into tears as Alex watched them with a deep sadness in his eyes. He thought of how Hillary was responsible for his new satisfying life. She'd helped him to see the light. If she'd been a vindictive person, he wasn't sure where he would be right now. He certainly knew he wouldn't be having such a wonderful relationship with Lois.

Alex walked over to Hillary and put her hand in his. "Hillary, thank you for giving me a life. I'm going to miss your radiating warmth around here."

She choked back a sob. "Alex, I never dreamed I'd ever be saying this to you, of all people, but I'll miss you, too. And, Alex, I didn't give you a life. You did that all by yourself. I just pointed out alternative choices. Take care of Lois. Guys, stay in touch."

Hillary turned to Lois. "I'm honored that you consider me a friend, Lois. My home is open to both of you anytime you'd like to visit. I don't want our friendship to end here," Hillary said as the two women hugged each other again.

"I plan to call you often and see you whenever your schedule permits us to get together. Hillary, shine, shine, shine like the brightest star in the universe. We'll be out there cheering for you," Lois enthused.

Brandon was waiting in the reception area when Hillary emerged from Alex's office. Seeing the painful look in her eyes, he quickly took her into his arms again.

A slight cold front had worked its way into the Los Angeles area, a welcoming relief from an unexpected heat wave that had sent temperatures rising into the mid-eighties over the past two weeks. While a silver moon shone brightly on the sands of Malibu Beach, the heavy breeze blowing in from the Pacific Ocean was relatively warmer than normal for the lateness of the hour and for the time of year.

Dressed in jeans, sweaters, and sneakers, Brandon and Hillary walked hand-in-hand on the beach. Minutes before, they'd been relaxing in the house when Brandon had lured Hillary outside for a moonlit stroll. Their eyes sparkled with the love they'd found between them. After walking several yards, they ran back to the spot where they'd left their blanket. Dropping down onto the checkered blanket, they held each other closely as they watched the high tide roll in. Hillary felt so serene here in this familiar spot she'd come to love.

To ease the slight cramping, Hillary stretched her leg muscles. "We have to start walking more. It's so invigorating. For sure, it beats those strenuous workouts I pace myself through."

Brandon gave her entire body the once over. "Those strenuous workouts definitely pay high dividends. You look like a million bucks!" She laughed appreciatively.

Opening the small Styrofoam chest, Brandon removed a chilled bottle of sparkling cider and two crystal flutes. After pouring cider into the two glasses, he had to nudge Hillary to get her attention. She appeared to be caught up in the spell of the silver moon. When she finally looked his way, he handed her a filled glass.

"What shall we drink to?" she asked, smiling.

"Us," he stated simply. Clinking the glasses in a toast, they sipped their drinks.

Suddenly, Hillary sputtered, spraying Brandon with cider. Something hard had come into contact with her tongue. While looking down into the glass to examine its contents, she discovered the object that had nearly caused her to choke. Sticking her fingers into the crystal flute, she retrieved a gold ring fashioned with a breathtaking cluster of sea green emeralds and baguette diamonds. Emerald was her birthstone.

Looking at Brandon, who wore an enchanting smile, her honey-brown eyes, filled with love, outshone the dazzling moon above. Jumping up, she landed on him, knocking him back on the blanket. She kissed him until she was breathless.

"Oh, God. I don't know what to say. It's beautiful! It's not even my birthday yet. Thank you so much. You've just managed to surprise me for the umpteenth time. You are a total surprise package."

"You're deserving of every one of them." He pulled her on top of him, showing her just how much she deserved to have her life filled with awesome surprises. He kissed her just as ardently as she'd kissed him earlier.

Breathless from his kiss, she lowered her lashes. "I'm sorry about all the time that we've spent apart over the past few weeks, Brandon, but I've hardly had a chance to catch my breath. Things at the studio should calm down soon."

She'd been in the recording studio ten to twelve hours a day, sometimes longer. She was recording her first album, and the company was working hard to have it released by early spring. She was also working on a single to be released around the holidays, which were fast approaching.

Hillary frowned. "I knew this was a tough business before I got into it, but I don't think I fully realized how demanding it would be on my time. For a girl who likes to come and go as she pleases, I find myself totally tied down. But it's been all good. I feel as though I'm being rewarded for something that I love to do."

He brought her hand to his lips. "I know that the photo shoots for the album cover, public relation matters, tough recording sessions, and arranging and rearranging of music has been hard on you, as well as our time apart, but I'm confident it'll get better. Some things take more time than others."

It has to get better, he mused painfully. He was already half crazed by her absence. The thought of her being around so many men for hours on end made him even crazier. He had worked hard on his jealousy, but the more they were apart, the harder he was finding it to keep his jealousy at bay. He actually feared the insanity of his feelings.

Hillary smiled. "We've selected a beautifully written, brilliantly arranged song for the single cut that will be featured first. The album will be entitled *Soulful Serenade.* The single is entitled 'Destiny.' " The words of the song perfectly described how her life was turning out; both Brandon and singing were her destiny.

"The titles are beautiful, babe. And I do appreciate you making it a point to be with me as much as you can, but it's been tough. I really miss you."

She looped her arm through his. "You've been so supportive. I know our times together have been short, and that's why we need to get back to our celebration, Brandon. We have to make each and every second count."

After their premature celebration of her May birthday, Brandon took Hillary home. He had some plans to design for an early morning meeting, so he didn't go in.

Hillary dressed for bed and went downstairs to the family room, where she stretched out on the sofa. She was happy enough, but because she and Cassie rarely got to see each other anymore, she felt a little blue. It hurt her not to be able to share herself as much with Cassie, but the timing had been all wrong during the times they talked about getting together. Cassie wanted her to succeed, she knew, but Cassie had said that she didn't want her success to come between their friendship.

Brandon had been crying foul a lot, too, she thought, recalling all the times she'd had to cancel their plans. He hated sharing her, plain and simple. She knew he missed her, but she didn't like all the spats they'd been getting into lately. She was glad that their evening had been stress free. Calling a halt to the "woe is me" party she seemed to be throwing for herself, she went back upstairs.

Lying in bed, her thoughts sailed backward to the time

on the beach. Smiling, she stared at the beautiful ring Brandon had given her. She could hardly believe all the wonderful things that had happened for her. Despite all the hassles, she was thrilled with the way her life had turned out thus far.

While there were many others who believed in her singing talent, Eric was the one who'd given her the opportunity to test her wings. She'd been soaring for weeks now; her wings proved to be well beyond sturdy. Hillary had always hoped she could share her voice with the world; it was the only worthwhile thing she had to offer. With the type of money she'd now be earning, she could offer so much more. Homelessness was a major issue for her, especially in a country touted as the world's superpower. The eradication of child abuse, in any form, was another cause she championed.

There were others out there with dreams that mirrored her own and they were to be included in her plans. She hadn't been able to go on the road with the special choir established to bring the joy of music to those who needed it the most, but she still planned to be involved in some of their local performances. The choir prided themselves on performing at nursing homes and entertaining those hospitalized for one reason or another.

Sleep didn't come for hours. When it finally did, she hadn't come any closer to finding a solution to sharing equal time with family and friends. Somehow, someway, she'd soon find a way to spread her time evenly among those she loved the most, she vowed before falling into a deep sleep.

Seventeen

Christmas was a special time in the Houston house, a time when the family all got together, sharing their hopes and dreams while showing even more love toward one another. This Christmas was to be a special one. The entire Houston family would be together for the first time in several years.

It was a Houston tradition for the entire family to pick out the Christmas tree together. They were all in their cars, heading for the tree lot. Everyone was excited as they exchanged stories from past holidays. With the sisters all in one car, they laughed about the nickname Hillary was given when she was very small. Her sister, Diane, had dubbed her "Baby Newspaper" because Hillary could never keep the secret about the gifts they'd purchased for their parents. She gave the surprise away every year, and often tattled to her parents when the older girls had been up to no good.

After several minutes of traipsing around the tree lot, the Houstons discovered the most majestic tree. Besides being magnificently tall, the tree had green branches that were full and sweeping.

Although Hillary was excited about the tree, she couldn't stop thinking about Brandon. When her thoughts zeroed in on the Thanksgiving holiday they'd spent with his family, she smiled. She'd refused to allow herself to be bogged down with too many things over the Thanksgiving weekend. She'd spent the entire four days with him between the beach house and her town house. It appeared that he'd finally made his peace with her busy schedule, and her life seemed to be easier with his acceptance. They had talked a lot over the long weekend, and he'd told her that business at his company was brisk. He had so many new contracts he'd had to hire more people to help out. His company had grown strong and solvent. He had already made more money than he knew what to do with, but he was a businessman, he'd told her. Besides, he loved all the challenges with which his profession presented him.

Hillary couldn't believe how great things at the studio were going for her. Dedicated to her career, she made sure that she was a hit with all the employees at her recording company. The single was just about finished, and hopes reigned high for it to be released before year's end. Her smile was warm as she thought of how St. John always tried to make things as easy for her as possible at the studio, lending her support at every turn. The public relations department was working overtime at his request, in an effort to get her as much publicity as possible. He wanted Hillary Houston to be a household name by the end of the year. Knowing he had a winner, he couldn't wait to see the fruits of their labor, he'd told her on the phone earlier in the morning. St. John was looking forward to the day when she would emerge as a "superstar."

Jackson, his son, and four sons-in-law dragged the tree from the car to the porch. As he looked at the tree, Jackson informed Alice that he would have to trim the trunk.

"Let's get the ornaments out while they're preparing the tree trunk," Alice told her five daughters.

Before long, the men brought the tree into the house

and installed it in the usual spot, in front of the window that looked out onto the streets below. For the next couple of hours, the Houstons indulged themselves in adorning the beautiful tree with all the lovely ornaments they had accumulated over the years. Everyone agreed that they'd chosen the perfect tree for the Houston home. The tree was so tall and full it took them longer than usual to decorate it.

After Hillary hung a few ornaments, she went off to decorate the marble fireplace in the living room of the Houston home, using several sweeping tree branches they'd purchased at the tree lot.

Jackson finally climbed the ladder and placed the golden angel on top. After completing the task, he plugged in the lights, rendering everyone speechless. Dressed with the most beautiful and unusual ornaments, the tree was magnificent. At that moment everyone knew why Christmas was the favorite Houston holiday.

Later, when the sisters sat down to discuss all the things that had been happening in their lives, the men were already engaged in a conversation of their own, with sports the topic of their choice. Alice was kept busy attending to all the grandchildren's needs.

Seated on the sofa, her legs drawn up under her, Hillary was engrossed in telling Lenore and Lynne all about Brandon. "He's absolutely adorable."

"When are we going to meet Brandon?" Lenore asked.

"He'll be here later this evening," Hillary enthused. "I want you guys to behave yourselves and not tell any of my childhood secrets."

Lynne laughed at her request. "Hillary, are you going to deprive us of embarrassing you to no end?"

Hillary hit Lynne playfully. "If you embarrass me, it will serve you well to remember I have a few things I can tell Russ," Hillary countered.

"Sister dear, I don't think anything you could tell Russ

would shock him after all these years," Lynne said. Hillary leaned over and whispered something into her ear. Lynne screamed. "Oh, no, you can't tell that one! I promise to keep all your secrets."

Hillary gave a little smirk. "I thought you'd see it my way."

Lenore and Diane laughed. Even though Hillary hadn't spoken out loud, they all knew to what she'd alluded; a blind date whom Lynne couldn't get rid of no matter how hard she tried.

"Where's Cassie?" Lenore asked. "I thought we would've seen her by now."

"Don't worry. Cassie will be here. She's so much in love there are times when she doesn't even remember her own name," Hillary said, laughing.

"You should talk," Jean chimed in. "We used to hear from you every day, but since Brandon, we're lucky if we hear from you once a week."

"Come on, girls, we're not too old to remember how it is when you fall in love," Diane said. "Give the younger girls a break."

Maurice, Hillary's oldest nephew, wandered into the room and tugged at Hillary's sweater. "Auntie Hillary, are you going to play with us?"

Hillary kissed Maurice on the head as she pulled him onto her lap. "Sure, sweetie. What would you like to play?" He pulled her by the hand so that she would follow him into the den, where the rest of the children played.

Smiling, Hillary dropped to the carpeted floor to amuse herself by playing with her nephews and niece. The children chatted happily while she showed them how to work some of the toys she had bought for them. When Hillary and the children began to sing Christmas carols together, the rest of the family came in to the den to join in the fun. The entire family joined in singing carols and playing games with the kids.

A short time later, when the kids grew tired and sleepy, Hillary and her sisters put the kids to bed. When the five sisters finally came back to join the rest of the family, the other members of the clan were busy going through old picture albums from past family gatherings.

Having been asked about her singing career, Hillary told her family all the things that had happened up until now. Lenore and Lynne were really excited about Hillary's new career, even though Lenore teased Hillary about all the times she'd caught her using an eating utensil for a microphone. The family shared several laughs at Hillary's expense, then Lynne asked her to tell them more about Brandon. Before Hillary could even get into the story, the doorbell pealed. Jackson arose from his cozy seat by the fire to answer the door.

Hand-in-hand, Cassie and Aaron popped into the living room. "Hey, Houston girls! What's up with my favorite people?" Cassie sang out, hugging the women whom she thought of as sisters. They felt the same as she did as they exchanged hugs and kisses. With the greetings all done, Cassie introduced Aaron to the rest of her second family.

Aaron was very familiar with the Houston family that he'd already met. As though he were one of the family, he had no problem settling in.

Cassie was disappointed when she learned the kids were already in bed. "I've been looking forward to seeing them all day. I've already told Aaron so much about them. I guess I'll have to wait until tomorrow at Christmas dinner."

Looking very nervous, Brandon stood outside the Houston home waiting for someone to answer the door. There was so much noise inside the house it took a while for someone to hear the doorbell. Alice finally opened the door and Brandon hugged her warmly.

"Good evening, Mrs. H."

She smiled, loving the name by which he fondly called her. "Hello, Brandon. It's good to see you. Everyone is in the living room. Come on in."

Feeling somewhat uneasy, Brandon followed Alice into the living room. When the room fell into a hushed silence, his nervousness grew. Seeing the discomfort on his face, Hillary jumped up and ran over to kiss him.

"Hello, Brandon," everyone said in unison.

He smiled as he wiped his forehead with the back of his hand. "Hello, everyone. For a minute there I thought I'd forgotten to use deodorant." Peals of laughter rang out.

"We're sorry if we embarrassed you," Lenore said. "It's just that we've heard so many wonderful things about you, we weren't sure such a charming creature existed."

He flashed Lenore a disarming smile and she immediately saw for herself what Hillary had been raving about when she talked about his beautiful smile.

"I exist," he assured her. "You can touch me if you're still not sure." He could see that he'd broken the ice with his last comment, feeling relieved when everyone began to laugh. His nervousness had just disappeared.

Hillary took Brandon by the hand as she introduced him to the rest of her family. Hillary's brother, Henry, and her brothers-in-law, Jesse, Russ, J.R., and Taylor, nodded their approval to her as they extended their hands to give him a warm welcome. Hillary smiled sweetly at all her family and friends, feeling lucky to have such wonderful, caring people all in one room together.

Much later, when they decided to continue their caroling, Lenore played the piano while everyone sang. Jackson brought in hot homemade cider for everyone to drink, and Alice served the cookies and cinnamon rolls she'd baked early that morning.

Henry Houston could sing as well. His deep baritone voice was in contrast to Hillary's soprano and alto tones, but they blended together well. Lenore played "Silent Night" and Henry and Hillary put on a duet fit for royalty. The room was totally quiet while they sang.

When they sang the ending, "sleep in heavenly peace," their voices took on an angelic sound, blending together in perfect harmony. Their listeners rewarded them with a standing ovation.

"You guys need to make a record together. That was fantastic," Aaron said. "And, Lenore, you play a mean piano."

"There's a lot of talent in this family," Alice boasted.

Jackson nodded in agreement. "Each of our children is unique."

For one of the best parts of celebrating Christmas day, everyone was seated around the Houston table as Jackson passed the blessing. The table then became an assembly line as dishes passed from one person to the next. There was turkey, dressing, mashed potatoes, yams, a variety of green vegetables, and other assorted foods. Waiting on a sideboard to be consumed, sweet potato and apple pies and three huge double-layered chocolate cakes looked almost good enough to skip the main event.

There wasn't much time for conversation since everyone's mouth was kept full.

Over an hour later, with dinner over, everyone retired to the spacious living room of the Houston home, where Jackson played Santa, passing out all the gifts. When everyone had their packages, the sound of paper ripping could be heard followed by shouts of joy and loud laughter.

Suddenly, Jackson paled at one of the gifts he'd received from Hillary. He looked at her with tears in his eyes. "Little lady, is this what I think it is?" With tears in her own eyes, Hillary nodded.

As Jackson hurried over to the stereo, he saw that no

one had been paying attention to the emotionally charged exchange between himself and his youngest daughter. When the noisy room suddenly filled with soft, tantalizing music, it drew everyone's immediate attention.

"Destiny" was making its public debut.

As Hillary's sexy, sultry voice leaped from the stereo, everyone looked at one another as though they'd been hit by lightning. Only the music permeated the room until the record finished playing.

Full of emotion and excitement, Jean found her voice first. "Hillary, you've finished your single! Why on earth didn't you tell us before now?"

Hillary beamed all over. "I wanted it to be a surprise. It's just a demo cut, but I thought it would be the perfect Christmas gift to all the people I love so much."

"Hillary, you couldn't have chosen a nicer surprise," Alice enthused with pride. "The song was absolutely beautiful."

While the rest of the group made their enthusiastic comments, Brandon was unusually quiet. He found it hard to believe that Hillary had finished her single but hadn't breathed a single word to him. Recognizing Brandon's mood, Aaron tried desperately to ease the tension of the moment as he discreetly whispered something to his friend. Whatever was said, it appeared to lighten Brandon's mood.

Fumbling in his jacket pocket, Brandon came up with a small, elegantly gift-wrapped present. He then asked for everyone's attention. The suspense in the room began to mount when everyone saw how small the package was.

Brandon smiled, though he looked terribly nervous. "I have a surprise of my own." Turning to face Hillary, he gathered her into his arms. "Miss Hillary Houston, you would make me the happiest man in the world by becoming Mrs. Brandon David Blair." He kissed her tears away as he handed her the small gift-wrapped package.

Her eyes positively glowed as she slowly removed the wrapping, driving everyone to distraction in the process. Opening the black velvet jewelry case, she discovered the most perfect two-carat, trillion-cut diamond adorned on each side with five diamond baguettes. Her eyes shone with glistening tears. Moaning softly, she looked deeply into his raven-black gaze. "Mr. Blair, I would be honored to become your wife," she announced breathlessly.

Happy beyond description, they locked into a kiss that wasn't broken until someone shouted, "Don't you need to come up for air?"

While congratulations were generously expressed to the couple, Brandon and Hillary appeared deeply enchanted with each other as they savored the moment. Engaging her in another passionate kiss, Brandon heard the happy group of family and friends clap and cheer.

Her eyes filled with tears, Cassie walked over and put her arms around her childhood friend. "Congratulations, dear heart," Cassie said in an emotionally unstable voice, "you now have all the wonderful things we grew up dreaming about!"

Hillary squeezed her tight. "Thank you, sweet Cass. I do feel as though I have it all! This is going to happen for you as well. Very soon, I must add."

Cassie had a devilish glint in her eye. "In that case, I guess we should go ahead and plan that double wedding!" Cassie then held her ring up for Hillary to see.

Hillary squealed in delight. "You have one, too!" she shouted, tossing Cassie a charming smile. The two women cried so hard, they began to shake.

Cassie put her arms around Hillary. "I've had mine since Thanksgiving, but I wanted to wait until you and Brandon were engaged before I announced it."

Hillary looked shocked as she and Cassie hugged each other tenderly. Hillary felt awful that Cassie had held off celebrating her own engagement for over a month, but she decided not to comment on the insanity of her best friend's decision.

The festivities at the Houston house went on till a very late hour, which gave Brandon plenty of time to stew over Hillary's finished record.

Hillary had agreed to spend the next couple of days with Brandon at the beach house, but he was very quiet on the way there. Once they were settled in the house, he sat across from her. His anger had gotten the best of him, and he desperately needed to confront her about the surprise she had sprung on him at her parents' house.

Hoping to control the anger in his voice, he tried speaking softly. "Hillary, why didn't you tell me you finished your single? Why didn't you think enough of me to let me in on your little secret?"

His questions surprised her, but his sharp tone put her on edge. "Brandon, I thought I explained that after everyone had heard the song."

"Hillary, you could have told me before then." His voice now turned petulant. "I can understand you wanting to surprise your family, but why me?" he challenged. "We've shared everything over the last few months. Doesn't that mean anything to you?"

She didn't understand it, but she could see that he was really hurt. "Brandon, I had no idea that keeping the demo a secret would upset you, but I don't understand why it has. I certainly didn't think you'd react this way."

He fought hard for control. "Hill, that's part of the problem. You don't think anymore!" he shouted, losing the fight. "You've been walking around here like a wound-up robot for weeks. You were so damn busy that Cassie had to put her news about her engagement on hold."

His remark cut her like a knife, making her wonder if Cassie had been lying to her about the reason for not sharing her engagement sooner. Her temper near the boiling point, Hillary gritted her teeth. "Brandon David Blair, how can you be so cruel? That's not the reason Cassie gave me for not sharing her news with me."

Highly agitated, he ran shaking fingers through his hair. "What the hell did you expect her to tell you? Cassie has been so understanding with you, but the ugly truth is you've let her down. You've let us all down in one way or another." Menacingly, he sliced his left hand across his neck. "I've had it up to here with you and your lame excuses."

Hillary was close to tears, but she resigned herself to the fact that she wouldn't give him the satisfaction of seeing her cry. He had wounded her deeply. "You'd better take me home now." Her voice was tight with control. "This type of behavior is not getting us anywhere."

Bristling like an angry bull, Brandon wasn't about to let her run away from yet another situation that needed airing. "Hillary, you can't run from everything that you don't want to face. I simply don't like surprises that make me look like a damn fool."

She no longer tried to control herself. "Now I see!" she screamed at the top of her voice. "This doesn't have a damn thing to do with Cassie. It's your larger-than-life ego talking. I can't believe this is coming from the man who's been surprising me since the day he walked into my life. You just surprised me at my parents' home with a marriage proposal. Now look at us. I can name several surprises I wasn't too thrilled about, but I accepted them in the spirit in which they were given. Are you saying it's okay for you to surprise me whenever the mood hits you, but it's not okay for me to reciprocate?"

Knowing she had hit home, all he could do was stare at her. Unreasonably so, he wanted her to tell him every detail of her life, he quietly admitted to himself. He didn't want them to have any secrets between them. He also knew that he'd really blown it with her.

His nonresponse made her even angrier. "Take me home now or I will walk." Sorry for the hurt he'd caused, he tried to take her in his arms.

Violently, she jerked away. "Don't you dare touch me. I never want you to touch me again." She regretted her caustic words as soon as they left her mouth, but she was too angry to even think about retracting them.

He looked contrite. "Hill, is the proposal one of the surprises that you aren't too crazy about?"

"No, Brandon," she cried. "I just want to go home." Angry as hell, she walked out the front door. After locking up the house, he followed after her, hoping they'd make up before they got to her house.

Neither one spoke a single word during the entire drive to her place.

Hillary couldn't help thinking how awful Christmas day had turned out, and how it was a time for love, not anger. Her parents had always taught her about love and forgiveness, which made her wonder why she just couldn't forgive him. At the door of her town house, Brandon tried to talk to Hillary, but she was still too angry to engage in any sort of show of forgiveness.

"You had a chance to say something at your place, but you just stood there like an overindulged, spoiled brat," she rounded on him. "You can't always have it your way." While reaching into her purse for her door key, she also took out a quarter, which she handed to him. "Call me when you grow up."

Her retort was so proper and fitting he almost laughed out loud, but he knew it would only add fuel to the fire already burning way out of control. Hillary made a last show of anger by trying to slam the door shut in his face, but he had her in his arms before she could complete her mission. With her back against the door, she slid from his arms and down to the floor. Dissolving into

tears, her sobs came hard and bitter. Feeling totally help-
less, he looked on as she started to cry even harder.

Writhing in emotional agony, she cried for her friendship with Cassie, for Christmas being ruined, and for their
bitter argument. She didn't even want to think about what
effect this would have on their engagement. How could
this happen on the very night he'd asked her to become
his wife? They should've been celebrating their love, not
arguing over something as silly as surprises. This was the
first serious argument they'd had in all the months of being
together, she realized with much regret.

She cried until all her tears were spent. Pulling herself
up from the floor, she began to ascend the stairs. Moving
behind her, he stayed her with a calm arm around her
waist, burying his face in her sweet-smelling hair.

He turned her around to face him. "Why are we going
through all this?" he asked. "Don't you love me enough
to work this out? I'm really sorry for acting so childish,
Hill. I thought I had my jealousy licked, but I guess not.
I can only promise you that I'll keep trying to beat it.
Can't you find it in your heart to forgive me, Hill?"

He sounded so sincere she couldn't do anything but forgive him and trust in the promise he'd made to her. She
reached down to take his hand as she searched his eyes
earnestly. "I do love you, Brandon. I hope you'll forgive
me for my part in this. I should've stayed to confront the
situation. You were right when you said that I always run
from situations I don't want to face. I was guilty of running
away from my problems with Alex . . . I'm guilty now. I do
forgive you, Brandon. I don't want to lose you over something so silly. You are quite a catch, you know."

He sighed with relief. "The only person I want to be
caught by is you! Hill, thanks for believing in me. I
couldn't have gone on with things the way they were.
We've already missed out on so much already."

For the first time in their relationship, Hillary was the

aggressor. Slowly, she unbuttoned Brandon's shirt while probing his mouth hungrily. Reaching for his belt to unbuckle it, she groped nervously at the zipper of his pants and waited for him to garner protection. Finished disrobing him, she pushed him back on the sofa, aggressively so. As she quickly pulled her sweater off, he saw that she wasn't wearing a bra.

Halfway naked, she pressed her hot flesh against his, causing Brandon to moan with pleasure. Pausing briefly to remove the rest of her clothing, she then unleashed the wild caged tigress within her, teasing and taunting him until his own desire to be in command took over. Their completion came as they capitulated to an uninhibited, frenzy-filled release.

In awe of the way she had seduced him, he gazed at her, his eyes smoldering. "Babe, where did all that fire and brimstone come from? You've been holding out on me, girl."

"Are you complaining, Mr. Blair?"

He threw up his hands in a halting gesture. "Not in the least. I loved every second of it."

"In that case, don't worry about where it came from. Just be glad that you were the recipient."

Brandon laughed loudly as he pulled her back on top of him. "Whoa, Miss Houston, you're kind of small to be talking so big, aren't you?"

"Mr. Blair, didn't anyone ever tell you big surprises come in small packages. So be careful who you call small."

"Yes, I have heard that. I've also been put in my place," he said, laughing. "You get no more arguments from me. Can I spend the night?"

"What took you so long?" she breathed seductively.

Eighteen

It was a beautiful, clear night in southern California. One could see the outlines of the large palm trees that lined most of the streets in Los Angeles. Tall and stately, the huge palms appeared to finger the skies above.

Cassie and Hillary had already seen a movie and were now pulling into the parking lot of their favorite restaurant. Cassie had been in an extremely good mood ever since she'd talked with her parents and they'd promised to come to California very soon.

Cassie put her car in park. "Hillary, I can't wait till my parents come for a visit. It's been two years. I can remember how upset they were when I first told them I was moving out here with you. It seems so long ago since I left our little home town."

Hillary smiled warmly at her friend. "Cassie, I can relate to their feelings. When my parents told me we were moving to California, I just about died. You and I had been inseparable all those years while growing up. I couldn't imagine living three thousand miles away from my best friend."

Cassie's brows furrowed. "Oh, boy, do I remember well. The day you all left Pennsylvania I was heartsick. Nothing could comfort me. I remember you sitting in the back seat of the car crying your heart out. When you all pulled off, I ran into the house and cried like a baby.

I remember being angry with you. I thought that somehow you could've stopped them from tearing us apart."

Hillary looked surprised. "Cass, this is the first time I'm hearing this. I'm sorry that you had to go through those emotions. Why didn't you ever tell me that you were angry with me? I always thought you knew that I tried desperately to get them to change their minds."

"I knew. I never mentioned my anger because I had come to the realization that there was nothing you could've done. Your mother was determined to make you go, and I knew her well enough to know that when she made a decision it was final. Hell, I practically lived at your house." Hillary laughed at Cassie's statement about her mother.

Soon after they entered their favorite restaurant in Marina Del Rey, they were seated at a window table. The two friends sat in silence while taking in the beautiful view of the marina. Several boats glided past the window heading for or returning from the open sea.

The waitress appeared to take their order. She was very attractive, and would've had a beautiful smile if it weren't for all the hardware she had in her mouth, Hillary assessed, trying to imagine her without the braces.

Both women ordered steak and lobster, sautéed mushrooms, and a Caesar salad. They always came to Marina Del Rey when they had a taste for lobster. The two friends resumed their chatter when the waitress left to turn in their order.

"Aren't you going to have your usual rum and Coke?"

Cassie pulled a face. "I'm on the wagon. I never really enjoyed drinking, anyway. It was just something to do. With all the drugs and alcohol problems that people are faced with today, I decided I didn't want to join the ranks of Alcoholics Anonymous."

"Cass, you never overindulged. You're a far cry from becoming an alcoholic."

Cassie shrugged her shoulders. "I'm sure there are a lot of people in this world who thought the same thing. Aaron and I both made the conscious decision to swear off alcohol after we saw how some of his colleagues carried on at a party one night. All it does is make you act stupid. A lot of people don't know where to draw the line. Alcohol is responsible for millions of deaths every year. Hillary, I just don't need it. It has no life-enhancing qualities."

Hillary nodded. "You said it. I'm proud that you stand up for what you believe in."

Hillary and Cassie sat quietly enjoying their meal. Then, out of the blue, Cassie appeared so sad for someone who'd been so bubbly earlier. Hillary noticed that her friend's mood had changed drastically.

"Cass, you've gotten quiet all of a sudden. What's troubling you?"

Cassie's eyes grew pensive. "I just wonder if I'm doing the right thing by marrying Aaron. I really haven't known him all that long. Do you ever worry about your decision to marry Brandon?"

Hillary folded her hands and placed them on the table. "As a matter of fact, I worry a lot. A few nights ago, after our big argument, Brandon and I had a big discussion about marrying so soon. He wanted to run off to Vegas!"

Cassie looked surprised. "I thought we all wanted a big wedding."

"I do, we do. He was just being impulsive, as usual. He wanted to do both. I had a nightmare about him and his old girlfriend, Lisa, that night. So I'm sure that's what prompted his sudden urge to run off to Vegas, coupled with the fact that he wants us to live under the same roof."

Cassie allowed a little smile to appear on her face. "That Brandon! He's as impulsive as they come, though it was a sweet gesture. How'd you convince him to wait? Or did you?"

"I was able to convince him to wait. We talked about kids, religion, commitment, and a few other important matters. After our discussion, we decided to discuss marriage as a whole, before setting a date."

Cassie eyed Hillary with admiration. "That sure makes me feel a lot better. I'm glad to know that I'm not the only one worrying about marriage. You have given me something to present to Aaron. I think we, too, should discuss what marriage means in detail. We've only scratched the surface. Thanks, friend. I can always count on you to keep my head above water. It looks like we're going to have this double wedding after all, even if it is going to be delayed a bit longer."

"Cassie, that's why we're so good together. We've always been able to help each other solve problems. When we put our two heads together, the world better look out. I'm so glad we've stuck together all these years. Cassie, I promise I won't ever feel I'm so important that I don't have time for us. I know I've let you down lately."

Cassie smacked Hillary's hand playfully. "Girlfriend, where is that garbage coming from? I just told you what I thought you needed to know. I was really concerned about your and Brandon's fight. I thought you were taking too hard of a line with him. He just can't seem to help himself where you're concerned."

Hillary grinned. "You're right about that, but I think we're back on the right track. The conversation we had did us both a world of good."

Cassie patted Hillary's hand affectionately. "I'm glad to hear you and Brandon worked your differences out. That man is crazy about you. We're so lucky to have two wonderful, successful—not to mention handsome—men in our lives. California has been good to us, thus far."

It was raining hard when the women left the restaurant. They were disappointed because they had planned to go to Hollywood just to hang out. Instead, they decided to go back to Cassie's place to listen to some of their favorite music.

After a lot of hard work, the compact disc entitled *Soulful Serenade* was released. The CD was finished much sooner than anyone ever expected. Although it had only been in the record stores for a short time, it quickly became the number one CD on the soul and rhythm and blues charts.

Hillary was delirious with excitement. All morning long, people buzzed around her excitedly. She was having a hard time believing that her dream had finally come true. The single cut from the CD, "Destiny," had already put her on the map. By the sales figures, it appeared that the fans were eager to hear more of her music.

Champagne flowed while the crew cut up in celebration of the latest sales figures. Eric St. John had given Hillary a dainty solid gold charm designed in a treble clef. The co-owner of the company, MacArthur Serrano, gave her a gold bracelet to wear it on. Serrano and St. John had collaborated on the expensive gifts. They knew they had a winner in Hillary and seemed pretty sure that *Soulful Serenade* would eventually make them all a ton of money.

Hillary Houston had the voice of an angel, and she now had the music world at her fingertips, Eric announced to the staff.

Without a word to anyone, Hillary slipped away from the celebration to phone Brandon. While her fingers trembled from the excitement, she dialed his number.

"Blair here."

"Hello, honey, this is the woman you've spent the entire morning dreaming about," she cooed in a sultry voice.

"Pretty lady, are you trying to seduce me over the phone? These phone lines are burning up."

Hillary laughed. "If you think the phone lines are hot, wait till I get you home alone!"

"I hope this is a promise. How long do I have to wait?"

"Not as long as you have waited. Now that *Soulful Serenade* is doing so well on the market, I have a few days off to stroke your ego and quench your burning fires."

"Keep talking, babe, and I'm going to jump right through this phone line." They both laughed. "What time can we get together, Hill?"

"Is six-thirty okay?"

"You bet. Do you want me to pick you up at the studio?"

"No, honey, I'm going to be leaving here shortly. I have some shopping to do, and I need to get to the bank. I should be home around five or so."

"I can handle that. Hill, before we lock ourselves away from the world, would you like to take Cassie and Aaron out to dinner? I'm sure they'll want to help us celebrate. You are coming back to the beach house with me, aren't you?"

"Brandon, I plan on coming home with you. Let me check with Cassie about dinner. She and Aaron may already have something planned, but that was such a sweet offer. I'll see you a little later."

"You know I'll be there. I love you," he said before hanging up.

Rejoining the celebration, Hillary sat at a table with Eric. As they discussed the upcoming concert and the public appearances she was scheduled to make in the near future, she was grateful for the few days she'd have off. She needed to be with Brandon before her hectic schedule further limited their precious time together.

Grabbing her purse on the way out of the studio, she ran to her car.

Her first stop was at the bank to make a withdrawal. First National was the only bank she'd ever dealt with, which made her well known by the bank employees. Several of the personnel raved over her song "Destiny," telling her how exciting it was to know a celebrity. After thanking them, she let them know she was still the same Hillary Houston they'd all come to know and that she would always remain approachable.

Hillary's next stop was the exclusive fashion boutique where Cassie worked. Cassie had taken some time off to spend with Aaron, but her absence wasn't a problem for Hillary, since she knew most of the salesgirls.

Connie Hill, the assistant manager, rushed over to offer Hillary assistance. The two women exchanged enthusiastic greetings before Hillary began her shopping spree.

Hillary checked out several formal evening dresses, instantaneously falling in love with a formal, black crêpe tuxedo trouser-suit designed by Cassie. The jacket, fully lined, had satin lapels and buttons; the high-waisted pants had a pleated front.

Rushing into the dressing room, she quickly tried it on. Looking into the mirror, she saw that the fit was smooth and elegant on her shapely, petite body. The other dresses she had chosen also fit perfectly, but she had a hard time making up her mind about which ones to buy. Minutes later, feeling a desire to splurge, she purchased everything she'd tried on. Once she'd written a check for her purchases, she waved to the sales crew and departed the store.

At home, Hillary showered and dressed for the evening in a tailored dress that had the appearance of two separate pieces. The surplice-notched collar was decorated in a rich scarf print of rayon challis, while the bodice displayed colors of black, gold, and red, complemented by a wide belt of the same material. The dress reeked of finesse.

Arriving a little late, Brandon explained there'd been an accident on the freeway. As he drank in Hillary's stunning appearance, she twirled around in front of him, laughing with glee. Today had been one of the most special times in her life, and she felt as though she'd drunk a full bottle of the best champagne. However bubbly she felt, she was sorry that Aaron and Cassie weren't able to join in their evening.

Hillary and Brandon shut the world out for the next forty-eight hours. They made love over and over, seemingly unable to satisfy their sexual appetites for each other. Showing off his culinary skills, he cooked dinner for her both evenings.

As it was their last evening together, he set the table beautifully, using fine bone china and Waterford crystal goblets. To further enhance the table, he used lighted candles and a huge vase of red roses as a centerpiece. He had chosen the most romantic musical selections for them to dine by, and he'd transferred several of Hillary's love ballads from her CD, including "Destiny," onto a cassette tape.

Hillary had been resting in the master bedroom while Brandon prepared the meal. When she walked in and saw how lovely the table was, she couldn't believe her eyes. "Honey, the table is absolutely divine. Who taught you how to arrange such a gorgeous table?"

His smile said that he appreciated her comment. "Hill, I've watched my mother set many a table over the years. She was always so creative with her hands. I guess you could say that I learned from watching, or I inherited her talent."

"That's very interesting. Men don't usually pay attention to domestic details."

"Well, this one does. I'm starving. Are you ready to eat?"

She licked her lips. "Honey, I am famished."

For the main entrée, Brandon had prepared London broil, new potatoes, and baby carrots. For dessert he had whipped up a delicious-looking chocolate mousse.

Hillary laughed with delight when she saw the beautifully prepared meal. Standing on her toes, she planted a kiss on his forehead. *He has so many of the same qualities that my father possesses,* she thought quietly. *I guess it's true that men and women alike marry people who have the same qualities as their parents,* she concluded.

Hillary ate till she was stuffed.

Knowing that the lazy days and nights filled with love and passion would be far and few between, they shared every waking moment in each other's arms.

As the schedule at the studio became crazier than ever, Hillary spent so much time recording, she and Brandon were only able to steal moments here and there. While she was busy making several appearances on talk shows, the studio heavily promoted the new CD in other ways. The record sales had skyrocketed after only a few weeks on the market.

With her concert coming up in a few days, spare time was nonexistent. Hillary and the band rehearsed for several hours each day. She had a free hand in selecting her costumes for the concert, and Cassie was instrumental in helping her decide what looked good. In the late evenings, when she returned home, she was too tired for anything. Her phone rang constantly, and her popularity had increased greatly. She was frequently recognized when out in public. Brandon had been called Mr. Houston a few times, but to Hillary's surprise, it didn't seem to upset him.

The ticket sales for her concert were brisk, and St. John expected a sellout. The personnel at S&J Records pulled together and got things done as a unit. There were no jealousies or silly backbiting; just a common bond to reach a common goal, which was to have Hillary's first concert be a total success. Fear set in on her from time to time. Because she had so many around to offer her support, her fears didn't get much of a chance to manifest themselves.

The big day had finally arrived. Several hours before the concert, Hillary was already in the large arena. As she walked around the near empty space, she found it hard to believe that she would actually be performing here. In the back of the arena, she sat down. Looking out at the stage, she suddenly became very emotional. To calm herself, she closed her eyes and imagined herself singing on the huge platform.

No opening act had been booked for her debut performance, simply because St. John didn't want her to have to wait too long, as he'd considered the possibility of stage fright. Therefore, the success of the concert rested solely on her shoulders. It was all up to her to bring about the most exciting, most entertaining, and most talked about concert of the year. As the old saying went, she had to go out on that stage and break a leg. Perhaps both legs, she mused.

Smiling at the soft expression he saw on Hillary's face, one of the stage crewmembers walked over to where she sat. He had to tell her that she was needed backstage, but he waited a few minutes before intruding on her wistful mood.

Fans packed into the arena while Hillary paced backstage, nervously awaiting her cue. A professional had been hired to take care of her hair and makeup and her wardrobe had been checked and rechecked. Her sisters and Cassie had been with her earlier, but they'd left to take their reserved seats in the front row, along with the rest of the family.

Several people from Atlantic Pacific Airlines were also in attendance, including Mr. & Mrs. Asher, Lois and Alex. Brandon and Aaron hadn't arrived yet, but they were expected momentarily. The band had just cued up when the guys slid into their seats. Brandon had arranged for red roses to be delivered to her dressing room.

The lights lowered and the crowd cheered as the master of ceremonies, tall in stature and immaculately dressed, entered the stage. Reaching the microphone, he easily removed it from the stand and began to speak. "Good evening, Los Angeles," he boomed. "Are we ready for a good time?" The crowd responded eagerly and positively to his enthusiasm. "All of you here tonight are about to experience stardom in the making. Are we ready for the show to begin?" The crowd stomped their feet in breathless anticipation.

"Tonight, in concert, I present to you the lovely, vivacious, extremely talented young lady who hails from the great state of Pennsylvania. Miss Hillary Houstonnnnnnnnn!" he announced, dragging her name out for emphasis. Spelling out her name, the multicolored bright lights blinked off and on. Whistling and cheering was loud and plentiful. If she'd had any doubts about her popularity, they should've been erased with the response that her name alone received.

Walking slowly out onto the stage, Hillary appeared to have as much confidence as any veteran performer. Wearing a sexy black gown fashioned with a high neck collar, cutaway bare shoulders, and a slit up the right side reaching midthigh, Hillary was stunningly beautiful.

In appreciation of her sexy attire, wolf whistles echoed throughout the building. Thrilled for her, family and friends smiled. Brandon's smile outshone them all as his heart filled with genuine pride, happy that she belonged to him. With their hearts filled with joy, Jackson and Alice hugged each other as they watched their very own daughter through the eyes of love. Cassie was speechless as Aaron held her trembling body close to him.

Holding onto the microphone tightly, Hillary greeted the crowd enthusiastically. As her effervescent personality spilled over into the audience, she thanked her fans for buying her CD and for their presence that evening. Looking toward the band, she gave a slight nod of her head.

Poised and confident, Hillary Houston began to sing her heart out. As her audience became her puppets, she exulted as the puppet master. Her ability to wow her audience came naturally as she dazzled and delighted.

Swaying seductively, singing with a level of passion that surprised even her, she worked the audience into an emotional frenzy. The song program was mixed with cuts from her CD and other popular tunes. "Hang On Sloopy" was added to the program after Cassie had reminded her of how much she used to love the song her parents had played when she was little. The music had been rearranged and she drove the fans wild with her sultry rendition of the oldie. As she sang the old Negro gospel "Swing Low Sweet Chariot," she nearly brought the house down.

Out of everyone present, Brandon was the most affected. In absolute awe of her performance, he fell in love with her all over again, receiving tremendous pleasure from watching the audience's near crazed reactions to her performance.

The single "Destiny" was the last cut to be performed. By far, it was the most popular of all the songs, and drew an even wilder response from the audience.

St. John nearly had a cardiac arrest when Hillary stepped off the stage during her performance of the last song. Because security was on top of the situation, she walked the aisles unmolested. Hands reached out for hers, but no one was overly aggressive.

Stopping briefly in front of Brandon's seat, she serenaded his soul. Pausing momentarily to kiss her family members and Cassie, she then returned to the stage. Finished soulfully crooning "Destiny," she proudly walked off into the wings. A deafening applause for an encore brought her back immediately. After singing two more songs, she disappeared backstage, where the crew waited to congratulate her on such a stupendous performance.

A small party was held backstage immediately following the concert for those who held backstage passes. Hillary felt dizzy with euphoria as she was congratulated over and over on her outstanding performance. Serrano and St. John appeared to be on cloud nine. As Serrano once again praised St. John for his discovery of Hillary, she smiled beautifully.

Several extremely popular African-American recording artists, male and female, joined in giving praise to Hillary on her electrifying performance. She was both flabbergasted and flattered to be in the company of such celebrated performers. Three hours had passed before Hillary was finally able to slip away.

* * *

En route to the beach house, Brandon and Hillary chatted up a storm.

"Hill, you were in your element tonight. You shone brighter than any star in the galaxy!" Without taking his eyes off the road, he leaned over and kissed her. "I'm so proud of you."

Remembering Lois saying something similar to her a while back, Hillary experienced a warm feeling inside. "Honey, I'm floating right now. I don't know how many times I've pinched myself to see if I was dreaming. My thighs may be black and blue. They will probably sue me for limb abuse," she announced, laughing.

Brandon laughed, too. "Precious, don't ever lose that dynamite sense of humor. It's one of your greatest assets. Your sense of humor brings so much enjoyment to me."

"Honey, if you give me any more compliments, I won't be able to get my head in the new hat I just bought."

"That's okay—I'll just buy you another one."

As soon as he parked the car, he ran around to the passenger side. Lifting her up, he carried her into the house. The door had barely closed when they fell into each other's aching arms.

Nineteen

Over the next several weeks, Hillary was busier than ever. Her life was no longer her own. Every time she turned around she had to make a meeting, a photo session, or something else. She took time to learn every aspect of the business because she wanted to prepare herself for life after live performances and recording. She learned quickly and was always accepting when receiving constructive criticism. There was no question too silly for her to ask, and she asked plenty of them.

The second album was already in progress, but a title hadn't been chosen yet. Writers were still sending in songs for consideration. Her fan mail was delivered by the truckload. In the beginning she did her best to respond to all of it, but it soon became an impossible burden on her time, and the public relations department took on the task. She still personally signed every photo that went out. A stamp with her signature, which was kept under lock and key, had been obtained for other fan correspondence.

Though she loved singing the softer love ballads, she knew she had to keep up with the everchanging times. To keep up with the competition, she had to be versatile. The studio hired a choreographer to teach her all the latest dance steps, and she learned them with ease. Several dancers were hired to dance with her on the more hip-hop tunes. She loved having her own dance troupe.

She loved the entire business, but her relationship with Brandon was suffering under the strain of her schedule. The hours she spent at the studio sometimes seemed endless. The more hours spent at the studio left her with less time for Brandon. No matter how hard the crew tried to keep things on schedule, often there were unforeseen matters that needed immediate attention.

Returning to her home very late in the evening, Hillary, in a panic, ran upstairs to check her answering machine. She was supposed to have met Brandon there at eight o'clock, but it was well after nine. Realizing she couldn't make it on time, she'd tried to reach him, but he'd already left his office.

The recording session had lasted a lot longer than she had expected, but lately that was par for the course. She'd already broken dates with Brandon twice this week. He had tried to play it off, but she knew him well enough to know that he had hidden his bitter disappointment.

After rewinding her messages, she threw herself across the bed to listen. When Brandon's voice came over the recorder, she thought he sounded disgusted. "I see you still haven't made it home. I've been there twice already and I doubt seriously if I'll come back again tonight. . . ." The message ended.

There was no "good-bye," "I love you," or "I'll call you later," she mused. Afraid of what she'd heard in his voice, she lay quietly, trying to calm her fears. In the next instant, when the doorbell rang, smiling, she leaped off the bed and ran downstairs. Not Brandon but Cassie, in her usual bubbly mood, stood there when she opened the door.

Taking one look at Hillary's face, Cassie knew trouble brewed as she followed Hillary into the living room, where they both took a seat. "You look as if you've lost your best friend," Cassie exclaimed. "I know that can't be true since I hold the title. I popped in to say hello, but what's happening with you?"

Hillary frowned. "I've messed up another date with Brandon. I was supposed to meet him here at eight, but I didn't make it until after nine. He left a message on the recorder, saying he'd been here twice. Cassie, he sounded so disgusted."

Cassie briefly thought over the things Hillary had said. "I'm sure that he knows by now how things work when you're recording. If he doesn't, shame on him, but I don't think you really have anything to worry about. He'll get over it. Just give him some time to cool off."

"But, Cassie, I've already broken two dates with him this week alone."

Cassie gave Hillary a serious look. "Girlfriend, I guess it's a little more serious than I realized. Still, he has to know you're not doing this on purpose."

Hillary sighed. "I sincerely hope so. We've been fighting over time spent, or lack thereof, for over a month now. He's been so supportive of my singing career thus far, but I think he's at the end of his rope. He hasn't been a happy camper lately. I can't stand the thought of losing him. Especially over my career," she wailed, her voice quaking with emotion.

Cassie put her arms around Hillary. "Just hang in there. If he loves you, everything will be okay. Just stroke his ego a few times and reassure him. I hate to leave you upset, but Aaron is waiting for me at my place. Are you going to be okay? You can come home with me if you don't want to be alone. You can spend the night."

Hillary got to her feet. "I'll be okay, Cass. Come on, let me walk you out. I don't want you to keep Aaron waiting."

* * *

Sitting on the terrace, his favorite spot when troubled, Brandon intensely watched the waves crash against the rocks below. He felt as agitated as the sea in front of him. His turbulent thoughts included Hillary's career and how much time they'd been spending apart. It seemed to him as though she ate, drank, and slept music. As he thought about the many dates she'd broken or been late for in the past several weeks, he couldn't help wondering if it was going to be like this the rest of their lives. Or at least until they were too old to get out of their rocking chairs. He was at his wit's end with the way the situation was now. It seemed that the more she gave to the studio, the more they wanted. She should have been the one making the demands, not the studio. They demanded to know where she was every waking moment . . . and she complied.

Knowing he couldn't go on sharing her with millions of people, his eyes became troubled as he thought about letting her go. With her as a celebrity, they'd never have a private life, and he wanted a wife with whom he could share quiet time. The best thing was for him to let her go so that she'd be free to pursue her dreams. While he knew it was the right thing to do, the last thing he wanted to do was break Hillary's heart. He loved her like crazy. He knew himself all too well, knew he was being selfish, but he couldn't control it any more than he could control his breathing. It was one of the things he detested about himself. An acute pain pierced his heart each time he thought of living without her. Willing his mind to go blank, he gave his attention to the one-man show nature performed for him.

Hillary could no longer fight the urge to call him. Picking up the phone, she dialed his number, hoping there wouldn't be another ugly confrontation. She briefly held her breath when he answered. "Hi, honey," she said, trying to make her voice cheerful. "How are you?"

"I'm fine," he said, his response dryly terse.

"I'm sorry I didn't make it home in time for our date. The recording session ran longer than I had anticipated. But then again, what else is new? Can you forgive me one more time?"

"Sure, Hill. Why the hell not? I'm becoming a pro at it." His voice still carried the same dryness, she noted. His bad attitude and sarcasm stung her hard.

"Brandon, I can tell you're upset. Please tell me what's on your mind."

"Drop it, Hill. I don't want to get into this over the phone."

Her feelings were hurt, but she struggled to remain optimistic. "Okay, let's discuss something else. How was your day at work?"

"The same as yours. Busy. I was awarded two new contracts today. That should keep me hopping for a while."

"What are the contracts for?"

"One is for a twenty-eight-story office building. The other is for a church."

"Congratulations, sweetheart!" She knew she might get into hot water with her next question but decided to jump in anyway. "Brandon, can we make another date to get together?"

"For what? So you can just break it again?"

She began to feel slightly exasperated. "You know I haven't broken our dates intentionally. I can't help it if the schedule gets out of whack. I've tried to apologize. Why are you giving me such a hard time over this?"

"Hill, I'm coming over there."

She looked at the clock and frowned. "Are you talking about now?"

"Yes, now," he said sharply. "We need to talk. It's long overdue. I'll see you shortly."

Needing something to do to calm her nervous stomach, she busied herself by putting her already neat house in order. Gravely concerned with what he wanted to discuss, sensing the foul mood he seemed to be in, she felt it wasn't going to be favorable for her. At one point she became so high-strung she broke down and cried. Waiting for him to arrive felt like waiting to be publicly executed by a firing squad, without a blindfold. She could see it coming, but there was nothing she could do to prevent it. Aware that it would take him a while to get there, she ascended the steps to take a shower, hoping it would help to make her less tense.

After her twenty-minute shower, she slipped into a green satin lounging robe. As she brushed her hair out, the doorbell rang. For some time now Brandon had been granted free access to the complex at Hillary's written request to security. Many times she had toyed with the idea of giving him keys, but she felt strongly about her need to keep her independence and privacy intact. She didn't want to have to go through the trouble of changing locks if they broke up.

Hillary raced down the stairs and flung the door open wide, noticing right away the rigid set of his jaw and his grim face. Stepping aside, she allowed him entry. It hurt when he didn't kiss or greet her in the manner to which she'd become accustomed. Instead of sitting in his usual spot on the sofa, he seated himself in one of the chairs. *So much for cuddling up with him,* she thought with growing agitation. For several seconds they stared at each other in silence.

"Hill, I honestly don't know where to begin, but I do know there's no easy way to tell you the decisions I've made." His voice sounded as though it came from inside a hollow tube. *Lover, you've just exposed your hand big-time,* she thought silently, nervously biting down on her lower lip. He rested his elbow on the arm of the chair. "I've been doing a lot of thinking about us. I've thought about all the things we've discussed over the last several months . . ."

Without giving him a chance to say anymore, she cut in, "Please be more specific regarding your thoughts."

"The things we've discussed about our roles in marriage." Her heart started beating rapidly and she prayed he couldn't hear it. "Hill, I love you, I'm proud of you, and I'm happy for your success, but I just can't commit to this relationship any longer."

Ready, aim, fire, her heart screamed. The firing squad had aimed straight for the heart, hitting and killing its target instantly. Mourning the tragic death inwardly, she moaned painfully, seeing herself lying on the ground, bleeding from the heart.

"Performing has become your life," he continued. "I feel like a postscript at the end of an old letter." Not realizing she was dead, he waited for her to speak.

Finally, her blood supply rushed to her heart, giving her another chance at life. "I thought we had worked all this through, but I see I was sadly mistaken."

He looked grief-stricken. "I did too, babe. Hill, it's plain and simple. I'm a selfish person and you've always known that about me. I don't want to share the woman I love with millions of people. Our time together grows less and less. Our private space is invaded on a regular basis by the studio or some adoring fan. I just don't know what to do anymore."

She shook her head from side to side, as though she were trying to clear the cobwebs. "I'm totally unprepared for what you're telling me." Her voice was barely above a whisper. "I thought we had all the right ingredients to make a wonderful life together. I believed we were going to spend eternity together. Weren't you the one who told me not to ever let go of my dreams? Didn't you encourage me to pursue a singing career? Were those just empty, meaningless words? I'm having an incredibly hard time accepting the things you're saying. It's like I'm sitting here with a stranger. You've done a complete one-eighty on me."

He lowered his gaze to the floor. "I did say all those things and I also meant them. I guess I didn't realize I'd be put on the back burner while you turned your dreams into gold. Hill, I just can't live like this anymore. I miss you. I miss us. I miss the spontaneity our relationship afforded us in the beginning. The way things have become hurts too much. If I don't let you go, I'll end up destroying us. Trust that, I know myself."

She could hear the raw pain in his voice, which made her want to take him in her arms and surrender her entire life to him, but she couldn't do that. To end his pain and suffering, she knew she had to say things that were in direct conflict with her true feelings. If he couldn't be happy in her lifestyle, then she felt dutybound to let him walk away while their dignities were still intact. For his sake and hers, she had to let go of him, let go of the man who was her world.

"Brandon, I have no intentions of trying to change your mind. It seems you've given this matter a lot of thought. I want you in my life, but begging isn't in my repertoire. If our relationship is causing you this much pain, I agree that we should end it. I love you enough to set you free. I don't understand any of this, but I certainly respect your right to choose what's best for you. I truly hope we can remain friends. I don't want to mar the beautiful times we've shared with bitterness and hard feelings. It's better to have loved and lost than to never have loved at all. I'm so glad that I first discovered love with you."

He was stunned by her beautiful, expressive words of

understanding. Yet he had imagined there would be anger and shouting, almost sure she would've resisted the breakup. *She's truly a lady,* he pondered sadly, his heart breaking in two.

She got to her feet. "Well, Brandon, I guess this is good-bye for us." Choking back a ragged sob, she slipped her engagement ring off and handed it to him.

The unexpected gesture stunned him as well. "Hill, I bought you the ring as a symbol of my love for you. I still do love you. This isn't about me not loving you. It's about my inability to handle our private lives and your career in an unselfish manner. The ring was a present to you from me. I have no intentions of taking it back. It's yours to do with as you see fit."

She laid the ring on the coffee table. "Brandon, this ring was also a symbol of betrothal, but we're no longer engaged. I'll never wear this ring again."

He sighed heavily. "Suit yourself, Hill, but I'm not taking it back."

Desperately searching for a flicker of hope, Hillary looked into his eyes, moved closer, and put her arms around his waist. Her gesture was almost his undoing. Her laying her head against his chest fueled his desire to take her upstairs to the bedroom and maniacally ravish her body with the white-hot passion coursing through him. How ironic, he mused. Hillary was the only woman he'd ever wanted to spend forever with and he'd somehow managed to destroy the chance of that ever happening.

Releasing her hold on him, she walked toward the door. He started to speak, but she cut him off before any of his words could escape. "Please, Brandon, don't say anymore. I understand what you must be feeling. I feel it, too. Please just go now."

With a painful expression on his face, he kissed her

forehead. As he stepped into the night, he suddenly felt very cold, and it had nothing to do with the weather.

Hillary was devastated as the closed door stood between them like an unconquerable force. As she began to mourn her lost love and the tragic death she'd just died, she knew she hadn't been lucky enough to make it to heaven. Hopeless feelings of despair assailed her as the flood of tears spilled over onto her cheeks. With trembling hands, she pounded the wall with her fists in uncontrollable fury, unable to stop until the pain in her hands became unbearable.

"Why?" she screamed over and over again. "Why is this happening to us?" Leaping from one emotion to another, she experienced anger, rage, pain, and sorrow, vowing inwardly that no man would ever con her into loving again, never again. While crying off and on through the night, she never found her old ally, Peace.

Brandon had a hard time concentrating on his driving; visions of Hillary's pain-filled eyes were branded deeply into his memory. While cursing his selfish nature, he even questioned his own sanity. Thinking of how much she'd trusted him and how sweet she was, he remembered the night she'd surrendered her innocence to him even though it was in direct conflict with her beliefs. He winced from the pain of that memory, undoubtedly knowing he was the only man to whom she'd ever given her heart and soul. Then he thought of that which he'd promised himself not to ever think of again.

Reaching his house, he hastily jumped out of the car, slamming the car door behind him. Instead of going inside, he ran hard on the beach for what seemed like hours.

He was so exhausted by the time he entered his house he couldn't make sense of anything that had happened.

While taking a long, hot shower, he wished he could wash all the incredible pain he felt right down the drain. In bed, he stared into the roaring fire burning in the fireplace, unable to stop thinking about Hillary or wondering if she was okay. Thinking about how well she'd handled the breakup, he wondered if her calmness was just a front for what she'd really felt. He knew he'd soon have to face the reasons why he'd really let Hillary go.

His thoughts turned to Cassie and Aaron and he wondered what they would say, but he already knew that Aaron was going to read him the riot act. All along, Aaron had been trying to get him to understand what Hillary needed from him. He'd warned him so many times to get control of his selfishness, to deal with the past, to move on. Shutting his thoughts out, he closed his eyes. As he conjured up visions of them making love, he could almost see the undeniable feelings between them. Imagining her soft hands on his face, stroking him gently, he fell into a troubled sleep.

Looking at the clock as she climbed out of bed, Hillary saw that it was only six-thirty A.M.; she wasn't due at the studio until nine-thirty. Walking over to the dresser, she looked into the mirror, horrified at her image. The lack of sleep clearly showed on her face, and her terribly swollen eyes had dark rings around them. Running into the bathroom, she turned on the cold water thinking a cold cloth applied to her eyes might reduce the swelling. At the same time, she wondered how she was going to face the people at the studio.

Getting the water as cold as she could, she placed a cloth under the water and placed it over her eyes, repeating the procedure several times. She threw the cloth aside. It was useless.

Needing someone to talk to, she started to call her

parents but changed her mind. Since they were so fond
of Brandon, she didn't have a clue how to tell them the
engagement was broken. However, how she herself felt
would be their biggest concern. She then decided it
would be better if she waited until later to phone
them . . . like a few light-years later.

Having wasted most of her breakfast, she scraped it
into the garbage disposal. Her appetite had deserted her,
just like Brandon had. This was just the beginning of her
anguish. It was going to take a long time, if not forever,
for her to get over their broken relationship.

Hillary arrived at the studio much earlier than scheduled. She hadn't been able to stand it at home alone.
Before going inside, she checked her personal problems
at the door, refusing to bring them into the workplace.
She'd done it once before, but she'd never do it again.
She'd just have to pick them up on her way out. If anyone suspected that something was wrong, it wouldn't be
because of any clues from her.

Hillary launched herself right into rehearsing, going
about her day in the usual manner. Several people noticed her swollen eyes but made no comment. Since
she'd been working so hard on the recording, most people thought she suffered from burnout. No one asked
any questions; she didn't offer any explanations. Hillary
was just glad it was the weekend so that she could take
her off time to sort things out. Right now, she needed a
break.

Eric St. John approached Hillary where she sat at a
table in the studio's break room.

"Hi, honey, how are you?" he asked cheerfully.

She looked up but didn't have the emotional strength

it would take to smile. "Eric, I'm fine. How about yourself?"

Eric tossed out a broad smile. "Hillary, I couldn't be better. I just received the latest sales figures on 'Destiny.' Honey, I think this record is going gold!" He was so excited that he kissed her hard on the mouth. When she flinched as though she'd been severely burned, St. John apologized, deeply concerned with her reaction. "Hillary, honey, I wasn't trying to seduce you. I was just a little overexcited about the record. Please don't take the kiss the wrong way. You almost jumped out of your skin. Is there something wrong?"

Hillary lowered her lashes, embarrassed by the way she'd reacted to Eric. "I'm sorry. I'm very tired. I think I need to get some rest over the weekend. I have plenty of reading material I can curl up with. I just need to relax."

He gave her a sympathetic smile. "I have a lovely beach house up the coast in Oxnard. It's very quiet and private there. You're welcome to use it. I want you well rested for your next concert." Noticing the dark circles under her eyes, he wondered if it was more than just her being tired. Though concerned for her, he had no intentions of challenging her explanation.

"Thanks, Eric, but I have to decline. I'm going to shut myself away in my little town house and sleep to my heart's content." Running away wasn't going to solve her problems, she knew. Besides, where would she run away to? Brandon was a part of her. Therefore, always with her.

Feeling she'd taken a long enough break, Hillary immediately returned to the sound booth and resumed her session. Several times during her performance her voice broke. Stopping for a few minutes, she cleared her throat and collected her wits. While she was at it, she tried to reclaim her courage. Her voice came through strong and clear on her next try. The meadowlark had returned to its nesting place in her throat. Her melodic voice once again sounded like the first day of spring.

As Hillary entered her house, she thought about the fact that she hadn't been able to tell Cassie about the breakup. Though she needed more time to get used to the idea, she couldn't help wondering if Brandon had already told Aaron by now. She'd hate for Cassie to find out through someone else, yet she couldn't bring herself to discuss her enormous heartache with anyone right now. However, she'd have to face her family and friends when the weekend was over. She'd have Cassie over for dinner on Sunday evening.

After undressing, she went outside to walk around the complex grounds, where she walked and walked until fatigue set in. On her way back to the house, she heard someone shouting. As she turned to see what the commotion was all about, she saw a tall, slender man running toward her. She didn't know him, and his advancement toward her puzzled her. He hadn't called her by name, but it was clear that she was the one at whom he'd shouted. When the stranger with the nut-brown complexion and the russet-colored hair reached her, she couldn't help but notice how fit his body was.

He smiled warmly. "Hi, neighbor. I'm Austin Taylor." Pointing in the direction of the town house a few doors from her own, he said, "I just moved here. I've seen you coming and going, but I've not had the chance to make your acquaintance."

It amazed her that she'd been so preoccupied with her own life that she hadn't noticed that someone had moved into the recently vacated town house. She extended her hand to Austin. "I'm Hillary, but I'm afraid you have me at a disadvantage. I've never seen you before now."

While shaking her hand, he gave her another warm smile. "Hi, Hillary. I guess you haven't seen me because I haven't been outside on the grounds since I moved in. I've seen you a couple of times from the balcony."

"How do you like the house and the complex?"

He looked around him. "I love the house and I like what I've seen so far of the grounds. I didn't look at the place before I purchased the property. I went on the recommendation of my Realtor. I just moved here from Atlanta." Discreetly, he looked at her ring finger and saw that she wasn't wearing a wedding band. "Hillary, could I interest you in dinner out this evening? I hear there are a lot of good restaurants in the area of the complex."

She frowned. "I'm sorry, Austin, but I'm going to do nothing but rest this weekend. I've been working too many hours lately. I just want to curl up with a good book and relax."

"Maybe another time, Hillary. Since we're neighbors, I'm sure we'll run into each other from time to time."

Not wanting to appear rude, she made polite conversation with Austin for several more minutes before deeming that enough time had passed. She didn't want any part of men this weekend. She wasn't sure if she ever wanted to have anything else to do with men, period. Brandon had seen to that, she mused. He had ruined her for any other relationship. She would never again find someone to love as much as she loved Brandon, and she wasn't about to settle for just any relationship. From now on, she would be wary of any man bearing a beautiful smile and lavish gifts.

Hillary locked herself away in the comfort of her house, where she spent a good deal of her time reading and listening to music. While she remembered every detail of her first date with Brandon, "The Look of Love" played on the radio. Though an old tune, the song had become their very own theme song. Remembering caused her a great deal of pain. Jumping up, she turned off the radio. Unable to get Brandon off her mind, she sat on the floor in front of the window and stared out at the lake.

Deciding she would just go to bed even though it was only early evening, she turned off the lights and climbed into bed, where she lay very still, hoping sleep wouldn't desert her like her appetite and Brandon had. Unable to sleep, she got out of bed, went downstairs, and lit the fireplace. As soft music played on the expensive stereo equipment, thoughts of Brandon crept into her head again. She tried wishing them away, but they refused to honor her desire. Tears ran down her face as the many beautiful memories of him rushed out to embrace her.

The time they had spent together in New York was uppermost in her thoughts. The road would be rough on the journey into the past, but she hunkered down, ready to take it all in. She decided to first start the journey in Manhattan, inside the fabulous hotel where they'd first made love. Then she'd wing her way west, to Santa Barbara.

Her eyes closed when Brandon suddenly hovered over her. Dressed only in his beautiful nakedness, she felt his mouth searing into her hot flesh as he held her tightly against him. His teeth nipped gently at one hardened nipple, then the other, causing her to arch into him. As her hands slid down his flat, sweat-slickened stomach, he moaned, taking her mouth with a wet, passionate kiss. Pushing his hands up through her hair, he held her head steady, making sure her lips stayed sweetly fastened to his. As he stole inside of her like a silent whisper, she buried her lips against his, kissing him deeply, intensely.

Twenty

It wasn't Brandon's warmth streaking down to kiss her face when Hillary awakened. It was the kiss of the sun. Although spring hadn't yet arrived, the weather was almost summer-like and it had already woven its magic over the city. The bright sun shining though the window appeared to fingerpaint strands of Hillary's lovely chestnut-brown hair in various shades of gold. Slowly, as though it took all of her strength, Hillary got up and made it to the bathroom.

Hillary showered before putting on a pair of blue denim jeans and a navy-blue Michigan State sweatshirt. Pulling on a pair of white sneakers, she sat down on the bed to lace them up. Then, she made up the bed and tidied the room before heading for the stairs. On her way downstairs she thought about making a full breakfast of pancakes, sausage, and eggs. Just as the pangs of hunger growled in her stomach, the phone rang. Though she hadn't been answering the phone all weekend, something in her heart told her that she should do so this morning.

"Good morning."

"Hillary, what the hell are you trying to prove?" a familiar voice on the other end screamed into the phone. "Frantically, I've been calling you all weekend."

Shaking her head from side to side, Hillary searched for the right words to say. "You know, don't you, Cassie?"

"What I know or don't know is not important. I want you to answer the question I asked you. Do I need to repeat it?"

Hillary sighed. "No, Cassie, I heard you the first time. I'm not trying to prove anything. I just needed to be alone. I'll explain everything when I see you."

"Hillary, you have to stop hiding from your problems. Yes, I do know about the situation with Brandon, but you should've been the one to tell me." Cassie began to cry, but quickly pulled it together. "However, we'll get to that later. Aaron and I are going out to brunch. We'll pick you up in a half hour. Don't even try to squirm out of it." The line went dead.

Hillary hated that she'd made Cassie cry. "I'm sorry. I never meant to hurt you. I just didn't know what to say. Our plans for a double wedding had gone up in smoke right in front of my eyes," she explained, even though there was no one on the other end to listen.

Just thinking about all the hurt made Hillary cry, too, as she climbed the stairs. Sobbing brokenly, she changed out of the jeans and sweatshirt. While pulling from her closet a gray pinstriped pants suit, she noticed a lavender silk shirt that caught her eye. Taking it off the hanger, she put it on and buttoned it up. After putting the pants on, she neatly tucked the shirt into the waistband.

She pulled a face as she sat down at the dressing table. Her face was pale and drawn, making her look like an escapee from Halloween. *This isn't working for me*, she thought, reaching for all the cosmetics she'd need to per- form the miracle of making herself presentable.

Aware that it was Cassie who stood on the other side of the door, Hillary opened it and threw her arms around her best friend. After pulling Cassie into the house, hand-in-hand they walked into the family room and sat down beside each other on the sofa.

Cassie squeezed Hillary's hand. "I want to hear it all, Hillary. You don't have to hold back with me."

Hillary was in tears when she finished the story of her breakup a short time later.

Cassie did her best to comfort her friend. "I just love you so much. When you hurt, I hurt. When I heard about the breakup, I just wanted to put my arms around my sister and console her. Then I find that I can't reach her. I wanted you to need me." Both Hillary and Cassie began to cry.

"Cass, I did need you. I need you now. I could use one of your old-fashioned hugs right about now. I remember the first hug you ever gave me. It was also the first time you called me your sister. It was when I fell on the ice and cut my knee, when we first learned to ice skate. You hugged me tight, then told the attendant that your sister was hurt. Do you remember?"

Cassie's heart broke for Hillary's very obvious sorrow. "Yes. I remember every minute detail of our childhood, sister dear. Aaron is furious with Brandon over this situation. I talked to Brandon myself and told him he's nothing but a coward."

Hillary couldn't believe what Cassie had said to Brandon. "Cassie, we parted as friends. Don't be too hard on him. I respect him for having the guts to tell me the truth. I could've been the last one to find out. Coming to one another with the truth was what we'd agreed on from the beginning of our relationship. Please don't harbor any ill feelings toward him."

"Ill feelings?" Cassie aped. "I don't have any feelings for him at all." Cassie threw her hands up. "I'm sorry. I shouldn't be saying these things. Brandon has always been sweet to me. One thing for sure is that he regrets it all.

He's downright miserable. He's fencing with the devil, girl-friend. I'm eager to see who's going to win." The doorbell rang. Looking puzzled, Hillary glanced at Cassie. "It's Aaron. I told him to give us a few minutes alone. Are you ready to go? We can finish our discussion later."

Hillary nodded. "Let me get my jacket. I'll lock up and meet you outside." While getting her suit jacket, Hillary had to take a minute to massage her aching heart.

They had already finished their meals when Cassie decided it was time to tell Hillary about the plans she and Aaron had made. Smiling gently, she covered Hillary's hand with hers. "Hillary, Aaron and I have some good news," Cassie announced with some reluctance.

"Let's have it. I, for one, can sure use some good news."

Cassie hesitated briefly. "We've set our wedding date. We're getting married in three weeks."

Hillary looked puzzled. "Three weeks?" she queried breathlessly.

Aaron, who sat on the other side of Hillary, decided to get in on the conversation. "Yes, Hillary, three weeks. We don't want to wait any longer. Cassie and I want to be together in every sense of the word. We love each other infinitely."

Hillary choked back the tears, unintentionally making Cassie feel like a first-class heel. "I'm so happy for you guys. You should be together. You've been waiting on Brandon and me for forever. I don't want you to worry about me. I can get through anything with you two by my side." Both Cassie and Aaron gave Hillary a hug.

Cassie looked at Hillary with concern. "Are you sure you're okay with this?"

Hillary kissed Cassie's cheek. "Of course I am. There's

no reason for you guys to have to wait. Brandon and I aren't getting married, so there's nothing to wait for."

Aaron hugged Hillary again. "I'm sorry about what's happened between you and my best bro, but I know for a fact that this isn't what Brandon wanted. He's got some issues to deal with, Hillary. He's no good for anyone until he deals with himself."

"What issues, Aaron?"

Aaron shrugged his shoulders. "I'm not at liberty to say any more than I have, Hillary. I've probably said too much already, but I don't want you taking any responsibility for the breakup. These are Brandon's issues, and he must be the one to deal with them. Do you understand what I'm saying?"

Hillary shook her head in the negative. "No, I don't, but I'm not going to ask any more questions of you. I don't want to divide loyalties here. I think that's why I found it so hard to talk to you in depth about the situation," she said to Cassie. "With you engaged to Brandon's best friend, I didn't want you to have to split loyalties, either. I didn't want to put either of you in an awkward position. And I don't want either of you to feel that you have to choose sides."

Cassie's hands went to her hips. "Wait a minute here, girlfriend. I'm always going to be on your side, no matter what. You and I have been best friends for forever. That's a fact that can't be ignored here. Without question, I am on your side in this."

Hillary shook her head. "There are no sides to take. Brandon and I parted as friends. I'm so glad for that. I couldn't bear it if we had parted in anger. I admit that I'm angry at the way things turned out, but not at him. I'm bitterly disappointed in his attitude toward my career, but I'm not disappointed *in him*. He was honest about his feelings, and that's important. Just be glad that he didn't figure out his feelings after we walked down the aisle. That would've been even more devastating. Divorce would've come at an extremely high price for me."

Aaron sighed. "I see your point. At any rate, I don't think Brandon thought this whole thing through. We all know how impulsive he is. He wants what he wants, when he wants it, which is usually immediately. He has to have instant gratification. That's gotten him into trouble more than once." Aaron rocked back in his chair. "Hillary, I can say this honestly, I've never seen him work on the defects in his character. That's because he's never admitted that he had any. That is, until he met you. He knows he's not perfect, but he's never been able to see all of his flaws clearly. Believe me, he's taking a good, long look at the man in the mirror. So far, he doesn't like what he's seeing. If I know him—and I do—he'll do something about it."

Hillary brushed the single tear away from the corner of her eye. "We better get out of this restaurant. We've been here for hours now and we finished eating a long time ago."

Cassie pushed her chair back and stood up. "You guys might be finished eating, but I'm just getting my second wind. I'm going to have some more food, then I'm going to move on to the dessert line. Anyone care to join me?" Aaron and Hillary laughed as they got to their feet.

Aaron swatted Cassie's behind. "I don't know where you put it all, girl. You're no bigger than a minute."

Cassie grinned. "At twenty-two-ninety-five a plate, I'll find plenty of places to put it. They're lucky I didn't bring my largest purse. I could put enough food in that bad boy to feed a family of six!" Cassie exclaimed, laughing along with Aaron and Hillary.

Hillary looped her arm through Cassie's. "You're too much. Thank you for not letting me get out of coming here with you guys. Putting all the sorrow aside, it's been fun. I can't wait to stand up for you on your wedding day. Congratulations, darling Cassie. Maybe we can have that double ceremony when you and Aaron renew your vows on one of your anniversaries. I love you!"

"I love you, too, Hillary Houston. You're the best friend a person can have." Both women had tears in their eyes as they embraced.

"Your wedding day is still going to be *our* day. We're going to make it so special!"

Hillary ran into Austin Taylor, her new neighbor, as she rounded the walkway. After leaving the restaurant, she'd spent some time with Cassie and Aaron at Cassie's place. Because it was so nice outside, she had decided to walk home. Seeing Austin before her made her wish she hadn't. No matter how nice he seemed, she didn't want to get involved in any sort of relationship with him.

"Hey, Hillary. It's good to see you. How are you?"

She smiled. "I'm fine, Austin. Are you all settled in?"

As though he'd remembered something, he snapped his fingers. "You know something, when I saw you face-to-face the other day, I knew I'd seen you somewhere. I couldn't get it out of my head. Then, when I went to play the new CD I'd just bought, there you were on the cover. Even after you told me your name I didn't put it all together. When it dawned on me that you and the woman on the cover were one and the same, I went nuts. I love your songs. When I called Atlanta and told my girlfriend that I lived a few doors down from you, she freaked out."

He's safe, she thought with relief, sitting down on the concrete bench. *He already has a girlfriend.* "I'm definitely the one on the cover. Thanks for buying my music. What's your favorite cut?"

He sat down beside her. "What's everybody's favorite cut? 'Destiny' of course. My girlfriend wants it bumping at our wedding. The first night she heard it she called me at two-thirty in the morning to tell me about it. She said it reminded her of us. That's why I went out and bought it. She was right. It's a real tight song. The whole CD's phat, but 'Destiny' is the cut that's got everybody pushing up in the record stores."

It suddenly dawned on Hillary that Austin was a few years younger than she was, perhaps quite a few years. It wasn't that he looked young, because he looked like a mature, older guy. All the hip-hop slang had given his age away. "Are you engaged, Austin?"

His eyes grew bright with love. "Not officially. Torri and I have been friends since the fifth grade. We started taking our friendship a bit further in our senior year of high school. I went to college in Atlanta and she went off to Florida. It wasn't all that far away, but it was too far for us to see each other every day like we had been. She's going to be moving to L.A. in the next few weeks, but we're not going to live together. Torri's going to stay with her aunt. However, we're talking about getting married next June. I bought this town house sight unseen, but we're going to have our dream house built to our own specs. Know any good architects?"

She knew that Austin had no idea what he'd just stirred up deep inside of her, but that didn't make it have any less impact. "As a matter of fact, I know a wonderful architect. I'll turn you on to him when you're ready to build that house."

Austin smiled. "It's not going to be that far off. If you don't mind, do you think you could give him my number real soon? I'd like to talk to him about our plans."

Looking perplexed, Hillary nodded. "I have to ask you this, but you don't have to answer, especially if it offends you. How can you afford to buy a town house and also build your dream house in such a short span of time? Aren't you just fresh out of college?"

Briefly, he looked down at the ground. When he lifted his head, the pain in his eyes mirrored the pain she'd seen in her own the night she'd died at the hands of Brandon's firing squad. "It's not a pretty story, Hillary, but I'll share it with you. My parents were very wealthy when they died together in a car crash last year. I'm their only child."

Hillary's hand flew up to her mouth. "I'm sorry, Austin. I shouldn't have pried into your private affairs. I hope you can forgive me. You have my deepest sympathy."

Fleetingly, he touched her hand. "It's okay, Hillary. I've made my peace with their death simply because I know I'll see them again. I don't want you to think I'm being frivolous with their money. I'm not. I do a lot of good with it. I've been privileged all my life, but my parents taught me that it was a blessing to be so. When I move out of this place, I'm going to put someone in here that needs a place to live. There are a lot of homeless families out there and I'm going to find me one to sponsor. When I find one, I'll start by putting them in an apartment, with the promise that they can move in here when my house is ready. You'd be surprised at the incentive that that will give them, not to mention the revival of their hope."

Hillary felt the tears in her eyes, but she didn't bother to wipe them away. "That was a very moving story, Austin. I'm sure your parents are smiling their approval down upon you. I do what I can for the homeless also, but nothing compared to what you have in mind. Like you, I plan to do so much more. Would you like to come in for something to drink, Austin?"

Hillary felt extremely comfortable with Austin. Now that she knew she had nothing to fear from him, she saw no harm in befriending him. She could use a friend of the opposite sex, too. Austin's obvious love for Torri was refreshing. That made her feel good about the future.

* * *

Just as Hillary and Austin disappeared into her town house, Brandon turned around and slowly walked back to his car. Looking defeated, he slid behind the wheel. He'd come there to beg her forgiveness, to tell her how wrong he'd been, to tell her that he couldn't live without her, to plead with her to take him back as her fiancé. Apparently she'd already learned to live without him, he realized painfully. He'd been right to fear Hillary, he told himself.

He'd also been right about her being the one who would pay him back for all his misdeeds. Even though he'd conned himself into believing it could never happen again, he'd been right about history having a way of repeating itself. Somehow, he'd failed her. In the process, he'd also failed himself.

Time flew by while Hillary and Cassie busied themselves with the preparations for the wedding. Most of the major tasks had already been taken care of. Hillary's sisters had helped Cassie out tremendously. Mrs. Houston had been instrumental in taking care of the catering and the flower arrangements and Cassie's parents had arrived to help with the finishing touches. Along with Mrs. Paige, Mrs. Samms had helped Cassie pick out her wedding dress.

Hillary felt awful that all this had taken place without her, but in looking back she saw that she wouldn't have been much help. She understood why things had to be done without her; she just wouldn't have been able to handle the stress, no matter how happy she was for Cassie.

Everyone seemed so cautious with her feelings, tiptoeing about her as though she might break in two, but Hillary assured everyone that she could handle things from that point on. She vowed not to let anything stand in the way of Cassie and Aaron having a wonderful day.

Once Cassie's bridal party was fitted for their dresses, the shoes were selected and dyed to match the gowns. White and two shades of lavender were her color scheme. Hillary's dress was done in soft lavender while the other dresses were a deeper shade of the same color.

Aaron's groomsmen would wear black double-breasted tuxedos by Dior, with white shirts and black buttons. The cummerbunds would be black, with the exception of the ones done in both shades of lavender for the groom and best man.

A group of Aaron's lawyer friends were in charge of decorating the church, the reception hall and all the cars. Fresh carnations had been chosen for the decorations.

Hillary sat quietly in her bedroom chair, looking out the window. It was a perfectly delightful day, perfect for Cassie and Aaron's wedding. Today would be the first day she'd be in the company of Brandon since their breakup, and she wondered how they'd handle seeing each other after such a long spell.

Brandon hadn't shown up for the rehearsal or the dinner that had taken place afterward, which had perturbed Aaron to no end. Aaron hadn't heard from Brandon the entire day, but they had talked the night before, Cassie had told her. While there was concern, the show had to go on without him . . . and it had. Hillary had mixed emotions about him not showing up, but she hadn't passed comment one way or the other. Her first emotion was relief, followed by disappointment. Maybe if they'd seen each other before the wedding, she thought, it might not be so awkward for them at the ceremony.

Hillary decided not to dwell on her situation with Brandon. This day belonged to Cassie and Aaron, she mused, promising herself to help make this the happiest day of their lives. Hillary moved away from the window and gathered all the things she had to take to the church, where the girls had all agreed to get dressed.

Less than an hour later, when Hillary arrived at the church, she was full of optimism. Since their childhood, she and Cassie had constantly talked about a double wedding and how they were going to marry twin brothers. Though neither would occur, Hillary was happy for Cassie.

As Hillary stepped into the chapel to have a look at the beautifully decorated room, her breath caught. Flowers and bows were everywhere and seemingly on everything. The gold candelabras trimmed with floral garlands in lavender and ivory tones rested on the altar. Tiers of lighted ficus trees graced the front of the church. Overwhelmed by it all, she felt the hot tears sting her eyes as she fled into the dressing area. This was going to be tougher on her than she'd imagined, she now knew.

Everyone had taken their places while waiting for the wedding party's entry. Looking absolutely dreamy, Aaron was in position, eagerly waiting for his bride-to-be. Aaron's groomsmen looked extremely handsome in their tuxedos.

The organist began playing softly, hushing the guests immediately.

Hillary, as the maid of honor, was the first to enter, looking exquisite in the soft pale lavender, off-the-shoulder foille sheath. Piled loosely on top in large curls, her beautiful hair was adorned with a circle of pale lavender flowers. Wearing three-pearl earrings in her dainty ears, she carried a delicate bouquet of lavender and white flowers. Adorned in the same dress as Hillary, only in a deeper shade of lavender, the three bridesmaids wore the same earrings as Hillary, which had been Cassie's gift to her bridal party.

Brandon, looking like a male cover model, stood next to Aaron. Keeping his eyes trained on Hillary, whom he thought was a vision of timeless beauty, he inhaled deeply to calm the butterflies in his stomach. More than at any other time he realized how much he truly loved and missed her. He tried to turn his eyes away from her, but his attempt was unsuccessful.

As the rest of the wedding party walked down the aisle, the pretty little flower girl strewed her lavender rose petals all around. The ring bearer looked adorable in his little tuxedo as he carried the pale lavender satin pillow with pride.

First, the organist softly played "Here and Now," Cassie and Aaron's favorite song. As she began the wedding march, Cassie appeared in the archway of the church on her father's arm. The guests gasped as they took in her magnificent beauty.

Cassie wore a sophisticated silk-faced, ivory-white satin gown with an off-the-shoulder, sweetheart neckline. Beaded lace trimmed the neckline and the capped sleeves and encircled the full gathered skirt. Dainty satin-covered buttons trailed down the back of the dress to meet a chapel-length train. Wearing elegant satin slippers on her tiny feet, she carried a bouquet of cream-colored baby roses and baby's breath.

Her father looked dashing in his black double-breasted tuxedo. His chest swelled with pride as Walter Paige marched his beautiful daughter down the aisle to the altar, where he handed her over into Aaron's care. Ena Paige looked on with tears in her eyes.

As if they were somehow magnetically drawn together, Brandon and Hillary stared into each other's eyes as Cassie and Aaron exchanged their vows. Tears slipped from Hillary's eyes before she could turn her gaze away from

Brandon's to fully concentrate on Cassie and Aaron. Wanting this to be their wedding day, too, Brandon ached to hold Hillary in his arms and kiss her tears away. Seeing her cry caused his heart to split wide open. Brandon had been watching Hillary from a distance for some time now, yet seeing her before him, without being able to touch her, was almost more than he could bear, more than he wanted to bear. He needed her desperately.

As the minister pronounced Cassie and Aaron husband and wife, they sealed their vows with a deep, passionate kiss. "I present to you Mr. and Mrs. Aaron Jonathan Samms." Aaron and Cassie floated up the aisle, smiling into each other's eyes.

As the attendants paired off, Brandon held his arm out to Hillary. She slipped her arm into his without so much as a glance at him. The wedding party and the guests followed the bride and groom outside to the waiting floral-decorated limousine.

Once everyone was outside, a pair of beautiful white doves were released into the blue sky. Everyone stood in silence, watching in awe as the doves took flight. It was at this moment that Hillary lost her composure. Unable to control it, her petite body shook with sobs. Brandon reached out to her, but she quickly turned away from him and ran toward her father.

Jackson gathered his weeping daughter into his strong arms, whispering softly to her. "Remember that this is Cassie and Aaron's day. A day for pure happiness."

Hillary hugged her father. "Thanks for the loving reminder, Dad," she sobbed.

Brandon stood by helplessly, watching as she suddenly flashed her father a dazzling smile. He could only wish that she'd smile at him the same way, the way she used to smile at him, but he knew he deserved the treatment she'd given him. However, the realization did nothing to ease the torturous pain.

* * *

The gala reception was held in the private ballroom of a prestigious hotel. Cassie and Aaron looked as happy as any two people could be as they took time to speak to each guest. Aaron and Cassie's parents watched their children with love-filled eyes. The Houstons and the Blairs were happy for the couple, as well, but their hearts were breaking for their daughter and son, Alice had told Hillary after the ceremony.

Cassie slipped her hand into Hillary's and took her aside. "How are you really handling things, Hillary?"

Hillary lowered her lashes. "It's hard, but not because of you. I'm deliriously happy for you and Aaron. It's just hard being in the same room with the man I love so desperately. We parted as friends and I shouldn't be feeling this anger right now."

Cassie squeezed Hillary's hand. "Why don't you talk to him. I know for a fact that he regrets breaking up with you. You two did part as friends, you know."

Hillary kissed her beautiful friend. "We shouldn't be discussing this now. This is a day for joy, a day for Cassie and Aaron!"

Cassie hugged her friend. "Thank you for being so wonderful. This day wouldn't have been possible without you. I love you!"

"I love you, too!" Hillary responded, fighting her wretched emotions.

As Cassie floated off on a cloud with Aaron, Hillary, desperately needing some fresh air, rushed outside to take a stroll in the hotel's lovely garden. Scents from the beautiful flowers and shrubs seemed to instantly relax her. While touching an exotic wildflower, she heard her name whispered to her on the gentle breeze. She didn't need to turn around to find out who'd called out to her. No one spoke her name like Brandon did. No one made it sound like poetry. No one called her Hill. As she turned around, he already stood very close to her.

His smile was as bright as the day. "Hello, Hillary. How have you been?"

Though dying inside, she gave him a halfway decent smile in return. "Fine, thank you." Forgetting her manners, she turned her attention back to the flower she'd been examining.

He gently touched her shoulder. "Hillary, we have to talk. We can't suffer in silence any longer. This hurts me too damn much. Way too much."

Unable to believe his gall, Hillary turned to face him. "Oh, no, no, this won't do. I won't have you believing I'm suffering when I'm not," she lied. "Brandon, you made yourself very clear the day you walked out on our relationship. I wanted so much for us to remain friends, but you've not called once, nor have you returned mine. I respected your feelings by staying away from you. Now you respect mine and stay away from me."

Handicapped by his aching desire to have her back, Brandon couldn't leave well enough alone. "Hillary, I need you in my life. I've been a fool. I know we can work this out. I told you my decision had nothing to do with not loving you. I'll always love you. I just needed to work through some things. I needed to work on my flaws. I love you, Hillary. Please don't be mad."

She wanted to throw herself into his arms, wanted to have him further rock her world if only for an instant, but that would be a big mistake. "Brandon, dogs get mad, people get angry. I'm angry, Brandon. I'm angry at this whole situation. I haven't heard a single word from you. Now, all of a sudden, you need me in your life. I think not. You hurt me deeply. I'm beginning to heal now and I'm putting the past behind me. I suggest you do the same."

Not wanting him to see her tears, yet wanting him in the worst way, she turned away and walked back into the hotel. She'd be damned before she'd give him the satisfaction of letting him know how much she wanted him back in her life. He hadn't bothered to call her back, even after she'd left Austin Taylor's phone number on his service. That had really spelled out the end for her.

Brandon remained in the garden, lowering himself into a chair. He was sure that Hillary still loved him, even though he'd convinced himself that she didn't when she'd refused to fight for their relationship. In spite of what she'd just told him, her eyes had told him something quite different. Seeing her today had brought back a flood of memories, making him determined to have her back in his life, permanently. First, he had to find out the identity of the man he'd seen with her and what he meant to her. He could only pray that it wasn't too late for him, too late for eternity.

As Brandon reentered the hotel, the happy couple was about to leave. He needed to say something to them both before they got away. He approached Cassie first. "Hello, gorgeous, you are one beautiful bride!"

Cassie couldn't stop herself from smiling. She missed him. "Hi, yourself. You're looking mighty gorgeous, too."

He bent his head and kissed her gently on the lips. "I should've been the first one to kiss you after Aaron and your father. You know that, don't you?"

Swiping playfully at his arm, she grinned. "Yes, I do know that."

His eyes grew somber. "Cassie, I just wanted to say I'm sorry for ruining this day for you and Hillary. I know how you two had planned a double wedding all your lives. I never meant for things to turn out this way. I'm truly sorry, babe."

"You should be sorry," Aaron chimed in, "but not as sorry as you're going to be if you don't get Hillary back.

You made a big mistake, man. Now it's time to rectify it. That is, if you still love her like I think you do."

Brandon shook his head. "Boy, do I still love her. I never stopped for a second. I tried to tell her that a minute ago, but she wasn't having any of it."

Anxiously, Cassie searched the room for Hillary. Brandon's confrontation with Hillary had her worried. Hillary had been doing okay, and she wished that Brandon had left it alone for today. Spotting Hillary sitting with her parents, Cassie saw that she had a smile on her face, which made her sigh in relief. It appeared that Brandon hadn't been able to do too much damage. Silently, she prayed for Hillary to get through the rest of the day.

She turned her attention back to Brandon. "Say, guy, could you give it a rest for today? Hillary needs more time. Don't try to rush anything. Okay?"

Brandon grinned sheepishly, like a child who'd just been scolded. "Okay. Whatever Mrs. Samms wants." He gave Cassie another light kiss, this time on the cheek.

He shook Aaron's hand. Then the two friends hugged, patting each other hard on the back. "Hang in there, my man. I think there still might be a chance for you, but you've got to take things slow. Hillary's not a faucet. You can't just turn her off and on like one. I don't think I need to tell you again what you need to do. You got some serious tasks ahead of you."

Brandon gripped Aaron's hand. "Thanks for the advice, man. Now you need to get back to your bride. It looks like she's getting ready to throw the bouquet."

Aaron laughed heartily as he saw all the single women waiting in eager anticipation, each one hoping to make the lucky catch. Aaron reached Cassie's side just as she turned around and threw the bouquet over her shoulder. Without any guidance on Cassie's part, the flowers headed straight for Hillary's hands. Seeing it coming in her direction, she stepped aside to allow someone else to receive it. She thought the catch was a bad omen for her, especially under the circumstances.

Brandon noticed her deliberate action of stepping aside to avoid catching the flowers. But it didn't stop him from deliberately stepping in front of someone else to catch Cassie's blue garter, which Aaron had tossed over his shoulder. While waving the garter in the air, Brandon flashed Hillary his most charming, disarming smile.

Not at all amused by his mischief, Hillary stuck her tongue out at him, which he found hilarious. Not wanting to maker her any angrier than she already was, he turned away from her so that she couldn't see his laughter.

While the newlyweds ran toward the waiting limousine, everyone threw birdseed at them. Cassie and Aaron laughed out loud, dodging the tiny pellets. As they reached the limousine, Aaron pulled Cassie into his arms and planted a deep, passionate kiss upon her luscious pink mouth. All the guests cheered and clapped as they watched the couple disappear into the limousine, off to the Virgin Islands for their honeymoon.

With tears streaming down her face, Hillary watched the limousine pull away, unable to keep from wishing that she and Brandon were in the car with them. If only Brandon David Blair had loved her as much as Aaron loved Cassie, she would've been the happiest woman in the city. If only he had loved her enough to make her his wife. If only . . . To avoid making herself even more miserable, she cut the rest of her morose thoughts loose.

Twenty-one

Only days after the wedding another nice day paid a visit to Los Angeles, nice enough for Hillary to sit outdoors by the complex's Olympic-sized swimming pool. The cloudy days that often came to the city when the month of June marched in were referred to as "June Gloom." Clad in black jeans and a yellow sweatshirt, her sun-toasted skin gleamed under the bright sunlight. With her legs drawn up under her, she sat in one of the colorful chairs, deriving untold pleasure from the beauty of her surroundings.

The complex grounds were beautifully landscaped with lovely plants, flowers, and trees. The red, purple, white, and pink ornamental bougainvillea vines ran rampant throughout the grounds, while the aromatic fragrance of the showy white gardenia bushes tantalized her sense of smell. On each side of her two fully bloomed acacia trees boasted yellow clusters of flowers.

Hillary stared into the shimmering, crystal-clear, aqua-colored water of the pool. The golden sun skimming off the water drew her into a hypnotic trance, making her eyelashes sweep slowly down over her eyes. Fully relaxed, she fell into a tranquil state.

Listlessly, Brandon stood beside one of the gigantic palm trees. Hillary, lost in her own world, had had no idea that he watched her from the other side of the pool. With his face full of yearning, his eyes thirstily drank in every inch of Hillary's beauty. This was the closest he'd been to her since the wedding. His thoughts were turbulent, which came from not knowing whether to approach her or just turn and walk away.

Noticing how the sun had run its fingers through her chestnut-brown hair, streaking it with bright golden highlights, he smiled. Running his fingers nervously through his own hair, he was powerless to stay in the background any longer. Slowly creeping closer to where she lay, he finally reached her. Instead of touching her, he just stood there quietly, watching over his solo singing angel.

After several minutes had passed, he turned to walk away. When his feet refused to take him away from the woman he'd come to love so completely, he knelt down beside the chair and brushed her cheek with feathery soft strokes. As his touch caused her to stir slightly, she shifted her position, causing him to withdraw his hand. It took all the strength that he possessed to keep from inebriating himself by kissing her inviting mouth.

Suddenly, a police siren went off somewhere in the distance. The offensive sound reached her ears before he had a chance to move away. The car's siren had scared the daylights out of her, causing a terror-filled scream to wrench loose from deep within her throat. Without the slightest thought, he pulled her into his arms. Instantly, without hesitation, she entwined her trembling arms around his neck, seeking comfort in the very familiar security of his arms. She pressed her head close against his chest, and he began rubbing her back in circular motions.

Now fully cognizant of what was happening, she willfully loosened herself from his loving embrace. "I'm sorry for the way I reacted," she said, seemingly embarrassed. "I'm still not sure what frightened me. My thought process is totally mixed up right now. What are you doing here, anyway?"

Putting one finger under her chin, he lifted it up. "Hill, the only answer to your question is an honest one. Pretty lady, I've missed you more than you can imagine."

Watching him closely, she contemplated her next words. "Brandon, now that I'm thinking clearer, I guess it was an obtuse question. But I was so sure we had settled all this madness."

"Hillary, there's nothing obtuse about the question. I think it's a perfectly legitimate one. Do you want me to expound upon the answer I've already given?"

She grew impatient with the trend of their conversation. "No, especially if it's more of the same rhetoric you spewed at the wedding. I'm simply not interested in hearing it." She bent over to pick up her shoes from off the deck. Without uttering another word, she moved toward the house.

Brandon stared at her retreating form with persistence shining in his dark eyes. Her stubborn attitude had only fueled his relentless determination. He chased after her disappearing form. Before she could close the door behind her, he pushed his way inside. She took his action as an attempt to force her to talk to him regardless of how she felt. It aroused a burning anger inside of her, which reached the depths of her eyes.

She slapped her hands on her hips. "Brandon, you have more nerve than any one person should be able to lay claim to. I would like for you to leave. I don't have anything to discuss with you. Everything I needed to say to you was said at the wedding."

"But I have something to discuss with you . . . and you damn well need to listen for a change." The anger in his voice scared her. "Hill, you're not the only one who feels hurt and betrayed. I have feelings, too. Did you ever once consider how I was feeling all those months you were establishing yourself in the recording business? Did you ever stop to think about what I might be needing from you?" Hillary opened her mouth to answer, but he sharply cut her off. "You don't have to answer. I'll be glad to do it for you. The answer is no, on both accounts. You accepted everything I had to offer, but you gave very little in return. All you were interested in was seeing your damn precious name in neon lights. You're the only one who is allowed to make a mistake. I made a mistake, I've admitted it, but that still wasn't good enough for you. Would you be happy if I penned an apology to you using my blood for ink?" Hillary thought the tirade was over when he started shouting again.

"I thought you were different from all the other women I've ever known. The women who want everything handed to them on a silver platter, yet they don't want to work for it. I can see now that I was mistaken. You're no different at all. Your damn holier-than-thou attitude makes me sick. I'm finished trying to convey to you how much I want you back in my life."

Having heard enough from him, she moved across the room with a vengeance, not stopping until she stood toe-to-toe with him. "You're so wrong about me. I'm glad you let me know how you really feel about me. I've never asked you for one darn thing. How could you have ever imagined yourself in love with such an outright opportunist?"

He glared fiercely at her. "It was easy. Your deceptions were gift-wrapped in satin paper, with a lovely red velvet bow tied around them. As far as I'm concerned, this conversation is over. You can go straight to hell with the rest of your conniving comrades," he spat out.

The words had flown out of his mouth before he'd had a chance to ponder them. Immediately, he wished that he could take them all back. He hadn't meant for this encounter to turn out this way any more than he'd meant the last ones to turn out badly. Not only could he see the rage in her eyes, he felt it. Still, he was totally surprised when she slapped him across the face, something he would've never expected from her.

"Don't you ever talk to me like that as long as you live. My father has never talked to my mother that way, and you won't talk to me that way, either."

He hadn't even seen the slap coming. He'd been too busy wishing he had all the words back that he'd spoken, knowing what he'd said to her was so terribly far removed from the truth. He'd only wanted to shock her into breaking down the barriers she'd erected between them.

As he started toward her, she cowered back in fear, thinking he was going to retaliate against her. Her hands flew up to protect her face from the assault she expected. Backing away from him, she tripped and fell down into the chair. It broke his heart when he realized what she'd been expecting from him.

Kneeling down beside the chair, he took her trembling hand in his, wanting desperately to kiss away her fears. "Hillary, I'm so sorry for what I've said, for what I made you think. I would never strike you. I just feel terrible knowing that I hurt you enough to cause you to strike out at me. I didn't mean anything I said, nor do I believe any part of it. I was merely trying to get you to break down the walls standing in the way of our happiness. I realize now that I've only made things worse between us. Hill, I promise you I'll never, ever speak to you that way again. You have my word, though I know I haven't kept my word in the past. That has all changed."

He pulled her into his arms. When she offered no resistance, he stroked her hair tenderly, hoping to soothe her rattled nerves. "I love you. Only you," he whispered softly into her hair. "I love you. I love you. How did I let it come to this?" he whispered over and over again. "Please, pretty lady, don't cry anymore.

Scared to move a muscle for fear that she'd move away from him, he didn't want to release her from his arms, or stop planting kisses in her sweet-smelling hair. She allowed him to hold her for a very long time before she found the strength to put a slight distance between them. Lifting her head up, she stared into his eyes, caressing his cheek with the back of her hand.

"Brandon, we can't do this to each other any longer," she said on a jagged sob. "We're destroying all the beautiful memories that we have. Each time we have one of these outrageous scenes we further damage our spirits. I'd be devastated if you really felt the things you said about me. Please tell me again that you truly don't perceive me in that way."

He brought her fingertips to his lips. "No, precious. I don't perceive you in that way at all. I couldn't love you and feel that way about you. And I do love you so very much."

Her eyes brimming with fresh tears, she looked into the depths of his raven-black gaze. "I need to know something. Have you been hurt before by someone you cared for deeply? If so, did that someone destroy your ability to trust?" As hard as it was to do, he tore his eyes from hers. Wringing his hands together, he paced the floor.

Walking up behind him, she wrapped her arms around his waist, just as she'd done the night he'd broken off their relationship. "You don't have to answer that. The answer is clear. I'm so sorry, so sorry that possibly your love wasn't valued."

Anguished over his despair, Hillary excused herself to go to the kitchen for a drink of water. He watched her as she moved gracefully out of the room, wanting to tell her the truth of the fears that haunted him. But he still wasn't ready, still hadn't worked it all through. Judging from what had just occurred, he hadn't completely conquered his fears. He was unsure of where he now stood with her, but more than anything he was wary of pushing himself into something that he just might not be ready to handle. How familiar those words sounded—Hillary's words.

Positioning himself in the chair in which she'd been

sitting, he thought over the last hour. It suddenly dawned on him that not once had she said she still loved him. Was it possible she didn't? Or worse, had he destroyed that precious love with his selfishness and arrogance? Knowing he still had some work to do on himself, he decided not to push the subject. Whatever the outcome, Hillary Houston was the only woman in the world for him, the one and only.

Wearing a warm smile on her face, she returned to the room. "The offer I made for us to remain friends is still open. I hope you'll take me up on it."

So sure he'd seen love for him in her eyes at the wedding, her statement crushed him like a bulldozer ramming a building. Could he have misread what he'd seen in her eyes? Running his hands down across his thighs, he cleared his throat. "I'd like to think we'll always remain friends. But, Hillary, one day I want to be your lover, your husband." If she wasn't interested in that happening, he didn't know what else he could say, nor did he know what he would do without her.

Hillary felt a sadness that she couldn't begin to explain. "Brandon, I think we need to continue to take time out as lovers. You need to be sure that you can handle all the things that come with my profession. I still don't think you're ready, and I'm not willing to give it up for anyone or anything right now. My life is extremely busy, and I can't imagine that changing any time soon. I've dreamed of being a recording artist all my life, just as you probably dreamt of becoming an architect. There are many things I want to do; so many far-off places I want to see. At this moment in time I can't offer you any more than friendship."

Her unintentional barbed arrow struck him right through the heart. That last statement convinced him she didn't love him, at least not the way that he needed her to love him. Her words caused him more distress than he was willing to show.

Removing himself from the chair, he crossed the room to stand in front of her. "Pretty lady, I better go now. I'd like to think over the things we've discussed here today. I'll be in touch. I want you to know that I'll always be there for you should you need me. I love you, pretty lady." He brushed her lips lightly with his. Crushing her to him, losing himself in her exotic scent, he kissed her as though it might very well be the last time. As he released her, he didn't dare look back. Looking as if he'd been sentenced to death, he walked out the door.

Appearing no less devastated than the man who'd become her morning glory, her midnight sun, the man she loved for all seasons, for all reasons, she closed the door behind him and ran to her bedroom. Walking out onto the patio, she sat in the chair and looked out at the lake. Remembering his last soul-crushing kiss, she closed her eyes and swept her fingers across her lips, her thoughts more confused than ever before. Of all the things that had occurred between them, she couldn't believe she'd been unable to tell Brandon she loved him, but there was no doubt in her mind that she did, endlessly.

Her mind flipped to the scene where he'd told her what he thought of her. Flinching in pain, she recalled some of the ugly things he'd said. Even though she believed he didn't mean them, the harsh anger in which he'd spoken them still made her suffer.

Wishing Cassie were there to talk with, she felt sorry for all the times she should've talked to her but didn't. In the past she and Cassie had shared everything that went on in their lives. She couldn't explain why she'd shut Cassie out, other than the reason she'd already given her. Aaron was Brandon's best friend, and she'd been afraid of dividing loyalties, she reiterated in her thoughts. Moving back into the house, she lay down across the bed. While her heart exploded into millions of fragments inside her chest, she promised herself that if he came back and still wanted her, she'd take him back in a heartbeat.

Pondering the things he and Hillary had discussed, Brandon walked along the private strip of beach in front of his home. This was the second time she'd refused to fight for their love, he told himself. Maybe what she felt for him wasn't as strong as what he felt for her. How could something so beautiful be over so quickly? Fully aware that most, if not all, of the problems they'd encountered arose from his selfish nature, he didn't blame her for anything that went wrong.

Like Hillary, he wished his best friend were there to help make sense of these last few painful weeks of his life. Cassie and Aaron weren't back from their honeymoon yet.

Finally, Brandon came to the conclusion that Hillary loved him, but perhaps not enough to make him a part of her world. He understood why she'd have doubts about his willingness to commit to the things that were a part of her life, or to marriage, or to being loyal to the family she loved dearly, among all the other responsibilities that came with marriage.

He returned to the house when the sea air caused him to shiver from the coldness.

Twenty minutes later, after a hot shower, he climbed into bed. Extending his arm to the place where she'd be lying if she were with him, he rubbed her sleeping place with open palms. Shifting his position, he moved over to cover her spot with the warmth of his body.

Twenty-two

Southern California had experienced a bitter cold, rainy spell. Mudslides had had disastrous effects on the coastal cities and rural areas. BDB Architectural Design had received more than its fair share of contracts for restoring houses and buildings damaged by the rainstorms. Cassie and Aaron occasionally updated Hillary on Brandon regarding matters that weren't of a personal nature, but only when she asked about him.

As much as it hurt, Brandon had accepted the fact that he and Hillary wouldn't get back together. He hadn't called her out of fear of rejection. Several weeks had passed since the last time they'd talked, but he constantly kept up with her career.

Though she didn't know of his presence, he rarely missed one of her local performances. She smiled at him everyday from the *Soulful Serenade* CD cover. He read all the articles written about her and watched every television appearance she made. Aaron would always let him know when she was going to be at their house so he wouldn't walk in unexpectedly and risk causing her embarrassment. The only social life that he had was that which directly involved his business, though he kept himself very busy.

Hillary worked hard to finish her latest recording project, *Heartbreak at Dawn*. Inundated with preparations for a very special personal appearance, she rarely had a free moment. Scheduled to appear for the first time ever in front of her hometown crowd, the performance was expected to be very unique, which was the sole reason for the unusual request she'd put in her contract regarding her home state. She'd wanted to wait until she was financially able to give her family and close friends in Washburgh a special evening at her own expense.

Taking care of all the arrangements herself, she had placed several long distance calls to her hometown. A ballroom in the only large hotel in Washburg had been leased for the entire evening. Gold embossed invitations had been printed and sent out to all the special people that had touched her during her years there. Her invitations included Mr. and Mrs. Asher and Lois and Alex, who were now married, but she wasn't sure if the younger couple could make it. Lois was several months pregnant.

Classmates, teachers, ministers, neighbors, and many others were expected to attend. All of her family from the West Coast would be in attendance, but her sisters who lived overseas wouldn't be able to make the performance.

Red and white was the color scheme she'd chosen for the event. Red and white floral arrangements were ordered for each of the tables and a pre-selected catering list had been sent to the hotel. Red roses had been ordered for some very special people who had encouraged her in her singing. Mrs. Harris, the church choir director, was chosen as one of the flower recipients. She often chose Hillary for solo parts, calming her fears before each performance. Hillary never forgot how wonderfully the choir director had treated her.

As Hillary walked into the ballroom of the hotel, she could see that all her hard work had paid off. She was pleased with everything, from the tables dressed up in white linen tablecloths with red napkins, to the floral arrangements of red and white dainty rosebuds and sprigs of baby's breath, which all looked exquisite. Encircled with wreaths of fresh red and white carnations, the gold candelabras held red and white candles. The white place cards with the name of each guest engraved in gold lettering added the finishing touch to the tables. Red and white helium balloons and streamers hovered above the tables and chairs.

Arranged by Cassie's parents, a large red and gold banner hung above the stage, welcoming Hillary Houston home. The banner read: WELCOME HOME, HILLARY HOUSTON, OUR VERY OWN HOMETOWN CELEBRITY!

Looking up at the sign bearing her name, she broke down and cried, overwhelmed by the significance of it all. She had a hard time believing all the things she'd actually accomplished. Being at home after all these years felt strange and sweet, all at the same time.

Before she could get too emotional over her homecoming, her band and dancers showed up for the scheduled rehearsal. St. John entered the room right behind the stage crew, smiling adoringly at the woman he'd discovered in a Hollywood restaurant. "Hey, sweetness," he called out to her. "Are we ready to knock your hometown crowd dead?"

Hillary laughed heartily. "I'd like to think I'm going to knock them alive! If they're deceased, we can't party hard after the concert, the way we've planned for months now."

St. John grinned. "I guess you got a point there." He kissed her cheek. "Look, I've got to make sure everything comes off just the way you've planned it, so I'm going to run along. If you need anything, holler loud. I'm never too far away from my 'superstar.' "

"Superstar, indeed," Hillary reiterated. How sad, she mused, a superstar with a broken heart, never to be mended, a superstar with no special lover to share in her superstardom.

St. John hated the tragic look that had made a permanent home in her beautiful eyes. More than that, he hated the reason it was there. "He's out there somewhere, honey. God has no intentions of allowing one of his most beautiful creations to spend the rest of her days alone. You're His special angel of music. You can believe He's already chosen the best man for you."

After rehearsing for an hour with her band and dancers, Hillary was ready to return to her suite in the hotel to lie down, but not before she checked out all the preparations once more.

Her family crowded into her room just before the performance to wish her well, to offer any support she might need. Cassie, Aaron, and Cassie's parents also dropped by. Everyone was excited. Even the air seemed to be charged with a powerful feeling of love and joy.

Once everyone had left to go to their own rooms to dress, Hillary began to ready herself for what she considered the most important night of her life. Using extreme care, she fixed her hair and applied her makeup to perfection, having refused the services of a makeup artist. The black velvet dress she'd first performed in, in New York, was the chosen one since it had also been worn the first night she and Brandon ever made love, she recalled with crystal clarity.

Looking dashing dressed in a black tuxedo, with a red rose in his lapel, white shirt, and red cummerbund, Henry Houston, who would serve as the master of ceremonies for the evening, entered the stage of the magnificently decorated ballroom. Taking center stage, he picked up the microphone. A hush came over the room as he spoke to the guests.

"Good evening, family, friends, and special guests. On

behalf of Hillary and the rest of the Houston family, I would like to welcome all of you and send out a very warm thank-you for joining us this evening. Hillary will be so pleased to see each and every one of you. This has been a long time coming for her." He laughed. "I know I'm not what you came here for so I won't put you through any more agony. Here to warm your heart and dazzle your soul is my baby sister and your very own hometown girl, *Miss Hillary Houston!* Let's give her a warm, hearty Washburg welcome."

Everyone stood, clapping and cheering their loudest to welcome Hillary Houston home. As Hillary appeared onstage, her guests gave her another hearty welcome. Smiling sweetly, her complexion glowed with the love and warmth she felt inside. Waving to everyone enthusiastically, she stepped to the microphone.

"I'm sorry it took me so long to make it back home." She held her arms out in an embracing gesture. "Tonight is for each and every one of you. I love you all!" As the cheers and whistles grew louder and louder, she remembered her childhood dream of long ago.

The music began and the audience fell into a complete yet almost tangible silence. Hillary surveyed the room before turning her attention to the head table, where her immediate family members, the Paiges, and the Sammses were seated. Smiling, she blew a heartfelt kiss.

Her confidence in her abilities to give an exemplary performance was never more pronounced as she flirted and flaunted her talent in front of her bewitched audience. Walking slowly off the stage, she stopped in front of the head table, performing for her loved ones like she'd never performed before. Going into the audience normally drove St. John crazy, but not tonight. No security was needed here. After all, this was her beloved hometown crowd.

Giving her family members a personal performance by

singing a cover of "We Are Family," she changed the lyrics to include her only brother, calling each of them by name, including Cassie. Mrs. Harris got a big hug and Hillary was thrilled to see Mr. and Mrs. Asher seated at the same table. As she worked the entire room before heading back to the stage, the pride she saw in her parents' eyes was unmistakable.

Pausing after a few songs, she introduced her band, asking the audience to show their appreciation of their extraordinary talents. Hillary also mentioned the names of several people she'd spotted in the audience. Everyone appeared to love the personal attention from her. Cassie and Aaron were seated in front, and Hillary embraced them with her eyes before introducing the newlyweds. She then sang a special song just for them.

As Hillary spotted the empty chair next to her father, her breaking heart began beating out of control, making her feel that a runaway freight train was loose in her chest. Though she couldn't help thinking that Brandon should be there with her, she continued to sing. As a constant reminder of what she'd lost, she had requested that one chair be left empty at the head table. Also at her request, there was always one empty front seat at all her concerts.

Her heart ached for him. She had heard something said once and she'd never forgotten it: "Success is nothing without someone you love to share it with." Nothing anyone could ever say could be closer to the truth, she mused, tears stinging her eyes.

Gesturing for the band to cease playing, she began speaking into the microphone. "I would like to do something special for you this evening. First, I would like to take a special moment to thank God for the many rich blessings that He has bestowed upon me. Without Him, I know I wouldn't be here this evening." Several hearty amens rang out. "Now, for what I think will be special." She looked over at her brother. "Henry, please join me up here on the stage."

Looking bewildered, Henry moved from his seat to join Hillary. As he reached the stage, she whispered something into his ear. Smiling, he hugged her tenderly. Presenting the audience with a duet, they sang "Amazing Grace." Pulling out all the stops on the popular gospel song, they saw that there wasn't a dry eye left in the house.

Hillary sang several more songs solo, then shared the stage with her dancers. While dancing together in perfect rhythm, they encouraged audience participation. During the intermission she went backstage to change her clothes. Her dress was soaked clear through with perspiration.

Hillary's band entertained the audience until her return. While she'd sung all the hip-hop songs earlier, when she returned to the stage she'd be singing all her love ballads from *Soulful Serenade*, showcasing her very special talent as a solo singer.

Wearing a formal length, blood-red crêpe gown, Hillary walked back onto the stage. Worn low on the shoulders, fashioned with a discreet slit up the front, the eye-popping gown had a deeply plunging V-neckline down the front and back. She positively loved the gorgeous gown that Cassie had designed with the intent of lending Hillary an air of sophistication.

The only jewelry she wore were the diamond earrings from her parents and her engagement ring from Brandon. This was the first time she'd ever put the ring back on her finger. She didn't know why she'd felt so compelled to wear it tonight. She had tried sending the ring back several times, but it was always returned to her.

A stool had been set onstage, and she perched her small frame on it. Reaching down somewhere deep in her soul, she began to pull out every emotion possible. Her voice took on a richness that didn't seem to be there before her broken heart. Knowingly, she tugged on the heartstrings of every person present. Crying inwardly, Hillary closed her eyes as she began to sing her golden single "Destiny."

Transforming herself into a sultry seductress, she sang the song with all the emotions she'd stored up for months. Wooing the audience with low guttural moans, she held them spellbound. Stroking their emotions as tenderly as a mother would her newborn baby, her voice thundered sweetly into the audience, sending out shivers of haunting pleasure. Her tears running free, Hillary continued to titillate the crowd beyond comprehension.

Before long, she had the audience's tears flowing once again.

Continuing to drive her audience over the edge, Hillary wrung out every bit of emotion of which she was capable from the crowd. Her broken heart had definitely added a whole new dimension to her singing as she mourned her lost love. Tireless in giving her audience what they had come to expect from her, her voice continued to cast its magical spell, drawing emotional responses from relatives and guests.

Coming upon the last words of her song, Hillary's eyes fluttered open, stretching in disbelief. Sitting next to her father was Brandon. His eyes, dark with emotion, pierced the edges of her sanity, sending messages of love that streaked through the core of her soul like a bolt of lightning. Suddenly, hitting a high note that could've shattered glass, she held the note as long as she could before shifting gears into a low moaning sound. Bringing the crowd to their feet, shouting for more, Hillary gave them more of the same, starting "Destiny" over from the beginning. Tears glistened brightly in her eyes as she finished, giving Brandon a bewitching smile, a smile that caused his heart to sing in rapturous harmony with hers. Going right into the song "Unbreak My Heart," recorded by Toni Braxton, she prayed that Brandon had come there to *unbreak* her badly shattered heart.

Feeling weak yet exhilarated, Hillary stepped back from the microphone. Walking over to the music conductor, she whispered something to him. He nodded in agreement as she stepped back to the microphone.

"Ladies and gentlemen, I would like to sing a very special song, to a very special person who's here in the audience. That special someone is Brandon David Blair!"

His desire to rush up on the stage and devour her was all too powerful, but he fought the battle hard and won. He only hoped that he'd read her signals right this time.

As Hillary crooned "The Look of Love," everyone was aware that she sang only to Brandon. No one seemed to mind.

Brandon couldn't take his eyes off Hillary. Long ago she'd made him a captive for life. As her sisters and Cassie were crying, Aaron beamed at his best friend, glad that he'd finally come to his senses. The others seemed pleased to see Brandon as well. Both wrought with emotion, Mr. Houston hugged his wife tenderly. It was easy to see that Henry and Hillary's brothers-in-law were thrilled for her, having missed the sunshine in her eyes.

Bringing her premier performance to a heart-stopping finale, Hillary watched Brandon rush up onstage to claim the woman he loved. Throwing her arms around his neck, Hillary kissed him passionately. As he responded with the aggression of a starving man having a meal set before him, the entire place was in a buzz over what was happening on the stage.

* * *

With the afterparty in full swing, Hillary mingled with all her guests. Smiling, Brandon remained faithfully by her side as she sat down to chat with many of her high school friends. While several of her elementary and high school teachers were present, she did her best to speak to each and every person in the room, warmly receiving the heartfelt congratulations.

This had been Hillary Houston's night. She had shone as the brightest star on everyone present. To her family and friends Hillary Houston had always been a "superstar."

Walking over to Aaron and Cassie, Hillary showered them both with affection. Cassie smiled at Brandon, who held on to Hillary's hand as if he was afraid to let go. "I guess we're going to have to allow you back into our little group," Cassie teased Brandon. "We've missed the four of us like crazy."

Smiling affectionately at Cassie, Brandon gave her a huge bear hug. "Thanks, Cassie. I've missed the dynamic foursome, too."

Aaron embraced his old friend. "I'm glad you're here, man. You look good."

Brandon placed his hand on Aaron's shoulder. "If you hadn't kept at me to do what I needed to do, I probably wouldn't be. Thanks for all the encouragement."

Hours later, after making sure she had fulfilled her obligations to her family and friends, Hillary slipped quietly out of the ballroom with Brandon. Holding each other in an intimate embrace, overjoyed at being together again, they strolled through the hotel lobby. She was surprised to find out he had booked a suite in the hotel, when he stopped at a room different from the one she occupied. Responding to the look on her face, he told her that he made it his business to know where she was and that he'd followed her career closely.

Inside the suite, Brandon sat down in a chair and

pulled her onto his lap, kissing her neck and ears tenderly. "Pretty lady, I've missed you. My life has been unbearable without you. Every time I picked up a magazine or turned on the television, there you were, smiling brilliantly at me from the cover or through the screen." His voice was husky with emotion.

Allowing a small breath to escape, she looked dolefully into his eyes. "Brandon, my life has changed drastically since we were last together. It's even more hectic than it was before. With the upcoming release of my new album, *Heartbreak at Dawn*, my schedule is going to be booked solid. I guess I'm saying all this to say that nothing has changed to allow us more time together. I wish I could tell you different." She took hold of his hand. "If you couldn't handle it when things were a lot less hectic, then how will you handle it now?"

Running his fingers through her soft hair, he took a deep breath. "Hill, I love you. I didn't know how much until you were gone. Remember the conversation we had about absence making the heart grow fonder?" Hillary nodded. "Baby, you were right. Your absence has almost driven me mad. The belief that you wouldn't take me back was the only thing that kept me away. I couldn't live with that kind of rejection."

"What made you risk it tonight?"

"Hill, I have something to tell you." His expression put Hillary on edge. "When I came to you that night to tell you I couldn't commit any longer, I really didn't expect it to turn out the way it did. I expected you to put up one hell of a fight. When you didn't offer much resistance, my ego was badly bruised. My bruised ego quickly turned into a broken heart. When you didn't fight for our love, I convinced myself that you didn't love me. I told myself over and over that this was my payback for all the women I'd hurt in the past.

"As our eyes locked together when Cassie and Aaron

gave their vows, I saw the love shining so powerfully in your eyes. It was then that I knew you truly loved me. Later, out in the garden, I saw how much I'd hurt you, especially when you walked out on me. That made me determined to get you back no matter what it took. Then I came to see you the day you were out by the pool. I had high hopes of us getting back together then. I was once again able to convince myself that you didn't feel the same way I did."

The edginess she'd initially felt disappeared. "Brandon, I see things clearer now. From the things you've just said it sounds like you were testing my love and my loyalty." His face showed his chagrin. "Honey, you really did hurt me badly. How could you not know I loved you? I entrusted my heart and soul to you, not to mention my innocence. I compromised many of my beliefs by engaging in premarital relations with you, yet you constantly questioned my loyalties."

He massaged the back of her hand. "Hillary, it goes even deeper than that. You once asked me if I'd been hurt before, but I never answered. It was because I couldn't. I guess you could say I'd been hurt, but more than that, I'd lost the ability to trust. This happened so long ago, but it's stayed with me throughout my life. For God's sake, it was a high school romance. I should've been able to deal with something as simple as infatuation. What I know now is that infatuation is all it could've been . . ."

Placing her forefinger against his lips, she kissed him softly. "Don't. A youthful betrayal is the worst kind of betrayal. Often the spirit can be broken. Simply because of our immaturity, it can hurt more than anything in the world can. At such a tender age, we're still forming opinions and making new discoveries about life in general. The teenage years are the most vulnerable time in a person's life."

He grimaced. "It sure as hell was a vulnerable time

for me. Here I am, captain of the football team, and my favorite girl dumps me for a non-athlete scholar. It might not have been so hard if the guys hadn't ribbed me day after day. That was when I lost my ability to trust. I never knew how to get it back."

His eyes grew soft. "Then I met you. That's when my inability to trust got me into the most difficulty. It wasn't that I didn't trust you, as much as it was that I was scared to trust, period. Fear has a way of turning you inside out and upside down. Before you, my inability to trust people didn't matter one way or the other."

She rested her forehead against his. "I know the feeling. I had vowed to never involve myself with a jealous man ever again. Then came you. I never told you about Tyrone Thompson because I wasn't in love with him. Our relationship only lasted less than a hot minute. Tyrone was jealous and possessive and he didn't trust women any further than he could throw one . . ."

"Much like me," Brandon interjected. "I'm sorry, babe, for what I've put you through. Do you think you can forgive me?"

"Brandon, no one has the right to take another person's feelings and batter them to satisfy their own egos. When a person is cut, they bleed. I love you and I will not settle for anything less in return. But I don't blame you for all that went wrong. I have to take some responsibility, too. I know now that I set myself up for a fall by always waiting for the other shoe to drop. I felt our relationship was too good to be true, that happy endings only happened in fairy tales. Most of the time I was terrified you'd run out on me. So when you did, I didn't fight because I had more or less prepared myself for the ending. So you see, I was just as responsible as you."

She got up from his lap and walked across the room, where she picked up the Bible. Instead of sitting on his

lap, she sat down in front of him, on the floor. "Do you
mind if I read something to you?"

"No, Hill. Go ahead."

She opened the paraphrased Living Bible and turned
to I Corinthians, thirteenth chapter. "Love is very patient
and kind, never jealous or envious, never boastful or
proud, never haughty or selfish or rude," she read softly.
"Love does not demand its own way. It is not irritable
or touchy . . ." As she finished reading the chapter, he
slid from the chair onto the floor to sit beside her.

His eyes glistened with unshed tears. "Hill, I'm committed to you, to your career, your family, and whatever
else it takes to have you by my side. I commit to living
by the words you've just read. These words I say are
all true. Hill, these aren't just empty words. Just like
you advised Alex, Aaron advised me to seek counseling.
And I did. Not for you, not for Aaron, I did it for
Brandon." He got up and moved away from her for a
few seconds.

Returning to where she sat, he handed her a bouquet of dried flowers. Recognizing it as Cassie's wedding
bouquet, she was astounded. He kissed her forehead.
"I had offered to pay a serious bribe to the woman
who'd caught the bouquet. After I explained why it was
so important for me to have it, she willingly gave it up
and wished me the best of luck. I thanked her for giving up the bouquet that undeniably belonged to the
woman I loved, the only woman I've ever loved, the
only woman I'll ever love."

Her tears flowed hotly as she pressed the beautifully
preserved bouquet to her chest. "Oh, my heart is so full.
And you're still full of so many wonderful surprises. With
the counseling and all it seems you've made a lot of personal sacrifices."

With tears falling from his own eyes, he looked deep
into her soul. "The best surprises are the ones yet to come.

As far as sacrifices go, sometimes the greatest love requires the greatest sacrifice. Pretty lady, will you marry me?"

Their tears mingled as Hillary drew his face close to hers, kissing him until they were both breathless. "Honey, what took you so long?" she cried joyously.

ABOUT THE AUTHOR

Author Linda Hudson-Smith sees romance writing as redemptive. Stories of love and hope have come to her rescue on several occasions. Married to a career Air Force meteorologist, Hudson-Smith was among one of many military wives who turned to romance novels for encouragement and entertainment during periods of separation from their husbands. Later, she would find that trying her hand at writing romances would help her through a debilitating illness, allowing her to occupy her time and imagination while discovering a talent and a voice she hadn't realized she possessed.

Born in Canonsburgh, Pennsylvania, and raised in the town of Washington, Pennsylvania, Hudson-Smith has traveled the world as an enthusiastic witness to cultures and lifestyles. Her husband's twenty-year military career gave her the opportunity to live in Japan, Germany, and other parts of Europe, as well as in many cities across the United States. Hudson-Smith's extensive travel experience helps her craft stories set in a variety of beautiful and romantic locations. It was after illness forced her to leave a marketing and public relations administration career, that she turned to writing full time.

Linda Hudson-Smith is a member of Romance Writers of America. *Romance in Color* recently chose her as Rising Star for the month of January. *Ice Under Fire,* her debut

Arabesque novel, has received rave reviews and earned rapturous letters from fans. Though novel writing remains her first love, she is currently cultivating her screenwriting skills.

Dedicated to inspiring readers to overcome adversity against all odds, Hudson-Smith is a member of the Lupus Foundation of America and the NAACP, and is a supporter of the American Cancer Society. She also enjoys her volunteer work at a local nursing and rehabilitation center. In her spare time she enjoys writing poetry, entertaining, traveling and attending sports events. She's resolved to visit all fifty states by age fifty and is a mere seven states away from her goal. Linda is the mother of two sons, and also has a son and daughter through her extended family.